TRAFFIC NORTH

Crime on the Alaska / Russia border

by

RICHIE GOLDSTEIN

ISBN: 978-1-5323-9692-2
Writer's Guild of America West - Registry #18776

A note on Russian names:

Russian men and women have middle names based upon their father's first name.

For women, *ovna* or *yevna* is added to the father's first name to make a woman's middle name. Example: here is Aleksandra whose father is Peter. She would be called Aleksandra Petr*ovna*. If her father were Sergei, she would be Aleksandra Serge*yevna*.

For men, *ovich* or *yevich* are added. Example: here is Boris, whose father is David. Boris would be called Boris David*ovich*. Or if his father is Sergei, he would be called Boris Serge*yevich*.

If I am a friend of Boris, I might drop the *ov* part and call him Boris Davidich. Or if his father is Sergei, I might drop the *yev* and call him Boris Sergeich. This doesn't work for women's middle names.

Almost every Russian first name has a nickname. So Aleksandra is Sasha, Boris is Borya, Valery is Valya, Mikhail is Misha etc.

A note on rendering Russian phonetically into English:

The main problem in rendering Russian into English is with the two (2) Russian letters for the English sound E. One is pronounced, one is not (at least in any way discernable to the English ear). Many Russian words end in both the pronounced E and the so called 'short E.' I have avoided the problem by smushing them together and using an English 'y.' Hence, Yury, Georgy, Veliky. All of which, in Russian, end in *both* the pronounced *and* the 'short E.'

With appreciation:

This novel is dedicated, with great affection and thanks, to my corps of volunteer readers—Barbara, Tandy, Michele, Jeff, Steve, Norda, Nancy and Penny.

This book is a work of fiction. The characters, incidents, and dialogue are drawn from the author's imagination and are not to be construed as real. Any resembance to actual events or persons, living or dead, is entirely coincidental.

Cover design, book layout and maps by Penny Panlener.

TRAFFIC NORTH

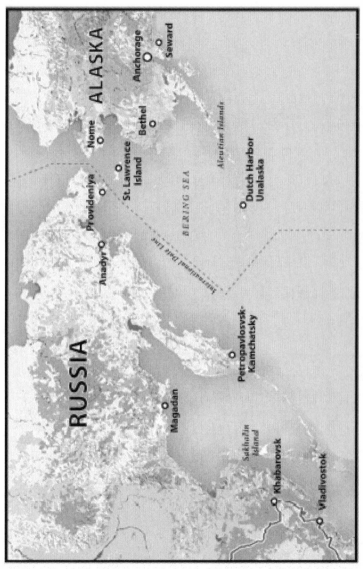

Russia and Alaska are divided by the Bering Strait, about 55 miles at its narrowest point. The closest official port in Russia's Far East is Providenya.

1

Neither of the two Russian seamen who were busy beating the shit out of Jimmy Lasorda knew a word of English. If they had, they might have appreciated Jimmy's plea, spat out through split lips and a fractured jaw, "Wait a minute. For God sakes. Wait a minute. I can explain. I can give it all back. I swear."

But even if they had understood, the two men were not negotiators. They had been hired to punish Jimmy Lasorda, then kill him.

The victim never saw it coming. Just before midnight, the American high seas fisheries observer assigned to the Russian trawler, *Pyotr Veliky,* had left his small berth on his way topside. There, Jimmy was slated to count, weigh, and determine the sex and health of tonight's haul of sable fish caught close to St. Matthew Island, in the heart of the Bering Sea.

Jimmy was properly outfitted with foul weather slickers and lined rubber boots. He was carrying his life vest and would certainly have put it on before going outside to face the northern ocean at one of its usual, nasty moments. He would have stationed himself aft, just above the rear deck where the trawl was being gathered after scouring the ocean floor.

But Jimmy never made it to work. Passing through a narrow corridor, he was yanked into a below-decks, small storage room where the two fishermen proceeded to pummel the young American as they had been instructed.

Now, nearly unconscious, Jimmy sensed himself being dragged by his feet, his head bump-bumping along the steel-plates of the passageway. He felt, more than heard, the bulkhead hatch fly open and slam against the superstructure, caught by the near gale force winds whipping over the boat. A moment later, when a freezing spray of salt water lashed his face, Jimmy was brought up to a state of blurred awareness. What he saw loosened his anal sphincter and sent his gonads into hiding: the Russians had tied his right leg to a two hundred pound steel crab pot and were pushing it to the edge of the heaving deck. Jimmy began to flail like an animal with its paw caught in a trap. Incoherent screams burst from his throat but couldn't pierce the blowing tempest that engulfed the vessel and carried away his shouts.

The Russians worked with murderous efficiency, sliding the crab pot toward the watery abyss even as the ship tilted steeply from side to side, gripped by fifteen-foot waves. As the heavy pot was slowly coaxed toward the edge of the ship with Jimmy in tow, the victim-to-be reached out frantically for a handhold, scrabbling for something he might latch on to. But the deck was water-slick smooth and the edge of the boat and the end of Jimmy's life loomed ever nearer.

Just as the pot was being tipped over the side, Jimmy saw a length of chain dangling from the trawler's railing. He grabbed with both hands as the steel box slid over the side, the weight of it wrenching his leg out of its socket. Jimmy howled in pain and would not have been able to hold on for more than a few seconds. But the two men assigned to end the life of the American fisheries monitor were impatient. One of them picked up a heavy gaff hook—brought along for just such a contingency—and swung it down on Jimmy's hands. Knuckles splintered and the fingers of one hand gave up their life-hold on the chain. Another blow delivered with terrific force and the second hand crushed. And now one final and very short shriek as Jimmy Lasorda followed the crab pot swiftly into the waves, disappearing into the inky ocean. The victim's lungs filled quickly with freezing salt water. He had time for a single, final thought as he sped to the bottom of the Bering Sea, "I can give it back."

~~~

Standing on the runners of his dog sled, Nelson Alexie couldn't help smiling. The fifty-year old Athabascan trapper was totally at peace this glorious spring morning. His five dogs loped effortlessly along, pulling their master's sled over the forest trail. A light snow had fallen overnight and the sled glided easily through sun-dappled stands of birch trees, ready to burst into bud.

The last cold snap was a distant memory. Today, in such mild weather, Alexie needed neither his heavy seal skin parka, his snow machine suit, his neoprene bunny boots, nor his heavy driving mittens. Those were clothes for January. This late April morning, with the days lengthening and the sun gaining strength, Alexie was dressed only in a hoodie, Carhartt overalls, felt-lined boots, and work gloves. And dark glasses, of course. For even at this early hour, the Arctic sun was burning with an intense brightness.

Go-Go, Alexie's lead dog, sensed his master's joy and responded with energy to all of his commands. The dog was an Iditarod veteran, as were the other four huskies. They all knew the drill: a few hours of easy running, frequent stops as Alexie checked his trap line, snacks along the way, then home for a warm meal of beaver tail.

The trapper whoa-ed his team to a halt at a place in the forest where the trees thinned out, next to a large, circular meadow. He buried his ice anchor deep into a snow berm. The dogs stretched themselves out, resting their muzzles on their front paws.

Alexie reached inside his sled bag and took out a thermos of hot cocoa, a ham and Swiss sandwich, and a bag of Fritos. He eased down onto a familiar stump and dug into his early morning snack. The cocoa was furiously hot and steamed up his glasses. As he was wiping a smear of mayo from his mustache, the morning stillness was broken by a single, loud caw. Looking up, Alexie saw three blue-black ravens sitting like ominous sentinels on the branches of a nearby spruce tree. "This is my breakfast, not yours, you thieves," he called to them.

Go-Go perked up his head and watched the birds, yipping at them.

"They are more clever than you, Go-Go," he gently chided his leader. The trapper had often witnessed how a pair of these birds, working in perfect tandem, would outwit his dogs and steal a piece of salmon or a hunk of moose right out from under their muzzles. One bird would taunt the dog and draw him to the limits of the five-foot chain that secured the husky to a post in front of his kennel. The dog would lunge futilely at the raven, the bird hopping exactly five and half feet away, as though measured. The raven would waltz around the dog, remaining just out of reach, cawing mockingly, an avian thumbing-of-the-nose. With the dog distracted, the second raven would brazenly snatch the husky's unguarded dinner.

The three birds ignored Alexie and his team. They were focused on something in the meadow. The trapper stood, walked to the edge of the berm, and followed their gaze across the treeless, snow-covered field. Toward the center of the meadow, three gyrfalcons were ripping at a carcass. A dozen ravens hopped nearby but didn't dare venture closer.

Whenever one came too near, the raptors flapped and hissed. Another large bunch of the black birds filled the branches of the surrounding trees, waiting patiently for scraps. From this distance, Alexie wasn't able to discern what was occupying the birds. *Probably a dead fox,* he thought.

He finished his meal, wiped his mouth with the back of his hoodie's sleeve, returned the thermos to his sled bag, and withdrew a small Ziploc, full of frozen tomcod. The huskies rose up and began shifting from foot to foot, ready for *their* usual mid-morning snack. Alexie lobbed them each a small tomcod, calling each dog affectionately by name: Go-Go, Smiley, Silver, Flip, and Buzzy. Five quick gulps and the dogs resumed their sprawled positions.

The trapper returned the Ziploc, took a gunnysack from his sled bag and removed a dowel-shaped piece of heavy wood and a pair of tin snips. He began wading into the meadow where two days earlier he had set his trap. The snow was deeper here than on the beaten-down trail and Alexie had to trudge his way slowly toward the thicket where he had set his wire trap. But after several steps, he stopped short. A few yards off to his left, a set of ATV tracks—covered with a light dusting of last night's snow—snaked into the meadow. Unusual because ATVs were out of place in this part of the forest. The more well-traveled trail was half a mile to the south, a hard-packed, straight shot through the woods where drivers always ran their snow-gos and ATVs too fast. Alexie never used that trail. Too many collisions between animal and machine.

He shaded his eyes and followed the tread marks, saw how they circled around the feasting falcons, before returning to the trail. His curiosity was aroused, but a flash of light in the thicket recaptured his attention. The wire-trap moved again slightly, the thin metal catching the sun. He had caught something, and recently.

~~~

Dressed in the blue-striped, heavy flannel pajamas his daughter insisted he wear at sea, Captain Yury Gregorovich Vronsky, long time master of the Vladivostok-based fishing trawler, *Pyotr Veliky*, sat on the edge of his bunk. His short legs dangled above a piece of remnant carpet that served to keep the captain's toes off the cold steel of his cabin's floor. With the tips of all ten fingers, Vronsky vigorously massaged his bristly scalp. A minute earlier, he had been deep in sleep despite the roaring sea on the other side of the hull.

The vessel's first officer, Valery Timoshenko, dressed from head to foot in a bright yellow foul weather suit, stepped back from his captain's berth. He removed his soaked woolen watch cap and stood ready to explain why he had done the unthinkable: awaken the ship's master.

"Well, Valery. Speak." Vronsky demanded.

"Man missing, captain. Almost certainly overboard. The ship has been thoroughly searched twice from stem to stern. It's the American fisheries observer, Lasorda. James Anthony Lasorda."

The captain of the *Pyotr Veliky* sat slump-shouldered and listened stoically to the report. In over twenty-nine years of commanding ships on the Bering Sea and in the North Pacific, not a single seaman had ever lost his life serving under Yury Vronsky. Not even in 1999, when his previous ship, *Vostochnaya Zvyzda,* nearly swamped off Magadan, in the Sea of Okhotsk. Vronsky had earned a commendation for his efforts. He righted his vessel, saved all on board, *and* delivered a record harvest of tanner crab. But that was then.

Now, not only had someone apparently disappeared, but it had to be the *one* person whose certain death would grab the attention of his joint-venture bosses from Vladivostok to Seattle.

"Details, Valya."

"He was last seen below decks around midnight. Never showed up at his station, top side. We were all working the net and only started looking for him when the trawl was emptied and stowed, around three hundred hours."

Vronsky tucked his pajama legs into his socks then grabbed his pants. His thoughts were filled with *'what ifs?'*

If he turned the ship around, it would take at least three hours to return to the area where the American *probably* went into the sea. If the captain chose that course, he'd get called on the carpet by the owners. They'd grumble and grouse about lost time on the fishing grounds. They'd remind him that the ship's hold was only a third full of sable fish. The *Pyotr Veliky* was scheduled to return to Vladivostok in five days and if Vronsky showed up with less than half capacity, the veteran seaman would probably get pushed into retirement. His company's owners were not fans of the captain, thought him too independent, too outspoken. His employers had been trying for the last five years to get him off the ocean. *Nothing quite so pathetic*, Vronsky thought, *as a seaman forced to redefine himself on dry land.*

Added to that, Vronsky weighed the odds of finding the careless American. They weren't small. They were non-existent. Even if the fool went over the side wearing a cold-water immersion suit–an exceedingly unlikely possibility–he might be alive, yes, but they would never find him in this rotten weather. And if they did miraculously come upon him, the man would have almost certainly succumbed to hypothermia and exposure.

As an exclamation point to the captain's considerations, the bottom fell out of the vessel as the *Pyotr Veliky* plunged into a deep trough. Twenty tons of freezing Bering Sea salt water washed the decks.

But if he didn't try to find the missing man, the Americans would be all over their Russian joint-venture partners. And ultimately, and more tellingly for him, he'd get an earful from his fellow masters. They'd be on his case for not taking all measures to rescue one of his crew, even though the American moron was not technically a crewman.

In his heart, Captain Yury Vronsky was a seaman first and foremost, and a commercial fisherman only after that.

The master stood up to his full five-feet four-inches, clenched his fists at his sides, and grunted, "Bring her about, Valya. Go to full speed. Backtrack our course. Turn out all hands, and pass out every set of binoculars on board. Then send a mayday alert and notify the American Coast Guard."

The first officer dashed out of the cabin, his captain's curses filling the corridor behind him.

"Cock sucking American . . . What's your name? Lasorda, huh? Fuck you, Lasorda. And fuck your mother, too!"

~~~

Nelson Alexie waded through the snow to his trap. The snared animal wasn't going anywhere. After another several paces through the knee-high drift, he could see most of a large, male snowshoe hare, caught by a foreleg and struggling to free itself. It thrashed weakly, its strength rapidly ebbing. It made sorrowful, weeping sounds.

The trapper knelt in front of the hare, raised the wooden dowel, and brought it down expertly on the animal's skull. A tap really, but hard enough to kill. Alexie loosened the wire from the bloody paw and placed the hare in the burlap bag. He snipped the wire trap from the brush, wound it up neatly, and put it, too, in the sack. He stood, brushed the snow off his overalls, and looked once again at the feeding frenzy, thirty yards away, in the center of the meadow. The falcons were still picking at the carcass. He shaded his eyes but could not identify the animal being consumed. A vague sense of unease grabbed at the trapper's throat. On the trail, the dogs sensed Alexie's apprehension. They rose to their feet, shook the snow from their bodies, and looked to their master as he stood in the brightening sunlight, gazing fixedly at something out of their view.

Alexie dropped the gunnysack and began walking slowly toward the birds. With his approach, the ravens scattered, but the gyrfalcons were not so easily chased from their meal. When he yelled at them, the big birds bounced into the air, flapping their wings, cawing defiantly. He reached around his neck, feeling for a chain with a small medallion: Hubertus, the patron saint of hunters. He held the revered talisman between thumb and forefinger, never taking his eyes off the carrion in the snow in front of him.

The dogs began barking and whining their alarm.

Alexie looked to his team. "Go-Go, shhhh. Good dog," he assured his leader. But his calming words could not mask the anxiety in his voice. The huskies continued their yelping.

The trapper resumed his advance, his focus riveted on the object in front of him. Another few steps and . . . "Jesus, Mary and Joseph," he uttered, closing his eyes, hoping to eradicate the image. But when he opened them again, there it was: the partially exposed body of a woman, upper torso and one arm exposed, flesh ripped off in a hundred places, her empty eye sockets pecked clean, staring blindly skyward. Alexie pressed St. Hubertus to his lips and began a prayer.

The falcons resumed eating, but kept a wary eye on the trapper.

The dogs were now hysterical, leaping in their traces.

And in the sky, a full conspiracy of ravens was circling, screeching their annoyance.

The noise shattering the spring morning was deafening.

~~~

On the way back from work to her doublewide mobile home, the woman stopped at the Oaken Keg. It was the first time in a year she was going to buy hard liquor. She began shopping at the beer cooler, her conscience going pang-pang. Not about the brew choice—she was a confirmed Corona drinker—but whether or not she should even be buying alcohol in the first place. The woman called to mind the event that had brought about this self-imposed, year-long abstinence: she had been severely hung-over on the job, and was saved from being discovered by a colleague. When she swore to be good, she earned his begrudging forgiveness.

And she *had* been good. Relatively good. For a year. An occasional glass of wine at a restaurant. No big deal. A beer with her co-workers, every couple weeks. Easy. But no hard stuff. Not a drop during the past twelve months.

Tonight, however, with a three day break from work stretching in front of her, she felt she might let her hair down. She believed she merited a celebration, a small-scale party to be built around a pair of Corona six-packs.

And a pint of Cuervo.

What the hell.

She'd indulge herself tonight, Saturday, and after a noon wake-up, she'd fly out in the afternoon to her family's homestead north of Anchorage. There, she'd catch up with her daughter and grandfather and get a good loving from the rest of her family. She'd return to town on Tuesday evening.

The woman lived in one of Anchorage's more sorrowful trailer parks, Bay View Estates. A triple misnomer. No bay. No view. And estates? Many of the sixty mobile homes were vintage Winnebagos, wheels removed and replaced by timber or cement foundations.

Six years earlier, she had moved to Anchorage and had rented—temporarily, she had wrongly supposed—the doublewide. Why she was still living there, despite her well-paying job, was mostly a function of her non-existent social life: few friends, fewer lovers. No need to entertain, to impress anyone. No need even to make the bed.

On either side of her, two single-mother families eked out a bare existence: a Samoan woman with two middle school boys, and a Hispanic teenager with a three-year-old girl. They were perfect neighbors—there when the woman needed them, invisible when she did not.

Then there was Mortimer, the feral tomcat that had glommed onto her when she first moved in. The two had bonded at first purr and quickly established a routine that defined the precise limits of their relationship. The woman provided a once-a-day can of tuna, served outside, *only* outside, on her tippy, wooden front porch. Denied the modest comforts of the doublewide's interior, the cat was made to suffer through the Arctic winter in the small, hay-strewn kennel she kept for him below the trailer.

Arriving home, she acknowledged the cat, received a *"squarl"* in reply, then went inside to prepare his meal. Over the years, she had occasionally tried to vary his dinner, spice it up—first with sardines, then chum salmon. The cat, however, turned up his nose at those offerings and insisted on tuna. Albacore, solid pack.

After showering, the woman emerged into her bedroom wrapped in a beach towel. She avoided checking herself out in the full-length mirror. She was certain she'd put on several pounds this past winter and didn't need to see them bunched around her waist and hips. Despite her reluctance to see her reflected image, she still imagined people saw her thirty-eight-year old body as tall and shapely. The last time she looked, her breasts were still winning the fight with gravity. Her ash blond hair hardly needed looking after—she'd kept it inch-long for the past fifteen years. She believed her face still worked: slanted, Tartar-green eyes over high cheeks inherited from her Cossack grandfather, blond brows and lashes that barely stood out against her fair and lightly freckled skin. And full lips that, when she smiled, she knew stopped traffic. Problem was, these days—these years, in fact—not much to smile about.

She threw on loose fitting gym clothes, grabbed beer number one, popped the top, took a long swig, then began preparing the usual—dinner for one.

In honor of the Mexican choice of alcohol, she opened a can of whole green chiles, stuffed three with grated Jack cheese, dredged them in flour, cumin and cayenne. She dipped them in egg whites and fried them briefly in hot Canola. After that they went onto paper towels to sop up the oil, and lastly, into a deep Pyrex. She smothered the chiles with salsa picante and placed the dish in the oven at 325 for thirty minutes. That gave her half an hour to catch up on her current reading, *Raylan*, the main character in a series of Elmore Leonard novels. He was her favorite literary law enforcement tough guy, a take-no-shit Kentucky-born U.S. Marshal.

The woman stretched to her five-foot nine-inch length on her living room's hide-a-bed and sipped at a second beer. The oven timer went off just as Raylan was having an interior monolog about whether he'd bother arresting the man he was pursuing or simply shoot the SOB. The woman could absolutely relate.

She book-marked the page, went to her kitchenette's nook table, and pushed aside the detritus of a solitary life. The smell of the rellaños had the predictable effect—her mouth began watering. She removed the casserole from the oven and set to, the third beer near at hand. She chugged four long swallows and turned on her TV for the local news. A young, good-looking Latino newscaster was standing in front of the Dena'ina Center in downtown Anchorage. He was reporting on the hundreds of international law enforcement personnel who would be coming to town in a week to attend the first half of a conference focusing on international crime up and down the Pacific Rim. The reporter added that the second half of the conference was to be convened in Vladivostok, in the Russian Far East. He introduced Nolan Cardozo, the director of the

Drug Enforcement Agency's small Alaska office, and asked the fed to comment.

Before the DEA director could open his mouth, the woman used the remote to shut him off. She knew Cardozo. "Nolan, you're a stuffed-shirt asshole," she said out loud.

She finished her meal and turned to dessert—a favorite she hadn't enjoyed in a year—French vanilla ice cream enhanced by a shot of tequila drizzled over the top. Almost from the first mouthful, the liquor began to produce the sought-after buzz. She felt the pressure of her work slowly ebb.

While still fairly lucid, she did her nightly, motherly duty—called her eleven-year-old daughter, Robin, living with the woman's large family north of Anchorage.

When she came on the line, Robin jumped right in. "We're repairing rudders and ailerons on the old Beechcraft. And I've been calling in everyone's flight plans. So cool."

The woman listened, recalling her own flight school training with her grandfather, Viktor, twenty-five years earlier. He was working on his family's third generation of students. Cool, indeed.

Mother and daughter chitchatted for a few minutes more before running out of things to report.

"Love you, mom. See you tomorrow afternoon."

"Love you, girl. Can't wait," the woman said, ending the call. She realized she'd been eyeing the bottle of Cuervo during her entire conversation with her daughter. With a strong sense of self-loathing, she returned to her drinking. She steadily worked her way through the tequila while watching *Prince of the City,* a film she'd seen often. By the end of the almost three hour movie, she'd finished the Cuervo and all but two of the Coronas. She reeled into her bedroom and without bothering to brush her teeth, climbed under the covers.

The plan was to sleep late, but *The Man Who Sold the World,* her Nirvana ring tone, began clanging just past 7:00 a.m. Kurt Cobain's wailing, *"I thought you died alone, a long long time ago,"* made it through her ear drums but stopped short of her temporal lobes. For all the waking it did, her cell phone could have been ringing in Calcutta. She rolled over and returned to dreamland.

Again and again, at ever-shorter intervals, the phone shrilled at her, went to voicemail and recorded the appeals of her partner, "Pick up the fucking phone, Sasha. We've got work."

Around 7:45, a seriously insistent thumping on her front door hauled the woman out of her hung-over stupor.

And thirty minutes later, after a shower that went from tepid to cold, a half-eaten fried egg she couldn't look at, let alone get down, and a cup of under-brewed and bitter coffee, Detective Sergeant Aleksandra Kulaeva of the Anchorage Police Department was being driven to some god-forsaken forest north of town to investigate a report of a woman's frozen and ravaged body.

2

Seven very large men with very large handguns tucked away in shoulder holsters encircled the small, seaside park. They leaned against fences and sat on benches. They spoke with one another through two-way radios attached to their lapels. The men were diverted neither by snacking nor by the occasional short-skirted lovely who passed through the park this sunny spring afternoon. The men were on full alert. The focus of their protective attention was Boris Davidovich Bunin, the balding, bespectacled man playing soccer with his sons.

For today's scrimmage, Boris wore red sweats with *Dynamo Moskva* emblazoned across the jersey. His sons, Misha, fourteen, and Petya, thirteen, opted for Nike gear.

The Bunins were joined by several of the boys' classmates from St. Margaret's, their private, Long Island, school. Filling out the squads were a few panting, out of shape fathers, clearly having a hard time keeping up with the younger generation.

When Petya broke free, took a long pass and dribbled unchecked toward the goal, Boris did the only thing a defender could do: he caught up with his son, grabbed him around the waist in a bear hug and swung him into the air.

"Papa, you can't do that," Petya yelled at him. "You'd be DQed."

"*Vinovat.* Guilty, Petrushka," Boris confessed, giving his son a huge kiss on the neck before putting him down. "But I was beaten. What could I do?" He turned to the other players, "Time out, coach needs a breather." He trotted slowly off the field while the game went on without him. On the sidelines, his wife, Larissa, sat at a picnic table, reading.

Boris took his time walking toward her, astonished once again by her elegant beauty. He thought himself the luckiest man on the planet, who, after sixteen years of marriage, could still be so moved by his wife's visage.

She heard his step, looked up, and smiled at her husband. He flopped down opposite her, took off his glasses, and mopped his face and neck with a towel. He noted the title of her book.

"Chekhov's plays again, Lara?"

"Again. As usual. And always," she said. She put a marker in the well-worn book and closed it. "I'm at act four of *Cherry Orchard*. They're chopping down the trees. Everyone is bummed. So what else is new? It's Chekhov," she laughed. "I remember once at the conservatory, in Saint Petersburg, my ballet teacher and I were improvising a short piece based on *The Seagull*. I told him I thought Chekhov was an optimist. He looked at me like I was crazy. I told him, compared to Shakespeare, Chekhov *is* an optimist. 'How's that?' he asked. I said, 'By the end of most of Shakespeare's tragedies–Hamlet, Lear, Titus, Macbeth–the majority of his characters are dead. All of Chekhov's characters, on the other hand, end up depressed, dejected, isolated, and inconsolable. But at least they're alive.'"

"And of course he was convinced by the brilliance of your argument."

"No, not by the brilliance of my argument, which, at the time, I thought was pretty damn clever," Larissa said. She replaced a length of wind-blown hair to its place over her shoulder. "But because he had designs on me–I was all of fifteen at the time–he allowed himself to be convinced." She put her forearms down on the table and bent toward Boris.

He took up one hand and kissed the up-turned palm. "Ah, you women. It's always the same with you. We're putty."

"Not all men are putty, Borya. But *you* are, my sweet, and you know it. And you wouldn't have it any other way." With her other hand she stroked her husband's stubbled cheek.

Their quiet regard for each other was interrupted by a deep voice splitting the air, calling, "Boris Davidich."

The couple looked toward a giant of a man who was advancing toward them. Boris turned to him and held up a hand. "Wait a second, Taras," he told the man. Boris looked back at his wife. "Lucky we found each other," he said, reaching into a nearby cooler and grabbing a bottle of beer. He popped the cap and took a long pull. "Tired," he admitted as he took a second swallow, then reached into her purse and retrieved a pack of Camels and a book of matches. He lit up, inhaling deeply, arching an eyebrow at his wife. She gave him a look of severe reprimand. He touched her chin lightly with the knuckles of his free hand. "*Dorogaya,* dear."

She reached to take the cigarette from him, but before she could snatch it away, Boris flipped it onto the grass and stamped it out. "How's that, Lara? Only one drag."

"Wonderful," she said, smiling. "Now if we can only do something about the beer and your growing pot belly."

He held up his index finger, "One vice at a time, Lara," he said, taking the towel off the table and wrapping it around his neck.

Boris and Taras walked to an old maple on the far edge of the soccer pitch. The tree was coming into leaf. Its bark was etched with half a dozen names of people swearing eternal love to each other. The men rested against the tree.

"The Americans are both dead," Taras said.

Boris wiped his perspiring head and neck. He was intent on the soccer practice. "Wonderful pass, Ivanko," he yelled to one of the boys, then spoke to Taras, "Dead and disappeared, as ordered?"

The bodyguard hesitated. He knew his boss would never blame him as messenger. Nonetheless, he didn't fancy giving Boris news that wasn't happy. "The American fisherman is at the bottom of the ocean. The woman was left in the forest."

"Just dumped in the forest? Where she might be discovered? Why didn't she vanish? Wasn't Kostya told what do to?"

Taras was Boris' brother-in-law, his best friend, and twice his size. But right now he felt short and vulnerable. "They left her body in the woods. Kostya said he's certain it'd be eaten by bears or wolves before it might be discovered."

"And maybe lions? Or possibly tigers? Oh, my." Boris wagged his head back and forth. "Are we now depending on the animal kingdom to clean up after us?"

When his bodyguard couldn't answer, Boris spoke again, with more authority. "Taras. Tell your dopey brother to stop watching shitty American cop shows. Tell him to do only what he is told. No more, no less. Tell him not to think. That's why *I'm* here in New York and he's in iceberg Alaska. When you talk to your twin . . . talk to Kostya tonight . . . tell him next time he has a bright idea to clear it with me first."

Taras nodded. "I'll let him know."

"And the last shipment the fisherman was holding? Have they collected it yet?"

"They're still looking."

"Why *still* looking? Didn't the man tell them where it

was before they threw him in the ocean?"

"The two seamen who Kostya hired . . . they don't speak English."

Boris' eyes went wide. "The devil! The *whole* idea, Taras, was to get the American to talk before they killed him."

"I'll scold my brother."

"Do more than scold. Tell him to get his ass out to Dutch Harbor right away. Tell him to find out where the American stayed and search his rooms. Tell them all. Tell Denis, tell Gerasim, and especially tell your knuckle-headed brother to search very, *very* hard."

"I'll tell them. I'll yell. Anything else, Boris Davidich?"

"Yes. The woman's brother, the drug addict. Take care of him, too."

"Certainly. His girlfriend was close to the woman and the fisherman."

"Fine. Her, too. Let's not leave any loose ends. The last thing we need is to have the program crash down around us."

On the soccer pitch, Misha slammed a goal from twenty yards out. "Brilliant shot, Mishka, brilliant," Boris shouted to his son. He then laid his hand on the arm of his bodyguard's jacket. The man's immense bicep filled the entire sleeve. Boris gently pulled him close and spoke softly into his ear. "Taras Dmitrich. Please. Old friend. Find my fucking heroin."

~~~

The morning sun had a voice, high pitched and incandescently eyeball-shattering as it bounced off the hood of the police cruiser and slashed through the windshield. The visor was down and she was wearing dark sunglasses.

Still, Detective Sasha Kulaeva viewed the world through a painful, hung-over squint. Her thinking was sluggish, her speech slurred and disjointed. The few coherent thoughts she could manage centered on her partner and his reaction to her post-drunken state. *I've let Gary down. Again. I swore to him I wouldn't be a repeat offender. We've been partnered for four years and I've gone and squandered his trust in me. I wouldn't blame him if he turned me in. Sasha, girl. You are such a worthless shit.*

She snuck a look at him. He was choking the steering wheel, barely containing his unhappiness with her. They stopped at the Fred Meyer Superstore in Eagle River for coffee to-go. The hot liquid went straight to her bowels, the last place from which she needed relief. She sprinted to the store's bathroom and spent fifteen minutes there before returning to the police cruiser.

~~~

Nelson Alexie met the two cops at the trailhead. As soon as he saw her lurch from the cruiser, he guessed the woman was hung-over. Then, when she walked unsteadily over to him, shook his hand, and mumbled her name, he was certain of it.

The trapper knew a lot about drunks, had been one himself until he got clean, nineteen years, two hundred and forty-five days earlier. And even after such an extended period of total sobriety, he was still thirsty.

Alexie led them to his snow machine. A long, wooden sled was hitched behind. The male cop carried an official looking bag, placed it in the sled, helped the woman settle down, then got in himself. The trapper started up the Sno-Cat and, for her sake, drove slowly.

When they arrived at the meadow, the policeman had to help his partner to her feet. She reeled for a moment before righting herself. She put her hands over her forehead, shielding her eyes, then headed for the shade of a spruce tree.

Alexie walked to the berm and pointed out what he had discovered a few hours before. He needn't have bothered. It was obvious. Ravens were feasting on the corpse, raising a racket, arguing over the choicest bits of flesh.

"When I found her, there were three gyrfalcons eating away at her and keeping the ravens off. Looks like the falcons ate their fill and left."

Gary walked to the edge of the field. He found a small, fallen birch branch and flung it at the birds, hoping to scatter them. His throw came up well short and the ravens ignored him. He needed to get closer. He returned to the sled and took high rubber boots from the trunk of the police cruiser. When he returned, he gathered several more pieces of dead wood and began plowing his way through the snow toward the body. Alexie carefully followed in the cop's deep footprints.

Halfway there, Gary resumed his shouting and throwing. One of his missiles scattered the birds. He turned to the trapper. "This is as far as we'll go for now. The police techs and forensic teams are on their way. We'll leave it for them to get to the body." He glanced back toward the trail where Sasha was watching from her shaded vantage. He looked at Alexie and, with slightly upraised palms and tilted head, made a mute apology.

"Do you outrank her?" the trapper asked.

"We're both sergeants, but I have more seniority. About

six years worth." Gary threw another broken limb at a few ravens that were sneaking back to their lunch. They flew away and settled on the branches of the closest alder, cawing their indignation.

"They'll wait all day," Alexie said. "They know a good meal when they see one." He looked back at the woman cop.

"Sergeant Hernandez. I think you have some difficult choices ahead."

Gary stared at his partner, her hand still shading her eyes. "So it would seem."

"I'm an AA counselor," Alexie said. "I've never had any qualms about intervening into the lives of drunks. Up 'til now, all my clients have been men, working-class Alaska Native men. But this here's different. A police officer. A white, *lady* police officer. Not certain it's my place, but . . . how 'bout I have a chat with your partner?"

"Give it a go," Gary urged.

The trapper retraced his steps.

Sasha was leaning against a spruce, eyes closed, rubbing the back of her neck. She sensed the trapper's presence, stood up as straight as she could, cracked her left eye a fraction, and smiled weakly. "Thanks for the help, Mr. Alexie."

He held her gaze but didn't speak for a moment. "Detective . . .? Please remind me of your last name. I didn't catch it earlier."

"Kulaeva."

"Detective Kulaeva. You're hung-over. Let me help you."

Sasha recoiled and tried to focus on the man. His tone had been kindly, without censure. She looked toward Gary.

"You're busted, Sash," he called back to her from the meadow.

"Don't worry about being busted," Alexie told them both. "There's only the three of us here. No need to fret about that." He turned back to Sasha. "But you *are* hung-over, ma'am, and if you'll let me, I can help you."

Without waiting for a reply, he took her firmly by the elbow and steered her to the stump, the seat he had used earlier that morning. "Sit yourself," he ordered, helping her gently down. She sat, turning away from the light.

The trapper went onto his hands and knees and began pushing a bank of snow toward her. He picked up a pile and put it into her gloved hands.

"Wash your face with the snow. Rub it in good," he said.

She paused, looked again at Gary, then did as she was told. At first, she rubbed only half-heartedly, but after a moment, her skin began to tingle and she felt herself revive.

"Again" he ordered. "Do your eyes this time. Just hold the snow there for a minute. Don't rub."

Sasha took the large handful of snow and looked again at Gary. She sensed her partner's conflicted feelings: seriously aggravated, but obviously getting a kick out of the trapper's home cure.

"Do it, Sash. Do your eyes," Gary said.

She did, and it worked. The numbed, brutal thumping that had taken root behind her eyeballs now eased. With the snow pressed into her face, she was able to assess herself more honestly. She *was* hung-over. Whether she was a drunk, or just drunk last night was a distinction without a difference. For purposes of her work as a police detective, either one had career-endgame written all over it. She let the snow drop from her hands. "Better," she said. "I'm obliged to you, Mr. Alexie."

"We're not done yet. Two more places. A minute on your temples and a minute on the nape of your neck."

Sold on the trapper's remedy, she applied the snow to the designated areas and three minutes later rose to her feet on her own. She could now squint without pain.

Alexie raised himself up. "I'll go collect the rest of your police team. They should be at the trailhead by now. Normally, it wouldn't take more than twenty or thirty minutes, back and forth." The trapper smiled at Sasha. "But if I take an hour, will that be enough time for you to get yourself presentable?"

She couldn't help herself. She laughed out loud. "Dear Mr. Alexie. I'm not sure I'll *ever* get presentable. But for now, yeah, an hour should work. Thank you so much. I'm indebted to you."

"Forget the thanks, ma'am. Twenty years of working with drunks has taught me one thing—talk is cheap."

"Nothing cheaper," Gary confirmed. "I've been hearing the same shit for over a year."

Sasha stood quietly, taking in the long overdue critique of her life choices.

Alexie walked toward his snow machine, then paused. He turned and appeared to be debating with himself. "Listen, detective. I'm an Al-Anon coordinator in Eagle River. Over the years, I've sponsored a dozen drunks. All but one are alive and sober. I can help you. If you want to be helped."

"You already have. And I'm grateful. AA would be a good option for most people, but not for me, not for a cop. Word gets out, I'm toast." She hesitated. "I know there's another option. Maybe I could . . ."

". . . go to Jack and ask for rehab," Gary said. "He likes you. He'd help."

"Yeah, I could do that," she said without enthusiasm, then spoke to the trapper. "I thank you again, Mr. Alexie, with all my heart."

"You're welcome, Detective . . .?"

"Kulaeva."

Alexie allowed himself a brief, self-deprecating grin. "Back in an hour." He waved and drove off at a leisurely pace.

The two cops watched the snow machine twist around a stand of birch before disappearing into the forest. They continued to look down the trail, neither wanting to face the other and both dubious that the scene enacted over the past few minutes would have the least effect on Detective Aleksandra Kulaeva's self-destructive habits.

Just past one o'clock. The sun's high arc across the spring sky bathed the meadow in a warming white, shortening the afternoon shadows. The light layer of snow that had collected the evening before on leaves and limbs was melting and dripping to earth.

The snow therapy Alexie offered to Sasha had helped. She was nearly ready to emerge from her shaded seclusion to dare the brightness of the meadow. She still needed her dark glasses and continued to use her hand as a visor, but at least she could open her eyes wide enough to take in the activity: on either side of the ATV tracks that led into the meadow, a pair of crime scene forensic techs were slowly working their way toward the body, gently sifting through the snow, looking for things of interest, objects possibly discarded by the ATV driver.

Sasha stepped into the field, nearly tripping over the berm. Gary and a second man, Assistant Medical Examiner

Shane Sanford, were standing about ten feet from the body. The sight of the assistant M.E. made Sasha wince internally. Six years earlier, when she joined the Anchorage P.D., she had made it a point to refuse all overtures from guys in the business. And because of her back-story, known to all, she was successful. A year ago, however, Sanford's insistence and sweetness won out. But two months into an affair she thought they were keeping under wraps, he shot his mouth off to another detective. Soon, the word was out. Although Sanford was contrite, no amount of repentance could delay the inevitable: she cast him off. Life in the station house changed radically for the worse and Sasha found herself constantly having to beat back the advances of most of her male colleagues, several of them married.

Sanford looked her way. "Something you ate?"

She sensed the slightest note of put-down in his tone. *You used to be sweeter.*

"Hi Shane. Yeah. Chiles last night. Went down wrong. But I'm on the mend." She walked closer to Gary and bumped him with her shoulder.

Her partner lowered his voice and faced her, his back to Sanford. "We both know he's an asshole. But listen real good, Sasha. We get a minute free, you and I are going to have a heart-to-heart. A serious one. Hear me?"

"I'm on the same page, Gary. We'll talk. Promise. Now what's going on here?"

He turned back to the body. "Shane and I have photographed everything except the vic. Soon as the forensic team has finished searching along the ATV tread tracks, we'll get close-ups of the body."

A loud "Awright!" from one of the tech-sifters drew

their attention. He was standing three feet from the corpse and pointing down into the snow where the smoked end of a cigarette was poking into the air. He carefully took hold of it with tweezers and held the butt up to the light: half smoked, black paper, a long, gold tip. He placed it into a clear evidence baggie. "Never seen one like this," he said, handing it to Sasha.

"That's because it's Russian," she said, surprise in her voice. "Sobranie. They're manufactured in England since Soviet times. Never known anyone except Russians to smoke 'em."

"Maybe we can lift a print from the cardboard tip," Sanford said.

The sifters advanced up to the body and began the work of digging it out from the snow. It was slow, tedious work, something akin to brushing the dirt from shards at an archaeological site. As each layer of snow was removed, photos were taken.

"Glad she's not frozen into the ground," Gary said. "God knows how we'd get her out. We'd have to wait for a thaw."

Half an hour later, the dead woman was moved onto a large tarp—her body still somewhat flexible. She was completely naked. One of her arms lay across her stomach, while the other—the one that had caught the eye of the trapper that morning—was raised, as though hailing a cab.

Sanford and the forensic team now closed in.

Although the pecked and chewed portions of her body were obviously prominent, it was a syringe, buried to the hilt, protruding from her left buttock, that drew their initial attention.

"They'll be trace evidence in the needle," Sanford said,

taking photos. "Always is." He moved closer to the woman's head. "Check this out."

Both detectives leaned in to take a closer look.

Sanford pointed to the woman's mouth. Although most of her lips had been eaten by the birds, there remained a crust of hardened, small pink bubbles where her lower lip should have been.

"This might be a foam cap. Usually caused by drugs that suppress breathing. Normally, we could verify by checking the vic's pupils. Give us a hint as to what might be in the syringe. But, since she doesn't have any eyes . . ." Sanford chuckled.

Not sweet at all, Sasha thought.

The Assistant M.E. began his preliminary post-mortem examination with a general description of the body, speaking into a voice-activated recorder on his collar.

"Hispanic or native woman, twenty-five to thirty. Looks to be no taller than five-foot one, approximately one hundred, fifteen pounds. Victim has long, straight black hair. Most of her upper torso has been eaten by birds, but the portions that were under the snow look relatively intact. Possible chaffing around her shaved pubic area. Faint trace of lividity spread throughout right rib cage, right side of face, and right thigh. Deeper lividity along spine and back of thighs." He paused and turned to the two detectives with a blank expression, as if daring one of them to ask about lividity. Neither took the challenge.

Sanford continued, "Victim has deep ligature marks on wrists and ankles." He turned to the detectives. "Someone bound her up pretty tightly."

Sasha felt her teeth start to grind.

"No jewelry," Sanford continued. "Painted toe nails. We'll bag her hands, hope to preserve whatever might be under her nails. Maybe she put up a fight. Might have scratched some skin off the perp." He asked two of the crime scene techs to turn her over on her other side.

Sasha said, "She's got a tat on her lower back: FSU."

"Could be the Seminoles, Florida State," Gary said.

Sanford circled the body. "Once she's totally thawed, we'll have a better idea what happened to her, and in what sequence. We can't do toxicology on her organs, blood work-up, or stomach contents until she's unfrozen. Meanwhile, we can speculate that those marks all across her chest and breasts are burns. And she's got multiple abrasions around both her vagina and her anus, so we'll test for semen residue in every orifice."

"Any idea when she was killed?" Gary asked.

"Really hard to pin point the time of death but it's clear from how supple her body still is that she couldn't have been here in the meadow more than a night. Two nights here, what with the low temps we've been having and she'd pretty much be a popsicle.

"And the cause of death?" Sasha asked.

"Hard to say. She's taken a beating, that's for sure. Dislocated jaw. But cause of death? Need to look at the syringe."

Towards five in the afternoon, the few remaining crime team members were wrapping up, packing their gear into a sled drawn by an ATV. The victim's twisted and half-frozen body was long gone, stuffed into an extra large body bag and loaded onto a game sled borrowed from Nelson Alexie. Gary and Sanford had accompanied the body back to the trailhead, leaving Sasha to close up the crime scene.

The trapper had remained throughout the afternoon. He approached Sasha. "You're looking better, Detective Kulaeva."

"Feeling better, too. Thanks, Mr. Alexie."

"You have a lot of work to do. Don't put it off."

"I hear you, sir."

Alexie regarded her closely, then turned, went to his snow machine, mounted and drove away.

Ten minutes later, being towed back to the trailhead, Sasha thought about her options. Option, really. Since AA was a non-starter, rehab was it. *Jack's going to be so disappointed. And I'm already on Gary's shit list. No way around it. Rehab. Christ, could I use a beer right now.*

~~~

On August 16, 1999, a Saturday, Boris Bunin met his wife. He remembers it was a gray day, drizzle in the forecast and a brisk wind blowing off the East River. Despite the unhappy auguries, he counts it the luckiest day of his life.

He and his entourage were in a three-car caravan, half way across the Brooklyn Bridge. Boris was in the middle car's passenger seat, Taras, driving. The other two cars, front and back, were filled with protective muscle.

"Boris Davidich, you asked me a week ago if I had a copy of Solzhenitsyn's short stories," Taras reminded his boss. "I don't, but I called over to Russian Bookstore 21, on Fifth Avenue. They've put a copy of *Apricot Jam and Other Stories* on hold for you. We can swing by right now."

Boris had read a few of the Nobel laureate's chestnuts:

One Day in the Life of Ivan Denisovich, and *The Gulag Archipelago*. But for some reason, Solzhenitsyn's collection of short tales had not found a place on Boris' night table.

"Thank you, Taras, but we haven't the time right now. We're supposed to be uptown in half an hour. Perhaps on the way home?"

"The bookstore's on the way. Ten minutes, tops. Trust me," Taras insisted.

"Fine. But if we're late, you'll pay for the book."

"I already have," the driver said.

They pulled into an underground parking lot on East 23rd. A steal at $7/half hour—weekend rates.

The six formidable bodyguards formed a scrum around the shorter Boris as they circled the Flatiron Building. A crowd had gathered outside the bookstore—older Russian men and women, clearly having a good time. Coming closer, Boris could hear the sounds from within—people applauding, cheering. He left his small army at the door and had Taras carve a channel for him. The bodyguard's bulk cleared the way.

The bookstore was packed. A moderator stood on a raised platform thanking an older woman—just stepping down from the improvised stage—for her declamation of three poems by Lermontov.

Boris cursed having missed the recitation. He adored Lermontov. The first poem he had ever memorized as a child was the poet's *The Sail.*

The moderator now invited to the stage a young woman, small, dark, intensely vibrant, lovely. He introduced her as Larissa Kirillovna Stolypina. He told the crowd she was born and raised in St. Petersburg and had arrived in America only in the past year. The man lowered the standing microphone a few inches to accommodate her, then left the stage.

The woman stepped forward and in an unexpectedly deep and throaty voice, thanked the man. She paused for a moment, looking down, preparing herself. Then she raised her head and without further hesitation began her recitation,

'I have come to you with a greeting to tell you the sun has arisen . . . .'

There was an audible sigh of joy and approval from the audience. Neither Boris nor anyone else in the bookstore needed to hear another line to recognize the chillingly seductive poem by Afanasy Fet.

The combination of the woman's striking looks, her Piaf-like presentation—hands at her sides, letting the words speak for themselves—and the husky quality of her voice worked a spell on the listeners. Not a sound, not a shoe shuffle, not a cough until the four stanza poem concluded,

'I myself don't know what I'll sing . . . I know only that a song has awakened within me.'

Having held their collective breaths, the crowd now exhaled, then exploded into a chorus of *'brava'* and *'hurrah.'*

Boris couldn't take his eyes off the woman. As soon as she descended from the riser, he moved toward her just as three other young men were also closing in.

Anticipating Boris' intention, Taras again preceded him, politely though insistently clearing the way. "Pardon me, please," the bodyguard said, laying an immense paw on the shoulder of one of the admirers. Nothing the young man could do but give way. Taras now stepped aside, allowing Boris to move into the woman's line of vision. She eyed him with an amused expression, gazed up at Taras and then back to Boris. "Good day gentlemen," she said.

Boss and bodyguard exchanged glances, confounded, wondering which of them was supposed to speak.

For their first meeting, Boris suggested a stroll on the Brighton Beach boardwalk. As soon as they began their promenade, Larissa noticed that three men were accompanying them, one in front, one trailing behind, and Taras, abreast of them, on the opposite side of the boardwalk.

All three had tried, wholly unsuccessfully, to remain discreetly out of view. But Larissa had spotted the escorts right away and stopped walking. "Well, Boris Davidovich. What's going on?" Her tone seemed to demand nothing less than a totally honest answer.

"Taras, you've met," Boris said.

"Yes, he's very sweet. But I don't recall you telling me that he was invited to our walk. And the other two? The one up ahead pretending to look in at the store window, and the one in back of us, buying an ice cream cone?"

Boris hesitated. In the face of her frontal attack, he couldn't even parry. "Actually, Lara, they are . . . my bodyguards."

She bridled and stared at him sternly. "Lara, is it? Really?" She straightened. "It's Larissa Kirillovna, until I say differently."

He bowed an apology for his unwarranted, and far too early intimacy. "I am well rebuked, Larissa Kirillovna. Forgive me, please."

She allowed herself a half-smile and they continued slowly strolling. "So again, Boris Davidovich, why would someone with a chain of dry cleaning businesses need bodyguards?"

He stopped and leaned upon the wooden guardrail that kept folks from falling off the boardwalk onto the sand, ten feet below. He looked far out to sea, watched a squadron of gulls as they raced over the waves, squawking at each other.

The truth is, Larissa Kirillovna . . ." He couldn't make the words come out of his mouth. Words he had never spoken before.

"We are speaking truthfully here, are we not, Boris Davidovich?"

"We are. Definitely," he rushed to assure her. *It's now or never with this woman. If I tell her the truth, what'll she think of me? But if I lie to her, she'll see right through me. She'll turn and walk away, and we'll never meet again.*

"The truth is . . ." He licked his lips and mumbled, just loudly enough for her to hear, "My father is the head of the Russian mafia here in South Brooklyn." There it was. He said it. It could not be recanted.

She didn't blink. Her expression was sober, unreadable.

"He'll be retiring in a year or two. At which time I'll take over." Another pause as he looked directly at her. "If this information offends you, Larissa Kirillovna, I'll have Taras drive you home right now," his voice caught, "and I'll never contact you again."

She didn't move to leave, but joined him in leaning over the guardrail, resting on her forearms. A salty gust blew off the ocean, whipping her long hair. She reached up, gathered a handful, and twisted it into a rough braid.

The gesture caused a delicious knot that filled Boris' chest. He continued in a hoarse voice, unsure of himself, yet hopeful, "But if you decide to remain here with me now

. . ." He left off, not knowing how to finish. Promises and declarations seemed out of place.

"Tell me everything you do, Boris Davidovich. Don't leave anything out. Tell me everything and I'll think about staying. At least until dinner time." She smiled and let her hand, hanging over the guardrail, move a fraction to the left to lightly brush his own.

For the next two hours, standing, sitting, and strolling along the boardwalk like any other courting couple, South Brooklyn's capo-in-waiting explained what he did. He never spoke the words murder, torture, fire-bomb, or extort. He never mentioned kidnapping, gambling, smuggling, narcotics, or prostitution. It was enough that he alluded to them, hinted at them.

She caught the meaning but remained unruffled, carefully assessing this man who seemed hell-bent on winning her heart. And the more she listened, the more it was clear to her that his words did *not* offend. If she had to choose an occupation for a boyfriend, a lover, a spouse, it would *not* be crime boss of South Brooklyn. Although his words didn't exactly thrill her, his impassioned honesty was making an impression.

It was past six when he finished, the eastern sky darkening over the Atlantic. A cooling wind brought out goose bumps on her bare, upper arms. Boris took off his sports coat and laid it gently over her shoulders.

"Thank you, Borya," she said, reaching up and straightening his shirt collar.

He felt as he had in the bookstore—like cheering. "You are very welcome," he paused, "Lara," he said in a hushed tone, drawing his coat more tightly around her.

~~~

A springtime Sunday night at the station house and everyone could feel the pace quickening. People were being wheeled in—cuffed or not, belligerent, freaked, stoned, embarrassed—in numbers not seen since autumn.

Alaska's long winters tend to make folks want to stay indoors and help keep the lid on, help keep the crime rate at a manageable level. But because of the warming weather and lengthening days—nine o'clock and still tons of light—the city's rowdies were out in force. People who had taken shelter for the winter, who had kept their lunacy in hibernation, now felt free to howl at the spring moon. Bikers vroomed their Harleys on streets that were barely ice-free; joy-riding kids celebrated the coming end of the school year and the state's legalization of recreational pot; panhandlers who had survived the winter in their lean-tos congregated on corners with their signs promising a day of labor for spare change and God Bless; prostitutes working the streets were now able to shuck off their bulky, formless parkas and show their wares to good advantage; and the city's drunks left the urine-stenched Brother Michael Shelter to stagger across the highways and clog the ERs.

Being a sometime drinker-to-excess herself, *and* being a police officer, Sasha Kulaeva was ambivalent about her vice. Because she was of Russian extraction, people naturally assumed she imbibed. She regularly had to field questions—usually friendly and joking—about liquor. *If they only knew.*

Sasha found she could abide the boozing class if they'd just keep to themselves, if they didn't stick their drunken snouts too noticeably into the public trough. What pissed her off as much as the crimes committed by drunks was the toll their self-indulgence took on community resources. *If you're going to be a drunk,* she thought, *don't make society pay for your liver transplant. If you're going to diet on Ding Dongs, we shouldn't have to cover your Type 2 diabetes treatment. And if you're going to smoke unfiltered cigarettes, we absolutely should not have to pick up the tab for the oxygen canisters you need to ease your COPD.*

She preferred to save her energy and the department's scant funds for the serious criminal class, those beasts of prey who commit heinous crimes, like the one perpetrated on the woman discovered this morning in the snowy meadow.

Over the past few years, she had developed her own, *very personal* version of the penal code, according to which criminals could expect to suffer the full force of whatever punishment *she, herself* might mete out. Sasha remembers the exact moment when she'd expanded the authority of her badge to include other, unassigned, duties—judge, jury, executioner.

In 2013, two nine-year-old twin sisters went missing, stayed missing for a month, then had their mutilated and violated bodies dredged up from Goose Lake, near the university.

The victims' stepfather, a local evangelical pastor, ultimately confessed after witnesses and DNA put him at the scene.

Detectives Hernandez and Kulaeva confronted the man with the incontrovertible evidence. He showed neither understanding of, nor remorse for the crime he had committed. He claimed his stepdaughters' fascination with popular music had driven him to try to instill in them the true love of Christ. Sasha wanted to gouge out the man's eyes. Luckily, Gary grabbed her and put her out of the interrogation room. She thanked him later, called in sick and stayed home for two days, alternately crying and inveighing against the gods of every faith.

The accused's parishioners came up with the half-million dollar bail, putting their church property up as surety. The flock was either unconvinced of his guilt, forgave the man his trespasses, or simply didn't give a shit that their religious leader was a murdering pedophile.

But Sasha Kulaeva cared. A great deal.

When the accused, out on bail, missed a scheduled court appearance, a bench warrant was issued. Police searched high and low, far and wide. Deacons of the church, faced with the forfeiture of their building, assembled a posse of 'fugitive recovery specialists,' aka bounty hunters. All efforts failed. The pastor was never seen or heard from again, the church property was forfeited, and Detective Kulaeva felt justice had been served.

Tonight, sitting behind her desk in the squad room, she began to document the progress of the current murder investigation. The detective in her would face up to the task of doing what a detective needed to be doing right now—assembling the information, distinguishing fact from speculation, writing the pertinent info onto the big white crime board in the squad room.

She could do all that. She was good at that.

But the avenging angel in her had re-awakened and was demanding her attention.

Sasha pushed away from her desk and tipped back in her chair, letting her head rest against a metal filing cabinet. She pressed the heels of her palms into her eye sockets, her fingers extending over her forehead. She let a minute go by, sat straight up, and vigorously rubbed her face. She came out from behind her desk, grabbed her carryall, left the squad room, and hurried down the dimly lit hallway to the women's restroom. It was empty. Sasha wrinkled her nose at the smell of fresh disinfectant. She locked herself in and rummaged in the bottom of her carryall until she found a small, unmarked bottle, one she'd purposely avoided for the past year. She uncapped it and sniffed the contents.

Minutes before, she imagined that at this precise moment she'd be faced with a 'Should I or shouldn't I?' moment of truth-seeking. *The hell with it,* she thought. She put the bottle to her lips and took a long swallow. The Cuervo hit the back of her throat and made her cough.

She rested her forehead against the cool of the mirror and waited for the liquor to flow its way into her system. She thought about Nelson Alexie's admonition about the work she needed to do. Work she was obviously not ready to begin. She opened her eyes and looked at her reflection, not liking what she saw.

Despite her self-critique, the shot of liquor worked its magic. The anger that had been building all day began to slide away. She took another gulp, smaller this time, then capped the bottle. She buried it back in her carryall and rooted around until she found the red and white tin of Altoids. She chewed up three of the mints, put the tin in her pocket, washed her hands and face, and returned to the squad room.

Sitting back at her desk, she was able to manage a slight smile. She resumed work on the crime scene preliminary report. She felt better, but hated herself for it.

"Lab thinks it's heroin and maybe something else in the syringe, but they'll know more tomorrow," Detective Gary

Hernandez reported over the phone. "And Shane, at the morgue, confirmed the body'll take a couple days to thaw completely, so no autopsy 'til then. He told us not to bug 'im. He'll call us when he has something."

Sasha held an Altoid between her teeth, spinning it with her tongue. "What about prints off the cigarette and the syringe?" she asked.

"Tomorrow. Same with anything they might find under the vic's fingernails. He'll be in touch."

"Okay. Sounds like progress. And you? What're you up to right now?"

"I'm on to something. I'm trying to get hold of a guy from Fish and Wildlife. Name's McKimmey. He called in a missing person yesterday, one of his field biologists. Been gone for several days. The description he gave matches the woman in the meadow. I've left messages at his home for a call back." Gary hesitated. "Anyhow . . ."

Sasha knew what was coming, what was on his mind. "Say it, Gary. I need to hear it."

He exhaled once, then launched. "You were fucked up today. In the woods. You were big time hung-over."

"You're right. I don't deny it." She felt tempted to offer an explanation, that she had been a good, sober girl for almost a year and that this morning's fiasco was an unfortunate lapse—start of a three day weekend and all. But she didn't think her partner'd buy it. *Why should he?*

Gary sensed her hesitancy. "Something you want to say? Huh? OK, Listen, kiddo. We're together nearly four years. You're a great partner Sash, and I love you to pieces. But . . ." He left it hanging.

"Go on. Don't be shy. I promise I won't take offense."

"I let it slide that first time, last year. I should have brought the hammer down on you then. My fault I went easy. This time you're pushing me into doing something I don't want to do. I don't want to go to Jack. But you're making it hard for me to keep quiet. It's one thing to be hung-over at the office like you were a year ago. We got away with that one. But it's something else entirely when you're fucked up at a crime scene. You were lucky no one else from the department was around when we got there. Lucky it was only me and the trapper. Anybody else there, you're blowing into a breathalyzer right now. Talking to IA. Suspended. You listening to me? Say something."

"I could try and find an excuse. But anything I might come up with, you'd call horse shit. And you'd be right."

His tone softened. "Come clean with Jack. He'll support you, so will Polly, if you go into rehab. Then take six months. Go on up to Big Lake, to your homestead. Fly your plane all over the state. Be with your daughter, your family, people who cherish you."

"You cherish me."

"'Course I do. Which is why I'm telling you to take some time."

"Listen, my good and faithful partner, how 'bout this? Let's you and me finish this case. Then I'll go to Jack. Meanwhile, I'll be good. Promise."

"Have I heard that one before?"

"Yeah. You've heard it before. A year ago. I was kidding you then, kidding myself. But this time . . ."

"This time you're serious? Is that what you're telling me? Is that what you'd like me to believe? The trapper today, Alexie, busted you good when he told you how cheap talk is."

Gary waited a beat. "I'd like to believe that you're serious, Sash."

"I'd like to believe it, too. Can we please talk more tomorrow, over donuts?"

"Count on it. I'm on your ass every day. Get that into your head. No mercy."

"I got it. And I appreciate it. Thanks for caring. See you for coffee."

"Yeah. In the morning."

Detective Alexandra Kulaeva put down the receiver, finished entering the pertinent data into the police report and uploaded it. Then she logged out and left the station. It was ten-thirty and the sun was sinking below the city scape.

Driving home, she could think only of the last two bottles of beer in her fridge. *I am so fucking weak!*

~~~

It took a little over four hours for the *Pyotr Veliky* to return to the approximate location where the American fisheries observer had likely gone into the ocean—a three hundred square mile chunk of a very dangerous Bering Sea.

Captain Vronsky's mayday alert had succeeded in drawing to the area all kinds of help: the American Coast Guard cutter *Hammersmith,* a twin-engine aircraft owned by Savoonga Aviation based on St. Lawrence Island, and a pair of helicopters from two Norton Sound off-shore oil platforms.

The rotten weather of the evening before had abated somewhat, the winds having dropped to a moderate—for the Bering Sea—fifteen knots, with waves cresting at only eight feet.

The hunt for the missing man, however, ended almost before it began.

The short-range helicopters based on the oil platforms eighty miles west of Nome spent only an hour searching before they had to return to refuel. They gave up after three trips, the availability of av-gas the determining factor.

And after only two hours searching the ocean, Savoonga Aviation's Twin Cessna 340, the air taxi service's longest-range aircraft, was called back to its St. Lawrence Island home. A newborn with acute breathing problems needed an immediate medevac to Providence Hospital in Anchorage.

The Coast Guard's *Hammersmith* would have continued the search but the cutter's computer propulsion control failed. Her engines were compromised and she was reduced to quarter speed. The captain called a halt to his rescue efforts, fearful of his vessel being swamped. Under reduced speed, the ship limped back to Dutch Harbor.

That left the *Pyotr Veliky* and a disgruntled Yury Vronsky in his ship's wheelhouse. The captain let his binoculars hang. They'd been a fixture around his neck since the morning before when the search for the missing man had begun.

"This is a load of shit, Valery. We've done our bit," Vronsky said to his first mate. "Maybe he's still out there. But even if he is, he's sure to have died from exposure. This is no longer a rescue. It's now a body recovery. Am I right?"

"You don't have to convince me, captain," Timoshenko said. "I'm thinking he's probably at the bottom of the ocean, part of the food chain by now."

"It was an accident, for sure. Comes with the job. Men have been lost at sea since people got it into their heads to see what was beyond the salty horizon." The captain returned his gaze out over the ocean and declaimed,

"Gleams white a single sail in the haze of the light blue sea. What does he seek in a foreign land? What has he left in his native strand?"

Timoshenko never failed to be amused when his captain waxed poetic. He turned his face from Vronsky, lest his smile give him away.

The ship's master shook his head. "It's possible the idiot was simply swept into the sea by a wave washing the decks. It was stormy."

Timoshenko scratched at his beard. "An all too common fate, captain. One should probably not even venture topside in such weather."

"Could be he lost his footing and slipped over the side."

"Happens all the time. I nearly went over myself, eight years ago, not far from Yuzhno."

"Or perhaps the man was disturbed, depressed, wanted to end it all."

"Not unheard of, captain. There was that Ukrainian, the assistant cook, shipped out with me on the *Pobeda,* nine, ten years ago. Morose son of a bitch. From Kharkiv. Always going on about his wife. She'd run off the year before, taking all his savings. He told a few of his mates 'goodbye' and jumped over the side."

Vronsky nodded. "I remember hearing about him. Litvinenko. Poroshenko. Something like that." The captain took up his binoculars once again and spent a minute scanning the ocean. Then he whispered, "Or maybe, Valery Stepanich," Vronsky paused a moment, "he was helped into the sea by one of *our* crewmen. Not a crazy idea, right?"

Timoshenko shrugged. "Well, Captain, it's a possibility, that last one. Though I'd be hard pressed to name a member of our crew who disliked the American so much he'd throw the man overboard."

"Right. You're right," Vronsky added hurriedly, unhappy with his own suggestion. "Some of these American fish monitors are smart asses. We've had a few. Crew hates 'em. But this kid wasn't the worst. He got along, didn't he?"

"He did, captain. I thought he was okay. So did most of the crew. At least, for an American fisheries observer. It's a rotten job in the first place. But he wasn't a bad sort."

"Well, *we* may not think it's much of a possibility, but the Americans are of a different mind. *They* think the idea of an angry Russian seaman tossing an American observer overboard is not beyond the pale. That's why they've ordered us to Dutch Harbor. They want to hear *my* version of the disappearance. Like I have a version! It'll be a total waste of time." Vronsky put his binoculars to his eyes and spent a minute searching the sea. "If it had been a Russian seaman overboard, you think those fucking Americans would search as carefully and as long as we have?"

"No way, Captain."

"Well, the sooner the man is officially declared dead, the quicker we can return to the fishing grounds for the few days left to us." Vronsky now practiced his limited English, *"This be the verse you 'grave for me: Here he lies where he long'd to be; Home is the sailor, home from the sea . . ."*

"Beautiful, Captain."

Vronsky smiled. "I'm happy you appreciate Walt Whitman. He's my favorite American poet."

Timoshenko was of two minds—to allow his captain to continue to believe the poem was by Whitman, or to tell him the truth—Robert Louis Stevenson.

Before the first mate could decide, the master of the *Pyotr Veliky* spoke, "The hell with the American, Valery. Let's end this foolish search right here and now. Take the bridge, steer us for Dutch Harbor. I'll be in the mess."

With the captain departed, Timoshenko turned to the helmsman. "Robert Louis Stevenson," he said to the man.

"If you say so, Valery Stepanich," the helmsman replied.

3

Two weeks after their boardwalk promenade, Larissa Stolypina took her new beau to the Metropolitan Museum to see an exhibition of German Expressionism. She had to drag him there.

"All that slow walking, Lara, picture to picture, makes my back ache. I can usually last about an hour before I have to take a rest. Besides which, I have a Russian's natural antipathy to anything Teutonic."

"I can't do anything about your inherent dislike of things German," Larissa said, "but perhaps I might interest you in something French. There's a room up on the second floor where there's a collection of paintings by Corot. It's the first gallery I visit whenever I'm here."

"Corot? Not sure I've heard of him. But let's have a look."

She led him by the hand up the Met's wide staircase and brought him to Gallery 803, to stand in front of Corot's *The Gypsies.*

Boris closely regarded the painting, hardly moving. Finally, "I like it, Lara. That little bit of flame in the twilight. He's good. Very good."

"I'm glad you like him."

They meandered through the other nearby European painting galleries until Boris began rubbing his lower back.

"I think we're nearing your sixty minute limit," she said. "Let's sit."

She steered him to a small gallery deep in the heart of the museum, in the middle of which stood a blue sofa. They were the only two people in the room. Three paintings by Francisco Goya were on the wall facing the sofa. Boris examined them. "Dark. Too dark. This one here—*The View of Toledo*—gives me the shivers."

"I think it's supposed to do that. But if you let it, it may grow on you," she said, sitting herself down, sinking into the plush sofa.

Boris came and sat close to her. He took her hand and pressed it to his cheek. "So here we are, Lara. We've known each other for such a short time. I have questions. May I ask?"

"Ask what you will, Borya. I'm an open book."

"Well, I know you were raised in St. Petersburg."

"Until I was twenty-one. Then we went to Israel. Stayed there for three years."

"Jewish? And a Refusenik? You could have fooled me," he laughed.

"I'm neither, Borya. But we wanted out of Russia and that was the only way. We know lots of non-Jews who did the same thing. All of us wormed our way out of the Soviet Union and landed in Israel."

"So, three years in the Holy Land? What was that like?"

"Too holy, but certainly better than the Soviet Union. Better food, better climate. But we had no interest in staying. So, we came here."

"I'm wondering, Lara. How did you manage . . .?" he trailed off.

"Manage what?"

"Well. This is not the most welcoming country in the world for immigrants these days, despite the *'give us your tired . . .'* on the Statue of Liberty. When my grandparents came here in 1905, they went through a simple process at Ellis Island and were done in a few hours. Today, it's a totally different story. Quotas, bans. It can take years. How did you arrange it?"

"We convinced the people at the American Embassy in Tel Aviv that we had sponsors—relatives and friends here in New York who would guarantee our safety and livelihood." Boris arched his eyebrows. "I've heard that one dozens of times. It almost never works. Why'd they believe you?"

Lara shrugged, smiling. "One man believed me. That's all it took." She dropped his hand and looked away.

"Ahhh. I get it now. Your feminine wiles, perhaps? Let's hear it."

She hesitated, stood, and walked toward *The View of Toledo*. "You're right, Borya. It *is* dark."

"Why do I sense reluctance, Larissa Kirillovna? Are you avoiding the question?"

She turned to face him. "It's true. I'm a little hesitant."

He gave back her own words, spoken to him a few weeks before, "We are being truthful here, are we not . . .?" His accompanying smile eased the moment. But it was out there. Tit for tat.

She looked at him and nodded. "Well then, if you insist."

The young man sitting opposite her, asking her questions, charting the course of her life, was far too young for the job, she thought. His US Embassy, Tel Aviv, badge named him and gave him a title: Warren Featherly, Jr., Asylum Assessment Officer. She guessed his age at twenty-five.

What Mr. Featherly Jr. had been assessing for the past half hour was the validity of the story he had been listening to out of the mouth of one of the most gorgeous women he had ever seen. Certainly the most gorgeous he had ever interviewed.

The man's judgment was clouded by the fact that the woman's loose fitting, not quite diaphanous blouse, was unbuttoned to the middle of her sternum. She wore no brassiere and her perfect, dark, and sharply pointed nipples could be easily discerned. The woman's eyes roved around the small interview room, allowing him ample opportunity to focus on her breasts. He continuously licked his lips. He was aware of it but could not help himself. He kept sipping at his bottle of Evian, hoping to keep his tongue from cleaving to his palate.

The woman, a Russian beauty in her mid-twenties, was claiming that she and her family had numerous relations in the United States who were willing to sponsor her. She had presented documents from a large Reform temple—B'nei Avram Stern, on Long Island—as well as testimonials from Hadassah in New York City, and from several Jewish lawmakers from Albany.

Featherly Jr. thought the story she had presented was drivel. Hogwash. Bullshit. He had reviewed similar testimonials presented by scores of Russians. He was fairly certain that the woman wasn't even Jewish. A phony Refusenik, one of the many he'd interviewed and turned down. He was about to stamp 'DENIED' on her application when the most remarkable thing in the up-until-then rather uneventful life of Warren Featherly Jr. took place: the woman got up off her seat, went to the office door and locked it. She then turned back to face her inquisitor and began, very slowly, to unbutton her blouse, taking a languorously long time with each button, never taking her gaze from the young man, whose eyes were, naturally, riveted.

Blouse unbuttoned, she let it fall off and laid it over her chair. Her magnificent breasts were . . . well, magnificent. Her hands now moved to the zipper on the side of her skirt.

Twenty minutes later, Larissa Kirillovna Stolypina and her family were permitted to enter the United States.

When she finished, Lara looked at Boris, trying to decipher the man's expression. "Well, Borya. If anything I've said has offended, you can let Taras know. He's in the next gallery behind us. He can drive me home and I'll never bother you again. Sound familiar?" She couldn't help smiling.

Nor could he. Boris began to laugh, at first a light chuckle. A minute later he was wiping tears from his eyes. He sat back into the sofa, put his knees together, and invited her to sit.

Larissa came over and straddled him, facing him. She put her palms on his shoulders. He put his hands on her hips.

"Last month, Borya, on the boardwalk, when you told me about your business, how did you think I'd react? How sure were you that I wouldn't walk away?"

"I thought there was only a one in five chance that you'd leave. Good odds, I thought. I was hopeful you'd stay."

"And I did."

"And you did. And I can't tell you how happy you made me. More than you can possibly know. But now, dearest, the same question for you. Before revealing to me this tale of your womanly powers, how did you think I'd react? Did you *really* believe I'd be offended?"

"About the same odds, Borya. About one in five that you'd find me somehow . . . unsuitable."

"The opposite, Lara. I find you absolutely irresistible. I am in awe of your strength and determination. And your trust in me, telling me this story."

She leaned forward, her forearms now resting on his chest, their faces close, their bodies pressed together.

Two teenage girls who were about to enter the gallery caught sight of the man and woman on the sofa. The couple were oblivious to the girls, who paused at the entrance, waiting. They watched as the woman's loose hair fell forward and swept the man's shoulders. Finally, he reached up to take her by the nape of the neck and very gently pulled her to him. The couple softly kissed.

The girls silently cheered.

~~~

"Here's the name of a terrific counselor," Gary said, handing his partner a pink Post-It.

Sasha took it and read out loud, "Katherine Manfredi. MSW, Clinical Psychologist, Licensed Professional Counselor."

"I'm serious, Sasha. She's the real deal."

The two detectives were meeting outside of *Borealis Espresso*, one of the scores of drive-up coffee trailers that materialize daily in empty lots all over Anchorage. The cops were dressed appropriately for the cool spring morning—light parkas, wool caps, and gloves.

"How do you know about her?" Sasha asked.

"I just know. Doesn't matter how. Go see her. She'll make time for you. You can phone her cold. She'll email you a questionnaire. Want you to get it back to her before the first session."

Sasha folded the Post-It and put it into her wallet. "Alright, thanks. I'll call her later. Do I give her your regards?"

They were on opposite sides of Gary's police cruiser, leaning over the hood, coffee cups, napkins, and a brown bag spread out before them. The early morning sun was raising steam from the cruiser's roof.

Gary took hold of the bag and tore it down the side, spreading it out and exposing two churros and two glazed donuts. He went for a churro, dipped it into his coffee, and took a bite. "She doesn't know me," he said with a full mouth.

"No? Okay. Go be all mysterious." Sasha smiled and grabbed a glazed donut.

She and Gary had started off rocky, four years earlier, his East L.A. creds not counting for a lot with her. They had distinctly different styles. She was rougher, enjoyed playing the hard ass. He was less judgmental. She worked from her gut, allowing her instincts to guide her. He was an evidence geek. She was the better writer. He, the better interrogator. It took six months, but things ultimately smoothed out to the point where they became after-work friends. Gary, his wife Flor, and their two girls often visited Sasha's family's homestead at Big Lake.

About her husband, Sasha remained close mouthed. Gary knew the bare details of Robin Hutchinson's death. Everyone in Alaskan law enforcement did. But he also knew there was a no-man's-land beyond the very few facts Sasha was willing to offer.

They worked well as a team. Until a year ago when they hit a bump in the road.

Gary had come in early and found Sasha bleary-eyed and hung-over. He caught the rancid odor of early-morning-after-a-night-of-drinking boozy breath. He was stunned. For all of their closeness, he never had any indication that Sasha drank to excess. Sure, a couple beers after work, a glass or two of wine when they were out together with their families. But here she was, shit-faced *and* at work. If caught, the sky would fall, compliments of the pricks from IA.

Gary hustled her to the nearest bathroom, forced her head under the sink's cold water tap, made compresses for her forehead, and shoved piece after piece of gum into her mouth to get rid of the damning scent of alcohol.

She accepted his help for a while, but then tried to force her way out of the room. He grabbed her, spun her around, and gave her two good smacks in the face—forehand and backhand. He drew blood from her lip and left a large, red welt on her cheek. She was stunned and submitted to his care giving. Ten minutes later, he snuck her out of the building, piled her into his own car, and drove her home. The next day she showed up embarrassed and apologetic. She abased herself, swearing, vowing never to allow this to happen again. "An aberration," she told him. "A one and only occurrence. Promise."

For a year or so, Gary believed her to be true to her word. Until yesterday morning.

Sasha was half way through her second glazed donut. "Did you get hold of the guy from Fish and Game?"

"Fish and Wildlife. Yeah. I think we got a positive match." He pulled out a small notebook, flipped through it. "The guy who filed the missing person, Judson McKimmey— he's in charge of migratory birds—says that one of his staff, Doctor Isabel Castro, has been missing for a week. Says she's from Florida and graduated from Florida State. FSU, the tat on the vic's back."

"Great work. Anything else?"

"He said that Castro's best friend is his administrative assistant." Gary again consulted his notes. "Rose Nakamura. He's sending her to the morgue this morning to help with the ID."

"No family?"

"There's a brother around, but no one knows where he is. So, it's the secretary. Go with her, hold her hand."

"I can do that. Captain wants to see me first."

~~~

Detective Captain Jack Raymond sat in his office with his back to the closed door. He faced a wall full of commendations. He puffed on a pipe, inhaling the aromatic Black Cavendish that had become his tobacco of choice after his wife, Marie, insisted he give up his two pack/day Camels. Although the station was ostensibly a smoke-free zone, everyone indulged the captain. They had to. But to placate the non-smokers, Raymond kept one of his windows slightly ajar. And because it was cracked open even in the winter, it was not unusual seeing people wearing their parkas in Captain Raymond's office.

Twenty-four hours earlier, his most able pair of detectives began investigating the death of a young woman—burned, beaten, tortured.

Raymond had a hard time making himself care. Equal parts callousness and apathy were at the root of his indifference. Too many murder investigations had carved out a void where his sympathies used to lie. Too many wife beatings, child molestations, armed robberies.

When he began as a street cop, in the early eighties, there were less than 160,000 people living in Anchorage. The police and the troopers were able to handle the load. But an expanding oil industry and an increased military presence had doubled the population.

Believing the battle now pretty much lost, Raymond was ready to throw in the towel. *Fuck it. Let me just retire, find somewhere quiet for me and Marie. Somewhere I can escape to, hoping the memories that I've accumulated will dissolve, will become unheard background music to the rest of my days.*

Six months earlier, his daughter, Janelle, living in San Diego, gave birth to triplet boys, Jack and Marie's first grandchildren. To his constant and nagging chagrin, Raymond had seen the babies only one time, for three days, when they were newborn and either slept, cried or ate—neither the time nor the place, he thought, to practice spoiling his grandsons. Marie bought him a smart phone so he could watch the boys long distance, in real time. But it wasn't enough. He needed to touch them, to hold them.

Raymond swiveled in his chair, refilled his pipe, tamped the tobacco and re-lit. He took a shallow inhalation as he eyed the two thin piles of paper stacked neatly in front of him. Atop one was an *Anchorage Police Department: Protect and Serve* ballpoint pen. Clicked open. Ready to write. He regarded the pen for a moment, picked it up, felt its weight, then clicked it shut, and returned it to the pile.

He turned his attention to the other set of papers and began re-reading the printout of the preliminary police report prepared by Detective Sasha Kulaeva. As usual with her work, the report was succinct, free of ambiguity, and informative. A good start.

He thought about this latest victim. Who was she? How was she killed? How did last week's alive young woman become yesterday's corpse? Perhaps she helped bring about her own demise. Did something stupid. Two-timed her volatile, fly-off-the-handle boyfriend. Took someone's money. Held out on her pimp. Maybe she got what she had coming to her. Maybe she was a total bitch, a pariah, a blight on society, someone who'd be better off dead.

Raymond reprimanded himself. *This is no way for a detective captain to think. She was the victim, after all, and I'm still in the Protect and Serve game. At least for the short term.*

The policeman had long ago come to a dismal and cynical realization: that just as citizens get the governments they deserve, so too, many victims often get the fate *they* deserve. An opinion clearly at odds with the public's popular notions about crime and punishment, but one that was more in line with what many cops feel, deep down, though they would be reluctant to share those ideas with the local news reporter.

After the second reading, he laid the three-page report neatly on his desk, next to the pen-topped pile. The freedom pile. His retirement papers. All filled out. Unsigned. He picked up the pen once more and positioned it above the signature line, where it hovered. *What am I waiting for? Get on with it on, for Christ's sake. Just do it.*

Which is exactly what his boss, Deputy Chief of Police Polly Adelson suggested at least once a month, with thinly disguised goodwill. "Perhaps Jack, you and Marie might like more time together. Maybe you'd like to wrap it up." *Yeah, fuck you, too, Polly.*

His smart phone rang. He saw it was from his daughter and his mood brightened at once. "Hi darling. How're our boys?" Raymond picked up the ballpoint pen and started clicking it open and closed.

When Detective Sasha Kulaeva stuck her head into her boss' office, Raymond was seated, holding his phone on his palm like any millennial, swiping his fingers over the screen, going from image to image. He was smiling, cooing. He saw Sasha and waved her over. "Whattya think?" he asked.

"Cute," she said, seeing the first picture. "Cute," for the second image and the same for the third and the next several photos he insisted she look at.

Raymond got the message. "Sorry. I know you're busy." He made excuses to his daughter and put down the phone. "I read your prelim, Sasha. Anything new since yesterday?"

She drew up a rickety wooden chair and pulled out a small spiral note pad. "A ton, and it's all pretty good shit. Gary thinks we may have the vic ID-ed. He followed up yesterday afternoon on a missing person report filed by someone at Fish and Wildlife. He connected with the guy last night. Man confirmed that one of his biologists hasn't shown up for work in a week. And he confirmed she's a graduate of Florida State University, FSU, the initials tattooed on the dead woman's lower back."

"Good work from Gary," Raymond said.

"Give my partner a raise."

"Or maybe promote him to detective lieutenant," Raymond answered. "There'll be an opening soon as Jordy gets the okay about the Bremerton gig he's angling for. Should be any day now." Raymond paused a moment, snuck a look at her. "Maybe even *more* changes coming."

"You're going to do it, aren't you?"

"Ninety percent certain." Raymond pointed to the smart phone, frozen with a picture of his three new grandsons. "Maybe ninety-nine." He laid a hand on the retirement papers on his desk, and slid them toward her.

Sasha picked them up and riffed through the pages. "Only one thing missing," she said, reaching over, picking up the pen from his desk and holding it out for him.

He smiled, but refused the offer. "You know, Sasha. How 'bout *you* taking Jordy's place? I could put in a good word for you with the selection committee."

"Detective lieutenant? An insane idea. Not nearly enough seniority, nowhere near enough experience, and *way too much* macho goin' 'round. Some of the guys have trouble enough with Polly as deputy chief. No, not my style, but thanks for the thought." Then tentatively, "Plus, I got a raft of shit I need to get sorted out. Personal stuff." Sasha waited for him to take the bait, to allow her to float the idea of rehab and a six-month leave.

But Raymond gave her a noncommittal look that she found strangely unsettling, as if he *already knew* about her problem. She suffered through the silence, then broke it by offering him the pen again.

"Best thing you'll ever do, Jack."

"Probably right." He took the pen but made no move to use it.

She stood and slung her carryall over her shoulder. "OK, then. I'm outta here. Gotta hit the morgue. Help with the ID. The missing woman's best friend, a co-worker from her office, is meeting me at the body shack in half an hour."

"Let me know what happens." He paused a moment. "Oh, Jesus. I forgot. Sorry, I completely spaced out."

"What's up?"

"The crime conference, here and over in Russia."

"What about it? You planning on going, after all?"

"Probably to the first half, here. I'll make a token appearance on the last day. Shmooze a bit. Just for an afternoon. You should, too."

"Maybe I can shake loose. Depends on how the case is going. But why'd you mention Vladivostok? I thought we couldn't afford it."

"We can't. But there's been a development. You have to go. You're needed to translate."

"What about Elena? I thought *she* was going to translate."

"She'll be there, too, but the DEA wants her to work for them exclusively. Cardozo's insisting."

"So who am I supposed to translate for?"

"You'll work for Emmitt. He asked for you. The FBI'll cover your costs. And he wants you and Elena to touch base, to get the program figured out."

"Emmitt? Christ. Well . . . I suppose that might be fun. The Special Agent in Charge has had the hots for me for as long as I've known him."

Raymond laughed. "He's too short for you. And besides, he's working on his fourth divorce, to go with his six kids. But watch yourself. He's available."

"Right. He's also closer to sixty than fifty. Just what I need, a father-confessor." Sasha checked her watch. "Gotta go. I'm late for the morgue. See ya later." She started for the door.

"Maybe I won't be here," Raymond said, rolling the pen over his retirement papers.

She turned, half way through the door. "I'd love to come back and see an empty desk. No shit, Jack. I really would!"

4

When she pulled into the Medical Examiner's parking lot, Sasha spotted Rose Nakamura's car right away—the red, Honda hatchback from which deep-throated sobs were emanating.

Sasha parked a few lanes away and waited until the crying subsided. Three minutes later, she got out of her police cruiser and walked over to the hatchback.

The sobbing woman was resting her head on the steering wheel. Her shoulders continued to heave sporadically, accompanied by convulsive gasping.

Sasha gently rapped on the driver's side door, "Miz Nakamura?"

The woman didn't react. Sasha tapped again, more forcefully this time. Rose Nakamura's head went up like a shot and she turned to her left, recoiling at the sight of the stranger banging on her car.

"Miz Nakamura. I'm Detective Kulaeva. We spoke an hour ago."

The young woman who had been tasked to identify the body of her best friend got out of her car. She dabbed at her mascara-streaked face. She was a petite size two, dressed in designer jeans with sequined back pockets. She wore a lacey, blue blouse under a heavy and overly bright cardigan ski sweater. Sasha believed the woman's clothes totally didn't work. *I should talk,* the detective thought, remembering the semi-crumpled slacks, the wrinkled shirt and the clodhopper shoes she had put on this morning.

Sasha began quietly. "I need to warn you, Miz Nakamura. The body you've been asked to identify is in pretty bad shape. She was left out in the open, in the forest. She's been pecked at by birds. Not pretty." The detective was unsure how much to tell the young woman. "And she was beaten. Badly." Sasha left out the torture-by-lit-cigarette detail. Rose would see the burn marks on her friend's chest soon enough. The detective also decided not to mention the needle in the victim's rear end.

Sasha gave her another minute to summon up whatever moxie the woman needed to enter the building. The detective placed a light hand on her shoulder. "Are you ready? Can we please do this, Miz Nakamura?"

They entered a low-lit anteroom where a middle-aged man in blue scrubs was waiting. His name badge identified him as Dr. Vance Maloney. Sasha thought he had hair weirdness—little on top, but pastures exploding out of ears and nostrils. Dr. Maloney was also just this side of being morbidly obese.

When he introduced himself, however, Sasha's initial assessment changed radically. She was beguiled by his voice, a surprisingly lovely and rich basso. She had grown up listening to Russian music and could picture Maloney in the back row of the Red Army Choir, *"Volga, Volga . . . ."*

The doctor brought them to the front desk, asked them to sign in. "You've come to identify a young woman who was brought in yesterday?"

"Right," Sasha said, writing her name and date. She passed the pen to Rose, who stared at it for a moment before taking it and signing in.

Maloney looked at Rose. She was chalky-faced and shaky. "Can I get you a glass of water?" he asked. "Would you like to take a minute?"

Although the question had been directed at the secretary, Sasha answered, "Thanks for the offer, Dr. Maloney. I think we'd like to get this over with."

"Sure. Please, this way."

They followed him down a hallway to an unmarked door that Maloney opened with his ID card. He held it for the two women.

The small viewing room was decorated in a no-nonsense fashion: two long tables and several metal folding chairs were scattered over an industrial strength, beige carpet. In the ceiling, banks of fluorescents hummed audibly. A long interior window with a curtain drawn down over the glass took up most of one wall. Next to the window was a door with a keypad lock.

Maloney moved a pair of chairs up to the window, went to the door, punched in the access code, and let himself into the next room. The door swung closed and locked solidly behind him. In a few seconds, the window curtain went up to reveal a gurney with a body on it, covered head to toe by a pastel green sheet. Maloney stood behind the gurney. "Ready?" he asked, his voice echoing tinnily through a speaker system.

Rose teetered, blinking back tears. Sasha nodded an okay to the doctor.

The doctor took hold of the two sides of the sheet opposite the cadaver's head and carefully withdrew the covering, stopping just above the corpse's breasts.

Rose choked, "It's her. It's Iz." A few seconds passed. "Jesus Christ. Where are her eyes? What are those marks on her chest?" She fell sideways into Sasha. The detective caught her and moved the small woman to a nearby chair.

Maloney replaced the sheet, closed the curtain and rejoined the two women.

"Maybe we can get that water now?" Sasha asked him. "Two glasses, please."

"Sure thing. Be just a minute," he said, leaving the two women alone.

Sasha held Rose's hand. "You're certain it's Isabel Castro."

"I'm certain." A long beat. "Who could have done this?"

"I'm hoping you might be able to help us with that."

Rose's face slowly hardened as if a dawning and unpleasant realization had burst upon her. She turned her body away from the detective. "I don't know anything about this," she declared.

Sasha was a fan of the World Series of Poker and knew that at the Texas Hold 'Em tables the pros call it *'a tell.'* It's the eye tic when you have a good hand, the ear scratch when you're bluffing. And in this case, the facial freezing and body aversion when you're lying. *A tell.*

Sasha helped Rose to her feet just as Maloney returned with two small Dixie Cups of room temp water. He handed one to each of the women. Sasha drank all of hers. Rose sipped, then passed her cup back to the doctor. Sasha said, "Miz Nakamura has positively identified the body as her friend, Doctor Isabel Castro."

"Do we have a next of kin?" Maloney asked, looking at Rose. She turned away again, unable to answer.

"We're trying to find a brother," Sasha answered.

After he left them in the lobby, Sasha turned to Rose. "How 'bout we both go on back to your office and you and I and your boss'll think about how this happened. There may be something you can tell us that might shed some light on this terrible event. Can you make it on your own, or do you want me to drive you over there?"

"I can manage. I have to make a phone call first," she said, then grimaced. A look passed across her face that told the policewoman, *"I wish I hadn't said that."*

"Great," said Sasha. "See you there."

~~~

The U.S. Department of Fish and Wildlife offices in Anchorage are in a fairly new, rambling three story, brown and green building stuck in a heavily wooded spot in the middle of town. Sasha was waiting in the lobby when Gary arrived.

"She ID the body?" he asked right away, showing his badge to the guard at the front desk.

"Positive ID," Sasha said. "She's here, inside. We drove over separately."

"We ready to go in?" he asked.

"Let's sit for a sec."

The two detectives found a sofa.

"What's up?" he asked.

"The secretary's got way more information about her dead friend than she's copping to. There's something going on here. I'd like a bit of time alone with her. Away from her boss."

"No problem. We'll figure it out. Meanwhile, I spoke again to the techs at the crime lab. There's probably both heroin *and* cocaine residue in the needle. A hot dose."

"Could have killed her for sure."

"More than likely. They're sending samples out of state for confirmation, so we won't know for absolute certain for a week. Let's go in."

Judson McKimmey, Fish and Wildlife's Director of Migratory Birds, was a tall, bald, geeky-thin man in his early fifties. He had an Ichabod Crane Adam's apple that yo-yoed up and down in time with his ever-moving eyebrows. Sasha had to stifle a laugh and couldn't look at him when he spoke.

McKimmey was dressed in a plaid wool shirt, a fishing vest, no tie, khaki pants, and lace-up boots. He was attempting to comfort his secretary, seated in a chair next to his desk. The young woman was hunched over and cried into a ball of shredded Kleenex.

"It's awful, awful," McKimmey said to the policemen as they entered. "This is a nightmare, a complete and total shock. To everyone. And especially for Rose, having to identify Isabel. The two of them were very close, best friends."

Rose looked up. "Why? God, no," she said between sobs.

Sasha moved a chair closer to the secretary, sat and laid a quiet hand on Rose's knee. "We're so sorry, Rose. It's hard, very hard, we know. But we need to ask you some questions, see if you can help us."

McKimmey went around his desk. "I think you can start with this," he said, pushing an expandable folder towards Sasha. "It's Isabel's personnel file. She was our sea bird specialist. Traveled to the Aleutians often. Six, seven times a year."

"Mr. McKimmey," Gary asked. "Did Doctor Castro have her own office?"

"Yes. And a lab, too. They're both one floor up, other end of the building."

"May we see those rooms, please?"

"Sure. No problem."

Gary turned to Sasha. "Detective Kulaeva, I'll go with Mr. McKimmey. If you'd stay here with Miz Nakamura?"

The detectives exchanged small smiles.

As the two men left the room, Sasha pressed a wad of fresh Kleenex into Rose's hands, squeezed tightly together in her lap. "Take your time," Sasha said softly, sitting back, not wanting to press. After a full minute, "Isabel and you were good friends?"

"Very," sniffling.

"She have anyone else but a brother here in town? Parents? Other kin?"

Rose hesitated. "Just a brother. Rudy." A long pause, then, "I used to go with him." The secretary's face registered the same *"I wish I hadn't said that"* look.

"Uh huh. Rudy's here now, in Anchorage?"

"Yeah. He's in town. *Somewhere*." Rose was about to add something, but stopped. Sasha waited. And waited some more. An old reporter/interrogator's trick. If you wait long enough, the person being questioned will invariably offer up something.

"He's probably up at the house," Rose said.

"Okay. And where would that be?" Sasha asked, pencil poised over her notepad.

"On the Hillside, way up above Potter's Marsh. At the end of Glazanof . . . something. Circle or Drive. He might be there right now. I don't know." Rose hunched her shoulders together and put her hands under her thighs. She shivered.

"Maybe you have a photo of Rudy?"

"There's some framed pictures on the shelf above my desk. In the next room. A couple photos of Rudy and Iz."

Sasha went into the adjoining office and easily found the pictures. One showed two women, Rose and Isabel, standing in front of a large, fire engine red SUV. The second showed Rose and another man—Rudy perhaps—standing in light snow in front of the Lincoln Memorial, smiling into the camera. The third photo showed four people—Rose, Isabel, the same man from D.C., and another man. The four, all dressed for warm weather, were seated in rattan lounge chairs next to a table in front of a pool. Palm trees and white sands in the background. Beers and limes on the table.

Sasha resumed her seat next to the secretary. "Where was this one taken?" showing Rose the photo of the four vacationers.

"Saint Croix. Just last December. Rudy invited me. We weren't getting along so hot, but it's hard to turn down a ten day vacation in the Caribbean." Rose stopped crying, perhaps finding some joy in her memories. "We stayed at the Three Palms Hotel. We had two bungalows down by the water. Me and Rudy. Jimmy and Isabel."

"Jimmy? Jimmy's Isabel's boyfriend? This one sitting next to Isabel is Jimmy?" Sasha asked, pointing.

"Yeah," Rose said. "Jimmy Lasorda."

"Where is he now?" Sasha asked, writing in her pad L A S O R D A, then showing it to Rose. "Lasorda? That right?"

"Yeah, I think that's how you spell it. He's out in Dutch Harbor."

"Lives there? Works there?"

"Works there. He's got some kind of government job."

"You know what agency?"

"Something to do with counting fish."

"Right. And Rudy? Isabel's brother. What does he do?"

Rose's face turned rigid. "Nothin.' He doesn't work."

She laughed once, derisively. "Never has. He and Jimmy . . . they share the place."

"Rudy and Jimmy are roommates?" Sasha paused. "You know the address on Glazanof?" Sasha pushed her pad and pen over to Rose. "Write it down, please. And the phone."

While Rose retrieved the information from her smart phone, Sasha stood and stretched, arching her back. "So. Rudy doesn't work. Never has, you said. And Jimmy supports the two of them by counting fish in Dutch. That it? Or maybe Rudy has his own money?"

Rose fidgeted in her seat. "Isabel stayed there, too," she said, as if in explanation.

Sasha turned to the desk and opened Isabel's personnel file. After a minute, "Says here Isabel lived across town, on Clay Products Drive, near Earthquake Park. Not on Glazanof."

"Yeah. She kept a place there but she stayed with Jimmy."

"Okay. I'd stay up on the Hillside too, I had the chance. Great neighborhood. Beautiful view. Anybody else live there? You live there?"

Rose shook her head.

"Jimmy own the place?"

"It's a rental."

Sasha got up and walked to a wall of east-facing windows. "So lemme see if I got this right. A rental house on the Hillside. Gotta be three thousand a month. No way it can be any less. Luxury vacation for four in St. Croix. Ten days. December would have been the high season. Sounds like two grand a day, give or take, just for the bungalows. Add in transportation getting there and back, food, fun stuff. Expensive vacation."

Rose didn't comment.

Sasha continued. "Isabel drove a Mitsubishi. That's her car in this other picture? This big red thing?"

"Yeah. It's her car. But it's not a Mitsubishi. It's a Lexus. An LX."

"An LX? Wow. Don't see many of them in town. Those suckers can run to ninety thousand."

Rose didn't respond.

Sasha looked at the last photo. "You and Rudy in D.C. When was that?"

"Few months ago. In February." The secretary stared into her hands as they worked the tissue.

"You know, Rose. I'm going to guess that Isabel was knocking down . . . let's say seventy thousand a year here at Fish and Wildlife. Maybe as much as eighty. Rudy doesn't work at all, you said. So that leaves Jimmy making . . . who knows how much counting fish?" Sasha walked from the window and stopped in front of Rose. She towered over her. "How'd they manage, Rose? Are folks living beyond their means here? Are their credit cards maxed? Are they robbing banks? Help me out, would you. Where's all this cash coming from?"

"I don't know," Rose said quietly, gaze fixed on the rug in front of her.

"You don't know?" Sasha repeated, staring down at the secretary. "I think you *do* know, Rose. Look at me," she said.

Rose kept her head bowed.

"Look at me!" Sasha commanded, grabbing Rose's chin and raising it roughly so that the secretary and the policewoman were now eye to eye, separated by less than twelve inches.

"You're not being square with me, Rose," Sasha said

coolly. "Your best friend was murdered, brutally. Beat up. Burned. Maybe raped. This is a fucked up situation, and you're not giving me the full picture. I think you're holding out on me."

"That's all I know," Rose insisted, pulling her chin away and swiveling her body toward the windows.

Sasha half-sat on McKimmey's desk and in a softer voice, "Okay. We're looking for a motive here. A reason someone would kill Isabel. Talk to me. What did she do after hours? Where did she play? What were she and Jimmy into?"

"They didn't go out much."

"Was there anyone who would want to hurt her? Here at work or maybe in her personal life?"

The secretary's neck sank into her shoulders. "I . . . no one I can think of who would kill her."

"Okay. How'd she get along with Jimmy? He ever smack her around?"

"Never!" Rose straightened. "Jimmy never laid a hand on her. He was crazy about Isabel."

Sasha nodded. "Alright. Let's do this. Make me a list of the names of all of Isabel's friends and acquaintances." Sasha took out her wallet. "Here's my card." When Rose didn't look up, Sasha laid it on McKimmey's desk. "That's it for now. We're going to meet again, Rose. You and me. Probably tomorrow." Sasha took up Isabel Castro's personnel file and started toward the door. "I'm going to hold on to these photos for a while. I'll get 'em back to you. Do that list of friends for me. And think about how you're going to help us."

Sasha left Rose seated in McKimmey's office and went out into the hallway just as Gary and the Director of Migratory Birds were coming down the stairs.

"I hope Rose was helpful," McKimmey said. When Sasha didn't reply at once, his expression clouded. "Anything wrong?"

"No sir, just thinking. Sorry. Yes, Rose was helpful. If you don't mind, sir, I'm going to borrow Isabel's file. I'll copy what I need and bring it back tomorrow. If that's alright?"

"Keep it as long as you need to." He looked from one policeman to another. "Anything else?"

"No, nothing right now. I left my card on your desk. We're going to stop by again tomorrow. I'll give you a ring before we come over. Thanks for your time, sir."

When he was gone, Sasha turned to Gary. "More than meets the eye, buddy."

"What's up?"

"There seems to be a pile of unaccounted for cash floating around. Folks are living the high life on workingman's wages." She showed Gary the photo of the quartet in St. Croix. "The one next to Rose is Rudy Castro, the dead woman's brother. He lives here in Anchorage with this other guy, Jimmy Lasorda, the woman's boyfriend. Here's the address," she said, passing the piece of note paper to Gary. "Isabel Castro had a place out in Earthquake Park. Lasorda has a government job in Dutch Harbor. Counts fish. He's there now, Rose says."

Gary examined the photo. "I'll do the brother first. I'll take someone and go on up, scout out the house. If the guy's there, I'll let him know what's going on."

"Okay. What'd McKimmey have to say about Isabel?"

"Says she was a good scientist. Great to work with. Beyond that, he couldn't say much about her. Didn't know anything about her private life, other than her friendship with Rose." Gary paused, "You call the shrink yet?"

"I did. She emailed me her questionnaire right away. Just a few questions. She said she's free tonight."

"Good for you, Sash."

"We'll see how it goes. But right now, I'm gonna get me a warrant and go over to Isabel's apartment. One more thing, Gary. Let's find out about Rose Nakamura, how she came to work here at Fish and Wildlife."

~~~

Earthquake Park in west Anchorage earned its name the hard way. On March 27, 1964—a not very good Good Friday—the most severe earthquake ever to hit North America devastated South-Central Alaska.

Located only seventy-five miles from the epicenter, Anchorage suffered immense damage from the 9.2 magnitude shaker.

The four and a half minute quake killed one hundred and thirty nine folks and caused immense tsunamis that destroyed several Alaskan seaside communities before barreling across the Pacific, to be felt all along the West Coast and as far as Hawaii.

One of the most spectacular local manifestations of the earthquake occurred when an entire neighborhood of Anchorage homes broke away from the shore and slid into the waters of Knik Arm. Those houses had been built on soil that turned to liquefied jelly under tectonic stress.

Redemption for the re-consecrated neighborhood came with the passage of time and the power of forgetfulness. In the fifty-odd years since the quake, the surrounding area has been rebuilt and now counts itself as one of the city's more stylish neighborhoods. It's a single family, residential collection of split-level homes with the occasional apartment house mixed in. One of the largest of these, and easily the biggest eyesore, is on Clay Products Drive, close to Hood Creek.

The structure is a run-down sixteen-plex, named—for reasons lost to history—*The Charioteer*. It was thrown up in the early seventies to house some of the thousands of welders, steel workers, and heavy machine operators who flocked to the state to build the eight hundred mile long oil Trans-Alaska pipeline.

The Charioteer never had much to brag about. Amenities? If you count doors and windows, then yes, the place had a few.

Apartment 11 of the two-story, U shaped structure is a second floor, one-bedroom rented to Isabel Castro. It looks down onto a forlorn patio in whose center a garden may, at one time, have grown. Today, with the earth still frozen, only gravel and a handful of skeletal bushes are showing through the last of the season's snow. The perimeter of the patio isn't any healthier—a straggle of leafless vines, not very upwardly mobile, and three pots of silk flowers.

At two o'clock in the afternoon, the day after the tenant's body was discovered in the woods north of Anchorage, Detective Sasha Kulaeva was standing in the middle of the dead woman's living room.

"How long she here, Mr. Garcia?"

Paul Garcia, the middle-aged, pear shaped, bushy haired manager of the apartment complex, raised and dropped his shoulders. "I dunno . . . nine months, maybe. Moved in July last year. On the first. I dint like her too good. She was kinda stuck up. Know what I mean? She wunt talk Spanish to me. I'm third generation and my Spanish is pretty crappy, but I enjoy talkin'. My great aunt Juanita, she was visitin' from El Paso? Isabel, she wunt talk Spanish even to her. I think she was from South America, maybe Honduras. I only saw her twice a month. Maybe three times."

The apartment manager had dressed in haste, having had both his lunch and his *Everybody Loves Raymond* interrupted by this nosy cop. He was wearing a three-sizes-too-large, black snow machine suit, open down the front, revealing an *'I (heart) Fairbanks'* pink T-shirt. An unlaced pair of Sno-Pac boots covered sockless feet.

Sasha surveyed the apartment. The austere vacantness of the living room spoke volumes about Dr. Isabel Castro's non-occupancy—no books, no clutter, no dishes in evidence, dirty or otherwise. Nothing in the fridge except an unopened box of baking soda. The only sign of any real life was the red light flashing on the land-line phone's answering machine.

"So what happened to her?" Garcia asked, without real interest.

Sasha toured the room slowly, stopping at the bathroom door, ajar. She donned nitrile gloves, then pushed the door open with a single finger and turned on the light. The vent fan rattled to life. She stepped into the tiny room. The linoleum flooring curled where it met the walls. The glass shower enclosure was heavily mildewed. An unused bar of Castile Soap, an Oral-B toothbrush in its unopened, plastic case, and a new mini-Crest were on the counter. The sink's faucet dripped, the red-brown stain in the bowl testament to the years the water had worked on the porcelain. A full bottle of aspirin and four Tampax were in the medicine cabinet. The toilet seat cover was down. Sasha left it that way. The detective turned off the light and returned to the living room. "Miz Castro is dead."

The manager seemed unmoved by the news, the only acknowledgement—raised eyebrows that asked, *"So what else is new?"*

Sasha took a photo from inside her coat—the four vacationers in St. Croix—and offered it to the apartment manager. "Who do you recognize in this picture?"

Garcia lowered a set of battered, wire frame bifocals from the top of his forehead, then reached for the picture. He examined the snapshot at arm's length for a few seconds before pointing, "Isabel and the midget. I think maybe it's her brother. He stops by once in a while. Just yesterday, in fact. When he dint find her, he came by my apartment, ast if I seen her. Ast if I'd let him collect stuff from her mailbox. I tol' him 'no.' He got pissed, tried to get tough. I tol' him to fuck off. That shut 'im up. The other two, the little chink and the white guy. I don't know. Like I said, I dint know nothin' 'bout Isabel. Now she's dead, huh? Well . . ." Garcia waved one arm around the room. "Are we done here? Can I get back to my lunch?"

"In a sec. First, *I'd* like to check her mailbox. You have a master key?"

"'Course I do. I'm the manager. But don' you need a sapeeny to look in a dead woman's box?"

Sasha thought of a tart reply but suppressed the urge. "All I need is a warrant, Mr. Garcia," she said, waving the document at the manager.

The detective returned to the room. And alone. Garcia was back at his cold lunch, *Everybody Loves Raymond* having given way to *The King of Queens.*

Sasha dropped herself into a caved-in La-Z-Boy and spread Isabel Castro's mail onto the stained coffee table in front of her. She handled each piece gingerly with gloved hands. She put aside bills and fliers and focused on three items—a letter to the victim from Maria Castro at an address in Miami Beach, a U.S. Postal Service Express Mail letter, and an embossed, cream-colored envelope from the Three Palms Hotel.

She opened the one from St. Croix first and found a letter and a copy of an invoice. In beautiful handwriting, the hotel's manager, a Mr. Joaquin Tordesillas, thanked Ms. Isabella Castro for her stay. He hoped she had "a wonderful time" and told her how "he was so looking forward to the future when she and her friends might once again come and visit." A copy of the bill, marked *'paid in full,'* itemized their expenses. Besides the rental of the two bungalows, there were charges for para-sailing, scuba lessons, a deep sea fishing half-day charter, a full-day circumnavigation of the island, four in-suite massages, two body scrubs, and nine room-service meals. The total was just under $21,500.

Sasha turned next, reluctantly, to the letter from Miami. The detective suspected it might be from a member of the victim's family—Maria Castro, Isabel's mother, perhaps?

Over the years, she found she was able to look at most evidence with dispassion. But the personal stuff, connecting victim to family, had always been a problem.

She had no interest in breaking the news to the victim's mother, to endure her initial denial, followed by the grudging acceptance, and finally the screaming. Always the screaming. It's not that Sasha didn't empathize with family members. She did. She felt deeply for the survivors—a daughter, a brother, a father, or a mother—who attempt to soldier on through life, hoping the cleft in their hearts will heal. *Never does. Too deep. I won't make the phone call. Gary can do it. Or Jack. I won't.*

The opened letter crystalized all of Sasha's fears. It *was* from Isabel Castro's mother, who at this moment, probably did not yet know that her daughter had met a gruesome and painful death.

The letter's tone was intimate, caring, and sweetly joking. Mother loved her daughter and the sub-text was unequivocal—*I'm proud of you.*

Not half-way through, Sasha put the letter down, returned it to its envelope, and sank into the reclining chair. She closed her eyes and imagined going into the kitchen, opening the fridge and discovering a frosty Corona. *What I wouldn't give.* In the surrounding silence she could just make out the canned laughter of the sit-com the apartment manager was watching.

She rose to a sitting position and took up the USPS Express Mail letter. It had a Dutch Harbor postal imprint but no return address.

Sasha opened the envelope and pulled out a second, improvised package—two small pieces of cardboard sandwiching a shallow lump of something in between. She used her switchblade to slice carefully through the clear, tape binding. When she removed the top piece of cardboard, she saw a Ziploc sandwich bag, half full of a bright, white powder.

Holy! Fucking! Shit!

She stared at the bag for a moment, then opened it, lightly licked her forefinger, tapped it gently onto the powder, brought her finger up close to her eyes and examined the shiny white crystals. *Heroin, most likely*, she supposed. That would be something for the lab to verify. She re-sealed the Ziploc and put it into her evidence bag.

The phone was the last item of business. She pressed 'Play Messages' on the answering machine. Sasha listened to a string of calls from Rudy, from Rose, and from McKimmey. The messages began seven days ago and ended yesterday evening. The first ones began with mild concern about where Isabel Castro was, why she wasn't at work or answering her cell phone. Through the next several calls, concern turned to worry, then worry to alarm. The last few, especially from Rudy and Rose, were near hysterical.

Sasha removed the cassette from the recorder and put it, too, into her evidence bag. Then she used her cell phone to call her partner. He picked up on the second ring and without preamble, Gary began in a rush.

"Listen to this, Sash. You won't fucking believe it. The vic's boyfriend, Jimmy Lasorda, the fisherman in Dutch, is *missing* off of his boat in the Bering Sea. I heard about it from the FBI."

"Missing? What's going on? How's he missing? And how do the Feds come to be involved?" Sasha flipped to a fresh page in her notebook.

"The Feds are in deep, all the way because Lasorda was a high seas fish counter, worked for the government. And because the foreign fishing crews usually hate these guys, his death is being viewed as suspicious. It's possible he was tossed overboard. It's happened before. I called the Coast Guard in Dutch and spoke to their mouthpiece out there, guy called Kozol. He said Lasorda was reported missing from the Russian fishing boat he was assigned to. The boat is searching for him right now. But the area where he went in is so big and the weather is apparently real shitty, so they're not giving it much of a chance. Kozol said he reported the incident to Coast Guard headquarters in Kodiak. And like I said, because Lasorda was a federal employee, the Bureau got involved late this morning. I filled Jack in and then called over to the FBI office. Spoke to Special Agent Charles Dana. I brought him up to speed as much as I could. He wants to meet."

"Okay. Okay. I'm keeping up with you," Sasha said, taking notes. "Now it's my turn. Listen real good, buddy. A blockbuster! I got a fat ounce of what I'm pretty sure is heroin in my evidence bag. It came in a letter from Dutch Harbor, addressed to Isabel Castro. No return sender."

"Christ! Not hard to guess who the sender might be."

"Right. Not hard. I'm gonna run this stuff over to the crime lab soon as I'm outta here. Couple more things. The apartment has *not* been lived in. Used, I think, as a mail drop. Meanwhile, let me have the FBI agent's phone number. I'll call him later. What else?"

"I got a warrant and went up to the place on Glazanof Drive, looking for Rudy Castro. No one home. There's something seriously fucked up here, Sash. The fisherman gone missing right when his girlfriend's body shows up dead? Too weird to be a coincidence."

"Absolutely too weird. Listen. I'll be back at the office in a couple hours. You be there?"

"I'll wait for you. And McKimmey's forwarding Rose Nakamura's job application."

"Great. Why don't you feed her name into the system, see if she's ever done something she shouldn't have."

"Already done it. See you soon."

Sasha signed off and began a more deliberate search of the apartment. Since the place was virtually empty, her search went quickly and without further discoveries. She stopped to let the manager know she was leaving.

Garcia had not changed out of his snowsuit, though he had discarded the Sno-Pac boots and answered her knock with bare feet. "Done?" he asked.

"Yes. For now. I've locked the apartment. The investigation into her death is on-going, Mr. Garcia. Me or my partner might be back to talk to you again." Sasha gave him her card.

"That's a loada crap," he complained. "I already tol' ya everything I know."

She ignored his displeasure. "You'll call me if you remember anything you might think pertinent. And if Rudy Castro comes around again, I want to know right away. Got it?"

Garcia took the card with a huff and returned to his apartment. *Friends* was just starting.

Sasha got into her police cruiser and checked her watch: 3:05. She considered stopping at the Oaken Keg. But when she was a block from the liquor store, she remembered her conversation that morning with Gary. *And* yesterday's talk with Nelson Alexie. *And* her appointment that evening with her new shrink. *Fuck.* She drove straight to the lab.

~~~

Boris' wedding gift to Larissa was an heirloom ruby ring that belonged to his great-grandmother.

Sitting in his favorite Manhattan delicatessen—P.J.

Bernstein's, on 70th near Hunter College—she nervously fiddled with the ring. She put down her half of a corned beef on rye with paper thin Swiss. Thinking the moment ripe, she spoke: "Borya. I'd like to talk about your business."

"Certainly Lara," he said, coughing and clearing his throat. He rearranged himself on his chair.

She knew he got nervous whenever she wanted to discuss his work. She gave him a reassuring smile, took a bite out of her half of the sandwich. "Do you remember our first date on the Brighton Beach boardwalk?"

"Of course. How could I forget? It was magic."

"Yes, it was." She took a French fry and dipped it in ketchup. "I asked you about the rates of growth of your various enterprises. I remember the look on your face. You were shocked by the question. It took you a moment before you could answer."

"You're right. I *was* surprised."

"What was your answer?"

"I think I told you we were earning maybe three percent a year. I wasn't sure. I told you the accountants handle it."

Larissa fell silent and concentrated on her sandwich. She vividly recalled that answer. It had not satisfied her and she spent the next several months—before and after their January 2000 wedding—thinking about his uncertain response. Now she felt herself ready to act. She dabbed her mouth with a napkin, put it aside, and sat up straight. "Tell me, Borya, what was my major field of study at university, in Leningrad?"

"You earned a PhD in economics."

"Good. And what was my thesis?"

"You wrote a three hundred and sixteen page dissertation on the short term positive effects, and the long term negative effects on American industry of off-shoring. Have I got it?"

"You have, indeed, my sweet. I'm proud of you." She smiled. "You remembered the exact number of pages. Good for you." Another French fry. "You'll recall, that my minor was the commodities market, specializing in minerals."

He avoided her eyes, paying attention to the basket of fries, pouring ketchup over several.

"So, my dear, given my expertise in finances, about which you have so sweetly reminded me, I'm ready, willing, and more than able to take control of *your* finances." Larissa took another bite of her sandwich, waiting for his reaction.

He pulled back into his seat and began rotating his neck as if he'd been sucker punched. He ate another handful of fries, buying time. Bought some more when he wiped his mouth, took a swallow of Coke.

"Larissa, while I recognize your expertise, this is really not a job for you. I appreciate your interest, but really . . ." Another swallow of Coke.

She put her sandwich down. "I have no wish to meddle in the day-to-day operations. That's the last thing I want. I'm not at all interested in the details—how you *get* the money. My only desire is to *manage* it. And I'm the perfect person for the job. I have the experience, the expertise in international finance, and the ability to put together successful business plans." Undaunted by his lowering brows, his turned-down mouth, she continued, "Who manages your finances now, Borya?"

"Old friends of my uncle Josef. They've been doing it for years."

"Are they trained accountants? Economists? Money managers?"

"I'm not sure, Lara."

"And you have faith in their honesty? What if they were to betray you?"

His face hardened. He looked her directly in the eye and whispered, "They fully understand the consequences of such an action."

"Are you reluctant to grant my request because you suspect *I* might betray you? And if so, would I face those same consequences?"

"If that were to occur, Lara, I would give you a pistol and tell you to shoot me in the heart. Because if you betrayed me, my life would no longer have the slightest value. I'd sooner be dead."

She smiled, but pressed her case. "From what you've told me so far, Borya, your business is sorely lacking any kind of financial cohesion. I can fix that. You told me three percent per annum. That is, simply put, no way to run a business with as much liquidity as yours. Anyone with any business sense will tell you the same. In addition, there doesn't seem to be sufficient investment in legitimate enterprises. We call it 'laundering.'" She took a sip of her Coke.

"I know what it's called," he snapped, He regretted his tone at once and sought to ease the moment. "Yes, dear. We *do* call it laundering." He mimed a *'sorry.'*

She nodded her acceptance of his apology. "Here is what I am suggesting, dear. And I fully believe that it's an idea you'll appreciate."

He waited, leaning forward in his chair.

"I will become the business' money manager for one year. I believe I can double your profits, to six percent per annum. At the end of that year, if I have failed, I'll withdraw and you can return to running the business in the way you are now operating it."

The offer on the table, Larissa resumed eating her sandwich. Her husband looked shell shocked. The ball was now in his court.

"Lara, dearest. Once more, I find I cannot agree. It's not in the nature of our business, my business, to allow—"

"To allow . . . .?" she interrupted, a knife-edge in her tone. She stared across the table, her gaze unwavering.

Boris backed off. If he were to finish the sentence with the word *'outsiders,* or *'strangers'* she would take offence, and rightly so. But his wife insisting on coming into the business? It was farcical. His father and his uncle would scoff. He looked toward the restaurant's front doors. Taras and the other two bodyguards were watching them intently, having sensed a change in their boss' mood.

"No, Lara. This cannot be. For any number of reasons. It simply cannot be. In all other aspects of my life, I welcome and encourage you to be an equal partner with me. But in business, impossible."

She continued looking at him steadily, steely in the way he was already becoming used to and admiring of. *She's tough.*

"Borya, you've got mustard on your chin. Go wash it off."

He reached up reflexively to his chin. He looked dazed, at sea. He pushed back his chair clumsily, excused himself, and followed the sign to the men's room.

When he returned five minutes later, his wife was gone. In the center of the table, a folded paper napkin with his name written on it. He unfolded it and saw, to his horror, the ruby ring. And written on the napkin, a note: *"My darling Borya.*

You are <u>not</u> Al Pacino's Michael Corleone. You are infinitely sweeter and I treasure you. And I, my love, for an absolute certainty, am <u>not</u> Diane Keaton's Kaye."

Larissa Kirillovna Bunina stayed gone for three days. Then four. Then five. Boris was crazy with grief. His wife had walked out on him.

He phoned her parents every day to hear the same story each time, "No. Lara is not here. She called and said she was going away for a while."

The head of a vast international criminal empire couldn't believe the depth of the hurt in his soul. He now fully appreciated the expression, 'heart broken.' His heart was not only broken, but shattered.

He didn't tell his family about Lara's disappearance, but two nights later, he spoke with Taras. The bodyguard was not as sympathetic as Boris hoped he might be.

"She's the best thing you've ever known, Boris Davidich. Far and away. And you've let her slip through your fingers." Taras shook his head sadly, looking at his best friend and brother-in-law with an easily read expression: *you fool!*

On the seventh day after having been abandoned, Boris once again called his wife's parents. Her father answered the phone and repeated to him what he'd heard every day, "Lara called to say she's having a wonderful time. She's not sure when she's coming back."

Boris laughed to himself. *She's tougher than I am.* "Kirill Yurevich, please tell your daughter that I agree to her suggestion. With all my heart."

"I will pass on your message," Larissa's father said, a smile shining through the phone.

Lara made him wait two more days before calling. "I'll be at the deli at seven this evening. Perhaps you'd like to join me?"

With bells on!

~~~

"Can I get you something to drink?" the woman asked.

"Water would be great, thanks," Sasha said.

"With ice? Or perhaps sliced lemon?"

"No thank you. Neat's fine," followed quickly by "Oops." *Shouldn't have said that.*

Katherine Manfredi stopped at her kitchen doorway, looked back and smiled. "No 'oops' here, Aleksandra. I also like my water neat. My scotch, too."

A moment later, Sasha met the counselor in the middle of her large, high-ceilinged living room. Sasha took the offered tumbler and took three large gulps. "Th . . . th . . . thanks. I n . . n . . needed that," she stuttered, demonstratively wiping her mouth with a purposely shaky back of her hand.

Both women laughed.

Manfredi took a seat in a padded swivel chair behind a cluttered desk. Her working library, floor to ceiling, took up the entire wall behind her.

Sasha remained standing and administered her cop's once-over of the psychologist: early fifties, tanned, well toned. Shoulder-length brown hair. Deep set, dark eyes. A long, angular face with a welcoming smile and a ready laugh. And a soothing voice that would calm a cobra. Sasha felt reassured. "How did you know my name is Aleksandra?"

"Easy. Kulaeva is clearly a Russian surname and Sasha

is the nickname for both Aleksandra and Alexander. You don't look like an Alexander, so . . ."

"Right. I often forget that some people actually know stuff." She walked over to a leather sofa, set at right angles to Manfredi's desk, and settled herself down. "Thanks for seeing me on such short notice. I mentioned in the questionnaire you sent that I need to pay in cash."

"Not a problem."

"Thanks. I was worried, because . . ." Sasha hesitated. *Here we go.* "I'm a cop. A detective. Anchorage Police. I can't go internal with my problems, for obvious reasons. Well, I guess I could. It's tricky. Complicated. I don't want them knowing that I'm seeing someone, especially for the stuff I'm going to throw at you. Plus, these visits can't show up on my health insurance reports. So, cash."

"Love cash, love problems. Throw 'em my way," the psychologist smiled. "Money talks."

"And bullshit walks," Sasha completed.

"I've heard that. But you don't impress me as much of a bullshit artist, Aleksandra."

"Don't jump to conclusions. We drunks are nothing if not bullshit artists. We invented the sport."

Manfredi nodded. "I'll reserve judgment. What makes you say you're a drunk?"

"I have many of the symptoms. I drink too much, drink too often. Although I don't black out. Don't wake up in the bushes. Still . . . ." Glass in hand, Sasha rose and began a leisurely stroll along the wall covered with Katherine Manfredi's academic credentials. After a careful read, the detective turned to the therapist. "I don't see a PhD, so I can't call you *Doctor* Manfredi."

"No PhD. Just a couple of advanced degrees in psychology and twenty-two years working with clients. I call myself a therapist. I'm not allowed, by law, to call myself anything more grandiose. Can't call myself a psychiatrist because I have no formal medical training. My title is 'therapist.' No more, no less."

When Sasha hesitated, Manfredi continued. "But if you feel you need someone with more training, I'd be happy to recommend some folks here in town. I hear nothing but wonderful things about them."

"No, no, it's not that. I'm just a little surprised by your room here. And your manner. Both are much more . . . intimate, I guess is the word, than I would have expected. I assumed I'd be seeing you in an office building."

"I know my approach isn't mainstream. If you'd prefer to lie on a leather couch and have me sit in back of you with pad and pencil, we can do that. But really, that's not how it works here." Manfredi gathered her thoughts. "Listen, Aleksandra. Whatever kind of therapist you might wind up with, the same basic rule applies: you'll do the work. No one, not a Freudian, not a Jungian, no one with a 'Frau Doctor' in front of her name is going to solve your problems for you, going to make you whole. All of them, in different ways, will try to help you discover why you've come to them. But, at the end of the day, *you* do the digging. And my job, as I see it, is to create an environment that will allow that to happen. Some therapists like couches, some do art therapy, others music therapy. Some combine their work with massage. Me, I like to make the work environment—this room and our time together in it—as calming and comfortable, as non-threatening as I can. And if my informality ticks off the traditionalists, well . . . tough."

Sasha had been watching the woman the entire time, focusing on her face and body language. *She knows what she's about. She knows her shit.* "I'm happy here."

"Good." Manfredi rose and walked over to the bay window that ran the length of the room, crammed with two dozen kinds of cacti, all bending into the west light.

The therapist turned to face her new patient. "So. You, Aleksandra. You're a cop. And you speak with a very, very slight accent. So I'm thinking that Russian was your first language. And you're a drinker."

"You have a good ear, Katherine. Russian was my first language. And I drink . . . Way less than I used to. But still . . . Mostly to help ease . . . " Sasha let it hang.

Manfredi waited, then gently encouraged, "Want to finish the sentence?"

"Help ease . . . life. A memory." She shifted her weight from foot to foot.

The therapist returned to her chair and sat quietly.

Sasha found a narrow sitting place on the wooden window sill, between a large aloe vera and a larger, spiky crown of thorns that reached to the top of the bay window.

Several minutes passed. The unlit room grew darker as the sun began its dip below the horizon. Sasha gazed out onto the vista, turned away from Manfredi. *Now I'm the one avoiding the questions.* Her head drooped forward. She looked away from the window, back into the room. The slightest tremble in her chin brought the therapist over with a box of tissues. She placed it on the window ledge then retreated to her seat.

Sasha took out several tissues. She wiped her eyes and swabbed her nose. "Christ, I can't remember the last time I got weepy."

Manfredi waited.

"I'm a wreck, Katherine. Yesterday, a guy busted me for being hung over while I was on the job. He told me to try and get *'presentable.'*" Sasha smiled at the memory. "A very wise man. Saw right through me. I told him I wasn't sure I could manage it."

Manfredi waited.

Sasha exhaled. Her shoulders slumped. "See. Twelve years ago . . ."

The windshield wipers on Patrol Officer Sasha Hutchinson's police cruiser were working overtime. To very little effect. This was Sitka, after all, the watery jewel in Alaska's southeastern panhandle. One hundred and thirty inches of rain in your normal year. And this year, 2003, was anything but normal. In the last two weeks of unrelenting downpour, they were getting over four inches a day.

Great currents of water spilled down her windshield, reducing visibility to not much beyond the front of the vehicle. All the patrol car's lights were blazing as it crept along Lincoln Street at a bare ten miles an hour. The waters of Crescent Bay, hard by the highway, were lost to sight in the slanting deluge.

Strangely, the weather never really got her down. You chose to live in Sitka, you chose water world. "Love it or shove it," as her grandfather liked to say.

And Sasha and her husband, State Trooper Robin Hutchinson, both loved Sitka, the small, tight-knit town in the middle of a multi-islanded archipelago. Great hiking and incredible fishing. She had her own plane and she and Robin flew out every opportunity to an unnamed lake, a hidden cove.

They'd camp, celebrating the pristine solitude offered by the Alaskan outback.

Born and raised here, Robin never complained about the weather. Came with the turf, and the turf included some of the most serious sea kayaking and glacier trekking in North America.

No amount of wet could dampen Sasha's current mood, made golden by the phone call earlier this morning from Anne Marie, Dr. Buchanan's nurse. The call confirmed what Sasha and Robin had hoped for—she was pregnant. Seven weeks along. For the first time.

Sasha tried to phone her husband as soon as she heard, but learned that he and his detachment were out on assignment.

She continued creeping along, smilingly unfazed by the elements, thinking about the unknown sex of her fetus and the name possibilities. Her meditation on motherhood was interrupted by her staticky radio phone.

"Sasha, come in please. Sash, are you there?" the dispatcher asked.

She picked up. "It's me. What's up, Millie?" An empty pause followed. "Millie, you there?" Sasha asked.

"Yeah, honey. Chief wants to see you. Come on in as quickly as possible."

It was not so much the words as the dispatcher's tone of voice that made Sasha bite her lip. Nervously, she asked, "Mill, what's up? What's the chief want?"

"Just come on in, Sash. That's all."

She found a shoulder and pulled over. She gripped the steering wheel with both hands and squeezed as hard as she could. "Please, please, please no."

Sasha turned to peer out Katherine Manfredi's bay window. The last rays of the setting sun lit the tops of the mountains on Point MacKenzie, on the opposite side of Knik Arm.

"Robin was killed and one other trooper seriously wounded. They were following up on a tip about a crack house south of town. Soon as they got out of their car, they were fired on." Sasha began nodding, as if to herself. "Robin died right away. The other trooper lost a leg. A third trooper, in the car, radioed for help. Turned out a couple douchebags zonked out on crack. They're still in jail. Out of state."

To herself, Sasha renewed an unspoken pledge: *And when they get their release, I'll be there, the meet and greet committee. Old Testament justice will be done.* Sasha looked at Manfredi. "You're a good listener, Katherine," she whispered.

"Thank you. Aleksandra. You have a child?"

"I do. Robin. After her dad. Smart like her dad. Tall like him. I see my husband every time I look at my daughter." She rose, went to her carryall, got her wallet, took out two photos, and brought them to the psychologist.

Manfredi lit a desk lamp, took one photo in each hand, examining them back and forth. "Lovely. Two peas in a pod," she said admiringly, handing them back.

Sasha took the snapshots and restored them to their place in her wallet. "I think I'm done for today. But you know something? I've never told that story to anyone outside of my family."

"How does it feel?"

"I'm not sure. Let me sleep on it."

"Do that. I hope you can come again."

"I hope so." Then, "I can. I will, for sure."

"I'll be here."

~~~

The *Pyotr Veliky* proceeded to Dutch Harbor at half speed. At this modest pace, the vessel would arrive in port the following day, mid-afternoon.

"No use straining the engines for this meeting with the U.S. Coast Guard," the master explained to his first mate.

"Correct Captain," Timoshenko answered. "The weather's turned fine, the crew's relaxing. No rush."

The two men sat in the ship's mess, taking a break from the monotony imposed on a fishing vessel that was prevented from fishing.

It had taken two days for Vronsky to emerge from the depression into which he had sunk after the disappearance of the American. Two days to become reconciled to his imminent land-based future. The transition would not be an easy one to navigate.

He had a large and supportive family who would help during the adjustment period: his own daughter, her husband, and their two children, as well as three of his own brothers and their large families.

And the captain was buoyed about getting back to his former passion—cooking, the job he started with upon entering the merchant marine.

The captain was about to say something to his first mate when a seaman burst into the mess. "Yury Gregorich. Come quickly and look at the sonar."

The master and first mate were in the ship's wheelhouse two minutes later. They went right to the scanning sonar, the device that shows the density, depth, and direction of schools of fish surrounding the boat.

One quick look was all the captain needed. "Good God, Valery. We're right on top of 'em. It's huge." Vronsky barely hesitated. "Forget Dutch Harbor, Valya. Call out the whole crew. Prepare the trawl. And have the radioman send the American Coast Guard our regrets. Tell them we've developed engine trouble. Make up something. Assure them that we're on the way, but we'll be delayed for at least two days, maybe three, while we make repairs. Let's go fishing."

~~~

Sasha entered the Rod and Creel Café at just past 7 a.m., ready for her rendezvous with FBI agent Charles Dana.

Never having met the man, she scanned the crowded restaurant looking for a likely suspect. She settled on someone—nerdy, conservative suit, buzz cut, official looking, sunglasses on the table, FBI written all over him. He was sitting by himself, reading a newspaper. Sasha approached.

"Excuse me. Are you Charles Dana?"

The man looked up from his Dispatch News, sat back and grinned up at the tall, blond, green-eyed woman who had, happily interrupted his reading of the comics section. "Charles Dana? No, I'm not." He paused, then with a suggestive smirk, "But I could be."

Sasha noticed his wedding ring and sneered, "And what do you think your wife would say about that, shit head?"

The man stiffened, huffed, flapped the newspaper, and returned to Dilbert.

Sasha continued searching the crowd until a high-pitched laugh coming from a window table caught her attention.

She walked closer. The laugher's focus was directed

toward a yellowing tabloid newspaper. He was dabbing at the tears in his eyes.

Seeing her, he put down the paper, took off his dark rimmed glasses, and stood up, gentlemanly. He was dressed in workout sweats with *'Fourth Grade Happens'* written across the front. He was unshaven, unkempt, and looked as if he had just finished jogging.

"Detective Kulaeva?" When Sasha nodded, he continued, "I'm Charles Dana." He extended his hand. Sasha gave him a stronger than her usual grip, appropriate, she thought, for an FBI agent.

"A pleasure meeting you," he said. "Thanks for making it here so god-awful early."

She started to take off her coat, but he beat her to it, hustling around in back of her and taking the jacket as she sloughed it off. He placed it neatly over the back of an adjoining chair. She smiled a thanks, slid into her seat, and gave him a perfunctory, "Nice to meet you too, Agent Dana."

With her eyes, she questioned the newspaper. "Entertaining reading?" she asked, a tad snarkily. She immediately regretted her tone, especially after his decorous behavior. She had been trying to get the snottiness out of her speech for a while now. It refused to leave.

The FBI agent seemed oblivious to her snidery. "It's the National Lampoon's Sunday Edition. It's a classic. Here," he said, offering her several pages. "Take the want ads home. You'll thank me tomorrow." He gave her a sweet grin.

Because of his apparent lack of guile, she took the pages, glanced at them briefly before laying the newspaper aside.

He pointed to a carafe. "Coffee?"

"Sure. Thanks," she said, turning her mug right side up and sliding it across the table. She continued her sizing up of the federal agent: over forty, but hard to say by how much. A shock of unruly black hair, probably too long for the FBI. Large, closely set hazel eyes. Floppy, Dumbo-esque ears. A schnoz you could open a can with, and teeth that could have benefitted from orthodonture when he was a teen. The individual parts were clownish, but taken together, for reasons that mystified her, they worked.

Sasha added cream and two packets of brown sugar to her coffee. "Seems the scope of the case has suddenly expanded," she said.

"Indeed. Your boss called mine last evening to let him know. Heroin sent to a dead woman from Dutch Harbor. Nickel says the missing man, Lasorda, sent it."

"No takers," she said. "Did Emmitt cream his pants when the heroin fell in his lap?"

Charlie raised a brow.

Sasha kicked herself for her choice of words. "Sorry. Cop talk. I should have said, FBI Special Agent in Charge Emmitt Esterhazy must be excited at the idea of heroin smuggling here on his turf."

"Got his attention."

"And did he call up the DEA right away to let them know?"

"I suspect not. At least, not right away."

"So Cardozo stays out of the loop for now, is that it?"

"Ours not to reason why . . ." he said, stirring his coffee.

"You don't look the FBI type, Agent Dana. I thought there was some kind of a dress code you people have." *Damn it. Snarky again.*

He nodded his agreement. "You're right, I believe there is. In fact, I'm sure there is. My mother warned me before I joined up. She's always worried about my wardrobe."

"Smart lady. She here in Anchorage?"

"Big Island. Kona side. She and dad run a two person maritime law office. Have for over thirty years. They came to visit last month for the start of the Iditarod. Loved the dogs, hated the race. My father volunteers for the pet rescue back home and when two of Mackey's dogs died during the race, dad started writing letters."

"Do any good?" she asked, picking up the menus and offering one to the FBI agent.

"Not that anyone noticed," he said. "Seems the Iditarod is one of those sacred cows in Alaska, part of the culture the locals here call *'The Last Frontier.'* I think the concept is total BS. But that's just me." He put down his menu and leaned into the sermon. "I mean, all you hear about is Alaskans being proud of doing it *their* way. That rugged individualism crap. Yet without the feds, this place would go under in a minute." He looked out the window. "See that barge, anchored just off shore? That's our lifeline up here. No barge, no *Last Frontier.*" He put up his hands defensively. "Sorry. Should have left the soapbox at home. I can get wound up sometime. The local hypocrisy drives me crazy. Hope I haven't offended."

"No. That's okay. No offense taken."

Dana looked briefly at his menu then put it down. "Listen, I eat here a lot. I always get the Canadian bacon and spinach omelet. It's wonderful. Funny thing. I try to be a vegetarian at home, but whenever I eat out, I go for the meat. Why is that, you think?"

"Chalk it up to lack of character. Or maybe your job

choice," she answered airily, reading her menu.

"Probably that's it. I'm so wishy-washy. Growing up is hard," he said, his attention shifting to the waitress who was coming over with a radiant smile wreathing a lovely face.

"Morning Charlie," the red haired, pony-tailed woman said with assurance, a lilting Texas drawl accenting her speech.

Sasha examined her closely. *A beauty, cheeks covered with freckles under sky blue eyes. Yowie!*

"Morning. I'm Melanie," the waitress said to Sasha. She turned her smile on Charlie. "Agent Dana."

"Morning Mel," he answered, grinning up at her. "How's work today?"

"Don't get me started," she almost snarled. "Had five BP execs in here earlier, talking nothing but oil. Brent crude. North Slope, North Sea. The proposed gas line. Fracking. The whole nine yards. Then they leave me a three buck tip for a sixty-five dollar breakfast. Bums!"

"Figures," Sasha said, liking Melanie right away.

"You folks ready to order?"

"Yeah, we're ready," Sasha said. "Two Canadian bacon and spinach omelets, home fries, rye toast, two large orange juices, and a side of sliced tomatoes."

Charlie Dana regarded Sasha with a wide smile of appreciation. "I'll have the same, Mel, thanks."

"Very funny," the waitress gushed.

Sasha sensed the rutting season was in full swing. Melanie, however, resisted the impulse to jump in Charlie's lap. She collected their menus and left.

Sasha poured more coffee into their mugs. "I know most of the agents but I haven't heard of you before. New up here?"

"Been here three months. And it's Charlie."

"Sentenced to Alaska for insubordination, huh?"

He looked at her, not getting the question.

"Well, some of you guys actually choose to come up here, enjoy the challenge. More often, this is the place naughty feds get shunted for the misdeeds committed in the *Lower '48*. Ask your boss. Emmitt knows all about it." She grinned mischievously.

He didn't bite. "No. Actually, my work with the Bureau got me up here."

"And that would be . . .?"

"CDC, a Chief Division Counsel, a resident attorney whose job is to keep the other agents current on criminal and constitutional law. I get to remind them how to apply and obey the law." He sat back. "That's my job, Detective Kulaeva."

"It's Sasha," she said, slowly stirring her coffee. "Obey the law. Is that what the FBI does?"

"Are you baiting me, detective?"

"Matter of fact, I am," she admitted. "But the question, Special Agent Dana, is a legitimate one. Let me repeat: does the FBI try to obey the law?"

"I think most of us actually try. I try. And some of us actually succeed. I succeed. Usually. And how about you, detective. Is that what you do, obey the law?"

"When it suits me," she said quickly and with finality.

Uncertain how to respond, Charlie held his tongue. Several minutes passed in silence until Melanie cruised back, loaded down with their food. She seemed less chirpy.

Charlie noticed. "What's up, Mel?"

"Colleen called in sick. Boss has volunteered me to work a double shift. I won't get outta here 'til eleven."

"That stinks," Sasha said.

"Not the first time. I'll manage. Meanwhile, enjoy," the waitress said, before sashaying off.

Charlie watched her departing backside with obvious appreciation.

Sasha's mood soured slightly, and with more acid in her voice than she meant to convey, she said, "Melanie's a sweetheart. Your type?"

Charlie's smile disappeared. "I'm not sure I have a type," he said.

Sasha thought she detected a note of something new in his voice: Regret? Disappointment? She broke the mood by diving into her breakfast. After a minute, "You spoke to my partner last night about Jimmy Lasorda, the missing fisherman. Want to fill me in?"

He put down knife and fork and from an intricately tooled leather briefcase, withdrew a black, three ring binder with 'Lasorda, Castro' neatly labeled across the front. He opened to the first page. "We ran preliminary checks on the presumed deceased, James Anthony Lasorda. Also on Isabella Juanita Castro, and her brother, Rudolfo Manuel Castro. Have you found him yet, by the way?"

"Not yet. He wasn't home when my partner went looking for him yesterday. It's possible he's laying low. I would if everyone around me's getting killed. I'm going up to his place to look for him soon as we're done here. Then I'm meeting with Isabel's friend, a colleague of hers from Fish and Wildlife. She ID-ed the body yesterday."

"Want some company?"

Sasha was about to take a sip of coffee, but decisively placed the mug back on the table. "We need to get something straight right off the bat, Agent Dana. While I *do* appreciate the FBI's interest in Lasorda—federal employee, missing off of a Russian fishing boat in American waters and all that—the woman's death is an Anchorage Police Department case. We can work together. I'm happy to do so. But don't fuck with my case."

If her language was an attempt to get a reaction out of the FBI agent, to provoke or intimidate him, it didn't work. He looked at her, never blinking.

"Wouldn't dream of fucking with your case, Detective Kulaeva," he said quietly, but with a sincerity she found disarming. "You're the last person I'd want to fuck with," he added, smiling at her in a way that set off a small charge in her chest. "But just so everyone at this here breakfast table understands the situation: Isabel Castro worked for Fish and Wildlife, which *also* happens to be a federal agency. If I wanted to take both of these cases, well . . ." he left the sentence unfinished.

Sasha realized the FBI agent had the whip hand. "Got it," she said.

"So, let's be partners, okay?" Charlie said, lightly. "After breakfast, we'll go on up to Lasorda's house and then talk to the dead woman's friend. Together. okay?"

"If we must," she said, returning to her food. Two bites later, "Tell me something. How come Emmitt assigned *you* to this case? You said you're a lawyer and not necessarily an action-hero agent. Why are *you* the one I'm talking with about murder and heroin?"

Charlie put on a guilty expression. "I was assigned to this case because the SAC wanted me to meet you."

Sasha sat back, stunned. "Emmitt Esterhazy is now a

matchmaker? What the hell is that about?"

"He likes you. He told me you're the best cop in town. He said I could learn more from you in a day than in a month at Quantico. He values you."

She was unsure how to reply. She left it and pointed her fork at his binder. "What else you got?"

"Not a lot. A Dade County, Florida rap sheet on Rudy Castro when he was young and silly in Miami. A little joy riding. A little grass. Nothing serious. His sister, Isabel, the woman in the meadow, was your clean-cut type. College, two advanced degrees, solid work history. No problems with the law. She rolled through a stop sign once. Her boyfriend, Jimmy the fisherman, grew up in Jersey. MS in marine biology. Had a few minor infractions. But again, nothing serious. They'll be more complete info by late afternoon. We could meet again this evening and compare notes," he said, looking sideways at her.

"I'll check my calendar," Sasha said, with a tinge of feigned boredom.

"One more thing," Charlie said. "I spoke to the Coast Guard in Dutch Harbor last night. The Russian ship that Lasorda worked on has been ordered into Dutch, supposed to get in tomorrow. Anyhow, I'm flying out there to question the crew. Emmitt suggested that you should come, too. To translate. How 'bout it?"

"I'll clear it with my parents," Sasha said, the snarkiness back.

"I'm sure they'd approve of me. You're not married, are you?"

Sasha gazed through the picture window at Fire Island. She could just make out the cluster of new wind turbines scattered on the island's hills. She shook her head in response.

"Boyfriend?"

She looked at him with exasperation. "Would that stop you from trying to hustle me?"

"Is that what I'm doing?"

"You deny it?"

He smiled. "No. It's true. I'd only stop trying if your boyfriend was a biker."

"Such commitment!" She shook her head. "No, Special Agent Dana. No current boyfriend."

He shook his head in disbelief. "What's with the men in this town? Are they all blind? Here you are, smart, sassy, filthy-mouthed, cynical, moody, a no-bull-shit, stunningly terrific looking woman. *And* you seem to be available. Why isn't there a line of guys a mile long, beating down your door?" He began spooning raspberry jam onto his toast, and not doing a particularly neat job of it.

Sasha realized he'd nailed her. Twenty minutes together and he'd divined the salient features—mostly negative—of her hard-edged personality. *Which is exactly why there isn't a line a mile long,* she thought. She looked at him without comment, but without her former animosity.

"So. Great," he said. "What are we doing for dinner?"

"I give you an A for persistence, Agent Dana. Tonight, like most nights, it's Lean Cuisine."

"Golly, sounds great. I like their sesame chicken."

"I thought you said you tried to be a vegetarian at home."

"I lied."

Melanie glided back to their table. "Anything else?,"

she asked, smiling brightly at Charlie.

"No thanks, Mel. We're fine," he said in a quiet voice, never taking his eyes off Sasha.

Melanie's body language showed disappointment that her presence didn't bring forth a more spirited reaction from the FBI agent. She wrote out the check and left.

Sasha watched her depart. "Why don't you ask her out? She looks ready."

"Too young. Besides, she's already turned me down flat. Twice."

The *'too young'* remark made Sasha consider her own thirty-eight years. *What the hell,* she thought, "What are *your* plans tonight?"

"Me? Oh, the usual," he ho-hummed. "Take-out chicken from Lucky Wishbone and a Dr. Brown's Cream Soda. Watch Jeopardy. I usually know all the answers, but about two seconds after everyone else. Synapses like molasses."

"Too much beef. Clog your blood vessels."

"I can't help myself."

"There's that wishy-washy thing again," she said.

~~~

At over a thousand feet above sea level, Glazanof Drive offers a view to die for—the entire Anchorage bowl, stretching up and down Turnagain Arm's shoreline. In the center of the Arm's waters, Fire Island, home to the state's latest experiment in alternative energy. And on a clear day, two hundred and thirty miles to the north, the Great One, snow crested Denali.

Standing in their destination's parking area, Sasha and Charlie surveyed the home they'd come to search—a six-sided geodesic dome, cedar shakes covering the outside, and six triple pane, vented skylights facing the heavens. Sasha admired the aesthetic attempt but from her own experience, she knew there was no such thing as a dome that didn't leak from its windows. She'd wait to inspect the ceilings from inside.

She rapped on the front door and announced herself. Nothing. One more time. Again nothing. Rudy Castro wasn't there or wasn't answering.

She tried the door handle. Locked. Sasha took out her lock pick set.

"Hang on a second," Charlie argued. "You're not going to pick the lock?"

"We have a no-knock warrant. Guy inside could be flushing the shit down the toilet right now. We need to get inside. And this door looks like solid oak. We ain't busting it down. So picking the lock is gonna get us in, quick."

Two minutes later, Charlie followed her into the Arctic entrance, the room that separates Alaska's harsh outdoors from its citizens' warm indoors. The walls were finished with cedar paneling, making the entry sweetly redolent. Benches ran down both sides of the room. Boxes of wool hats, gloves, and heavy socks were lined up atop the benches. And tucked underneath were a variety of footwear—neoprene bunny boots, lace-up hiking shoes, Sno-Pacs, felt liners, steel-toed rubber galoshes, ice skates, and several pair of house slippers. An assortment of parkas, hoodies, and rain gear hung from pegs on both sides of the room.

Sasha and Charlie passed through the interior door into the main room—an airy and spacious fifty-foot-diameter dome built on top of an eight-foot high riser wall.

Around the interior circumference of the dome, copper

tubing revealed baseboard heat. And in the center of the dome, on a foundation of thick bricks, a giant wood stove. Thirty feet of Metalbestos pipe went up from the back of the stove and through the roof. Neat piles of dried spruce and birch were at hand, as well as a box of kindling.

She walked up to the stove, a cast iron Rightway. It was cool to the touch. In the winter, fully banked, it would warm the entire dome, helped by the giant ceiling fan overhead that would push the heat down, spreading it throughout the interior.

Against the north side of the structure, stairs led up to a loft that looked to be the sleeping area.

Sasha's gaze continued upward. She had her suspicions confirmed about the efficacy of skylights in domes: below each of the six windows were long, darkened streaks caused by leaking water doing its thing.

She walked over to the only room with real walls. It was crammed with toilet, shower, a stacked washer/dryer combo, a fifty-gallon water heater, and a gas-fired boiler.

Sasha turned to Charlie and fished out two pair of nitrile gloves from her evidence bag. She put on a pair and tossed the other to the FBI agent. "Anything you find that's out of sight, in drawers or closets, pull out and leave exposed. Less hassle that way."

"We going to fudge on the parameters of the warrant?" he asked.

"Calm down. It's just you and me here. Fudging is what we do."

"I don't like it," he grumbled.

An hour later and the kitchen table was covered with the large collection of objects they'd discovered.

"There seems to be quite enough here to bring substantial charges against the residents," Charlie said. "At least the one who's still alive."

"*If* Rudy Castro's still alive," Sasha said. "Looks like an addict's wet dream. Syringes, alcohol swabs, cotton balls, thirty-two full dime bags and two, larger sandwich baggies, stuffed with a bright white powder."

"Can you identify heroin from the taste?" Charlie asked.

"I can, but tasting's verboten. I'm sure it's the same for you guys." Sasha opened one of the bags and, for the second time in two days, dabbed a moistened finger into the white powder and took a long look. "Seems to be the same stuff I caught yesterday from Dutch Harbor. The lab'll verify."

Charlie pointed to the pistol on the table—a Kimber Micro .380 with a rosewood grip, along with four full magazines. "Think these bozos ever bothered to get a permit?" he asked.

"Only if they bought the gun in a store. If they got it at the local gun and ammo show, they won't have had to register ownership."

"A seriously screwed up system."

"Amen to that."

The final items they examined were eight checkbooks Sasha found hidden under a stack of clothes in a loft/bedroom drawer. Three were from Aruba, belonging to Jimmy Lasorda; two from Nassau, belonging to Isabel Castro; and two from Antigua, Rudy's. Together, the Caribbean banks had over a hundred and fifteen thousand dollars and change socked away.

"Guys made a good living," Sasha said, checking her watch. "Listen, we have a little time before we see Rose. I spotted some Danish in the fridge. I'll heat 'em up. You work the Mr. Coffee. Maybe Rudy Castro'll show."

Charlie followed her to the kitchen. "Be sure and read the National Lampoon I gave you at breakfast. You'll get a kick out of it."

"I probably won't read it," she said, putting two apple turnovers on a plate and then into the microwave. "But my daughter might." *Why'd I offer that?*

Charlie stopped pouring water into the coffee maker. "Whoa. A surprise. I didn't figure you for a family kind of cop."

Sasha looked away. "You figured right. I'm not," she said quietly. "Not really. Not as much as I'd like to be."

"Just one kid?"

"Just one. My daughter, Robin. She'll be twelve this summer."

"Anything like her mom?"

"Happily for her, very little like her mom."

"Too bad," he said. "Want to tell me about her?"

"She's a sixth grader. Super smart in a people way. Good at reading folks."

"She doesn't live with you, does she?"

"No. How'd you figure?"

"At breakfast, you spoke about making dinner for one."

A pause, then flat-voiced, "No. Robin doesn't live with me."

The microwave dinged and Sasha removed the warmed pastry.

Charlie held up an apologetic hand. "Sorry, I'm getting too close to home. You don't have to answer any more of my dumb-ass questions." He resumed his coffee prep.

A minute later, Sasha sighed an explanation. "She lives

with my family. We have a big spread, hundred and forty acres, a homestead, on Big Lake. North of here."

"Your parents there?"

She shook her head. "They died in a plane crash when I was three. I was raised by my extended family, mostly by my grandfather."

Charlie took it in, not responding right away. After a minute, he asked quietly, "And Robin's father?" As soon as he said it, he regretted the question. "Sorry I brought it up. I'm stupid sometimes."

"No kidding," she said, slicing the warmed Danish into halves. *Go ahead, girl. Just say it.* "He died twelve years ago." *That's twice in twenty-four hours you've spoken about Robin's death. Both times to strangers. Maybe this is what proper mourning is all about.*

"Christ. I'm so sorry," Charlie said. "Was he ill?"

"Line of duty."

"Oh, fuck."

"Yeah, oh fuck."

They spent the next several minutes silently watching the coffee percolate into the pot. When there was enough for two cups, Charlie poured.

"Raised by your grandfather. What's he like?"

"Viktor? One of a kind. I'm lucky. He's still hale and hearty at ninety-one. He was born in Russia. Cossack blood. If they made a movie about his life, people wouldn't believe it."

"If you're telling it, Sasha, I'll believe it. We have a little time."

"It can wait. It's only history. It'll be there later. We need to check in with Rose."

~~~

Leonid Bulgarin was tall, blond, stoop-shouldered, thin of face, thin of body, sadly dark-eyed, with an elongated, pointed nose over a sensitive mouth.

The most significant day of his life was October 2, 2004, the day before his wife's fortieth birthday. He was planning to take the train into Manhattan in the afternoon, to Macy's, to buy Dorotea a gift.

But that morning, a surprise—a phone call from his cousin, Boris. Could Leo please meet him for lunch in Manhattan? At Lanza perhaps, on First Avenue? He had an idea he thought might interest his cousin.

Leonid rejoiced. An invitation from Boris was something to get excited about. But when he mentioned it to Dorotea, the woman began to froth.

"Leo, he's *never* invited you anywhere," she said, clasping her fingers together in front of her, imploring. "Why now? Whatever he wants, tell him thanks, but no. Do not, under any circumstances, get involved with that man! He'll be the death of both of us."

Leonid argued on Boris' behalf. "We're first cousins, for God's sake." He reminded his wife of the debt he owed to Boris and the Bunin family: in 1979, Leonid went to flight school, to the Higher Civil Aviation Academy, in Ulyanovsk, Russia's preeminent training program for would-be pilots. David Bunin, Boris' father, pulled strings to get him in and then sprang for the tuition. Leonid owed the Bunins.

Five years later, certified in fixed wing aircraft, he and Dorotea were brought to America, sponsored by Boris' family. Leonid owed them.

His cousins arranged work for him in a New York air taxi service, ferrying the well-heeled back and forth from their up-state homes to Manhattan, to Boston, and occasionally to Washington D.C.

"I owe the Bunins," Leonid insisted.

So, lunch at Lanza, where, over a dish of perfectly prepared calamari, Boris began outlining 'the idea' at which he'd hinted. He explained that he'd prepared the way for cousin Leo's dream to come true—owning his own flight service.

"Marvelous. Fantastic," Leonid gushed. "Where. Upstate New York. Maybe out west?"

"Northwest."

"Seattle area? Wonderful."

"No. Not Seattle. Further north."

"Canada?" Leonid skeptical now and not so thrilled.

"Not quite. Alaska."

If Leonid was shocked, Dorotea was apoplectic, furious, crazed. "Alaska?" she screeched. "Where the hell am I supposed to get my hair done in Alaska?"

But when Cousin Boris fronted Leonid a princely sum to buy two small Beechcraft, to rent an office and hangar space at Anchorage's Merrill Field, and to incorporate his business, Dorotea was mollified. Somewhat. And when there was money enough to hire Dorotea as staff, the woman was won over. She still managed a weekly rant, however, naming Boris Bunin as the person who would ultimately bring death and destruction to her family.

~~~

Two hours after the discovery of a treasure trove of what

the crime lab would almost certainly identify as heroin, the detective and the federal agent were outside the U.S. Fish and Wildlife building, waiting for Rose Nakamura. They had stopped briefly at the Federal Court Building where Charlie had arranged for a warrant for the arrest of Rudy Castro, suspected user and seller of heroin.

Rose met them on the tree-shaded front steps of the building. She was wearing white jeans with a brown suede coat over a pale yellow sweater. And around her neck, a billowy, light green scarf that matched her green Nike Lunar Epics. *There's no accounting for taste,* Sasha thought.

The secretary handed Sasha a piece of yellow, lined paper. "Here's a list of Isabel's friends. Everyone I could think of."

Sasha took the page and briefly read over the numbered list of twenty-eight people and their contact information. "Very good, Rose. This'll be big help. Thanks." She pointed to Charlie. "This is FBI Special Agent Charles Dana."

"How'ya doin'?" Rose said, glancing his way. Then, "FBI? Why the FBI?"

Sasha came closer and stood next to her. "Rose. Bad news. Jimmy Lasorda is missing off of his ship in the Bering Sea. They're searching for him but it doesn't look likely he'll be found."

Rose put her hand over her mouth to stifle a scream. It came out anyhow as a muted choking that started in her stomach and got strangled in her throat. Her legs wobbled, knees almost giving out. Charlie caught her under her arms.

"Come on," Sasha said. "Let's find a place to sit and talk." Gertie's Lounge and Diner on Lake Otis Boulevard was built during the war and had acquired a seventy-year-old musty-damp smell that no change of furniture, change of paneling, change of curtains, or change of clientele could erase.

When the trio arrived, it was quiet inside the diner, most of the lunch crowd having come and gone. Three middle-aged women, dressed in light parkas and khaki trousers, sat at the bar sipping white wine, watching TV. The bartender was polishing glasses. A waitress was busy restocking sugar and salt. "Sit anywhere," she said. "Same prices, any seat."

"We'd like one of the back rooms," Sasha said. "We're expecting several other folks here soon. We'd like some privacy. Will that work?"

"No problem. Any of those three back rooms are good. Get you coffee?"

"No thank you. Nothing for now," Sasha said. She took Rose by the elbow and steered her toward the back of the diner. Charlie brought up the rear.

The room they entered was dim, whatever light the five long, alley-facing windows allowed in was suffused. Charlie tried the light switch. One of three overhead fixtures flickered to life.

There was a single, long table set for ten. The tablecloth was vintage gold rush—red and white checked gingham. The chairs were heavy curled wood and came in a variety of shades of well-used brown. A fine layer of dust had accumulated on all the room's surfaces.

"Let's sit," Sasha said, bringing out a chair for Rose.

The secretary sat and looked from Sasha to Charlie, not sure what to expect. She held a clinched fist to her mouth and in a tremulous voice, "What happened to Jimmy?"

Sasha moved closer to Rose and took a seat opposite her. "We don't know yet exactly what happened to him, but we believe his disappearance and Isabel's death are connected."

Rose visibly shrank back into her seat, trying to distance herself from this information. "No, no. Wait a minute. What are you saying? There's a connection? That's crazy. No way. No way."

Sasha took her time, an edge in her voice. "Oh yeah, Rose. Way. Believe it."

Rose stared down the length of the table. "I don't know anything about any of this. Why are you asking me?"

Sasha said, "Two of your close friends are dead. One murdered. The other *probably* murdered. Listen to me, Rose. Pay real close attention. We were just up at the Glazanof house. Guess what we found?"

The secretary stiffened. "How am I supposed to know what you found? Why should I know anything?" she said in a rush.

Charlie nodded. "I'll tell you why. Because you and Rudy and Jimmy and Isabel vacationed together in the Bahamas, a vacation that cost . . ." he turned to Sasha. "How much Detective Kulaeva? Remind Rose."

"Something over twenty-one grand. For ten days. Not including airfare," Sasha said.

Rose was now gnawing at her lower lip.

"Chew that lip, girl. Keep faking it and see how far it gets you," Sasha said, a clear threat now apparent in her tone.

"I'm not saying another word to either of you. You want to talk to me anymore, you can contact my lawyer."

"A lawyer? Why would you need a lawyer?" Sasha asked. "You haven't done anything." She paused, glanced briefly at Charlie, then back to the secretary. "Or have you?

Maybe if we dig deeper, we'll find *your* fingerprints on some of the stuff we found at Rudy's this morning."

The secretary flinched, her head jerked, her eyes bugged open. "You won't find my prints on *anything*. I haven't done a damn thing."

"I guess we'll see, won't we? But lawyering up—whether or not you've done anything illegal—is always a safe bet. See, here's the deal, Rose. Two of your friends are dead and we've collected a ton of incriminating evidence that connects them to drug dealing. I'd say we have here some unusual circumstances." Sasha looked over at Charlie. "Agent Dana, would you give us a minute please. I'd like to talk to Rose alone. Girl to girl."

Charlie hesitated, wary. "I think I'll hang around, Detective Kulaeva."

Sasha stared at him for a few seconds.

He had never understood the expression 'hard eyes,' but looking at the Anchorage detective now, he knew for a certainty what she had in mind. "I'll stick around," he said, firmly.

Rose looked from one to the other. "What's going on? I told you I'm not going to say anything else without a lawyer."

Sasha ignored her, kept looking at Charlie. "Agent Dana, please," she said, nodding toward the door. "Give us a couple minutes. Please."

Charlie shook his head. "Unh-uh. I'm staying."

"Suit yourself," Sasha said.

Rose, a quaver in her voice, "Wh . . . what are you going to do? Why'dya want him to leave? I don't want to talk to you." She tried to rise but Sasha shoved her back into her seat.

"Sit the fuck down and don't open your mouth again," Sasha ordered.

Rose looked over at Charlie as someone adrift on the open sea might watch a boat disappearing over the horizon.

Sasha leaned toward Rose and in a single fluid motion, grabbed the much smaller woman by the front of her jacket, lifted her from her seat and slammed her against the wall. The secretary's head audibly thumped against the high, wooden window sill. Rose was on her tiptoes, gurgling as Sasha twisted her scarf, driving a fist into her throat.

FBI Special Agent Charles Dana couldn't believe his eyes. He cracked open the door to see if anyone in the lounge had heard. The bartender and the three morning drinkers were watching *The Price is Right* on TV. "Come on down," Drew Carey encouraged. Charlie shut the door.

Sasha leaned heavily into Rose. "Listen to me, you little shit. You're gonna help me connect the dots—Jimmy, Isabel, Rudy, and heroin. Right here and right now, or I'm going to do two things. First, I'm going to punch your lights out. Then, I'm going to call your boss and get your ass fired. You don't help me, I'm going to fuck you up something terrible."

It was hard to say which of the two federal employees— the FBI agent guarding the door against intruders, or the Fish and Wildlife worker being strangled against the wall—was more shocked by the ultimatum delivered on behalf of the Anchorage Police Department.

Sasha lowered the secretary to her feet, righted the overturned chair with her free hand and shoved Rose roughly down into her seat so that her head whiplashed.

The detective sat next to her and began speaking in a monotone, as though reading from a police arrest report.

"Been checking up on you, Rose. How you come to work at Fish and Wildlife. Almost didn't get the job. Because in 2008, in Seattle, you got busted for possession for sale of a controlled substance. Turns out, you had a bag of peyote buttons cleverly hidden in plain sight on the front passenger seat of your car. In all honesty Rose, I have to tell you. You don't look like you qualify for membership in the Native American Church." Sasha paused. "You lied about that, Rose. Six years ago on your employment application to Fish and Wildlife. We got a copy. In the little box that asks whether you've ever been arrested, you marked 'no.' That was a lie. How 'bout that, Agent Dana?"

At this moment, the FBI Agent wished he had never come to Alaska, had never met Detective Kulaeva. But here he was. He stepped closer to the woman being questioned and swallowed hard. "Grounds for dismissal, Rose. Every federal employee has to account for prior problems with the law. Your boss hears about it, you're out on your keister, your career with the government over."

Sasha smiled a 'good job' at Charlie. He didn't smile back.

"Please don't get me fired," Rose said, her lips trembling.

"Depends entirely on you," Sasha said.

The secretary tried to regain some stability by placing her palms on the table, but couldn't stop them from jittering up and down. She looked to the window for some kind of out. There was none. She bent over, cupped her face in her hands, and whispered, "They killed 'em. Both of them. I know it."

"They? Who's they? Who killed them?" Sasha demanded.

Rose hesitated, raised her head, and directed her remarks to Charlie. "Russians killed them."

"Russians? Why would Russians kill them?" he asked.

Barely audibly, Rose sighed her answer, "Jimmy was skimming."

"Say it again, Rose. Louder. One more time," Charlie ordered.

Now with more force, the dam burst, "They were skimming! They dealt dope! Jimmy . . . and Isabel . . ."

Sasha filled in, " . . . and Rudy."

Rose broke into tears, her carefully applied deep blue mascara smearing her cheeks.

Sasha took a paper napkin from the table and handed it to the woman. "If we're gonna to keep meeting, Rose, you and me, you're gonna have to get yourself some non-streak mascara. Either that or man-up." Sasha pressed on. "This is all about heroin trafficking, right?"

The secretary blew her nose. "Yeah. They dealt very good, very pure heroin."

"And where did they get this very good, very pure heroin?" Charlie asked.

Rose touched the napkin to the corner of an eye, sniffled. "I don't know exactly. I think Jimmy collects it from some Russian ships. Then Isabel brings it in from Dutch. *Brought* it in." The switch to the past tense, necessary to describe the deceased, caused a series of throaty moans and shoulder heaves.

"Did they deal here in Alaska?" Charlie asked.

"No. I don't know. Maybe."

"Jimmy use?" he asked.

Rose shook her head.

"Isabel?"

Rose became indignant. "Never. Not one time I ever knew her. She didn't even smoke grass. She was way too smart."

"OK. How 'bout you, Rose? You use?"

Adamantly, "No fuckin' way I use. I got better things to do with my life than stick needles in my arm." She lowered her tone. "And better things to do than go with someone who did."

"You mean Rudy?" Charlie asked.

Rose nodded once. "He used to. Up until last year. He's trying to get clean."

Charlie clasped his hands on the table. "So. Isabel and Jimmy were bringing in heroin from some kind of Russian connection in Dutch Harbor and were killed because they kept some for themselves. Is that what you're telling us?"

Rose licked her lips, nodded. "Yeah. Each load they brought in, they'd take half an ounce or so before they moved it on. That's how we went to St. Croix. Rudy knew some rich kids from Miami. They bought three ounces."

"So Rudy's a salesman," Charlie said. "How big would a shipment be? In weight?"

"I don't know exactly. A lot. Fifteen, twenty pounds, maybe. Maybe more."

"What happened to it?" Sasha demanded. "Who got it? Who did Jimmy pass it to?"

"Somebody here in town."

"He got a name? You ever see him?"

"No. I never saw him. Only Jimmy met with him, said he was older. That's all I know."

"Rudy ever see him?"

"I'm not sure. Maybe."

"Your boyfriend wasn't home when we went up to find him on Glazanof. Know where he might be?"

Rose stiffened. "I don't know."

Sasha grabbed the secretary by the wrist, gave it a twist. "Bull shit. Where's Rudy?"

When Rose shook her head, Sasha took out her notepad and flipped it open. Finding what she was looking for, she got out her cell phone and punched in a number. A moment later, "Hi, Judson McKimmey please." Sasha waited. "OK. Let me have his voice mail." Another short pause. "Hi Mr. McKimmey. This is Detective Kulaeva, Anchorage Police Department. Would you call me back at this number, please. I'd like to talk to you about Rose Nakamura." Sasha closed her phone and glared at the young woman.

Rose weakened. "If I tell you where Rudy is, what'll happen to him?"

Charlie answered, "If *we* find him, we'll arrest him and charge him with heroin trafficking. If he's found guilty, he'll go to jail. For a long time. Heroin's serious business. But if the *Russians* find him before we do, they'll almost certainly kill him. They seem to be in a going-out-of-business mind-set.

Rose considered for a moment. "He's staying at the Alyeska Prince Hotel, in Girdwood."

"You speak to him lately?" Sasha asked.

"I called him yesterday, told him about Isabel. And again this morning."

"Great," Sasha said. "We'll drive out and talk to him, right away. And if he's not there, Rose, I'll assume that you phoned to warn him. In which case, I call McKimmey and make sure you get canned. Are we on the same page here?"

"I told you. He's at the Alyeska Prince. He's registered as Richard Carlisle. RC. Smart guy, huh? I won't warn him," Rose said. "Please don't call my boss."

~~~

The highways in and out of Anchorage are few. Two, in fact. One north, one south. The one north splits and leads either to the oil-dense North Slope or out of state, into Canada's Yukon Territory. The highway south also splits, dead-ending in two cities—Seward and Homer—on either side of the Kenai Peninsula.

To drive to the Alyeska Prince Hotel to collar Rudy Castro, Sasha and Charlie headed south on the New Seward Highway. Detective Gary Hernandez and Patrolman Busby Moranis followed in a second police car.

Named for the American Secretary of State who convinced the Russians to sell Alaska in 1867, the Seward Highway is a road that offers numerous unique vistas—Dall sheep on the steep and very rocky slopes of the highway's land-side. And on the road's water-side, beluga whales are occasionally visible in the shallows of Turnagain Arm.

In the lead police car's passenger seat, Charlie Dana gazed at the mud flats that extended out half a mile to his right, to the west. It was low tide but in a few hours, one of the planet's strongest bore tides would begin surging up the Arm, moving in at over twenty miles an hour. In mid-summer, surfers on long boards and in full body wet suits would grab a wave—sometimes more than six feet tall—and enjoy a ride that might go on for half an hour.

They drove past Beluga Point, Anchorage's prime

whale watching vantage, where a dozen cars and RVs were parked. The hopeful passengers, cameras and binoculars in hand, were alternately searching the cliffs for sheep, or the water, for beluga, maybe a whole pod, maybe just a fin.

"You ever see a whale from here?" Charlie asked.

"Been here dozens of times," Sasha said. "Not a glimpse. Not one. Best time is when the salmon are running. Still too early. Though it *does* get exciting when someone gets stuck in the mud flats."

"How so?"

"Dangerous. Very dangerous. There can be a difference of nearly forty feet between high and low tides. You get stuck right now, for instance, at low tide, and you don't get yourself free, the high tide sweeps over you. Finito."

"So how do you get out if you're stuck?"

"With the help of friends or bystanders. But if that doesn't work, a helicopter comes, drops you a line. You tie it around your chest and they yank you out."

"Sounds simple."

"Normally is. Except if you're stuck too deep in the mud, helicopter'll rip your body in two."

Charlie looked long at Sasha. "You're serious? They actually pulled someone apart trying to rescue him? This is not an urban legend?"

"Believe it. And it was a her."

"Shit," he said, though not totally convinced.

They drove on a few miles. "You a family man, Agent Dana? Kids?"

He shook his head. "No such luck. Always wanted some. Always thought I'd have a couple, at least."

"Never met someone to help you realize your dream?"

"Been married twice. Both times to women who didn't like kids. Can I pick 'em or what?"

"Is that the reason you split from them? Children?"

"Not at all. Both of my wives split from *me*. And for all kinds of other reasons. My wives left *me*."

"Probably because you're stupid and can't keep your mouth shut," she suggested, with a smile to soften the jab.

"I'm sure that's part of it. My first wife, Ellen, left me for a dentist. Owns three clinics in the Bay Area. She goes in for a cleaning one day and never comes home. Really. Heard from her a week later. She wanted to come and collect her clothes. Asked if I please wouldn't be there when she came. We were married five years."

"And number two?"

"That'd be Linda. A lovely lady. Linda left me . . . just because."

"Just because what?"

"Besides being stupid, I'm sort of a louse."

Sasha glanced over at him. "Geez. A louse. You rarely hear men describe themselves so negatively. No one's been able to delouse you?"

Charlie gazed out his window. No belugas in sight. "There's always hope," he said without conviction.

Another silent interlude, then, "Oh, crap, look up ahead," Sasha said.

A mile up the winding highway, brake lights were flashing, traffic slowing, then stopping. She eased off the gas and continued for another quarter mile, slowing gradually and bringing the police cruiser to a halt behind a semi.

"What gives?" Charlie asked.

"Well, two or three things usually bring this highway to

a halt. Could be a rockslide. More common during the winter. Then they have to bring in the earth moving machines. That, or someone's hit a moose. Happens hundreds of times a year. Car's usually totaled."

"Do the drivers get to keep the moose meat and the antlers?"

"God no. Meat gets donated to charity."

"And the third reason?"

"Third reason. Someone crossed the divider and skidded head-on into an RV with possible dramatic results."

The wail of a nearing siren interrupted the conversation. A minute later a fire engine and an ambulance eased slowly past on the road's shoulder, followed by a police car and a large tow truck.

When the sirens had faded, Sasha heard a honking from the rear. She looked out her side mirror. Gary was signaling her.

"Sit tight. Back in a minute." Sasha exited her vehicle and walked to the trailing cruiser, fighting the wind as it whipped open her coat. She zipped up as she came abreast of the second police car. Gary rolled down the window and Sasha leaned in.

"Hey Moranis," she greeted the patrolman sitting next to Gary.

The officer nodded back at her. "What's with the fed?"

"Along for the ride." She hesitated, considering. "Listen, Gary. When we get to the hotel, you and I'll grab Castro. I want us two, *without* Dana, to talk to the guy."

"No problem." Gary turned to Moranis. "Buy the fed a cup of coffee. Keep him busy 'til we come out with Castro."

Sasha grinned at the patrolman. "Can you manage to keep him occupied?"

Moranis shrugged. "Sure. But, doesn't he kinda outrank me? FBI and all?"

"Do your best."

"I'll see what I can do."

"Great," Sasha said. She placed a hand on Gary's arm. "Bring your . . . you know. We cool?"

"Got it," he said.

They watched Sasha return to her car, the gusting wind almost pulling her door off its hinges.

"Tell me something, Hernandez," Moranis said. "She got an old man, a boyfriend?"

Gary turned to the patrolman, not speaking. Staring.

"What? Just asking," Moranis said.

"Busby, don't hold your breath. She ain't never gonna fuck you."

Busby Moranis, thirty-six-years old, blond, trim, good looking, made a face. "And why the hell not? What makes her so fuckin' special?"

Gary watched the semi, two vehicles ahead, rock in the wind. "My partner, Detective Kulaeva, enjoys a joke. You're not funny. She likes people with heart. You're a brute. And most of all she likes people with brains." Gary looked directly at the patrolman.

"Fuck you, Hernandez," Moranis spat out.

"Listen Busby. Stick to your own kind. You can usually find 'em Ladies' Night at Center Bowling.

Moranis snickered. "I was actually there couple nights ago," he said, grinning. "Met a lonely widow."

They both laughed.

In the lead car, Charlie asked, "What's up with your partner? Why the parlay?"

"Just sorting out some shit we have to do when we get back to town."

"Uh huh. What's he like?"

"Gary? Gibraltar. Always been there. Always will be."

"He from here?"

"Nah. You know East LA?"

"A little."

"Boyle Heights. El Monte. They've been Chicano neighborhoods since before the war. His grandfather was a Zoot Suiter, mixed it up with the sailors. Gary becomes a cop, gets assigned to his own neighborhood, tries to make things better. Tries to get the gangs to stop killing each other. Good luck with that! Gets shot in the hip for his efforts. Still limps a little. Survives and brings his family north. Been with the department about nine years. We've been partners for four. Trust him. Love him."

A helicopter appeared above them, arced over Turnagain Arm, banked and headed back to Anchorage.

"A medevac, probably flying to Providence Hospital with the remnants of whatever happened up ahead," Sasha said.

The semi in front of them came to life and began inching forward. Sasha started up the cruiser. Ten minutes later, they crawled by a brand new Ford 150 pickup with an accordioned hood and every window smashed. It had come to rest perpendicular to a vintage VW van whose entire driver's side was stove in. Paramedics were attending to three walking wounded.

"T-boned," Charlie said. "Christ."

Once past the drama, they picked up speed and after fifteen minutes Sasha turned left onto the Alyeska Highway, into the ski resort town of Girdwood.

Charlie sat up in his seat. "Something's eating me and I have to ask you about it."

"Shoot."

"I'm a little worried. What if she files a complaint about how we treated her? Gets a lawyer, talks about how we roughed her up?"

"What if *who* complains? Rose? Are you naïve, or what?" Sasha said, totally surprised. "What happens is I deny it. The bitch's word against Detective Kulaeva. You back me up. It's us two against her. Who's gonna believe her? Jesus, Charlie. Get with the program. Is that what's really eating you, Agent Dana? Spit it out."

He wished now he hadn't broached the subject, but pushed ahead. "Well, correct me if I'm wrong, but I thought there were certain boundaries we didn't cross when questioning witnesses."

Sasha slowed down, pulled the car onto a gravel siding, put it in park, and turned off the engine. She opened her window and waved Gary's car to pass and go on ahead. He slowed and stopped next to them. The passenger window rolled down.

"What's up," Moranis asked.

"Just getting some things straight. We'll be there in a minute. Wait for us at the hotel entrance."

After the second car drove off, Sasha turned to face Charlie. She picked up her aggression where she had left it. "Certain boundaries, huh? No kidding? Is that what they taught you at Quantico? And is that part of the course work you teach the staffers here in town?" Sasha shook her head in disbelief. "You know something, Dana? If you hadn't been there I would've busted that little shit's nose."

Charlie, incredulous, "Really? Busted her nose? Tell

me, detective. What kind of excuse would you have invented for *that* one?"

"Resisting arrest."

"Are you kidding me? The woman is all of five feet tall and doesn't weigh a hundred pounds."

"She was probably on PCP."

"Jesus Christ, you've got an answer for everything, haven't you?"

"Do my damnedest."

Charlie felt as if he were swimming against the tide. "Listen detective. These kinds of interrogation methods, besides being completely illegal, are . . ."

"Are what?" she jumped in. "Medieval? Soviet? Or how about, very effective in helping us solve a brutal murder?"

He nodded, grudgingly, acknowledging in a whisper, "I guess."

"Thanks for your vote of confidence, Agent Dana." Sasha relaxed and poked her head out the window, breathing in the spring air. She turned back to the FBI agent and spoke in a more modulated tone. "Listen, Charlie. Rose knows the whole score. Knows all about what Rudy and Lasorda and the dead woman were doing. We're not done with her. She has lots more to tell us."

"You're sure?" He watched Sasha closely and thought her smile devilish.

"Sure as shit. She'll tell all. It's her job on the line." Sasha rolled up her window and started the engine.

"Emmitt told me you're an education, Detective Kulaeva."

"Stick with me, kid. You'll make a decent cop."

"If I don't get busted for terrorizing witnesses or

tampering with evidence first."

"Relax. We're cool," she said, pulling back onto the two lane and heading toward the Alyeska Prince Hotel, there to find, interrogate, and arrest the junkie brother of a dead woman found two days earlier, a syringe stuck in her rear end.

~~~

"Good afternoon. I'm Detective Alexandra Kulaeva of the Anchorage Police Department and this is Special Agent Charles Dana of the FBI. You have a guest here, Richard Carlisle."

The clerk—short and stocky, wispy hair of indeterminate color, with watery blue eyes and a pitted face that would never quite recover from acne—looked at the policemen with much-practiced indifference. He had been sorting odds and ends. He continued for a few moments, then, "Let me check my computer," he said, bother in his voice.

Sasha stiffened.

Charlie noted her changed body language. *Uh oh.*

There was a too-long wait as the clerk scrolled through the guest rolls. He finally found what he was searching for. Although Sasha had asked, the clerk directed his response to Charlie. "That is correct, sir," he said. "Richard Carlisle is a guest."

"What room?" Charlie asked, politely.

"Room 604."

"Is he there now, in his room?"

"I don't believe so, sir."

"Where do you believe he might be?"

"I believe I saw him about twenty minutes ago pass

through the lobby on the way to the aerial tramway. Through those doors, there," the clerk nodded in the direction of doors leading to the tramway. "There's a very fine restaurant at the top of the mountain."

Before Charlie could move toward the tramway doors, Sasha took hold of his arm.

"Just a moment, Agent Dana," she said, turning back to the desk clerk. She stared at the man for twenty seconds, without a word. The clerk began shifting his weight, foot to foot.

A word at a time, she asked, "If you know him well enough to recognize him walking through the lobby, why did you have to consult the computer for two minutes to tell us if he was a guest here?"

The clerk retreated a step.

Sasha pressed. "Well? Answer my fucking question, asshole."

Charlie couldn't help himself, and smiled. *An education.* The other two cops, standing behind, were both shaking their heads, grinning.

The clerk's eyes rounded, his mouth fell agape. He took another step back from the desk and stammered a reply. "I b . . beg your pardon. I was unsure . . ."

"Right. You were unsure," Sasha interrupted. "*I* asked the question and you answered my partner. Don't do that again. Woman asks a question, answer *her*, not her male companion. Got it?"

When the clerk didn't or couldn't answer, Sasha repeated. "I asked you if you got it?"

"Yes, ma'am, of course," the man vigorously nodded.

"Great. Now, restaurant at the top of the tramway?"

"Yes, ma'am. The Seven Glaciers," the clerk answered.

"Through that large set of doors. They open out onto the tramway loading area. The cable car can hold sixty people." Words now tumbling out. "It takes about five minutes to get to the top, twenty-three hundred feet up. Would you like some ski lift tickets?" he asked.

Sasha turned to Charlie. "Bring your skis, Agent Dana?"

"Darn. Left 'em in town," he said, chuckling.

Sasha turned to the clerk, "We'll take a pass on the lift tickets, but thanks."

"Anything else I can tell you about the tram, the restaurant? I have a menu if you'd like to look at it. The halibut is quite good. I can comp you a meal."

Sasha checked the nametag pinned to his uniform. "Thanks, Mr. Detweiler." She gave him her warmest smile. "You've been a terrific help and I appreciate it."

The terrified man could only bleat a response, "Yes, thanks. Thank you. Very much."

Sasha graced the man with a final smile before she and Charlie began a slow walk toward the tramway doors. The other two cops trailed, laughing.

"How to win friends and influence people," Charlie said to her.

"Fear is a great learning tool. He'll be a nicer person." A few more steps then she stopped him half way to the tramway doors. "Listen, Charlie. Gary and I'll go up to the restaurant, see if he's there. You and Moranis hang out, grab him if he comes on down. Keep in phone contact."

Charlie considered a moment. "And if you find him? What then?" a note of concern in his voice.

"Gary and I'll talk to him."

"You're going to *talk* to him? What am I to understand about *that?* Will you Mirandize him?"

She hesitated, "Sure, we'll read him his rights. Then we're gonna talk to the man. You know, chat. Converse. Speak. Communicate. Talk."

When he couldn't manage a response, Sasha turned from him and walked toward Gary, waiting by the tramway doors.

Charlie stood there, confused, conflicted. He'd already sampled how his *ad hoc* partner had questioned Rose Nakamura. He hadn't liked it one bit. He didn't want to consider how the unorthodox Detective Kulaeva might 'talk' to Rudy Castro. For the second time that day, the lawyer in him worried about a suspect's guaranteed rights. On the other hand, he felt relief—he'd be spared participating in an interrogation that he knew might be rough, possibly illegal. He didn't need to be part of that. The one earlier, in the diner, was already one too many. As he watched the two detectives disappear through the tramway doors, Charlie felt someone gently touch his sleeve.

"Let's get some coffee, Agent Dana," Moranis said. "My treat. I'll spring for a piece of pie if they have anything decent."

Charlie looked at the patrolman, then back at the now closed doors. He realized that his nonattendance in the questioning of Rudy Castro had been well orchestrated. He allowed himself to be led by Moranis toward the hotel's café.

Gary and Sasha stood on opposite sides of the tramcar, looking out onto a darkening late afternoon. A Japanese family of five was along for the ride, all dressed in stylish winter attire.

The car rocked gently back and forth as it climbed, revealing an ever more expansive view—all the way back down the length of the valley to the waters of Turnagain Arm, and closer at hand, mountains covered with forests of spruce and birch.

Forty feet below them, a bull moose was grazing on birch twigs. The animal took no notice of the tram and moved slowly, his six-foot-wide rack brushing the lower branches and knocking snow onto its back.

A minute later they docked and the detectives passed into the Seven Glaciers restaurant, a medley of steel, dark wood, mirrors, plants, and above all, windows presenting diners a breathtaking view.

The restaurant was full, the end-of-season dinner crowd noisily recounting the day's adventures on the slopes.

The detectives worked their way past the bar and spotted Rudy Castro at the far end of the room. He was by himself at a window seat, picking at a zit on his chin, an iced drink and a bowl of peanuts in front of him. The detectives approached casually from either side. Sasha stopped at an empty table next to Rudy and leaned toward the window. "Great view, huh?" she asked him.

He looked up at her. "Yeah, sure. If you like snow and ice and cold weather."

Sasha continued gazing out the window. "I happen to love all that stuff." Then, taking a seat next to Rudy, she showed him her badge. "Why don't you keep your hands right there in front of you where I can see them. I'm a police officer and you're under arrest. Be a good boy and come with us quietly. Or we can do it the hard way, give the guests a show. Your choice."

It was a well-appointed, four-hundred-dollar-a-day, one bed-room suite with kitchenette. Rudy Castro was sitting on a wooden chair, his hands cuffed behind him. Detective Gary Hernandez was sunk into a deep sofa, gazing balefully at his prisoner. Rudy couldn't meet his eyes.

Gary began slowly. "This is way more than the coincidental deaths of two people, Mr. Castro."

Rudy looked shocked. "Two? Whattya mean two?"

"Oh, right. Forgot to tell you," Sasha said. "Besides your sister, your roommate's missing in the Bering Sea. We think the Russians arranged for him to be dumped into the drink."

Rudy began to gasp for air, his face drained of color. He looked from one detective to the other.

"You could be next, Rudy," Sasha said.

Gary continued, "We have every reason to believe that your sister and your roommate were both murdered because of their trafficking in heroin." Gary kept his voice calm. "James Lasorda was bringing some excellent drug into the country from Russia. We believe he's been doing it for a while. He'd mail some to your sister and she'd fly the rest to Anchorage."

Sasha came to stand at Rudy's side and immediately wrinkled her nose and began waving her hands. "You got the nervous stink-sweats, Rudy. A sure sign of guilt. Right, Gary?"

"I'd say so. You know, Mr. Castro, you're not only a user, but you're also a salesman. So the charge'll be possession of a Schedule I controlled substance *for sale*. You're looking at fifteen years, at a minimum."

Rudy let his head slump between his shoulders. "I want a lawyer," he whispered.

Sasha ignored the request. "But before you'd sell it, you

took some for yourself. Not a lot. Just enough to get Isabel and Jimmy killed. And if the Russians find you, Rudy, you're gonna get dead, too. Quick."

"I need a lawyer." A little louder.

"I'll say you do," Gary said. "About five or six of the best money can buy. They might get you off, true. But the Russians'll be waiting for you. They seem to be taking care of loose ends. That'd be you, Mr. Castro. A loose end."

"Detective Hernandez is right, Rudy," Sasha chimed in. "You're not careful, you could find yourself like your sister, face down in the snow with cigarette burns all over your chest and a needle in your tush. That's how we found Isabel."

Rudy turned away as if experiencing a great pain in his face.

Sasha walked around to the other side of the man, the way he was turned.

"We were at your place earlier today. Snooped around. Found some stuff."

He came alert. "What stuff?" His eyes swept back and forth between the two cops.

"Let's see, we found syringes. Cotton swabs. And . . . oh, yeah. Thirty-two dime baggies of a white powder. Heroin, I'm supposing. Ready for sale. And two other sandwich bags, full of the same shit. I'm betting your prints are on the bags and all over the fixings. We also found a pistol and a ton of ammo, which'll compound the seriousness of the charges." She sneered at the handcuffed man. "Especially if it's unregistered."

A noise came out of Rudy Castro's throat, like a kitten whose tail has been stepped on.

"I was at your sister's apartment yesterday," Sasha said.

"You were there the day before, according to the manager, asking about her mail."

"So? I went to her apartment. That a crime?"

"You weren't able to get into her mail box. But I got in. Found a letter from your mother. I'm not sure she knows yet that her daughter was murdered and her son is headed for jail. Poor lady."

Rudy bit his lip.

"Also found an Express Letter. Your former room-mate—the one who's now at the bottom of the Bering Sea—was the sender. It was addressed to Isabel, but we're certain the contents were meant for you. Package contained an ounce and a little more of horse." Sasha looked at Gary. "Detective Hernandez, what do you think Rudy's chances are for getting out of jail before 2030?"

Gary shook his head. "One in a thousand. Maybe." He rose and went to stand in back of the handcuffed man. He leaned over and whispered into his ear, "You're not only a user, but a salesman. We know all about how you and your sister and Jimmy spent the money you made through the sale of heroin. Druggies from Miami supporting vacations in St. Croix. Profits used by you and Rose to travel to D.C. Money for Isabel's new LX."

Rudy began to whimper, snot dribbling down onto his upper lip.

Sasha kneeled in front of him. She had two plastic cable restraints in her hand. She wrapped one around the chair's front leg and started to secure Rudy Castro's left ankle.

"Whattya doin'?" he demanded, trying to kick his leg free.

From in back of him, Gary grabbed the small man

around the throat and squeezed. "Relax Mr. Castro," the detective gently ordered.

Rudy stopped kicking, gurgling.

Sasha strapped both ankles tightly to the chair's legs then stood and faced the man. "Yeah, Rudy. You're super fucked, but if you help us right here and now, we'll do our best to help *you* with the DA."

"Here's what we want to know," Gary continued. "Where does the heroin come from? Who gave it to Jimmy? Who collects it, and what happens to it once it's in Anchorage? Simple questions. You know the answers to all of them. And you need to tell us."

Rudy Castro shook his head. Too much information. And all bad.

Gary said, "You know, Detective Kulaeva. Like many drug cases, this is also an IRS matter. There are always piles of money in the hands of drug-dealing boneheads who haven't got the faintest idea what to do with their ill-gotten loot, except spend it on expensive vacations, drawing everyone's attention. Or squirreling it away in some Caribbean bank account."

Right on cue, Sasha produced the recovered checkbooks and fanned them out, like a deck of cards, in front of the handcuffed man.

Whatever small bit of bravado Rudy Castro might have been able to summon up, this latest news caused his backbone to give way.

"Look at the amounts of money in these bank accounts," Sasha said. "You've got over a hundred and fifteen K socked away here. That ain't spit. Have you let the IRS know about this income? No? I didn't think so."

"You ever go up against the IRS, Rudy?" Gary asked. "Ugliest bunch of people in the world. Worse than customs agents, if possible. IRS gets on your case, forget the good times. And you know, they won't only go after you. They'll want to look at your parents' returns. Eduardo and Maria in Miami. Hope they've kept good books."

Sasha picked up, "Your folks are émigrés, *Marielitos*. Came over in the summer of 1980. Your dad runs a meat market on Calle Ocho. Probably worked his ass off for you and your sister. And how do you repay him? You deal heroin."

At the mention of his parents' names, Rudy began sobbing in earnest.

"I don't know, Gary. I think this guy here's a meatball. Doesn't want to help himself."

"Looks that way," said Gary. He went to the chest of drawers and found a pair of socks, one tucked into the other. He took a roll of duct tape from his pocket, ripped off an eight inch piece and placed socks and tape on the arm of the sofa, opposite Rudy. Then he returned to the back of the seated man and quickly grabbed him around his forehead with one large arm. With the fingers of his other hand, Gary pinched Rudy's nose shut. With his air supply cut off, the prisoner opened his mouth to breathe, allowing Sasha to cram the socks into his mouth and tape it shut. Gary released his grip. "Relax and breathe through your nose," he advised.

Bug-eyed, Rudy now watched as the two cops removed their watches, jackets, rolled up their sleeves. Gary came in back of Rudy's chair and tipped it onto its two rear legs and dragged the struggling drug dealer backwards into the linoleum-floored kitchenette. Once there, he carefully laid the man down so that Rudy was effectively on his back, legs in a chair-sitting position. Sasha was at the sink, soaking a hand towel. She knelt down next to the muzzled man.

"You know stuff, Rudy. If you refuse to share, we'll water board you all night. It'll be awful. But if at any time you want us to stop, just nod your head up and down. Got it? Sasha put a large bath towel under his head and then laid the wet hand towel over the man's face. Okay, Gary. Looks like he's ready."

Muffled screaming as Rudy swung his head back and forth, trying to shake off the cloth. Sasha held down the two ends of the towel on either side of his head. "Just nod and you'll save yourself a ton of grief."

Rudy began nodding vigorously.

"You ready to cooperate?" Gary asked.

A dampened affirmative from Rudy.

Sasha took away the towel, carefully removed the tape, then the sock. Gary picked him up and sat him upright on the chair's four legs.

"The fuck kind of cops are you?" Rudy sputtered.

"Determined ones," Sasha said, drying her hands.

"Let's start at the beginning," Gary began. They were back in the main room, Rudy still handcuffed. "Where does the heroin come from?"

"Russia."

"Russia's a big country. Be more specific."

"I don't know. Jimmy didn't know. He collected it in that port city, Vlad something."

"Vladivostok," Sasha suggested.

"Yeah."

"Who'd he collect it from?" she asked.

"Some old sailor. Jimmy told me he thought he was prob'ly mob connected."

"Why'd Jimmy think that?"

"The sailor never came alone. Always some goons with him, coverin' his ass."

"OK. Got a name for the sailor?"

"I think Jimmy called him Ivan."

"Well that's narrows it down," Sasha said. "How 'bout a description?"

"Short and old."

"Super."

Gary asked, "How big were the shipments?

"Usually twenty pounds. Sometimes more."

"And the two of you would skim . . . how much?"

"Never more than an O-Z. We was careful."

Sasha laughed. "Right. That's why your sister and your roommate are dead. How often did this happen?"

"Five, six times a year."

"And you've been doing it for how long?"

"Four years. And a half."

"So you've collected between, let's say, twenty-five to thirty ounces, give or take. That about right?"

"Yeah. Maybe."

"And you'd use some and sell some, right?"

Rudy avoided her eyes.

Sasha grabbed Rudy's face. "Listen up, meatball. We got you on both scores. We got the baggies of dope in your house *and* your income tax records *and* your bank records *and* a bill from some four star hotel in St. Croix thanking you for spending a small fortune. All compliments of some kids from Miami you sold three ounces to."

Rudy's entire body cried 'uncle.' Sasha let go.

Gary asked, "Your sister brought the heroin to Anchorage?"

"Yeah. She'd go out to Dutch Harbor for Fish and Wildlife, meet up with Jimmy. They'd spend some time out there together."

"Who did the skimming."

"Jimmy. Always, Jimmy. He'd skim in Dutch Harbor, mail the skim to Isabel's apartment. Then she brought the rest to Anchorage and hid it away from me. She wouldn't let me near it. Sit on it 'til Jimmy got back to town. Then he'd take it to the connection."

"Why didn't they send the whole thing in the mail? Why only the skim?" Sasha asked.

"Jimmy said he didn't trust the mail. Said he thought they might leave the package in front of Isabel's apartment when she wasn't there. Somebody might take it, he thought. Sounded crazy to me."

"Sounds crazy to me, too," said Sasha. "Let's get back to the connection here in town. Who'd that be?"

"I seen him once only. I followed Jimmy one time when he went to deliver the shit. I was feelin' left out. The two of them worked the scheme and I felt like they dissed me. So I followed Jimmy one time to see what I could see."

"And what *did* you see?" Gary asked.

"Not much. Jimmy met the guy at Kincaid Park. It was hard for me to follow him there. I had to park far away. Didn't want to get spotted. I see a guy gets out of an old four door Subaru. Dark color. It's night so I can't see too good. He's tall. Maybe six one, six two. Wearin' work clothes. It was cold and rainin' a little, and he was wearin' a wool cap with flaps on the ears. Gloves. Dint see what he looked like. Dint hear nothin'.'"

"Anyone else with him?" Sasha asked.

"He was alone."

"Go on."

"So Jimmy opened his trunk. Man took the package from Jimmy's car, dropped in an envelope, put the package into the trunk of his own car. Drove away. Then I had to get outta there 'cause they was gonna see me if I didn't move my car."

"That's it?" Sasha asked.

"That's all I know."

Gary asked, "Did Jimmy always meet him at Kincaid Park?"

"No. It was a different part of town every time. Jimmy said sometimes he'd get to a spot and wait and the guy wouldn't show. Then he'd call Jimmy and tell him to go to a new spot. Bein' careful, I suppose."

"What other spots?"

"All 'round town. The parkin' lot at Mulcahy Stadium, the Fifth Avenue Mall parkin' lot. The one at Wal-Mart. At Costco, on Debarr. Always a parkin' lot."

"Jimmy ever mention his name?" Sasha asked.

"No. He just called him 'the connection.'"

"'The connection,' huh? So where did the heroin go from there? Was it sold locally, or shipped out of town?"

"Jimmy ast one time and the guy told him it was none of his fuckin' business. Those were his exact words, Jimmy said, 'none of your fuckin' business.' Jimmy never ast again as far as I know."

"But *you* sold locally, didn't you, Rudy? The skim." Sasha said. "Big collection of dime bags at your place."

Rudy kept silent.

"How'd Jimmy meet the connection?" Gary asked.

"No idea. He was working this scheme before I met him."

"Guy talk with an accent?"

"Not that Jimmy ever said. He said they didn't even say hello. Jimmy said they'd see each other, guy would take the shit and leave Jimmy an envelope in his trunk with the cash."

"How much?"

"Seven grand, in twenties and fifties."

Sasha did the math. "Seven thousand times twenty-five times. Near two hundred thousand. How'd it get divvied up?"

"Jimmy and Isabel split it. Isabel gave me a grand each time."

"Which you supplemented by selling what you and Jimmy skimmed."

Rudy didn't answer.

Sasha looked at Gary. "Whattya think, Detective Hernandez?"

"He knows lots more than he's telling. I think we should drown him."

Rudy looked from one cop to the other, pleading, "Honest. That's the whole thing. I don' know anymore than what I just tol' you."

Gary signaled to Sasha. "Let's talk," he said. They went into the bathroom, left the door ajar.

Gary whispered, "Like all drunks and junkies, Rudy's a good liar. He's been around the law enough to know that he needs to save some choice information for the DA. Giving it to us reduces its value."

"I agree. He's holding back. What's your feeling about the connection?"

Gary thought a moment. "I think the pick-up, drop-off scenario is probably right. Wide open parking lots—usually a good place for that kind of stuff. And the connection would change spots without notice. Sounds real."

"But the description of the guy? A total crock, wouldn't you think?" Sasha said.

"Total. That's what he's saving for the DA. He might even have a name. Rudy may be stupid but he's not going to give up his life line."

"OK," Sasha said. "Let's get back to town."

Outside the hotel, the lit-up slopes were packed with skiers, their shouts bouncing across the snow. Folks were riding the chair lift or holding onto the T-Bar, stepping off at different downhill starting points.

Sasha and Charlie walked to their car, not sharing a word, a glance. Gary, Moranis and a handcuffed Rudy Castro headed to the second police car.

Charlie seemed content to stew. He sank into his passenger seat, arm on the door's windowsill, staring out at the forest, the dark trees now indistinguishable one from the other.

Although Sasha felt a little badly for him—his ego battered—she also felt completely justified in having arranged for him to miss the interrogation. She and Gary had learned some things that might help them with the case, things they might not have learned had they adhered to the legalities that the FBI agent held so dear.

Past ten o'clock now as the two police cruisers left Girdwood and turned north onto the New Seward Highway—forty miles back to Anchorage on a winding and occasionally headlight-blinding road.

"We got some good info from Rudy," Sasha said to a stoic Charlie. "He gave us some starting points for tracking down Jimmy Lasorda's connections in Vladivostok *and* here in town."

Charlie looked her way, but didn't speak.

"He said a sailor in Vlad brought the heroin to Lasorda. Ivan's the sailor's name, if you can believe it." She looked to her left onto a calm Turnagain Arm. "No belugas in sight. I think it's a chamber of commerce rumor, entice the yahoos up here." She turned to Charlie. *Not funny, I know. But you might smile anyhow.*

An eighteen-wheeler, lights blazing, came at them from the on-coming lane and passed in a whoosh. The police car shook.

"I hate this highway," she said. "Awful in the day. Way worse in the dark." No reaction from the passenger seat. She plowed on, "The water out there is part of Cook Inlet, named after you know who. He got to Hawaii and they loved him. Maybe too much." *Ha, ha. I know, it's not funny. Humor me. I'm trying.*

At last he spoke. "You'll bend the law however it suits you, won't you?"

She thought a moment, then raised and lowered her shoulders. "Bend it. Beat it. Shake it. Break it." She laughed. "I sound like Dr. Seuss."

"Yeah, you're a real riot, Sasha. There are no rules with you, are there?"

A glance his way. "You're dead wrong, Charlie. There *is* a rule. But only one. Get the bad guys off the streets." Eyes back on the road. "However it gets done. Everything else is commentary, just window dressing. Made for a public that likes to pretend it supports the rule of law, stands solidly behind the Constitution."

When Charlie didn't react, Sasha took it up a notch. "Jesus Christ, Dana. You're telling me the great unwashed has read that document? Like they could begin to tell you what the Eighth Amendment is."

"Cruel and unusual punishment, excessive fines and bails."

"Sure, *you* know. *I* know. But Joe the mother fucking plumber?" She blew out a breath. "Listen, Charlie. There's something you ought to see. I've been thinking about it. A good movie for you to watch. Ever seen *Prince of the City*, with Treat Williams? He's a cop on the take."

Charlie shook his head.

"Well, there's one scene you really need to see."

A motorcycle overtook them on their left, crossing the solid dividing line, passing them on a curve and going far too fast.

Sasha shook her head. "Asshole probably thinks he's immortal because of his full body leathers and helmet. Jerk."

Another quick look at Charlie, not sure if she should continue selling the film. Then, after a moment, "Anyhow, a cop is suspected of stealing money from a drug dealer and is being questioned by Internal Affairs. The cop looks at the two IA pricks and tells them the following . . ." She paused. "You listening, Charlie?"

"Go on," he said.

"Right. Cop tells them that there's never been a successful drug conviction made without a cop lying on the stand, under oath."

"That's *total* crap," Charlie said vehemently. "You really believe that?"

"Are you *kidding* me? I not only *believe* it, I *support* it. And you know who else believes it?"

Charlie didn't answer.

"You know who *else* believes it, Charlie? Emmitt Esterhazy, your boss."

"What's that supposed to mean?"

"Here's what it means. Next time you see Emmitt, ask him how come he got transferred to Anchorage. You ever wonder, huh? Well, here's why. He was the SAC at the Bureau's field office in Albuquerque. Great job. But then he broke *your* rules, Charlie. Broke 'em? Shit, he shattered 'em. Do I have your attention?"

He looked at her, clearly not liking what he was hearing but unable not to listen. "So?"

"So one day he goes to the FISA court with a bullshit story about someone the Bureau was after. A Korean techie from Santa Fe, Syngman Park. Emmitt does a snow job on the FISA judges, gets his warrant, executes his search. And doesn't find jack shit. Tech's clean. Totally clean. Turns out the probable cause that Emmitt took to FISA was completely fabricated. Made up by your boss. And if you don't believe me, go to the Albuquerque Journal. Happened about nine years ago, before your time with the Bureau. The paper started to dig. They put pressure on the DOJ. Washington had to make a move, meaning Emmitt had to go. Winds up here. But you don't need to take *my* word for it. It's in the public record." Sasha's voice had become strident, harsh. *I need to ease off.*

Charlie didn't react.

"And you know who else believes my version of the

penal code?" she asked, her voice rising again, getting sharper. "The other special agents in your office. Every one of them. The agents who every day leave your class amazed at what a sucker you are. You think you're helping them learn how to obey the law? Wake up. They're laughing at you."

He looked at her. "You're merciless."

With a softer voice, "You're right, Charlie. I *am* merciless. And you? You're a good guy. I know that. But you're in the wrong business, buddy. Do yourself a favor and get out of law enforcement. Try private practice where the rules may have some validity."

They were now close to the city, driving past Potter Marsh. The homes on their right, on the Hillside, all lit up.

"You believe you're right, Sasha. I can see that you seriously believe you're right."

She nodded. "I do. I seriously believe I'm right."

"And because you truly believe in your skewed version of the law, I'll never be able to convince you otherwise."

"Probably not."

"Certainly not. True believers, like you, can't be swayed from the catechism. They can't be reasoned with. I can think of any number of reasons for using my version of the law. You wouldn't allow any of them to penetrate the brick wall of your belief system. I'd be wasting my time and energy."

"I think that's true. So, can we leave it? Can we just agree to disagree and go on with the job?"

"Not that simple, Sasha. This is not some kind of hypothetical. Rudy is real. Isabel Castro was real. Jimmy Lasorda, if he's alive, is real. And I can't . . . I won't abandon my version of the law to make accommodation with yours. Or with Emmitt's."

Sasha considered. "Like I said a minute ago, you're a good guy. And if I could wave my wand and change everyone's thinking to yours, I'd do it in a minute. I really would. But if all my years of police work have taught me *anything*, it's taught me that some people are just bad fucking apples, menaces to society. How they got that way—nature, nurture—is not my concern. My job is to clean up the mess they make and get them off the street. And you know what Charlie? The niceties of the law sometimes get in the way."

"Too simple, Sasha. Life's not that simple. The law's not that simple."

"For me it is. In the lobby this afternoon, you were worried that I might not read Rudy his Miranda warning. The constitutional rights lawyers, like you, and the ACLU lefties, you all love Miranda. Protect the suspect, you think. But for law enforcement, Miranda's an obstacle, an impediment."

He gazed through the windshield. "Did you read him his rights?"

"I can't remember. Ask Gary. See what he says. We probably did."

"Why am I doubtful?"

They drove without speaking for ten minutes. Sasha watched in the rear view mirror as Gary's cruiser, trailing them the whole way home, peeled off at the Tudor Road exit and made for the station house. Gary'd book Rudy Castro for possession for sale of a Schedule I drug.

They continued into downtown, turned west on Fifth Avenue, and a minute later, turned left on Barrow Street and stopped alongside the FBI's fortress-like offices. A cooling mist had descended, the moon's light forming a shimmering, veiled curtain around the squad car.

Sasha gave Charlie a soft smile that she hoped might temper the raking over the coals she'd administered. "I'm talked out. But I think we made good progress on the case."

He sat staring through the windshield, and without looking at her, "I got a text back at the hotel. The Russian ship is delayed. Won't get into Dutch Harbor for a couple days. I'll make us plane reservations and fix us up with lodgings. I'll call you tomorrow with details." He got out of the car.

"OK. Good. We'll talk soon. See ya, Charlie." She waved lightly with her right hand, extended over the passenger seat. *He could reach in, take it, shake hands. Give it a squeeze. That would be nice. Dream on, girl.*

He turned without a look back and walked into the building.

Sasha sat for a while. *Dinner for two? Forget it. I deserve my solo Lean Cuisine. How'd he describe me this morning? Moody. Cynical. Foul-mouthed. Let's add a few: Stupid. Needlessly assertive. Undesirable.*

Her cell phone went off just then with the Beatle's *Good Day Sunshine*—her daughter's ring tone. Robin's lovely contralto echoed through the phone. "Hi mom. What's up?"

"Hi darlin.' Just winding down for the night. Gotta finish some stuff at the station then I get to go home."

"How's your day been?" Robin asked.

"Probably not as interesting as yours. What's new at home?"

"Viktor's gotten over whatever it was he had. Feeling lots better."

"Great. Give him a hug for me."

"For sure. I thought we were going to see you yesterday. What's up?"

"I'm deep into some stuff here. Working with an FBI agent. *Why did I tell her that? Robin never misses a trick and will ask me about him.* Maybe I can break off soon, fly home. Meantime, I'm lovin' you."

"Love you, too, mom. Miss you."

"Miss you, too, sweets. I'll call tomorrow when my brain's cooled down. Bye for now."

Sasha sat for a good two minutes, mulling the events of the day, thinking about Special Agent Charles Dana. *A square. But cute. Shit!*

~~~

The neon lights in the restaurant's window blinked from green 'Open' to red 'Closed.'

A quartet of late diners exited, laughing loudly. They pulled up their collars against the night mist. One pair walked hurriedly down the block and disappeared around the corner. The other couple paused at the curb. The woman clicked her remote starter. A new Nissan, parked across the street, purred to life. They waited while a late-night bus passed, then walked over, piled in, and drove off.

Several minutes later, Melanie came out of the restaurant and began walking to the side of the building, to staff parking. She wore a dark green, down parka.

A man who had been sitting in a car parked down the street from the restaurant got out and called to her.

She recognized his voice at once and relaxed, waiting for him as he came near. She smiled.

He stopped opposite her, said something that made Melanie laugh. Her body bent slightly toward him. He took a half step nearer and spoke once more. She laughed again, pretending to be embarrassed, then cocked her head, posed a question. He nodded. The two of them started towards his car. He offered her his arm. She took it and looked up at him. "What's on your mind, Agent Dana?" she asked.

"All kinds of things. We'll improvise," Charlie said.

"I like improvising," Melanie answered, pressing into him.

As she bent to get into his car, Charlie buried his nose in her red hair.

~~~

Driving home after a long and tiring day, Sasha felt a craving, almost a need, for a beer. At the same time, she brought to mind the words of the trapper, Nelson Alexie, her promise to Gary, and the session with her shrink. It didn't take her long to decide. *Fuck it. Time to restock the larder.*

Two minutes later, she was at the cash register of the Brown Jug, her favorite booze emporium. She bought a six-pack of Corona. *I can show some self-restraint, drink one or two. One or two? Really? Who're you kidding?*

She pulled up in front of her mobile home. On her doormat, a large vole, half-eaten, supine. Clearly a gift from Mortimer. *At last, a little acknowledgement.* Sasha searched the bushes, wanting to thank the big tom, but he was nowhere to be seen. She toed the carcass into the weeds. Once inside the doublewide, she opened a Corona, placed it on the table. She put the other five in the fridge, took out the foil-covered Lean Cuisine and a Tupperware of three-day old broccoli.

She dumped the heat-and-eat meal onto a plate, added the greens, and put the dish into her toaster oven. She regarded the just-opened bottle of beer, beads of frost inviting her. She studied it for a moment, took it up, and drained the contents without a pause. *Weakling!*

A huge belch interrupted her self-deprecating thoughts, the too-quickly-drunk beer returning with a gassy vengeance. A foul aftertaste spread across her tongue and made her shudder. She took a second Corona from the fridge and carried it with her, unopened, into her bedroom. She dropped her outer clothes onto her bed. The inner ones, wrinkled and smelly, went into the hamper. After a quick shower, she donned pajama bottoms and t-shirt and with the still-capped beer in hand—*to open or not to open, that is the question*—she returned to the kitchen. The infamous Lean Cuisine that was supposed to have been part of a shared meal was ready to be eaten.

Raylan, Elmore Leonard's bad-ass marshal, waited on the living room couch where she had left him. But Sasha's thoughts were elsewhere—the successful interrogation of Rudy Castro, and her *un*successful connection with Charlie Dana.

She'd been hard on both of them. Rudy, the little shit, deservedly so. But her scathing critique of Charlie's understanding of the law—*mis*understanding, as far as she was concerned—now seemed to her unnecessarily harsh. The two of them had markedly different ideas when it came to their work, differences that both believed could not be bridged. She had stupidly rubbed his nose in those differences. *Not the smartest thing I've ever done. Especially since I had hopes . . . for sex? Yeah, right. Silly girl.*

She admitted she wasn't particularly interested in what

Charlie had to say. She found his ideas theoretically correct, but from a practical point of view and for the way she operated as a cop, she thought them counterproductive.

But she craved his physical company. He had a way about him that was cozily charming. And he exuded a brooding attractiveness that made her stomach do flips. *Father, forgive me. I'm horny.*

She'd had sex with six men since moving to Anchorage six years ago. *One a year.* Had sex but hadn't made love one time. Not even close. Not since Robin.

Robin . . . .

Twelve years earlier, after her husband was shot and killed, Sasha quit her work with the Sitka Police Department and returned home to Big Lake, seeking comfort in the bosom of her family. Her grandfather, her aunts and uncles, her cousins formed a protective barrier around their Sasha, insulating her from the world, keeping her close, ever in view. And when she wanted solitude, it was available in abundance in the wilds around the compound and in the skies above Alaska.

A half year after leaving Sitka, her daughter was home-birthed, ably handled by aunt Annie and cousin Ben, both nurses. Robin-girl was born on the summer solstice, June 21, 2004.

Slowly, motherhood and the influence of her family worked to drag her back from the precipice. Around the time of Robin's first birthday, her mother could manage a smile, faint and evanescent.

But the only place Sasha felt relaxed, felt semi-whole, was in the air. She flew daily. In the winter, weather permitting, her preferred route was north, up the Susitna

River to Talkeetna, then a bank over Skwentna and Yentna, two stops in the Iditarod where in early March, she had an aerial view of scores of competing dog teams strung out along the snowy trail.

And in the summer, when she switched her plane's wheels to floats, she flew into her family's compound on Beluga Lake, occasionally ferrying customers to the Kulaev hunting and fishing lodge.

In 2007, on Robin's third birthday, Sasha announced she was returning to work. She'd been hired by the Anchorage Police Department and would be starting back as a uniform at the end of the summer. She was looking forward to the work, but it would mean moving away from Big Lake, and separation—only temporary she believed—from her daughter.

During those first years away, she tried to fly home every chance she got—only twenty minutes from Anchorage to the homestead. But she was low cop on the seniority totem pole, working the graveyard shift, 11:00 p.m. to 9:00 a.m., making it difficult to schedule extended time off. And vacations? Even harder to arrange.

She kept promising herself she'd bring Robin to live with her, but the longer they were apart, the more unlikely that became. Her parental guilt was assuaged by the knowledge that her daughter was thriving in Big Lake. Yes, she loved and missed her mom, but Robin was managing beautifully without her. With a passel of first cousins, aunts and uncles, and a doting grandfather, Robin lacked neither for care nor affection.

Living alone, Sasha had too much time on her hands, time she spent reliving and obsessing about the events that had overtaken her in Sitka. At first, it was the two crack heads—the ones who shot and killed her husband—who bore the brunt of her animus. Gradually, however, the breadth of her indictment came to include the entire criminal class in general, and drug dealers in particular. To escape her obsessive behavior, she began to drink. In moderation at first, only after work and on days off. And only at home. She believed she kept her vice to herself and under control.

But even as her home life became dominated by a festering anger and a growing dependence on alcohol, Sasha's day job was advancing. She passed the detective exam in 2009 and three months later was assigned to fill an empty slot in assault/robbery. Two years after that, she moved to homicide and was teamed with Gary Hernandez, up to Alaska from LA.

She set the heated plate of food in front of her and opened the second beer, the one she'd been carrying from room to room. Not as frosty anymore.

She ate automatically, without interest. She wasn't even sure what the meal was supposed to be, a concoction of noodles with tomato sauce. *Weren't all Lean Cuisine meals built around pasta and tomatoes, just in different configurations?*

After five minutes of poking at forgettable food, she gave up. The half-drunk bottle of warming beer followed the half-eaten pasta into the garbage.

She used the remote to turn on the TV and flopped onto the couch. She covered herself with the crazy quilt afghan her grandmother had crocheted. She watched Jimmy Fallon chat with a big-boobed ingénue, star of the latest super-hero, comic book-to-film extravaganza. The young woman kept tossing her tresses, laughing nervously, trying to be as engaging as the host. No soap. Fallon was having to do it all himself.

Sasha muted the TV and closed her eyes. She thought about Charlie Dana, imagining where he might touch her. She let her fingers go exploring, but fell asleep before becoming aroused.

5

After agreeing to his wife's proposal—*ultimatum, a more precise word*, he thought—Boris Bunin spent a month showing Larissa how his business was run. She took it all in easily, listening, questioning, taking copious notes. She learned the origins of the enormous amounts of money—invariably cash—that flooded the Bunin coffers: Euros, Swiss francs, Deutsche marks, British sterling, yen, renminbi, and dollars from everywhere.

The next two months were devoted to fashioning an Excel accounting system. In the remaining months of that first year, Larissa set to work vitalizing the stagnant finances of her husband's international criminal syndicate.

By the end of the year, the promised six percent increase in revenue had come in at seven and fraction. Larissa told Boris that from here on, she could guarantee an annual growth rate of ten percent. Boris' father and uncle, who at first had been deeply skeptical, were ecstatic. They thought the woman a gift from heaven.

Over the next two years, Larissa was content to manage the funds, move money around. She mastered the arcane financial art of 'layering,' shifting cash between banks in the Bahamas, Bahrain, Panama and Singapore. With each transaction, a different fictitious company was created out of thin air, impossible to trace.

When the funds were washed sufficiently, she legitimized them. By the end of her third year of money managing, Bunin enterprises had acquired more than eighty legal businesses in nineteen countries.

Although she generally kept herself removed from the day-to-day workings, Larissa would occasionally make suggestions about operations. At first, they were minor proposals: an intensification of activities here, a change in collection procedures there, moving manpower from one area to another. Boris always listened, weighed his wife's recommendations, then took them to his father and uncle, his counselors.

One morning in 2003, they were sitting in their den, enjoying coffee and fresh croissants from *The Almondine*, on Water Street, three blocks away from their condo penthouse.

Larissa invariably prefaced a suggestion with the same announcement, "I've got an idea, Borya."

He put down his cup and gave her his attention. "I'm listening, dearest."

She un-tubed a pair of large maps and spread them across the table. She weighted them down at the corners with a butter dish, a bottle of orange juice, and two jars of marmalade. The top map showed the United States, Canada, and Mexico. She used her fork as a pointer.

"Right now, Borya, virtually every federal and local narcotics policeman is focused either on the east coast or on the Mexican border. Some, but not many, are on the Canadian border, especially where it meets Vermont. And although we've enjoyed a fairly high success rate penetrating those defenses, the payoffs along the way are eating into our profit margin."

"This is true, Lara. I've read your numbers. Even with the increasing demand for our goods, our profits have *not* grown as they ought to."

Larissa smiled. *He's learning the language. Another year or two and he'll get the big picture.* "Exactly, my dear. So let's consider something new, a different approach." She furled the first map to reveal the second—Alaska, the Bering Sea, and the Russian Far East.

"What's this? A new Klondike gold rush?" he laughed.

"Better, Borya. Much better. Look," she said, her fork resting on the Bering Sea. "The nearest point between the US and Russia is Alaska, the state with the longest coastline—over six thousand generally unregulated miles—and the weakest federal police presence. The FBI has their main offices in Anchorage, smaller ones in Juneau and Fairbanks. But their focus is on counter-terrorism and Russian cyber crime. The DEA has a very small office, just a branch of their Seattle bureau. And customs is a joke."

Boris understood the direction his wife was heading. He began smiling in a way that told her she was on the right track.

"There are many easy exit points from the Russian Far East—Vlad, Nakhodka, Yuzhno, P.K. And further north, from Provideniya, on Chukotka."

"Provideniya? Never heard of it."

"Look here," she said, pointing. "It's a small town with a airfield and it's just fifty miles from American territory, St. Lawrence Island. Fifty miles across open water. An easy crossing in good weather. And the Americans and Russians are now allowing visa-free visits between American Eskimo families on the island and their Russian relatives on the mainland." Larissa fell silent. The essentials had been spelled out.

Boris spent a good ten minutes examining the map, occasionally posing questions for which his wife had ready answers. He looked west from Russia's Pacific shore, tracing the Trans-Siberian Rail route all the way to Moscow.

"I'll need a business plan, Lara. Covering all aspects of the venture, from Afghanistan, through the neighboring countries, into Russia, across Siberia, to Alaska and then here, to New York."

She was ready. "I think you and David and uncle Joseph will find everything you'll need here, Borya," she said, passing him three binders.

Boris Bunin quickly riffled through ninety typed pages, footnoted, full of graphs, charts, maps, drawings. Words failed him. He could only smile. Hugely.

"This is miraculous," said David Bunin. "The idea is so incredibly simple."

"The best ideas often are," Uncle Josef said, examining the map of the Bering Sea.

Boris was serving coffee and strudel to his father and uncle. "The plan Lara has prepared lacks only the people who will implement it. She expects us to take care of those details."

"Goes without saying," said Josef. "To move the goods from Afghanistan into Russia, we won't have to change a single thing. Our old friends in Helmand and Kandahar are dependable, as are the supply lines. Borders, no problem. And once in southern Russia, in Chelyabinsk, we need only redirect a portion of the goods east, to the Pacific. From there, we'll establish a new network."

"That means including our friend in Vladivostok," David said.

"He'll ask for ten percent," Boris said.

"We'll offer two," said Josef.

"What about the oligarch on Chukotka?" Boris asked.

His father shook his head. "Let's see if we can't keep him out of the loop for now. If he finds out, he can deal with Vlad."

Joseph bent forward to make his point. "Don't forget. Getting the goods into and out of Alaska, we'll need someone on site. Someone with great expertise."

David Bunin smiled. "I think I have that one covered," he said.

~~~

Mehmet Ozil's slum origins were in Istanbul's Gazi Mahallesi, on the outskirts of the megalopolis where fourteen million people were crammed on the European-Asian borderlands.

Like many bright kids, Ozil hated school, hated the regimen, thought formal education a waste of time. The youngster preferred roaming the streets and highways of his country, especially near the borders, where he acquired a conversational knowledge of the languages of Turkey's seven international neighbors. Seeing how easily one could earn a living off of illegal commerce, Ozil saw his career, his future.

His first foray into crime came about when he was just eleven years old—Marlboros, eighteen large cartons, liberated from the back of a lorry destined for American servicemen stationed at Incirlik Air Force Base. The buyer was the thief's uncle, Kamal, who paid his nephew the Turkish equivalent of three cents a pack. Pin money, for sure, but enough for the young man to begin to dream of bigger and better scores.

Next, sheep skins, ninety-five of them, stolen from the *pazar* in Kapitan Andreevo, in Bulgaria, then smuggled into Turkey, barged down the Maritsa River, and sold in Edirne. Profit? Seventy cents a hide. Enough to treat his cousin, Artun, and himself to quickies at the local brothel. Mehmet was growing his business.

Over the next decade, an increasingly more challenging series of crimes saw the young man through his apprenticeship: two hundred microwaves lifted from dockside at Gemlik, on the Sea of Marmara; a van hijacked with twenty bolts of fine silk headed for the Zara store in Ankara; seven Peugeot 504 autos driven into Turkey across its sandy border with Syria.

His move into the big time came when he was nineteen. Someone—a shadowy someone from West Africa—reached out to Ozil. Four hundred Kalashnikovs were wanted. Could Mehmet, please, make arrangements?

The young man had never dealt in arms but knew people who did. He approached several before finding a partner, Jabbril Effendi, a second tier crime boss in Varna, on the Bulgarian Black Sea coast.

The target was a military armory in Sofia, Bulgaria's capital. Bribes were paid, tasks assigned, times set, transport and storage arranged. The six men who were to assist—all Mehmet's cousins—rehearsed for a week. Everything was in place. Yet, Ozil was nervous.

He needn't have been. The Goddess of Arms Trafficking smiled down on him that day. Everyone did precisely as they were told. The goods were cleanly spirited away and after a two-week ocean journey from the Black Sea, through the Sea of Marmara, and into the Mediterranean, they were delivered to the buyers without incident. Profit: twenty-five thousand American dollars, cash. The new star of contraband went right out and bought his mother an apartment on the Golden Horn, walking distance from the Topkapi Museum. What a good son!

Ozil's continued financial success allowed him to move freely around Europe. He settled in Paris, married a French woman of Moroccan origin, helped raise their two daughters, and continued happily working on the continent for the next twenty-five years. He loved his work, loved moving contraband across European Union borders, made so much easier in 1990 by the Schengen Convention that eliminated many custom controls and visas.

But in 2003, Ozil experienced an unprecedented and unexpected reversal of fortune and wound up, surprisingly, on the run. And for someone of his girth—two hundred and forty pounds on a five-foot six-inch frame—being on the run had its down side.

The Turk found himself being hounded by a group of Basque separatists. *Really?* he thought. *This can't be happening to me.*

The problem had its origins when Ozil carelessly agreed to be the middleman in a transaction between groups unknown to him. A job that the usually cautious Turk would never have taken. But Nicole, his wife, wanted to take the girls to Bermuda for a month.

Ozil agreed to broker an arms deal between the buyers, ETA Basques, and the sellers, a Marseilles-based gang of mercenaries. The Frenchmen were more used to dealing with *Maghreb* dissidents in North Africa than with their Spanish neighbors, right next door.

The contraband consisted of thirty rocket propelled grenade launchers and three thousand grenades, four hundred each of a pair of Fabrique Nationale-manufactured small arms—an assault rifle and a light machine gun, with a million rounds of ammunition for each model, and three hundred night vision goggles. The price was just above two and half million Euros, payable by the Basques *in advance*.

The French didn't believe in escrow.

Though they grumbled, the Basques agreed, wired the money to Ozil, who passed it on to the French, less his agent's fee of eight percent, as per their agreement.

The goods were laded onto a small boat off of Capbreton, in the southwest corner of France. The vessel should have easily crossed the Bay of Biscay and arrived in Lekeitio, in northeast Spain, thirty hours later.

But the captain of the boat—a man obviously unsuited to the job—had apparently failed to consult the weatherman. Because midway through the voyage, a storm crashed down on them. Twelve foot waves. The boat swamped, then sunk. Crew lost. Captain lost. Cargo at the bottom of the bay.

Naturally, the separatists who had paid upfront demanded their money back.

The French mercenaries pooh-poohed the Basques, telling them they had never received the two and a half million. "If you want any money, talk to the broker, talk to Mehmet Ozil," they told the irate Iberians.

The Turk insisted he had already paid the French, and that the sinking of the boat was an *Act of God*.

The Basques wanted their money back.

Ozil explained that legally, an *Act of God* is considered a mitigating circumstance in all negotiations.

The Basques wanted their money back.

Ozil was torn. He was not worried about the separatists— their influence not that great, their reach not that long. If he had so wished, he could have returned to Turkey. *Thanks, but no thanks. A nice place to visit, but . . .*

Because he considered himself a *European* smuggler, Ozil wanted, above all, to continue to live and work in any of the several EU countries for which he had passport and fluency of language. The Basques were making that difficult.

But the Turk had friends. And one in particular from the old days. One with whom he shared a meal in April, 2005, at Nathan's, Coney Island, Brooklyn.

David Bunin, *capo emeritus* of South Brooklyn, recognized his Turkish friend right away—Mehmet Ozil was hard to miss. The two hugged, pinched cheeks. Bunin joked about not being able to get his arms around the Turk. Ozil countered that gray had taken control of the little hair the Russian had left.

Bunin ordered hot dogs for two. Ozil decided not to make a scene. *Maybe kosher. Certainly not halal. But now's not the time to stand on ceremony.*

The two friends sat on a beach-side bench, surrounded at respectable distances by a defensive cordon of five armed men, discreetly out of earshot.

The spring day was warm. The breeze coming off the ocean, a delight. Despite Ozil's doubts, he found the wiener delectable.

The two international criminals waxed nostalgic: a load of IBM mainframe computer parts smuggled into Izmir in 1984; sixteen hundred cases of Johnny Walker Black waived through Salonika customs in 1988 by an agent-paid-to-look-the-other-way; and in 1992, six hundred kilos of Egyptian hashish carried by camel across the Sinai Desert to Taba, then floated up the Red Sea to Eilat, in Israel, on a glass bottom boat.

There were other ventures, big and small. Good times. But now Mehmet Ozil needed a favor. David Bunin listened.

Ozil explained. Two million euros. Bad luck. An *Act of God.* Mother fucking Basques. Cock sucking French. Two million euros.

The Turk was greatly relieved to see that his old friend and oft-times business partner appeared sympathetic. The Russian nodded in all the right places, tsk-tsked when appropriate.

After the second round of hot dogs—*Really fabulous. I'll have to tell Nicole*—Ozil spread out his hands, as if waiting for the contentious Euros to magically appear on his upturned palms.

Although the money did not materialize, David Bunin's smile kept the light of hope burning in the Ozil heart. After a lengthy pause, the Russian put his arm around his friend's shoulder.

"Tell me, Mehmet. Ever been to Alaska?"

~~~

When he got to work the next morning, Charlie Dana taught a small class of six of his agent-colleagues. The topic was the latest changes—*erosions,* he believed—to the Fourth Amendment's 'search and seizure' provisions. Charlie explained to the agents a 2014 Supreme Court decision, *Heien v North Carolina,* a case in which evidence accidentally seized by a police officer was allowed to be used against the defendant. Charlie thought the Roberts court had erred grievously.

After the agents filed out of class, Sasha's words, spoken in the car with such assurance the evening before, rang in Charlie's ears: "They're laughing at you." *Were they?* he wondered. *Were the agents absorbing the lessons or simply mailing it in, going through the motions?*

For lunch, he walked the three blocks to Kumagoro, sat by himself, ordered the small bento box and iced tea. The young Japanese waitress was tall and willowy, with exquisite skin and lustrous eyes. He asked her name.

"Atsuko," she said, with a smile that to him, to Charlie, to the self-confessed louse, encouraged him to imagine that what she *really* meant was: "Please come again. We should see each other."

He left her a ten dollar tip and when he got back to the office, he found a message from the Coast Guard in Dutch Harbor—the Russian trawler was still having engine problems. The soonest the vessel would arrive in Dutch Harbor would be in two days.

Later that afternoon, he went on line in search of accommodations in Dutch Harbor. He found *Bering Bridge Bed 'n Breakfast,* went to their website, liked what he saw, phoned and discovered that there were vacancies galore.

"Just let me know when," said the tiny, female voice at the other end of the phone line. "We have only one guest right now. A photographer. We've got lots of room."

Charlie told her he'd get back to her.

The last thing he did before he left for the day was to call Sasha and briefly fill her in.

~~~

That night, after her shift, Melanie returned to Charlie's apartment. She brought a bag of groceries. She made dinner. They made small talk. They watched *Prince of the City,* the movie Sasha had recommended. He enjoyed the film, but had difficulty accepting Sasha's contention that police officers might commit perjury in order to get a defendant convicted. *Maybe I am naive,* he mused.

Melanie was lovely, sweet, caring. Wonderful in bed, creative and warm. He watched her do a slow and seductive striptease. Her overt sexuality allowed him to live in the moment. Melanie made him hard. What else was there? He felt himself a slave to his erection. *Louse.*

Afterwards, when they were naked, limbs entwined, damp and recovering, Charlie's thoughts drifted to Sasha. He pictured her in a centerfold. He could taste her—a bitter, acrid sweetness. He realized it was impossible for him to stay angry with the woman. He thought her immensely appealing in a way that his current sleep-over partner was not. Somehow, Sasha's blistering tongue and insolent putdowns were much more inviting, a greater turn-on, than the waitress' solicitude and kindness. *Louse. And fucked up, too.*

6

By late morning, Sasha had finished examining the two hundred crime scene photos taken and uploaded by her partner. It was quickly apparent, however, that there was little to be gleaned from the images. Neither the surrounding meadow nor the pecked body of Isabel Castro told the investigator anything she didn't know already. She'd have to wait until the corpse thawed and a proper autopsy could take place.

Gary showed up at noon with two boxes of donuts from Anchorage's new Krispy Kreme. Sasha grabbed two.

He sat opposite and began on a cinnamon twist. "I called over to the ME's little while ago. Talked to Shane. He thought the woman's body should be thawed enough for an autopsy by late afternoon. Toxicology'll take a while. As well as a check for semen and stomach contents."

"And the burns and the cigarette butt?"

"Shane says he's trying to connect 'em. He's looking for help from the FBI on that one."

"ATV treads?"

"Sent to the FBI's data base."

"And fingerprints?"

"Tricky. Forensics are trying to lift latents off both the cigarette and the syringe. Whatever they get'll go to AFIS. Results by tomorrow. Maybe." Gary finished a twist, started a second.

Sasha fiddled with a pencil, eyes fixed on the phone.

"What's with the fed?" he asked. "How'd he take being shut down yesterday?"

"He didn't like it much. Can't blame him. How's our boy, Rudy?"

"He's over at Fourth Avenue. Jepson, the public defender's been assigned."

"Competent PD, Jepson."

"He'll do. And the DA's drooling."

"Who can blame him?"

Her phone buzzed with the call she was waiting for.

Gary recognized the FBI's prefix and gave her some privacy.

Sasha sensed that Charlie's voice had softened from the night before. He wasn't saying exactly what Sasha was hoping to hear. No *'How are you doin' Sasha?'* No *'Sorry we couldn't do dinner last night.* No *'Gee, I miss you. Would love to see you.'* None of that. Instead . . .

"The Russian fishing boat is still at sea so we won't be flying out to Dutch right away. I'm making reservations at a local B and B." Then he fell quiet.

"Anything else?" she asked.

"No. That's it," he said. "I'll be in touch about Dutch tomorrow."

Not exactly an audio love letter, but after he hung up, she felt slightly better. She left work at six and decided *not* to stop at the Brown Jug. She congratulated herself on her forbearance.

Back in the doublewide, she settled in, drank only a single bottle of beer, watched an old Bette Davis movie, *Dark Victory,* on TCM, spoke briefly with her daughter, then called it a night. She crawled under the covers, picturing Charlie's naked body. The first two fingers of her right hand slid between her legs. She took her time. Success.

~~~

The man who booked a room at *Bering Bridge Bed 'n Breakfast* claimed to be a photographer. He gave his name as Arkady

Archenko. He told the hostel's owner, Verna Westinghouse, that he was on assignment from Audubon magazine, come to Dutch Harbor to chronicle the unprecedented and unexplained die-off of the lesser murres that abound on the Aleutians' rocky shores.

If questioned closely, Archenko would have had trouble distinguishing a murre from an ostrich. He had been ordered to Dutch Harbor two days earlier to find a missing shipment of heroin, missing because of a greedy American fisherman, in permanent residence at the bottom of the Bering Sea. Archenko began his quest in Unalaska's bars.

Since Jimmy-gone-swimming was the talk of the town, it had been no work at all discovering that the American fisheries observer always stayed at the *Bering Bridge Bed 'n Breakfast.* Archenko checked online, found the phone number, called, and booked a room.

When he arrived at the B and B, he spent time chatting with the owner about the unfortunate vanished man. He gently probed about Lasorda's activities when in Dutch.

Because of sniffles and a constant dabbing at eyes, the hostel owner was only semi-coherent, going on at length about Jimmy and his lady friend.

"Poor Isabel," the woman sobbed. "I wonder if she's learned yet that Jimmy's missing?"

Archenko smiled to himself. He didn't bother telling the hostel owner that Isabel Castro was no longer among the living, that he and his friends had been present when she died, and that, in fact, they had been the instruments of her demise. Details better left unsaid.

The man, whose real name was Konstantin Zhuganov, was using an alias. But not just any alias, not one simply plucked from thin air. The chosen name, Arkady Archenko, was actually the coach of the school soccer team on which he and his twin brother, Taras, had played.

But where Taras had found a way to get to America, Konstantin had remained in Russia. He stumbled through an undistinguished career in Alpha Group, a counter-terrorism unit attached to the Russian Federal Security Services, the successor to the Soviet's KGB.

In late October, 2002, a maladroit Lieutenant Zhuganov was in charge of one of the commando units that stormed the Dubrovka Theater in Moscow. It was there that Chechen militants took hostage more than eight hundred Russians. The Chechens demanded the withdrawal of the Russian army from their homeland in the northern Caucasus.

A direct assault on the Dubrovka proving impossible, the FSS decided to subdue the hostage-takers by pumping a gaseous chemical agent into the building. It worked, but with unintended and dire consequences. Although most of the Chechens were knocked out and were later shot by the Russian troops, the fumes also worked on the theater-goers, killing one hundred and thirty of them.

The bodies of the unlucky Russians were removed from the auditorium and laid out on the streets around the theater. While the corpses rested there, their valuables mysteriously vanished.

"Lieutenant Zhuganov, front and center."

The accused body robber was given the choice—a single rank demotion and redeployment to front line duty in Chechnya, where things were decidedly dangerous, or a two rank demotion and voluntary retirement.

Because Taras, his twin, was doing so well for himself

in a place called Brooklyn, USA, Kostya Zhuganov opted for demotion and retirement. And emigration.

After a bit of finagling, a visa was arranged by Taras' boss, along with the promise of a job in Bunin industries. The former soldier was brought to America to do the same things he had been trained to do in Russia: kill, maim, threaten, bully, and generally scare the living bejeezus out of people.

Kostya proved more than capable, pleasing Boris Bunin. So when someone had to go to Alaska to find a quantity of missing heroin, Taras' brother got the nod.

During his first evening in residence at the B and B, with the hostel owner having gone to bed, Kostya crossed from his room to the one Jimmy Lasorda had occupied. He tossed the room but found nothing. Nor was the missing heroin in the bathroom. Nor in any of the other second floor rooms. And the next day, when the old woman left to run errands, Kostya was able to thoroughly comb through the entire premises. Nothing.

He phoned in the results of his efforts to his brother. Taras put Kostya on hold while he went to convey the bad news to Boris Bunin.

Waiting for his twin, Kostya felt thankful for the chain of command. He didn't envy Taras having to tell Bunin that his heroin was still missing.

But when his brother returned and delivered an ass whooping that made Kostya's innards gurgle, the former FSS bruiser knew there would be no further room for failure.

~~~

Boris Bunin was fuming and chain smoking.

At these moments, the bodyguard always hoped that

Larissa might show up. Boris rarely exposed his dark side to his wife.

They were in the den of the Bunins' spacious, two-floor condo in Brooklyn Heights, both men standing in front of floor-to-ceiling picture windows. Twelve stories below them, the Brooklyn Bridge was a short jog north.

"Let me hear it all, Taras."

"The woman's brother has been arrested. He was taken by an FBI agent and an Anchorage detective."

Boris began pacing. "FBI. Shit. I don't suppose we know a lawyer in Alaska?"

"Not one. We have limited assets in Alaska with the means or talent to get the brother out of jail. Once out, no problem disposing of him. But while he remains a prisoner, with the possibility of serious jail time, he'll be tempted to cooperate, to tell what he knows."

"What do we *think* he knows?"

"Uncertain. He lived with the fisherman and was an addict for sure. And since his sister was helping bring the goods into Anchorage, he might know a lot."

"Complicated." Boris dug his hands into his pants pockets and rocked on his heels. "Remind me of the size of the missing shipment the American fisherman brought in. Over ten kilos, wasn't it?"

"Slightly more than eleven. Kostya's still searching. I conveyed to him the urgency of the situation, *and* your displeasure."

"Alright. Here's what we need to do. First and most importantly, the brother. Tell Denis to go to the brother's girlfriend. What's her name?"

"Rose Nakamura."

"Nakamura. Tell Denis to remind the woman what happened to her friend—the one your twin stupidly left in the meadow. And what awaits *her* if she says a single word about what she knows. Denis should tell the woman that she needs to convince her boyfriend to keep his mouth shut. Next. Our missing goods. Alert Leonid. Tell him he'll need to fly some folks to Dutch Harbor. But don't tell him who or why or Dorotea will make life a misery for him. Tell him to be ready to fly on very short notice. Then let Denis and Gerasim know that in a day or two, Leonid will contact them about going to Dutch Harbor to help Kostya look for our goods. Got it all?"

"I'm on it."

Boris kicked at an invisible soccer ball. "The fucking FBI is now involved. Just what we don't need. Who's the other policeman?"

"Some woman cop," Taras said, hurrying away to carry out orders.

~~~

Bobby Carl Jepson, a displaced Alabaman, was the public defender assigned to represent Rudy Castro. Jepson was a tall drink of water, in his late thirties, with a disappearing hairline, straggly beard, light brown eyes, moist lips, and a craggy face of a man twice his age. Somewhere along the line, his eyebrows had vanished.

He'd graduated from the Birmingham School of Law in 2002, finishing twenty-ninth out of sixty in his class. "Top half," he told folks. He passed the bar on his third try and, gripped by a wanderlust, wound up doing pro bono legal aide work in Nome. He moved four years later to Anchorage after the Public Defender's Office offered him a job.

Lawyer and client were sitting alone in the Fourth Avenue Jail's third floor visiting room. They were separated by a thick wall with built-in Plexiglas windows.

Rudy Castro, dressed in a bright yellow jump suit, was apoplectic.

"If I cop a plea, I want the charges dropped to simple possession, *not* possession for sale. And I wanna treatment center, maybe a half-way house. Not jail. I can't do jail." The inmate shook his head vigorously back and forth, demonstrating to his lawyer that hard time in the slammer was a non-starter.

"That ain't gonna happen, buddy," Bobby Carl calmly told his client, speaking through the land line phone. "The DA's bein' a total prick. Even if you was to cooperate, even if you was to name names, he's fixin' to send you away for a while. Not for a long while, mind you, but he wants you to do some time. Learn your lesson."

"I don' wanna serve *any* time," Rudy yelled into his phone. "Not another day. You gotta work on him, man. I mean, what the fuck are you good for?"

Jepson was in his sixth year in the Anchorage PD's Office. In that period, he'd represented a dozen Rudy Castros, all happy to do the crime. But when it came to doing the time—scared shitless.

"That dog won't hunt, buddy boy," the public defender explained to his client.

"Whattaya mean, huntin' dogs? What the hell you talkin' about?"

Jepson slowed down, took a deep breath, and tried again. "See, the problem for you Rudy, is that this ain't just a matter of your normal small-time heroin pusher gettin' busted with a couple dime bags. If that was the case, you might do as little as a year. No sir. This is considerably more serious. You were caught with a goodly quantity of a Schedule I drug, over eight ounces of heroin. Enough to earn you four to five years behind bars. Add to that an unregistered weapon, which'll bump things up. Ya see, Rudy, you're wrapped up in an international drug smugglin' conspiracy in which two people are dead. Well, one dead and the other missin'. Both, somehow, tied into your case. And you're the only one who can start puttin' things together. Are you with me, son?"

The dispirited prisoner slumped in his chair. "Go on," he said.

"Well, the DA is an ambitious punk who'd love to advance his career by being able to make a dent in this quite sophisticated drug traffickin' case. But he needs your help. If you talk, if you help him out, he'll go light on you."

Rudy sat up. "Light? You mean I won't hafta do any time?"

"No, Rudy. Light means he's offerin' you three years, with two and half suspended. You'll only do six months, less time served, and probably right here in Alaska. Maybe down at Spring Creek, in Seward. You might get yourself a cell there with a scenic view of Prince William Sound, catch sight of some otters, maybe an orca or two. You could do worse, buddy. Will do worse—a lot worse—iff'n you don't tell what you know."

"I'll tell 'im what he wants to hear, but six months? That's whack. I don't wanna do *one* month. Not even a week."

"Rudy, Rudy, Rudy," the lawyer nearly shouting at his

client. "You need to *listen*, buddy boy, and *hear* what I'm tellin' ya. You *will* do some time. That's a given. As sure as God made little green apples."

The prisoner looked wonderingly at his lawyer. "Apples? What the fuck?"

Jepson regrouped. "One more time. You had thirty-two dime bags and two Ziplocs loaded with heroin. And your fingerprints all over them." Jepson paused, took a breath. "You don't cooperate, Rudy, we're talking here about a sentencin' range of four to five years. Maybe more if the state turns the case over to the feds. *And* you had a weapon. Since it's your first offence, maybe the minimum, four years with some suspended. But I wouldn't count on it. The judge won't like you because you're not cooperatin', not helpin'. The jury will hate your guts, because between you and me, you're a dirt bag. They'll recommend the Full Monty jail time. No, buddy boy. Be smart, give up the info, cop a plea, avoid court at all costs. Do that and the DA'll recommend a three-year sentence, two and half suspended. He's told me that already. Guaranteed it. Ready to put it in writin', if that's what it takes."

Rudy looked dazed. "I gotta think."

Jepson stood. "Don't take forever, buddy boy. It's a good deal. Best you're gonna get."

~~~

Buster Kopanuk's grandfather loved to tell stories about how he and his family would regularly cross the fifty miles of open seas that separated his home on America's St. Lawrence Island—in the middle of the Bering Sea—from the east coast of Russia.

Kopanuk, a Siberian Yup'ik Eskimo, born and raised in Savoonga, one of his island's two villages, had an extended family on the Russian mainland.

Before World War II, visits back and forth were frequent. After the war, however, those visits between American Eskimos and their Russian cousins came to an end with the onset of the Cold War. If Europe was divided by an Iron Curtain, then the Bering Sea was cut down the middle by an Ice Curtain, one that didn't completely thaw for over forty years. During that time, contact between the families all but ceased.

Then, in the 1990s, permission was granted for the Siberian Yup'iks on both sides of the water to resume their visits. Kopanuk resumed his generations-old tradition—four times a year, he and his family would sail over to the village of Provideniya, at the tip of the Chukotka Peninsula. They'd spend a week in Russia in the bosom of their rediscovered family, and then return with a boat full of subsistence foods that had been gathered, hunted and fished by their cousins in Russia.

And beginning in 2005, there was something else Buster brought back home from Russia.

Often packed among the seal pokes, reindeer carcasses, and bags of eider feathers was a forty or fifty pound bundle, carefully wrapped in oilskin. Sometimes two bundles.

Before he'd set sail for Russia, Buster would call an Anchorage phone number and let someone know he was on his way to Provideniya. Once there, a man would show up, give Buster a parcel and an envelope containing twenty, one hundred dollar bills.

Buster had an idea what the packages contained, but

he played the innocent and never asked. Back home on St. Lawrence Island, he'd deliver the goods to a Grizzly Air pilot, a tall, thin, sallow-faced man named Leo, who was always in a rush to get back to Anchorage.

Four times a year, eight thousand dollars. Enough to pay for the college education of the three Kopanuk children. And in 2015, enough to cover the costs of his granddaughter Julia's final year of nursing studies at the University of Alaska Anchorage. So proud!

~~~

The cop and the federal agent sat across the aisle from each other, on their way to Dutch Harbor. The thirty-four-seater Saab turbo-prop was half-full. Most of the other passengers were a girls' high school sports team, many wearing Unalaska *Raiders* hoodies.

Charlie leaned into the aisle. "I'm a little afraid to ask, but how did you convince Rudy to talk?"

Sasha looked around to see who might be listening, then craned toward him. "If you must know, Agent Dana, we water boarded him."

"No. Christ. Please, no."

"Well not quite. There was no water and no board."

"So you *didn't* water board him?" he asked hopefully, confused.

"In a manner of speaking. We had him trussed to a chair. Couldn't move, cuffed behind his back. Laid him down. I put a wet towel over his face. Told him I'd drown him if he didn't cooperate. He yelled. We stopped. He talked. Simple."

"I don't know if I should be relieved or offended,"

Charlie said. "You really would have water boarded him if he hadn't talked?"

"Maybe. Maybe not. But I didn't have to, did I? The thought of what might happen to him if he didn't cooperate made him see the light." Sasha sat back in her seat. "You know, Charlie, when the Spanish Inquisition was at its height, not a whole lot of people actually got tortured. The *sight* of the instruments of torture was enough for them to blab whatever you wanted to hear."

He looked at her, uncertain, but interested.

"It's true," she said. "The Jesuits who ran the show would roll a table into your cell, loaded with the tools they'd use to convince you to betray your own mother, your kids, your god." Sasha paused for effect. "Especially if the prisoner saw a clyster."

"A clyster? That's a new one on me."

"Kind of a metal funnel that got shoved up your butt. A variety of hot liquids—sometimes molten—were poured in. Couldn't have been much fun."

"How the hell do you know all this shit?"

"I just know. Persuasion's my middle name." She grinned.

"And I suppose you own a clyster?"

"Not an authentic one. Hard to find a real one these days."

"Do the ends always justify the means with you?"

"Always. But I thought we settled that on the drive back from Girdwood."

"I'm not sure we settled anything. Anyhow, I talked again this morning to Kozol, the Guard's PR guy in Dutch. He thought the Russian ship was only a few hours out. Should be getting into port right about now."

"That'll leave us whatever's left of the afternoon to talk to the crew, and maybe a little into the evening. I'm not sure we can do it all in a day. How many crew we talking about?"

Charlie pulled a sheet of paper from his briefcase. "Says here on the manifest, there are nineteen, including the captain and first mate. Interesting that there are three new crew who came on board just before sailing. I'm figuring about a quarter of an hour, twenty minutes for each ought to do it. Comes to about five hours, give or take. It's sure to bleed over into tomorrow morning. Maybe you can use your powers of persuasion on the sailors."

"I doubt it," Sasha said. "They're probably way too big for me. I like 'em small, like Rudy and Rose. Persuadable."

"I get it now, Detective Kulaeva. You're a bully, hiding behind a badge."

She considered a moment. "I'll own up to that, Agent Dana," she said.

"The crew then, these big guys, ought to be pretty safe from you. Unless you improvise a clyster, of course."

"You hold 'em down, I'll pour the boiling coffee."

"Pass. But thanks for the offer." Charlie stretched in his seat, arms to the cabin's roof. "We've got about forty minutes before we land. You promised to tell me about your grandfather, how he got to America."

"Okay. You ready for a great story?" she asked.

"Let 'er rip."

At any one time between 1942-45, several hundred Russian airmen were stationed at Ladd Air Force Base, near Fairbanks, Territory of Alaska.

One of those airmen was Viktor Kulaev, a twenty-year-old pilot from Morskoi, a small village outside of Vladivostok, in the Soviet Far East. Viktor was one of the last remaining members of the Soviet-US Lend Lease mission who had flown more than eight thousand American-made planes from Alaska, over the Bering Sea, across Russia, ultimately to be used in battle against the Germans on the Eastern Front.

In late July 1945, the young airman was scheduled to fly back to the Soviet Union in the cockpit of an American-made Bell P-63 Kingcobra.

On Tuesday, July 31st, Kulaev was at the base canteen, sharing a table with a bevy of young American service women. Among them, Virginia Ann Bergson, a blond, blue-eyed, and leggy twenty-one-year-old Army Air Corps nurse from Lincoln, Nebraska.

Viktor pointed to the saltshaker. "Please to give sugar," he said. Virginia and her friends exchanged smiles. The nurse took both the saltshaker and the sugar jar and passed them to the pilot, explaining which was which.

The Russian bowed his head. "I thanking you deep," he said. "Very deep."

More smiles from the women.

Viktor's English was generally limited to the words and phrases he needed to fly the Kingcobra. For her part, Virginia knew only how to communicate in Russian about medical problems. She could ask, "Where do you hurt?" but not, "Where do you live?"

Neither of them, however, found their linguistic limitations the slightest obstacle, and they spent all their free time over the next few days exclusively in each other's company.

Two evenings later, with several more hours of light available at that latitude and in that season, he took her flying. Cruising at four thousand feet, they sailed in and out of the Arctic's protracted mid-summer twilight.

On Sunday, while riding a paddle wheeler down the Tanana River, Viktor proposed. Virginia wondered what had taken him so long. She told him she'd think about it.

The next morning, Monday, August 6, 8:15 Hiroshima time, the Americans opened the age of atomic warfare. Later that afternoon, Viktor received an order from Soviet Air Command-East, delaying his return until the end of the month. That evening, Virginia accepted Viktor's proposal.

The following morning, they borrowed a Jeep, drove to the Alaska Territorial Court House in Fairbanks, obtained a marriage license, and presented themselves before Judge Allan R. Bascomb, Jr.

His Honor was delighted at the novelty of marrying a Russian soldier and an American nurse. But he was nonplussed moments after the ceremony when Viktor petitioned him for political asylum. Judge Bascomb stammered that this was an unprecedented request and might take years to make its way through the system. Exactly what the two were counting on.

With the end of the war, the newlyweds became civilians. Virginia was demobilized in October at the Presidio, in San Francisco Bay. Viktor borrowed some civilian clothes from Judge Bascomb and demobilized himself, treating everyone at Mickey's Bar and Grill to countless rounds of vodka brought from the old country, and near-beer chasers, from the new.

The bride continued on to Nebraska to see her family and more completely fill out the news: she had married a Russian pilot; he was not a communist; he had no family left in the Soviet Union; she and Viktor would be living in Fairbanks; all were welcome to come and visit.

In November, she returned to Alaska—by train to Seattle, by boat to Prince Rupert in British Columbia, and then thumbed her way up a frosty Alcan Highway back to Fairbanks.

Viktor found work right away as a pilot and mechanic for a local flight service. Virginia opened a birthing clinic.

Their family thrived: son Peter was born in early 1949, followed by Marat in 1952, and Dmitri in 1954.

Viktor's legal status remained in limbo for years, becoming more complicated with the arrival of each new dependent. In 1956, after having his petition for asylum shunted from Fairbanks to Juneau to Seattle to Washington D.C., someone at last decided 'the hell with it,' and made him a permanent resident. Five years later Viktor Kulaev became an American citizen.

Virginia and Viktor's life together was serene and predictable. Their first grandchild, Alexandra Petrovna Kulaeva, was born in 1980.

It was readily apparent that Aleksandra more resembled her grandparents than her parents. In body type, she was a clone of her corn-fed grandmother, coming out of her mother's womb long, blond, and peachy-skinned.

Facially, Viktor saw himself when he held his new granddaughter—the same almond shaped, green, Tartar eyes, the same high cheekbones.

Sasha ended the story there, the forefinger of each hand pushing up the skin under her cheekbones. From there, they went to the outer edges of her almond shaped, green eyes. "It's me," she said.

Charlie was staring at her, smiling, taking in the story.

"What are you thinking?" she asked.

"I think, Sasha, it's as romantic a romance as I've ever heard. If I hadn't gotten it from you directly, I'd have thought it was some kind of invented Harlequin novel."

"It *is* pretty great," she said. "Grandma Ginny passed away twenty years ago, but Viktor's still alive, not quite as dashing, but still . . ." She drifted off.

"Still?"

"Still the best guy in the world," she said. "No one even comes close."

"I'll stop trying," he said.

They felt the landing gear drop down and engage. Dutch Harbor was five minutes away.

7

In early July, 2005, in honor of his new posting in Alaska, Mehmet Ozil brought with him a new identity—Jacobo Kabiri, born in Greece, a naturalized American, and a dealer in jewels. The Turk had assessed the variety of passports he kept stored in his Citi Bank safety deposit box in Paris and determined that Kabiri would work well. Ozil was fluent in Greek and hadn't used this particular ID for eleven years when he and his cousin, Artun, made off with four, 7th Century BCE Greek amphorae, lifted from a poorly guarded private home near Ephesus. How the jugs ultimately wound up in a Malibu villa is anyone's guess.

His first full day in Anchorage, the new Alaskan opened checking and savings accounts at Credit Union One, depositing a $120,000 cashier's check from Long Island Premier Industries, LLC, one of the many dummy corporations set up by Larissa Bunina. *Such an artful and astute businesswoman,* Ozil thought.

Next, he bought a four-year-old Ford extended cab pickup. Accustomed to small European cars, the Turk reveled in the size and power of his new, full-throated purchase. He drove for hours every day, exploring Anchorage neighborhoods, learning the streets, the parks, potential meeting places. He drove past the police stations, scoped out their routine, scouted the FedEx complex at the airport, as well as the rail and bus terminals.

In the autumn, with the help of a real estate agent, he found a suitable living space—a three-bedroom home on Bannister, in Rogers Park, one of the older neighborhoods in Anchorage. The spacious backyard extended two hundred meters down a hill to the city's densely wooded trail system that paralleled Chester Creek. In the rear of the property stood a small cottage, perfect for cousin Artun.

After being shown the house, Ozil met with the owners—a crusty sourdough in overalls and boots, and his similarly clothed and sour-faced wife, wearing a Seattle Seahawks wool cap. They wanted a two-year lease at $2,000 a month, first and last up front, $4,000 security deposit. After an hour of haggling, they agreed to a six-year lease at $1,400 a month, first and last, $1,500 security deposit. Utilities thrown in. They told their grandkids that night that bargaining with Mehmet Ozil had been "a real fun experience."

As soon as the place was officially his, Ozil texted his wife, Nicole, and sent her photos of the place, including one of a mother moose and two yearlings that had wandered into the yard to browse.

Nicole emailed back, asking about a suitable winter wardrobe. Ozil told her that the furriers in town, especially David Green, seemed to know what they were doing. Nicole was reassured, went to the fur dealer's web page and found a full-length red fox coat she just had to have.

The Turk's next task was finding an office—a place as lock-down secure as was electronically and mechanically possible.

Over the course of his long career, he had outfitted more than two dozen such places in as many cities all over world. Cousin Artun, electrician and all around handy man, was due in Anchorage in a few days.

Ozil scoured the outskirts of Anchorage until he found the perfect office in a two-story building near Ship Creek, far from traffic, near the rail yards. There were seven offices in the building, only two of which—both on the first floor—had occupants. Ozil chose a second floor walk-up with double access—one through the hallway and the other through a rear fire exit.

He signed a five-year lease then drove straight to Home Depot where he bought and ordered everything he'd need to make the place secure: steel doors for front and back, serious dead bolt locks, rebar for the windows, overhead cameras to be placed outside the two entrances, silent alarms, and movement sensitive lights. And the biggest safe available, a Mesa 7.6 cubic-footer.

~~~

Rose Nakamura hadn't the slightest intention of visiting Rudy Castro in jail. She was so done with that loser. Although she valued her job—the best, by far, she ever had—she was determined to flee, to put as much distance as possible between herself and the murderous events in Anchorage. Not even the warning by the woman cop to remain available for further questioning affected Rose's decision to disappear.

She went to her boss to request the next several days off—bereavement the excuse.

"Of course, Rose," a sympathetic Justin McKimmey said. "Take a couple weeks if you feel you need it."

But as she was leaving work that afternoon—for the last time, she believed—a man showed up. A stranger.

He was waiting by her hatchback, leaning against the fender of the pickup in the next parking lane. He looked to be in his early to mid-forties, close cropped brown hair, a small scar over his left brow, deep set dark eyes, and a cleanly shaven face. Good looking. He was wearing work clothes, a light wind breaker, and running shoes. When he saw Rose approach, he smiled and bowed his head sweetly. A smile and a voice, she remembered later, that were pleasant, non-threatening. She wasn't sure she knew him, but she felt no sense of alarm—there were many staff still in the parking lot, her coworkers. As she neared her car, the man stood and faced her. Relaxed, hands easy, by his side.

"Do I know you?" she asked, fishing her car keys out of her purse and activating the remote door opener.

"I don't think so," he said in his very soft, very musical voice. "I'm a friend of Rudy's. I'm wondering how he's doing. I heard he's in jail."

And now the first twang of suspicion. She had been going with Rudy Castro for three long years and as far as she knew, her ex had no friends other than her, Jimmy, and Isabel. And the last two were currently dead.

"Really, how do you know him? What's your name?"

"I'm Ron, Ron Carter. I know Rudy from Florida."

It was the way he pronounced his Rs. Not American. Though his English was perfect, Rose detected a very slight accent, not unlike the one that piece of shit woman detective had. And the dawning knowledge that this man was probably Russian made the bile rise into her throat. She swallowed it back down.

The man realized the effect he was having on her, that she was understanding who he was and precisely why he had come to see her. His smile broadened.

"Good," he said softly, the faintest trace of menace in his voice. "You know why I've come."

She was standing in the narrow lane between her hatchback and the pickup, her back to the dwindling number of cars that were passing behind her, full of federal workers hastening to leave the job site.

He was five feet away. She noticed that his wrists were thick, his fingers rough. And he continued to smile at her, a smile, she now thought, of someone who was used to getting his way.

A passing car in back of her honked. The man looked over Rose's shoulder to see a woman yell from her car window, "See you tomorrow, Rose. Don't forget to bring the ice cream."

"Yes, Rose," the man said in his gentle voice. "Don't forget to bring the ice cream. What flavor to they prefer in Fish and Wildlife? I like mint chip, myself."

Rose looked around at the rapidly emptying parking lot.

"A call for help, Rose? Is that what you're thinking? There's really no need. I have no intention of harming you." He paused and took a half step toward her. "At least, not at the moment. But tomorrow? Well, that might be a different story."

She felt wobbly, losing her balance. Her body was in full 'flight' mode but she was paralyzed. She needed a bathroom.

"What? What do you want?" she was able to get out.

"What I want, Rose, is simple. I want you to visit Rudy tomorrow. He's at the jail on Fourth Avenue. Go there and be as persuasive as you possibly can. Because your life depends on it." The man never changed the subdued tone of his voice. The threat was spoken as naturally as if he were ordering a meal at a restaurant.

He looked around, stretched his back, then took another small step forward. He inclined slightly toward her. "Rudy knows things he should not know. And he needs to keep them to himself. If he speaks about them to anyone, even with you,

Rose, that would be a serious and irreversible mistake. In fact, a fatal mistake."

Her throat constricted but she was able to gasp, "What does he know? He doesn't know anything. He's too *stupid* to know anything."

The man appreciated her burst of gumption and deigned to give her a well-deserved, "Nicely done, Rose." He took another small step toward her. He stood now an arm's length away. "But, actually, he *does* know certain things. Things that are important to the people your friends *used* to work for." The man paused, allowing a vision of Isabel and Jimmy to take hold in Rose Nakamura's memory. "Those two made a mistake. And paid for it. If Rudy makes a mistake and opens his mouth, he *and* you will pay." The man's voice now dropped a further half tone, seeming to her more ominous for its being barely audible. He inclined toward her, his arms still relaxed by his side.

Rose wanted to back up. "Why me, why . . . ?"

He put a finger to his lips to shush her. "Here's what will happen if Rudy talks," the Russian said. "It will be ugly. And painful. Extremely painful. And I promise you, before he and you die, you will beg me to stop the pain. You will beg me to kill you. Isabel begged. But it did no good. Have you seen her body? Nasty burns." The man straightened and took a step back. "So, tomorrow, Rose, you will go visit Rudy. Go early, before his lawyer gets there. Visiting hours begin at nine. Explain to him carefully what awaits the both of you if he shares what he knows."

The man reached forward and opened the hatchback driver's door and held it for her. "Please," he said. "Get in. Go home. Have dinner. Prepare what you are going to say to

Rudy. Perhaps write down some notes. But above all, Rose, be convincing. A lot depends on it. I'll call you tomorrow evening, after eight. You will have good news for me."

Rose fell awkwardly into her car. Before the man closed the door, "One more thing. It's natural at moments like this to consider flight. I assure you, Rose, that will *not* work. If you try to run, we will find you, and you will regret it for days and days before death comes." He glared down at her for emphasis, then shut her door and walked back through the parking lot. Rose tracked him in her rear view mirror until he turned out of the lot and disappeared. She sat in her car and shook uncontrollably.

~~~

At quarter past nine the next morning, Rose was sitting on a metal chair, bolted to the floor, one of four such chairs in the Fourth Avenue Jail's visitation room. In front of her, a cement wall with Plexiglas windows and a land-line phone. She was waiting for Rudy Castro to be delivered to her, so she could deliver to *him* the Russian man's threat.

Rose took out the notes—the talking points she had jotted down the night before. *This has got to work,* she kept repeating to herself. *But Rudy's so fucking stupid.*

Three chairs down from her, the only other visitor, a Hispanic woman holding a month-old infant, was ranting at an inmate. The woman was seriously pissed off and kept holding the baby up with her free arm for the man to see.

"This what you leave me with?" she screamed into the phone. "I didn't want this baby, Ramon, you prick. And now you goin' away for sixteen months. How the fuck am I gonna get by? Huh? Your drunk of a mama gonna help? Or your papa? He already in the slammer. Answer me, you shit. Tell me how I'm gonna get by!"

Rose thought: *Bitch. You think you got problems? I'd give the world to change places with you.*

The door to the inmate side of the room opened and Rudy Castro was led in by a guard twice his size. "You got 'til ten o'clock," the guard said, leading his prisoner over to the chair opposite Rose.

As soon as the guard was gone, Rudy picked up his phone and started explaining, complaining, whining. Rose listened, trying to appear sympathetic.

"I been in jail for only a couple days. No way I can do a month." Rudy's voice was full of self-pity.

"And the public defender?"

"That jackass. He tol' me the only way the charges might be reduced was for me to plea bargain. In other words, I gotta tell 'em what I know."

"You don't wanna do that, Rudy. You don't wanna tell 'em anything."

"Right. And even if do, they still want me to do six months. That's a lotta crap!"

Rose clenched her teeth. "Listen, Rudy. I got something very, very important to tell you. You have to listen good."

For the next ten minutes, Rudy Castro heard a blow by blow recounting of Rose's meeting with the Russian man in the Fish and Wildlife parking lot. She described the death of Isabel and how the same thing awaited the both of them if Rudy didn't shut up about what he knew.

"Your sister, Rudy, she begged these guys. Isabel begged them to kill her it hurt so bad. That's what the Russian said. She begged. They burned her chest and her boobs, for Christ's sake."

But the prisoner, for reasons Rose couldn't fathom, seemed not be listening. *He isn't getting it. He isn't hearing what I'm telling him. He doesn't understand the danger.* She wanted to bust through the window and slap some sense into him. She growled into the phone, "Listen to me, jackoff. You tell them what you know, I'm dead. You're dead. Why don't you understand that, you moron? Dead! As in Isabel and Jimmy dead. You can't be thinking of cooperating."

He refused to meet her gaze.

"Rudy. Look at me. Tell me you won't open your big mouth. Promise me."

He spoke in a quiet voice, "Listen Rose. I got an idea."

"No, Rudy, no. No ideas. The time for ideas is over. You just need to keep your mouth shut."

"No, really. I got a plan. This can work. I'm sure it can work." He paused for a moment. "Can you call the Russian? Did he leave you any way to get in touch with him?"

"He said he'd call me tonight. After eight. Ask about what you're thinking of doing. What am I supposed to tell him, Rudy? That you're going to cooperate with the DA? Or should I tell him you promise to keep quiet? You think you can lie to the mob? Look what they did to your sister, for shit sakes. They tortured Iz." Rose now yelling. "They burned her body. They beat her face in. That's what's in store for me, you dick head, if you open your mouth."

The woman with the baby glanced at Rose.

"Fuck off, bitch," Rose screamed at her. "You got nothing to complain about."

The woman looked away, gathered her baby and her

purse, and hurriedly left the visitation room.

Rudy sat, unmoved by Rose's words. "Tell him I swear I won't say a word. Tell him I guarantee I won't talk."

Rose was confused. "You mean you'll do the time? You'll keep quiet?" she asked, unbelieving, but hopeful.

He came closer to the Plexiglas, and whispered into the phone, "No. I'm gonna make bail and disappear."

Rose sat back in her seat. "You're out of your fucking mind. Where you gonna go? You think you can hide at your dad's meat store on Calle Ocho? Right, they'd never bother to look for you there." She tried again, more slowly. "As soon as you get out, Rudy, they'll kill *you*. They'll kill *me*. The guy yesterday told me if I run they'd find me and torture me until I pleaded with them to kill me. Is that what you want?"

"That ain't gonna happen, Rose. You'll see. We're gonna go so far away . . . ."

"We? You and me?"

"Yeah, the two of us."

"You're as crazy as a shit house rat, you know that, Rudy?"

"Whattya mean, Rose, we'll . . . ."

"No," she interrupted, waving her hands in front of her. "I don't want to know anything about this. I don't want to know you. I don't want to have anything more to do with you and your bullshit. This can't work. You'll get us killed."

"I'll make bail and . . ."

"And where's the bail money coming from?"

"I got the dough."

"You? You got two hundred grand? From where?"

"No. I don't need the whole two. All I need is ten percent, twenty thousand if I use a bail bondsman."

"Where the fuck you got even twenty?"

"It's Jimmy's money. It's hidden up in the house, twenty-two, twenty-three thousand, in cash. It's in a tin box under the wood stove. There's a loose brick. The box is under it. Cash inside. Go get it and do my bail."

"Jimmy's money," she said. "Makes total sense you would use someone else's money to save your ass. You're a piece of shit. You know that?"

He straightened in his chair and sat back. "And if I am? So what? Jimmy can't use the cash. I can. Just go get the money and get me outta here."

Rose shoved her chair away from the dividing wall and stood. "This is mob stuff, Rudy. You stole from them. You used their dope." Rose broke off, her mouth set into a thin-lipped sneer. "You're a loser, Rudy. I knew that right away I met you."

He was unfazed by her assault. "Rose. Tell the Russian what he wants to hear. That I'll keep quiet. You'll see. This'll work."

"I'll tell him. Don't worry, I'll tell him." Her arms fell uselessly to her sides. "We haven't got a chance, not a fucking chance, you jerk."

~~~

The cousins were having breakfast in their home in Rogers Park. Artun had just come over from his back yard bungalow and was brewing a cup of coffee in Mehmet's Nespresso machine. "What's with the woman?"

Mehmet was washing his breakfast dishes. "I heard from back east. She was told to go to the jail and try and talk her boyfriend into keeping quiet. I don't think he knows about us, but Brooklyn doesn't want to take any chances, wants them both axed." Ozil finished the dishes and dried his hands.

Artun began attacking a bagel and cream cheese. "You want me to take care of her?"

"Eventually, but not yet. She may help us get the brother out of jail. Let's just follow her closely. Stick a bug in her car and let's keep tabs on her. We'll see what she does."

"No problem. You want the other half of this bagel?"

~~~

"The work of the Coast Guard's Marine Safety Detachment, Dutch Harbor, is to oversee federal laws in the Bering Sea as they pertain to fishing and waterways. Among other duties."

The speaker, USCG Public Affairs Specialist Lieutenant Butch Kozol, had a squeaky voice that was full of pent up rancor. It matched his appearance. He was a skeletally thin man with compressed lips on a narrow face. He had slits for eyes and his ears seemed to be pinned to his head. A short shock of straw blond hair, sticking straight up, magnified the impression. His opalescent skin made Sasha wonder why he had chosen the Coast Guard, a usually full-sunshine job that would probably send the man to the melanoma ward by the time he was forty.

The two Anchorage investigators were sitting in the Guard's tiny office, in a corner workspace that Kozol kept fastidiously neat.

"We're kind of a small operation right now. The station at Kodiak is the main Guard base in the state, but just wait a year or two," Kozol said with an anticipatory grin. "Plans are in the wind to beef up Kotzebue, and maybe build a giant port on St. George. I know it's a screwy thing to say, but global warming's been very, very good to us here in Unalaska. The North Pole's ice minimums and maximums are shrinking by leaps and bounds and the Northwest Passage is going to be one of the major ocean corridors on the planet. You've probably read that a luxury liner is set to sail the passage next summer from Seward to New York City. And that's just the beginning. We're going to see traffic on the Bering Sea you can't imagine. And that means this station here in Dutch is set to grow big time. I can't wait."

The public mouthpiece of the Coast Guard picked up his open can of Pepsi, took a swallow and continued. "But, as you've noticed, at present, we remain an afterthought," he said, with more than a touch of petulance.

Sasha shook her head in mock sympathy. Wanting to get him back on track, she asked, "Lieutenant Kozol. Can you tell us about Jimmy Lasorda? What was his job? How long he'd been doing it? What people thought of him?"

The PA Specialist sat up in his chair. He cleared his throat and interlaced his fingers around the Pepsi can.

"James Anthony Lasorda worked for the National Marine Fisheries Service, a branch of NOAA, the National Oceanic and Atmospheric Administration. He worked on various American fishing vessels from 2005 to about 2010. He was tasked with making sure the *actual* harvest taken—in tons and in species of fish–didn't exceed the amount *allocated* to the vessel." Kozol paused, looked from Sasha to Charlie, took a long sip of soda, smacked his lips, and went on. "I'm certain you both know that there are mandated allocations. Fishermen can't just go out and catch whatever they want, whenever they want. They tried that in the nineteen eighties right here in the Bering Sea. They overfished pollock in what's now called the Donut Hole. It was the largest example of overharvesting in the history of the American fisheries industry. Drove the species right to the brink." Another sip of Pepsi, another lip smack. "There are now quotas and designated seasons for fishing. As well as specified areas that open on such and such a date and close after so many tons are reeled in. Get it?"

Both cops nodded.

Kozol smiled. "The main problem that Lasorda would have encountered is a common one—the crew's resentment. Fishermen want to take more than the amount allocated to them. And in fact, that's exactly what they do in most parts of the planet. Something like eighty percent of food fish are being harvested beyond their sustainable limits. And a good portion of that is illegal fishing. That's why the Guard is here. Protect the fish stocks." He looked from one cop to the other. "How're we doing?" he asked.

"Great," said Sasha.

"Super," said Charlie.

Kozol was warming to the sound of his own voice. "So here's how I see it," he said in a tone that suggested the imparting of a closely guarded confidentiality.

But before the secret could be shared, Charlie raised a hand to stop the sailor and get him back on topic. "What was Lasorda's job, exactly?"

"Sure," Kozol said, clearly disappointed that his end-of-fish-as-food story wasn't gaining traction with the two cops. He finished the Pepsi and moved the empty to the side of the desk. Now, with less enthusiasm, "Because he knew a little Russian, Lasorda became part of an American-Russian joint-venture program that was started up again around five, six years ago."

"Started up *again*?" Sasha asked.

"Right. The program began back in the nineties, but was cancelled after only a few years for political reasons. It was resurrected about five years ago."

"And Lasorda's job? How did it work?" Charlie asked. "How many times would he have shipped out with the Russians?"

"Probably thirty, forty times."

"What kind of salary did he pull down?"

"Beginners can make about four grand a month. Plus room and board. And all the tedium you can stand.. And if you signed up for second tour, more money."

Charlie looked up from his note taking. "Is there a way of checking dates and names of the Russian fishing boats Lasorda worked on, home ports, captains, things like that?"

"For certain. That's all in the project's database. Since it's such a politically hot program, we need to keep close tabs, so there are mountains of paperwork."

"Can we get that information, and how soon?" Charlie asked.

"I can get you the stuff by tomorrow. Everything you want, and more."

"That'd be great," Charlie said. "And besides Lasorda's records, we'd also like the names of all the other American fish monitors who ever worked on Russian boats. And one more thing that's crucial. Where did he usually come aboard the Russian trawlers?"

"It would have been in either Vladivostok or PK.

Petropavlovsk-Kamchatsky."

"How did he get to those cities in the first place?" Sasha asked.

"Commercial airlines. From either Anchorage or Seattle. Usually through Japan or South Korea. Might take days and crazy expensive. He'd arrive in Russia a couple days before the fishing vessel would put out to sea, go through the harvest guidelines with the captain, and settle in for however long the fishing might take."

"And where was he dropped off, afterwards?"

"Very often, he'd get put ashore in the Pribilofs. St. George has a pretty long runway so we'd collect him and fly him back here to Dutch. Sometimes he got dropped in Kodiak. Once in a while on St. Lawrence Island. But wherever he was dropped, he almost always ended up back here in Dutch."

"And is he the only casualty of this program?" she asked.

"The only one I know of." Kozol looked questioningly at Charlie. "Are you two here because of Lasorda's disappearance, or is there something I'm not seeing? I mean, you two, Anchorage police *and* FBI. That's a lot of interest in a missing fisherman."

The cops exchanged glances. Charlie spoke.

"We're not at liberty to say anything right now. Let's just keep this conversation between us, okay?"

Kozol shrugged his disappointment. "I guess," he said.

~~~

After her visit with her ex, Rose drove straight to the Hillside, to Glazanof Drive. She used her own key to let herself in, walked quickly to the wood stove, went onto all fours and found the loose brick described by Rudy. She removed the stone, reached in, and brought out a round tin box, painted over with flowers. Inside, she found several thick rolls of hundred dollar bills. And a surprise—twenty-two coins with *'Krugerrand 1 oz fine gold'* stamped on each. She went to her iPhone and in less than a minute, learned that at today's price, an ounce of gold was worth one thousand, one hundred dollars. The value of twenty-two coins came to almost twenty-five thousand dollars! She sat and began to seriously reconsider her options. She could leave Rudy in jail, keep all of Jimmy's money *and* the surprise gold coins. She'd have enough cash to flee to the farthest corner of the planet, with enough left over for a small nest egg. Leaving him behind bars would guarantee he'd talk. *No way that pussy would take his punishment. He'd cop a plea. Tell what little he knows.*

She tried to imagine what that alternative might mean for her. She imagined the Russians would continue to come after her, no matter where she might run. She'd be forever looking over her shoulder in a constant state of fear.

But.

If she used some of the money—Jimmy's cash, not the gold coins—for Rudy's bail, he'd be free. And more importantly for her, *he* would be the Russians' primary target. Perhaps he could run fast enough to stay alive for a month or two, giving *her* sufficient time to drop out of sight. He'd be a diversion and might give her a chance to slip away.

She felt no guilt about using her ex as a decoy. *Why should I? What has he ever done for me except involve me in a life and death struggle?*

After hardening her heart, she decided that tomorrow she'd bail out her ex, the sacrificial lamb. And then take a powder.

~~~

The master and first mate of the *Pyotr Veliky* watched the approach of the U.S. Coast Guard patrol boat cutting through the waters of Iliuliuk Bay.

Low hanging clouds masked the hills of Unalaska Island and cloaked the town of Dutch Harbor, half a mile shoreward. The sun had failed to burn off the morning haze, leaving a gauzy, damp film that covered Captain Yury Vronsky's pea coat with a million microdots of water.

Despite being ordered to come to Dutch Harbor, Vronsky was content. The forty hours they had spent fishing had been hugely productive—the ship's holds were bursting with fish, enough to mollify his bosses back in Vladivostok. They might even allow him to remain at sea, he thought. Perhaps. Perhaps not. Vronsky-on-land seemed to be the safer bet.

The Coast Guard launch, a long and sleek white cutter—all polished wood and shimmery brass—slowed to a crawl as it neared the Russian trawler. Vronsky couldn't help but compare the American vessel to his own. Perhaps some chipping and scrapping on the way back to Vlad was in order.

This would be the second meeting between a ship under his command and the U.S. Coast Guard. The first had been thirteen years earlier when a small American purse seiner, *Molly Z*, out of Kodiak, had lost power and was wallowing in high seas fifty miles east of Sand Point, off the Aleutian

Peninsula. His vessel, *Oktyabr,* a seiner, had been the closest ship and had rushed to the rescue. The American five-man crew had been taken aboard his boat just minutes before *Molly Z* split in half and disappeared.

When the Coast Guard arrived, more than twenty-five hours later, the Americans were reluctant to leave their hosts. They had been extremely well cared for and had become quite adept at differentiating between the eleven kinds of vodka provided to them by their new Russian shipmates.

Now, an hour after dropping anchor in Iliuliuk Harbor, the *Pyotr Veliky* was being boarded by two men and a woman. One of the men was wearing a heavy wool jacket covering his working blues. The other man and woman were in civilian clothes. Of the two, the woman was suitably dressed: long, heavy coat, heavy canvas pants, high work boots, wool cap and mittens. The civilian man was dressed foolishly: suit, tie, low-cut shoes, hatless, no gloves. *He must be freezing his ass off,* Vronsky thought.

The three Americans clambered up the steep, steel ladder. When they were aboard, the ship's master approached.

"I Vronsky, captain," he announced in clunky English. "This," he said, pointing to Timoshenko, "First officer. Who you?"

Both Charlie and Kozol looked to Sasha. She removed her cap, bowed slightly to the captain, then introduced herself and her two colleagues in perfect Russian, all the while beaming down at the diminutive ship's master in the most properly respectful fashion.

The captain was charmed. *An American who not only speaks Russian, but native Russian.* He returned her nod and re-introduced himself in his own language.

Sasha told the captain they could talk freely in Russian and she would provide the translations. "We are exceedingly grateful for your cooperation," she ended, laying it on thick.

Vronsky suggested that they adjourn to the vessel's small mess for coffee and raspberry torte.

When they were seated and had politely sampled both coffee and cake, Sasha began, "Captain Vronsky, I want to assure you that we have no interest in delaying your return to your home port. We will be investigating the disappearance of the American fisheries observer. That will require us to interview each member of your crew." She looked at the manifest Kozol had given her. "All nineteen of you. Help us out, here, Captain, and I promise you can leave Dutch Harbor in less than a day. But if you drag your heels, we'll tie up your ship 'til every fish in your hold rots. I don't believe that is to be desired by either of us." Sasha gave the captain her most winning, *can't-we-just-get-along?* smile.

It was clear to Vronsky that he was cornered. He could complain, but given the veiled threat so sweetly delivered by this woman, his remonstrations would be a total waste of time. "You are correct," he admitted. "Neither of us wants that. Can you begin right away?"

"We can," she said, taking a swallow of coffee and grabbing up the last torte. "May we start, Captain, with you?"

It took Vronsky less than ten minutes to fully explain what he knew of the disappearance of the American fish monitor.

"I left the bridge around eleven hoping to grab a short nap. I told my first mate to take in the trawl at midnight, and if all went well, wake me at five. But just after three, he came into my cabin and gave me the bad news. I immediately ordered the ship to reverse course and gave orders that the radioman signal a mayday alert to all nearby vessels and to the American Coast Guard. We proceeded under full speed back to the area where we believed the man had gone into the sea. We continued the hunt for a day and a half. Without success."

While Kozol sat and observed, Charlie had become the default court recorder, a demotion from his usual lawyerly interrogations. But he was enjoying watching Sasha sweet talk the vessel's master, a far cry from the two other times his *ad hoc* partner had been in action. Previously, with Rose Nakamura, she had used the bludgeon with unstinting brutality, and later with Rudy Castro, the threat of water boarding. But here, with Captain Vronsky, Sasha was all kindness and propriety. *An education, indeed.*

After their interview, and with the captain gone, Sasha and Charlie compared notes. Vronsky had provided the names and some background information on all the members of his crew. He had sailed with most of them before. But about the three new crewmen, the master of the *Pyotr Veliky* knew nothing.

They next interviewed first officer Timoshenko and learned that the missing American was a get-along guy, unlikely to be the object of the crew's anger. The first mate accurately corroborated the captain's account and his time-line of events.

After a further six interviews, they wrapped it up, saving the eleven remaining crew members for the next day.

Before returning to shore, Sasha went to the wheelhouse to find Vronsky. He greeted her with a smile.

"So tell me, Alexandra Petrovna, how does an American woman come to speak perfect Russian?"

"It was my first language. I spoke only Russian 'til I was eight. My grandfather was Russian, from Rostov."

Vronsky nodded. "I suspected as much from your accent. You've got some Cossack in your tongue."

"My great-grandfather was a cavalryman in the Red Army, with Budyonny."

Vronsky shook his head. "And *my* grandfather was on the other side, with Kolchak, the White's Volunteer Army. He was killed at Ufa. Seems our forebears were on different sides in the civil war."

"I'm wondering what they'd say if they saw the state of affairs in Russia at this moment."

"A question, Aleksandra Petrovna, that *you* can ask without consequences. You live in America. I, however, cannot. My president has big ears."

"I've heard President Putin hears very well," she said.

"Too well, for some. So your great grandfather fought in the revolution and survived. And what of his family?"

"His son, my grandfather, became a pilot in the Great Patriotic War. He was stationed part time in Alaska. He flew American aircraft to the Soviet Union. He stayed in America after the war. Raised a family. He's still alive. Still a pilot."

Vronsky smiled at his own memory. "*My* father was a tank driver at Kursk, summer of forty-three. A great turning point. We prepared well and beat the Germans at their own game. My father described to me what the Kursk battlefield looked like after six thousand tanks spent nearly two months shooting at each other. After the battle was won, our soldiers walked through the ruins, collecting keepsakes, remembrances of the victory."

"What did your father collect?"

"Oh, this and that. Nothing valuable. A bayonet, a helmet, a pair of pistols, shoulder patches, some personal stuff. A lot of Germans died. And a lot of our boys, too."

"Where is your home now, Yury Gregorovich?"

"Vladivostok. I live alone. My wife passed some years ago."

"I'll be in your city next week for several days. I'm being sent to a police conference as a translator."

"Wonderful! In that case, you must come and visit," Vronsky insisted, writing down his address and phone number on a piece of paper torn from his pocket notebook. "I'm serious, young woman. I usually keep to myself, but I would be grateful for a visit. My daughter lives close by. She's a teacher. She would love the chance to practice her English."

Sasha took the paper scrap, stuck it in her wallet. "I promise to be in touch, Yury Gregorovich. Right now, however, I believe we are done for the day. If it pleases you, we will return early tomorrow morning to complete our interviews. We have eleven more. I suspect that you'll be able to leave Dutch Harbor soon after, as long as nothing unusual shows up."

He nodded gratefully. "The earlier tomorrow, the better. Even seven would work."

"How about eight, captain?"

"At eight, then. Will you need breakfast?"

"My compliments to your cook, but coffee and perhaps more of that wonderful torte will be plenty."

"Until tomorrow, Aleksandra Petrovna."

8

Before arriving in Alaska and for months afterwards, Mehmet Ozil read and re-read Larissa Bunina's binder. He knew it by heart and found her conclusions convincing: getting the contraband into Alaska was not difficult; shipping it from Alaska to New York was a bit more complicated.

Moving the drug by land was out. She'd reasoned that having to pass through both Canadian *and* American customs at highway borders was dangerous, presented too many chances for discovery.

And transporting the heroin by air seemed no less troublesome. Ozil knew from previous experience that America's Transportation Safety Administration was a disaster, its undertrained agents generally incompetent. He had read how Homeland Security had conducted numerous tests and found that they were able to smuggle weapons past the TSA ninety-five percent of the time. But those damn sniffer dogs could be trouble. So air, too, was out.

Larissa's plan argued that a direct sea passage from any of several Alaskan ports to other American ports in the Pacific Northwest—avoiding Canada altogether and bypassing all customs inspections—was the surest way to move the goods. And the three most productive sea routes Larissa Bunina suggested were containerized shipping vans, the state-run ferry system, and any of the numerous cruise lines that bring tourists to Alaska in the summer.

Within a week of his arrival in Anchorage, Ozil visited the Crowley and Lynden Freight companies and learned just how safe it was going to be using steel container vans. The customer loaded a van in Anchorage, without inspection, and put on a padlock. The container—a twenty or forty-footer—was hoisted onto a barge, and less than two weeks later, arrived in Seattle or Bellingham or Portland where it was unloaded and waited for the customer or his assigns to come unlock it and carry away the contents. Trouble-free smuggling.

Princess, Norwegian, and Holland America's immense passenger liners presented another, customs-free option. Ozil loved the accommodations but found the clientele unavailable for his purposes.

Finally, the Alaska Marine Highway System ran a fleet of ferry boats from Alaska to ports in the Pacific Northwest. Ozil made the trip several times, in each cabin classification. He even went deck passage one time, sleeping in the ferry's heated solarium.

It was on a return ferry trip from Seattle in 2005 that the Turk met a young man on his way out to the Aleutians. An ambitious young man with an MS in marine biology. They introduced themselves.

"By your name, sounds like you're Italian," Ozil remarked.

"My grandparents were Sicilian, actually," replied Jimmy Lasorda.

They spent the next three days enjoying the Inland Passage along Canada's forested coast. Ozil learned a great deal about the young man, eager to talk about himself.

Lasorda boasted about being his high school's most successful drug dealer—grass, hash, the occasional hallucinogen.

Jimmy described to Ozil the drug-lust of many of his college classmates. He said that his time at university convinced him that crime could *really* pay. In just over five years, he had earned himself an MS *and* a small fortune. Both his bank account and his ego were bloated. The kudos received for his master's thesis—*The Effects of the Decline of Pelagic Phytoplankton Stocks on North Pacific Marine Mammal Populations*—won praise throughout the scientific community from Seattle to Nome.

That's what got him into the fishing business. That's what was taking him to Alaska. And that's what got him his job: high seas fisheries observer.

Ozil said an inaudible 'thank you' to the gods of Karma.

~~~

Bering Bridge Bed 'n Breakfast, just off Ptarmigan Road, was a two-story building that was converted into a hostel in 1990 by Verna Westinghouse, after her good-for-nothing husband died of alcohol poisoning the year before.

The two Anchorage policemen showed up towards dusk in their rent-a-car and surveyed the building through the windshield.

Charlie shook his head. "Looks like it couldn't decide– a Colonial wannabe or the Bates Motel."

"And way too much gingerbread on the siding," Sasha added. "But it looks to be in good repair. Paint on the trim looks fresh. Windows seem recently Windexed, and the roof looks as if it's securely fastened. Let's go."

When Sasha got out of the car, she was greeted by a mesmerizing silence, broken only by the wind buffeting the grass and the occasional far-away shrieking of a gull. The B and B sat atop a low promontory overlooking Unalaska Lake. The property was bordered on three sides by lush meadows, the tall grasses dancing in the Aleutians' steady winds.

The slamming of a screen door broke the mood.

A tiny woman came out onto the covered porch. She was dressed in denim pants under a knee-length fleece coat. She was shod in slippers and heavy woolen leggings over her child-sized feet. A New York Yankees baseball cap kept bare control over a mass of graying hair. She had a ruddy complexion on a round face with a dimpled smile.

Charlie waved a hello as he walked up to the porch. "Good evening to you, ma'am. We're Kulaeva and Dana. We've taken rooms for the night. Are you Ms. Westinghouse?"

"I know who you are," she said, the remains of a Boston accent broadening her speech.

"We saw your web page online. The porch and the view sold us," Charlie told her, standing with one foot on the lowest of a dozen steps up to the landing.

"My grandson designed the online ad just a few months ago. The business is far from a gold mine, but perfect for a single, older woman of modest desires," she smiled slyly. "And it's quiet here, too. The nearest neighbors—a young couple from the hospital—are fifty yards away. We're kinda isolated. But I like it that way."

"We the only guests?" Sasha asked.

"No other guests at present, but three're due tomorrow. Come on up for coffee and fresh scones. And if you haven't eaten yet, I can fix you up a quick crab salad. No biggie," she said. "No trouble."

"Never, ever refuse crab," Charlie told her.

Seated around a sturdy oval table, with dishes now cleared, Verna Westinghouse and her guests drank from mugs of very strong, very hot coffee. A plate of snickerdoodles sat in the center of the table.

"So now, what brings you folks out to the Chain?" she asked.

"We're investigating the disappearance of a fisheries observer," Charlie said.

"Jimmy," the woman said quietly, her voice quavering. "Jimmy Lasorda, that dear, sweet boy. Lord, when the news broke that he might be gone, I went right on down to St. Christopher's, prayed all morning. Then I came home, went to bed and just cried my eyes out."

At this new information, Sasha and Charlie exchanged surprised looks.

"Ms. Westinghouse . . ." Charlie began.

"You can call me Verna."

"Verna. How well did you know him?"

"Why, I knew him *very* well. Very well indeed. For four years, at least. He rented a room with me whenever he was in port."

"Jimmy stayed with *you*?" Sasha said. "We assumed when he was here in Dutch, he stayed in the fishermen's dorm, the one down by the docks. We were going to go there tomorrow."

"Don't waste your time. He never stayed there. Not one time, I know of. He *always* boarded with me. Him and his lovely lady friend, Isabel. I gave 'em the upstairs corner, with a view of the lake. They doted on each other, those two." The old woman smiled sadly at the memory. "Isabel'd fly all the way from Anchorage just to spend a day or two with him."

"What can you tell us about him," Sasha asked. "I mean, when he was ashore."

Lost in her memories, the hostel owner ignored the

question and continued rhapsodizing about the missing young man.

"That sweet boy always brought me something special off the boats—crab legs, black cod, halibut cheeks. Sometimes something from the by-catch. Squid. Maybe octopus. Sometimes he'd bring me so much, I wouldn't have room in my freezer. He'd take it over to *The Sea Turtle*, put it in their walk-in. I'd go by and chip off a hunk of whatever I needed. What a Jimmy that was," she sighed. "What a nice boy. Just breaks my heart. Does Isabel know yet?"

"Verna," Charlie said. "I have bad news. More bad news, I'm afraid. Isabel Castro is dead. We're also investigating her death."

The woman had been sitting with her elbows on the table, but now, as if the life force had been punched out of her, she fell back into her wooden chair, put both hands over her face and began moaning, "Lord, lord, lord." She rocked from side to side, vocalizing in time with her swaying.

Sasha, in as tender a voice as Charlie had yet heard from the detective, said, "We are so sorry, Verna. We understand how much they meant to you." Sasha gave the woman a moment to collect herself. "We believe that Jimmy's disappearance and Isabel's death might be connected somehow. We're not sure how. Can you tell us anything about their actions when they were together here. Anything that might help us?"

The B and B owner let her hands fall gently onto her lap. She took a yellowed-with-age lace handkerchief out of her pants pocket, touched the corners of her eyes, inhaled, then spent the next twenty minutes telling the two law enforcement officers absolutely nothing of value. For all the woman knew, Jimmy counted fish, Isabel counted birds. They were a loving couple and treated each other with kindness and respect.

Charlie asked, "May we look at the room where Jimmy and Isabel stayed?"

"It's upstairs. Follow me."

Ten minutes later, they were back in the kitchen, none the wiser for the fruitless examination of the room where the missing man stayed several times a year.

When they were again seated, fresh cups of coffee just poured, Charlie asked, "Anyone besides Isabel ever visit him here?"

"No. It was just the two of them," Verna answered, then stopped and gazed off into space for a moment, closed her eyes, conjuring a lost thought. "Funny thing," she said.

"What's that, Verna?" Charlie asked.

"There was a guest here. Stayed for two nights. Said he was a photographer for some nature magazine. Audubon, I think he said. I gave him the room upstairs, opposite Jimmy's. He checked out this morning."

"Why is that funny?" Sasha asked.

"Well, I sleep downstairs, directly under Jimmy's corner room. Two nights ago, I heard footsteps and movement above me, in Jimmy's room. Which was empty, of course. I always held it for him. Never knew when he'd show up. He'd try to give me notice, but most of the time, just showed up."

"Go on," Sasha encouraged.

"Well, the noise went on for about five minutes before I decided to check. I should have gone up earlier to see what was going on, but I had a headache." Verna looked at the two policemen. "Actually, truth is, I was a little tipsy," she confessed. "My book club met last night and we sometimes drink a drop too much. Meryl brought us half a bottle of Chivas."

"Good for Meryl," Sasha said, nodding approvingly. "And? The noises?"

"Yes. Well, I got myself up, put on a robe, and started up the stairs. They squeak like the dickens so I'm sure I announced myself. When I got to the top of the landing, I lit the hall light and looked down the corridor, towards the corner rooms. The door to the photographer's room, opposite Jimmy's, was just closing. I'm sure of it. Jimmy's door was also closed. I walked down the hall and went into Jimmy's room, turned on the light and noticed right away that the place looked . . . well . . . not the way I usually leave it. The pillows were a tad askew and the bed spread was a little rumpled. I got a real creepy feeling and scooted outta the room and went back downstairs, lickety-split. I own a Smith and Wesson revolver. A six shooter. A .22. It's older than Methuselah but it works real good. Some of us girls go target shooting in the summer. I'm not bad inside of twenty feet. Beyond that, ain't much good at all. Well, I took the gun out of the closet where I keep it, loaded it up, and slept with it next to me. I also locked my door. I tell you frankly, I was spooked."

"And the photographer? What do you remember about him?" Charlie asked.

"He was a nice looking man. Really good looking, actually. Late thirties, I'd guess. Maybe forties. Very tall and strong looking. Blond, scruffy. He was wearing a red and black Pendleton shirt and a blue wind breaker. He was very charming. Spoke with an accent. Said he was born in a place called . . . . now let me think. Odessa, I believe he said. Isn't that in Texas?"

"Yes it is," Sasha said, exchanging a quick look with Charlie. "There's also an Odessa in southern Russia."

"Did he sign in? Do you remember his name?" Charlie asked.

"Don't need to look at the register. I remember his name. Archenko. Arkady Archenko," she pronounced carefully. "I remember it because it sounds so beautiful when you say it. Arkady Archenko. I thought it was a little unusual that he said he was a photographer 'cause he didn't have a scrap o' luggage. No camera. No tripod. Nothing. Not even a backpack. I'm not sure he had a toothbrush. But I didn't question it. People come for an overnight, they can come however they want. Don't even need pajamas in my place."

"When he checked out, did he mention where he was going, what he was going to do?" Sasha asked.

"I didn't see him when he checked out. I had already collected the two night's rent, hundred and ninety dollars. He paid in cash, left me two, one hundred dollar bills."

"Do you still have them?" Charlie asked.

"I do. Right here in my wallet. Wasn't able to get to the bank today."

Charlie took out his own wallet and removed a hundred and two fifties. "Can I trade you, Verna?"

"Don't see why not," she said, walking over to the kitchen counter where her wallet and keys were piled.

"If you don't mind," Charlie asked. "Could *I* take the bills out of your wallet? We'll check them for fingerprints. The Audubon photographer might be exactly who he says he is, but we'd like to double check."

Verna slid the wallet over to Charlie. He took out his Swiss Army knife, accessed the tweezers, and removed the bank notes. "Can I trouble you for a baggie, Verna?"

After a second round of coffee and cookies, their hostess excused herself and retired, letting her guests know that she'd be up for cooking just about anything the two of them might want for breakfast.

For the next hour, Sasha and Charlie compiled six pages of notes, first hand-written, then entered into the FBI agent's laptop. They began with their interview of the Coast Guard's Butch Kozol, then their time on the Russian fishing vessel talking with Captain Vronsky and the seven crew members they were able to question. They finished with the surprise of the day—the discovery that the recently vanished Jimmy Lasorda stayed in the *Bering Bridge B 'n B*, and that his room might have been searched by another guest, possibly a Russian.

"What's your take on the photographer," he asked.

"Here's what I'm thinking," she began. "Lasorda brought in heroin and delivered it to *'the connection,'* according to our boy, Rudy Castro. If the last shipment of heroin had *already* been delivered, there'd be no reason for anyone to be looking for it."

Charlie nodded. "And if he *hadn't* delivered it," he smiled at her, "then there'd be every reason to believe it was still here and reason to check out Lasorda's room. Verna told us that Archenko left the way he came–without any luggage. So, we can assume he did *not* find anything here."

"But his not finding it here in the B and B," Sasha offered, "doesn't mean that it's *not* here, somewhere in the house."

He considered. "OK. I'll take the kitchen. You scout out the other parts of the place you can get to without waking Verna."

After a quarter hour of unproductive searching, they reconnected back in the kitchen. Sasha yawned again, mightily and for the tenth time. He'd counted.

"It's twelve-fifteen Charlie. I'm done. I think that's all I can take for now." But she remained standing there, watching him.

Charlie felt himself stuck to his chair. *Come on. Just don't sit there, get up and go on over. Reach for her hand. She'll respond. Move, for Christ's sake,* his libido demanded.

"I'm going to go over the notes one more time," he said. "See you in the morning." *Charlie, you chickenshit.*

"Right." Sasha said. She stood there another few seconds more, turned and left the kitchen.

Charlie did not go over his notes. Instead, he sat there damning his own failure to act. This was not new territory for the FBI agent. He had been told 'no' often enough. But a 'no' from this woman would hurt. And then thinking about it, he realized that a 'yes,' might have proven equally unnerving.

~~~

They used the ship's mess to finish interviewing the remaining eleven crewmen. They learned nothing new. Sasha had even saved the three new crewmembers for last, hoping they might incriminate themselves, fall to their knees and confess their heinous crime. But they turned out to be nothing more than not-very-well-educated seamen.

Interviews all done and logged, Sasha asked to see the captain one final time. Vronsky came to the mess.

She and Charlie had debated informing him of Jimmy Lasorda's narcotics trafficking. Charlie argued against it. He couldn't dismiss the possibility that the ship's master was part of the program. What better cover for the American seaman, he suggested, than to have his captain's connivance in moving heroin into the United States?

It wasn't the craziest idea Sasha had ever heard but she didn't buy it. "I'm certain Vronsky's clean," she said. "I can't prove it, but my gut tells me. I think he'd be horrified if he knew the truth. I think we should let him in on what's been going down on his boat. He might have insights into Jimmy's activities in Vladivostok."

"Well, I'll trust your gut. Let's see how he reacts."

After her explanation of the missing American's smuggling, the ship's master jumped to his feet, a shocked expression on his face. He began storming about the small mess and in the most forceful epithets he dared use in front of this Russian-speaking policewoman, he let the world know just how furious he was.

"So, you're telling me that this Lasorda bastard brought drugs—heroin, of all things—into America. And on *my* boat. This is cause for deep shame for me personally, Aleksandra Petrovna. I feel, as the master of this vessel, that I'm an accomplice to his crime. It was bad enough to lose him overboard. But now, to learn that he was a smuggler . . ." The captain closed his eyes. *I don't deserve this fate. When the joint-venture partners find out about this, they'll want to know how I let this happen on my ship. I'm screwed.*

Charlie looked at Sasha. "Please ask the captain what he can tell us about Lasorda *before* he came aboard the ship. Where did he stay in Vladivostok? Did the captain ever see him with anyone on shore other than the crew?"

Sasha translated.

"He sailed with me on four different occasions. I'm not sure of the dates, but we've been at sea together four times, including this last time. My first mate keeps track of the crew. He might have better answers for you."

Five minutes later, Valery Timoshenko entered the mess, cap in hand. "He's been crew four times," the first mate confirmed.

"Do you remember where he stayed in Vlad? A hotel, maybe?" Sasha asked.

"He stayed at the same place all the American fishermen stay, the Slaviansky Bazaar."

"Can you describe it," she asked. "Where is it in relation to the port? What kind of people stay there? Is it an upscale place?"

Timoshenko smiled. "Definitely *not* upscale. It's a place for travelers, and for folks . . ." the first mate looked at the captain.

"It's a place where prostitutes and their pimps do business," Vronsky explained. "Everyone knows of it. It's as Valery says, definitely low class. Cheap."

"And where?" Sasha asked.

"Three blocks from the pier," Timoshenko answered. "On Aleyutskaya Street. You can see it from our usual berth, Pier Twenty-Six. It's a tall building, very run-down, with a fire escape that almost works."

"And how do you know that Lasorda always stayed there?" she asked.

"It's my job to keep track of the American observers when they get to Vlad. They're supposed to arrive a day or two before we ship out. The hotel manager calls me when they get in. I go and meet them, get them settled before we sail. They usually have a free day before they need to be on board."

"Any idea what Lasorda did while ashore?" Charlie asked.

"I know he was seeing a woman because three times she dropped him off at the ship. She had a really neat car. A Mercedes, I think. Four doors. Blue."

"Can you describe her?"

"I didn't get a real close look. But she was a brunette. Young. Short brown hair. Dark skin. She could have been a native, maybe Chukchi. She wore sunglasses, even in the winter. They'd get out of her car. They'd kiss. He'd grab his bag and come aboard."

"How much gear did he usually have?"

"Couple duffel bags, seemed pretty heavy."

"Anyone else in the car?"

"Not that I could see."

"Besides the girl, what else was Lasorda into when he was in Vlad?"

"Don't know," the first mate said.

Charlie thanked the man. Timoshenko seemed relieved and left the mess.

Sasha turned to the captain. "Yury Gregorovich. I know how much you did *not* want to be here, but, believe it or not, you have helped us a great deal. We are very appreciative."

"You are very welcome Aleksandra Petrovna. And you're right. I did *not* want to come to Dutch Harbor. But, after all is said and done, I'm thankful that I got a chance to meet you. You are . . . special." Vronsky smiled at her.

Sasha eyed Charlie with a 'See, somebody likes me' look.

He also smiled. "Yeah, somebody."

Vronsky said, "You told me you'll be in my city next week, for a conference. I want to repeat my invitation. I'd be happy, very happy if you would stop by, say hello.

Please, I'm serious."

"I know you are and I promise you that I'll do my utmost to find time to come and visit."

They left the mess and came out on deck just as the Coast Guard launch cruised up to the side of the Russian trawler.

"Not a total loss," she said to Charlie. "We got something. How many blue, four door Mercedes do you suppose there are in Vladivostok?"

"Driven by lovely brunettes," he added.

~~~

Back in Kozol's office, a sense of inadequate resolution pervaded. "Where do we go from here?" the guardsman asked.

Sasha said, "Unless Jimmy Lasorda washes ashore showing bullet holes in his chest or a knife stuck in his ribs, there's not a hell of a lot we can do. No witnesses to his disappearance. Any ideas, Charlie?"

"Not a one. Legally, since there's no body, no evidence of a crime, no witnesses, then what we've got is a simple presumed drowning. An accident."

"Fine. That's enough for the Coast Guard," Kozol said.

"We're on our way back to Anchorage in the morning," Charlie said. "Don't forget the list of Lasorda's previous berths and the same info for any other Americans shipping out from Russian ports."

"Almost done. Soon as I finish, I'll shoot it to you in Anchorage. Meanwhile, let me know if I can help in any other way."

"We will," the FBI agent said.

Back in their rental car, Sasha asked, "You were working your phone this morning. Learn anything?"

"No surprise that no one named Arkady Archenko has arrived or left Unalaska by commercial air in the past three weeks. Audubon magazine never heard of him. I called the local cops and asked their help in finding the guy. I gave them the description Verna Westinghouse provided. I called the rent-a-car. He hasn't returned his car yet. And, so far as we know, he hasn't committed a crime. Unless checking into a B and B without a toothbrush constitutes a misdemeanor."

"Right," she said. "But we still need to find out what he was doing in Jimmy Lasorda's room."

"Can it wait until after dinner? I'm starving."

~~~

Rose was numb, parked in front of the TV, sound off, watching a CNN anchor mime the news about the latest suicide bombing in the Middle East. Rose was indifferent to the bloodletting. She was absorbed in planning the most important phone call she'd ever make. *A life line? I wish I had one to use.*

The tea she had brewed to soothe her nerves wasn't working. She gripped the mug with trembling hands and scarcely kept them from sloshing Oolong all over her lap. She felt queasy. *No way in hell this is gonna work.*

The Russian man said he would call after eight to find out how persuasive she'd been, how she'd convinced her ex boyfriend to keep his mouth shut. *Right. And all Rudy wanted to do was make bail and disappear.*

It was now half past six. She had ninety minutes to

practice what she was going to say to the man. So the Russian wouldn't kill her.

Her eyes moved to the second hand on her kitchen's wall clock, dragging her, inexorably, into a future she wanted to avoid at all costs. She now understood what it must be like for someone's last hours on death row, waiting for the jailer with the syringe or the noose to come knocking.

Finally eight o'clock. No call. Five past. Nothing. Then at a quarter past, her cell phone chimed. She let it ring three times, then punched the green button. "Hello," she said, astounded at how composed she sounded.

There was no immediate response. In the empty background, she thought she heard the swish/scrape of windshield wipers. And then a muffled blast from something that sounded like a foghorn. *What gives?*

"How did your talk go with Rudy?" the man finally asked.

Rose quickly scanned the scripted notes in front of her. She took a deep breath. "Went okay. He's not as stupid as I thought. He understands what'll happen if he talks. He's agreed to keep quiet." She read the words slowly, trying to make them sound natural, unrehearsed. "I didn't have to be that persuasive. When I described our meeting in the parking lot, he panicked." She had written, 'pause.' She waited a moment, then kept on with the text. "He's worried about my safety. He said he'll never say anything."

"And . . .?"

She was ready for the tough part, the hard sell. "He said he's ready to do the time the prosecutor warned him he'd get if he doesn't cooperate."

There was a long silence on the other end. "I'll call

back in a few minutes," the man said and hung up.

Rose closed her phone and walked to the bathroom. She dropped down onto her hands and knees in front of the toilet, put her head over the bowl, and purged the tea and the little bit of rice that had been dinner. She flushed, struggled to her feet, and washed her face. She quickly returned to the toilet, dropped her slacks and panties, sat down, and purged again. Everything that had been inside was now outside. She was officially empty. She shuffled back to her living room as a frail ninety-year-old might shuffle, sat on the sofa, and jittered. A minute later, the Russian called back.

"Good work, Rose. I'll be in touch with you soon." The line went dead.

Rose lay back onto her sofa, curled her knees into her chest, and covered her head with a blanket.

~~~

"Best food in town is at *The Sea Turtle*," Verna Westinghouse explained. "Get the seafood chowder. Nothing beats it. Jimmy and Isabel ate there all the time. I'll call Sean, the owner. Let him know you're coming."

After quick showers, a change of clothes, and a short drive into town, Sasha and Charlie rolled into the restaurant. The place was full up, all nine tables occupied, with another half a dozen expectant customers crowded around the front counter.

Verna's call to alert the owner brought Sean Carmody right over. He was a large, ginger-bearded and affable East Coast Irishman with an affected brogue he put on for the clientele. He led the two cops to a just-vacated table in front of a huge picture window.

Sasha watched many of the waiting-to-eat diners grumble to each other, clearly annoyed at the preferential treatment given to these two, obviously, out-of-towners.

Charlie and Sasha didn't bother with the menu. They ordered the recommended chowder and beers. When the bottles of Pauli Girl showed up, Sasha had to clamp down on her desire to chug straight from the bottle. She allowed Charlie to pour her beer into a frosted mug, then took a polite sip. *So dignified.*

The chowder came piping hot and savory smelling. They dug in without preamble and spent the next ten minutes sampling the variety of fresh-caught seafood. Between mouthfuls, they dunked chunks of warm sourdough bread into the chowdery broth. They only paused when Carmody stopped by. After receiving praise for his culinary skills, Charlie told him about the death of Isabel Castro. He took the news hard. Not with as much heartbreak as Verna Westinghouse, but with enough sadness in his face and in his tone of voice to tell the Anchorage investigators that the two deceased had a good friend in Sean Carmody.

"That both Jimmy and Isabel should perish in the same few days. It's inconceivable," the restaurant owner said. "I'm thinking their deaths might be related. Am I right?"

Charlie was noncommittal, shrugged. "Could be." He downed half a scallop. "Verna mentioned that Jimmy would occasionally store fish for her. In your freezer."

"He did. Several times a year Jimmy'd bring large packages of fish, put 'em in our walk-in. Verna'd stop by, take some for herself. Jimmy marked those packages with her name. But more often he left packages for Isabel."

"How often would that be?" Sasha asked, a small antenna rising. "That there'd be something here for Isabel?"

"Maybe every other month, maybe more frequently. There's actually some fish in the freezer for Isabel right now. It has her name on it. What should I do with it?"

"Let's take a peek," Charlie suggested.

"Jack, it's Sasha." She was back at the table, speaking into her smart phone, a second beer in her off hand.

"Hey Sasha. Tell me that you've solved Lasorda's disappearance and that I can justify the expense of sending you to Unalaska," the detective captain answered.

"Best we can do is to write it off as an accident. I'll fill you in on the details tomorrow when we get back to town. But I'm bringing you a present."

"Make it about half a dozen crab legs and you can have the rest of the week off."

"Better than crab legs."

"Impossible."

"How 'bout approximately twenty-five pounds of the same stuff we found in Rudy Castro's place, all packaged nice and neat."

There was a long silence on the other end of the line. "You shittin' me?"

"Meet me at the airport tomorrow. You'll see if I'm shittin' you. We're catching the morning flight."

"You're *not* kidding. Has Dana phoned this in to Emmitt yet?"

"Not yet, but Emmitt'll know soon enough."

"And the big mouth at the DEA, Cardozo. I'm not in a rush to let him know."

"No one is. Let him stew. But do me a favor and tell Gary. He'll get a kick."

"I will. Alright then. We'll see you tomorrow at the airport. I'll let TSA know what's in your baggage."

"See you, Jack. Mark one up for the good guys."

"An amazing score, Sasha. We're happy."

At the intersection of West Broadway and 4th Street, a brown Toyota rental was parked, its windshield wipers working just fast enough to allow the two passengers in the front seat to watch *The Sea Turtle*, across the street and midway down the block. The man in the passenger seat used a set of Nikon binoculars to bring the dining couple into clear focus. The two men had arrived by private plane from Anchorage, five hours earlier. In the Toyota's back seat, a third man was snoring.

The watchers had gotten lucky: the FBI agent and the woman cop they were keeping in view were sitting at a table by a large, street-facing window. They were served dinner and were soon joined by a red-headed man who sat down and said something that caught the attention of the other two. All three stood and disappeared from view.

The man with the binoculars checked his watch, then made a phone call. As he was dialing, rain began pelting the car. He ramped up the wipers. They thumped noisily with each back and forth stroke. In the distance, the sound of a fog horn rumbled in from the coast.

A woman answered his call. He listened while she described to him her visit with her incarcerated boyfriend.

"Good work, Rose. I'll be in touch with you soon." The man disconnected and turned to the driver. "Bitch is lying. Says the brother's gonna clam up and do the time. No way that'll happen."

"Look, they're back," the driver said, pointing at the restaurant.

The passenger raised his binoculars.

The cop and the federal agent returned to their table. The woman carried a large package. She was smiling. She said something to the other man as they sat down. He laughed. She placed the package under the table, then used her phone. A minute later, the FBI agent made a call.

The watcher in the Toyota's passenger seat, with close-cropped brown hair and a small scar over his left eye, squirmed. He put down his binoculars, took out his cell phone, and called Brooklyn again. "The two from Anchorage have found a large package, wrapped in the usual way."

There was a short reply, then the line went dead.

The Toyota's driver looked at the passenger. "Well?"

"We're waiting for an answer. We're to stay with them. They'll get back to us right away."

The man in the back seat, a large blond man in a red Pendleton shirt and blue windbreaker, continued snoring.

Less than five minutes later, the cell phone rang. The man in the passenger seat listened closely. "Understood," he said, then ended the call.

"So?" the driver asked.

The man in the back seat, sat up and rubbed his eyes. "What's up?"

"The two cops have the package. We get it and fly out," said the man in the passenger seat.

"The two cops have the package?" The man in the back seat sounded intense. "Taking it from them could be risky."

The man with the binoculars turned to face the rear seat. "You have a problem with that, Kostya?" he asked.

"Not in the least, Denis. I look forward to it."

~~~

They were giddy. They'd won the lottery. The Power Ball millions were waiting to be collected.

The detective and the FBI agent couldn't stop smiling. They drove back to their lodgings full of themselves, full of each other. And a twenty-five pound package of smuggled heroin, resting on the back seat of their rent-a-car, was the reason.

"We got lucky, Charlie," Sasha said from the passenger seat. "I mean, I wish I could say we were great cops, that we had taken a page out of Sherlock's book and *deduced* where to find the shit. That would've been cool. But, really, we got lucky."

"Somebody once said, 'I'd rather be lucky than good.' I think it was a ball player," Charlie said.

Sasha looked through the windshield. The late afternoon's downpour had softened to a damp mist. "We don't eat at *The Sea Turtle*, that box in the back seat is still in the freezer."

He looked over at Sasha, her eyes closed, smiling. For the next minute he shifted his view back and forth, highway/ Sasha. His earlier critique of her interrogation methods, her flaunting of the constitutional guarantees he so valued seemed less important at this moment. Right now, he was swimming in happy waters, happy to be in her company.

Perhaps sensing she was being watched, Sasha opened

her eyes, her smile getting even broader, stretching ear to ear.

"You look like the cat that ate the cheese," he said to her.

"That's how I'm feeling," she answered quietly, then slowly extended her left arm toward him. Very gently, she stroked his right hand as it gripped the steering wheel, her nails lightly scoring the backs of his fingers. He let his hand come off the wheel to take hers. He steered lefty the rest of the way to the B and B.

By the time they drove up to their lodgings, the mist had evaporated, leaving the air fresh and smelling of the sea. A half moon slipped in and out between clouds, alternately illuminating then darkening the meadows around the hostel. An unseasonably warm breeze floated up from the water, fanning the tall grass bordering the parking lot and bringing with it the sound of an occasional fog horn.

They held hands on the way to the front steps, Charlie carrying their precious cargo in his other hand.

At the bottom step, Sasha unlaced her fingers. "Can't give Verna and her girlfriends too much gossip at their next ladies' night," she joked.

Charlie reached down for the hand she had just freed, took it back, and pulled her gently to him. He kissed her once, lightly, on the lips. "I've got bubble bath," he said.

A breeze fluttered his hair. She cleared aside a thatch that was covering his forehead. "'Bubble bath', the man says. Think that'll get me into the tub with you, Agent Dana?"

"I bought it two days ago." He paused. "In anticipation."

She pressed into him. "I knew all along you were a Boy Scout. *Be Prepared.* Isn't that the Scout motto?"

"*It is. Lavender bubble bath.*"

"Oooh. Lavender," she said. "My fave."
They had adjoining rooms, upstairs, at the end of the corridor. Charlie was in the last room, the one occupied recently by the elusive Arkady Archenko. If that was his real name. From Odessa. If that was his real birthplace.

Sasha had the next, adjoining room, nearer the stairs. A large bathroom, trimmed with Mexican tile and accessible through interior bedroom doors, was sandwiched between their rooms. An ancient claw foot tub–easily big enough for two–was the bathroom's main feature.

Since they were the only guests, there was no shortage of hot water, now steamy, bubbly, and lavender-fragrant. Charlie was sunk up to his neck. The only light in the room was a single, rose colored candle on the bathroom's sink, oozing wax down onto the sink's tiled surface.

Sasha, still dressed, prepared the bed in Charlie's room, turning down the heavy comforter and top sheet. Then she went to the window, cracked it open to the spring breeze. She half-closed the dark drapes. The idea of rustling curtains providing a backdrop to what was coming in the next few minutes appealed to her.

The bedroom ready, she went into the bathroom and burst into laughter. Charlie's entire head was now covered with bubbles. Only his eyes were visible.

"Don't be frightened, little girl," he said in his creepiest voice. "You'll be safe in the water, here with me."

She began unbuttoning her blouse, then knelt by the tub and gently parted the bubbles that surrounded his mouth. She leaned over the tub and kissed him deeply. At the same time, she pushed up her right sleeve to the elbow and went fishing. She reached below the water and delicately scratched his left nipple, then slid her fingers down his stomach. Finding what she was seeking, she grabbed hold. She was thrilled, relieved, happy. *The Boy Scout's prepared.* She began slowly stroking him and with her left hand, began to unbutton her blouse.

The gravel-crunching sound of a car entering the B and B's parking lot caught her attention. The engine idled a moment, then quit.

"Those'll be the guests Verna told us about," she whispered to him. "So you'll have to keep your screaming to an acceptable level."

"Boy Scouts never scream," he said. "We just moan."

"Moaning is permitted," she said, laughing, continuing to stroke him, and working on her shirt's fourth button.

The sound of a short, guarded conversation—a few unintelligible words—came up from the car park. Sasha froze. Another snatch of conversation—familiar sounding this time—then the sound of footsteps on gravel. She rose up quickly and rushed to the window. She peeked through the curtains just as the clouds parted enough for the moon's light to shine down on three men moving at a trot toward the building. One carried a rifle, the other two, hand guns. Sasha raced back to the bathroom and grabbed the guest robe hanging from the door.

"Russians, Charlie. With guns! Get up. Now!" she commanded, tossing the robe next to the tub. He hesitated long enough to earn him a rough, "Move it. And douse the candle." He moved, then doused.

Sasha found her belt and holster and with quivering fingers strapped on her weapon. She popped and checked the Glock's magazine. Satisfied, she rammed home the clip and pumped a round into the chamber, then went to the bedroom door, cracked it ajar.

Charlie emerged from the bathroom a moment later, robe half open, bubbles sticking to his hair and neck. She thought to comment but decided against it. "Get your weapon, check the magazine," she whispered. "And dry your hands first."

The constitutional law teacher realized he was seriously and dangerously out of his element and decided he needed to do exactly as the detective ordered. He ran to his briefcase, took out his Glock, released the magazine, verified it was full, pushed it back into the grip.

"Chamber a round," she ordered.

"Christ," he said, then complied.

"You have an extra clip, I'm hoping," she asked urgently.

"No. This is it." His shoulders rose and fell with each rapidly drawn breath. He stood there in his half-open bathrobe, pistol in hand, waiting for her to tell him what to do.

The downstairs screen door creaked open, and a moment later, closed with a bang. Light footfalls in the entrance hall. And now the B and B owner's voice, kindly at first, inquiring, then agitated, argumentative. A yell. The sound of a blow striking flesh. A body hitting the floor. Then the report of a silenced gun shot, dampened, but unmistakable. Then a second gun shot.

"They shot Verna," Sasha gasped. She looked frantically around the room, then dashed over and lit the table lamps on either side of the bed. Charlie looked at her, wildly, wonderingly.

The detective explained in a frantic whisper: "All the other rooms, toward the stairs, are dark. We need to lure them down the hall, toward this room."

"And then . . . ?"

"I hope they'll think we're the only two here and come straight toward the light, won't check every room. I'll wait in my room. When they pass my door, heading here, I'll come out. I'll be in back of them."

"What do you want me to do?"

"Lock the door and get behind the bed. If there's firing, shoot through the wall and the door where you think they are. They should be right in front of your door. Don't come out into the hall. Stay in the room. We'll have them in a crossfire. Got it?"

"I guess."

"Take your time. We can do this, Charlie. You with me?"

"Yeah. I think so," he gulped.

"OK." Sasha glanced out the door, down the hall, toward the stairs. The men were in the stairwell, giving notice, squeaking as they ascended.

"Here they come," she said in a hushed voice, and ran quietly into the bathroom and to the door that connected to her bedroom. She eased herself into her darkened room and went over to the hall door. She could sense them now in the corridor, gliding along the carpet toward their two rooms. She adjusted her grip on the Glock. Why did her weapon seem lighter than usual? Had she forgotten to put in the clip? With her off-hand she felt for the magazine. It was there, of course. *Calm the fuck down. Breathe.*

Sasha heard the floor in the hall give as they slid past her door, heading further down the corridor, toward the light, toward Charlie's room. When she sensed they'd come to his door, she grasped the doorknob, tested the turn slightly, then yanked it open and sprang into the hall, crouching, gun up.

Everything now in super slow motion.

The two men had just arrived at Charlie's door. They never saw her coming until it was far too late. Sasha was firing her weapon as soon as she was able. No warning. No announcement. No "Drop you weapons." Just nine millimeter bullets ripping into easily yielding flesh.

She was no more than ten feet from the men. The Russian closest to her was standing sideways. He was carrying a pistol in his right hand. Sasha's first bullet struck him high in his left shoulder, spinning him around to face her. An astonished expression on his face, a gaping, pained mouth. Before he could raise his gun, Sasha fired a second time. The bullet struck him square in the middle of his chest and with such force that he was knocked backwards into the other Russian, the one carrying a shotgun. The collision drove the second man to a position directly in front of Charlie's room. Shots from inside that room exploded through the door and wall. Sasha's third shot, aimed at the second man, missed. Her fourth did not. It struck him in the lower throat, sending a geyser of blood spraying the window at the end of the corridor. She fired once more into the second man, hitting him in the stomach.

"Charlie, stop firing," she yelled. "Cease firing. They're down." The entire action had taken less than five seconds. Charlie's door was riddled with bullet holes.

The downstairs screen door slammed shut—the third man. She ran to the window at the end of the hall, next to Charlie's door. She had to climb over the two men and slipped in the pool of blood that was spurting out of the second Russian's throat. *Hit his carotid artery. He'll be dead in less than a minute.* She got to the window just as Charlie opened the door and stood, his entire body shivering wildly.

She ignored him and looked out the window. The third Russian was running toward his car at the edge of the parking lot. Sasha saw the window was painted shut. She kicked out the single pane of glass, aimed and fired at the fleeing man. The first two shots were wide, but when he got to his car and stopped briefly while trying to open the driver's-side door, Sasha's third bullet found the back of his thigh. He bellowed in pain and fell to the ground.

"I'm going after him," Sasha said. She had to once again step over the Russian shot through the throat. Dead or close to it. The other, the first man she shot, groaned slightly. As she passed over him, she paused, glanced at Charlie, lowered her weapon, and from a foot above the man, shot the Russian once in the heart. She noted the surprised look on Charlie's face. Then she spun around and ran down the hallway.

At the bottom of the stairs, at the entrance to the living room, the body of their hostess, bullet holes in the stomach and in the forehead. Sasha didn't need to check Verna for a pulse. The woman was gone. The detective exited the B and B carefully. *Maybe there are more than three.* She changed magazines on the fly as she ran crouching, down the steps and across the gravel, to the man she had just wounded.

Charlie Dana, FBI agent/law teacher, never dreamed he would ever have to shoot anyone. The last thing he wanted to do. He stared at the Russian man near his door, bleeding out from half a dozen wounds, major and minor. His bullets or Sasha's? Would he ever know? Did it matter? He examined the weapon in his shaking hand, as if it had a life of its own, as if *it* had shot the Russian without Charlie's involvement.

Then, a pained voice from the parking lot made him

snap to. He carefully stepped over the Russian, trying to avoid the rapidly enlarging pool of blood that was collecting on the hall carpet. The smell of warm blood, now mixed with the stink of fecal matter, brought up a biley taste of seafood chowder. He forced it back down and looked through the shattered window. The clouds had cleared and the half moon lit the parking lot, clearly etching the wounded Russian. He was lying face down, next to his car, holding his thigh, writhing and screaming.

Sasha advanced carefully toward the wounded man. He was on his stomach near the car. She could see he was a big man, light hair, wearing a red Pendleton shirt and a blue windbreaker. Arkady Archenko. Just as Verna had described him.

She kicked away his weapon, noting the silencer. "You killed Verna," she told him, frisking him for other weapons.

The man was clearly in agony, though his wound was more fleshy than fatal. She put the Glock to the back of his neck.

"Stop complaining, ass wipe. We have some talking to do."

She took a plastic zip tie from her belt and secured his hands behind him, then lifted him into a sitting position and propped him against the car. She kneeled in front of him. "Name?" No response. "You don't tell me your name, I'm going to bust you in the nose with this pistol." She brought the weapon close to his eyes. "Name?" she repeated. Silence. Sasha stood, reached back and swung the Glock against the man's nose. Whack. His head banged against the car's door.

She wiped her weapon and resumed her kneeling position in front of the man. Blood was cascading down his nose and into his mouth.

"Let's try it again. Name?"

"Arkady. Arkady Archenko," he sputtered.

"No, that's not your name," Sasha said, putting the barrel of her weapon on the man's pants zipper. "You have one more chance before I blow your cock off."

"Konstantin," he said quickly.

"Family name?"

"Zhuganov."

"How can I be sure you're not lying? Maybe I'll just shoot you in the knee," Sasha said, sliding the pistol down the man's leg.

"Christ, no," the wounded man begged. "Zhuganov is my name. I swear."

Sasha noticed a slight bulge in his shirt pocket. She reached over and removed a pack of cigarettes. Sobranie.

"Your two friends," she asked, "they smoke Sobranie, or just you?"

The Russian seemed surprised by the question. "Just me," he said as she replaced the pack in his pocket. Blood was dripping into his mouth. "My brother is going to cut your cunt out when he hears about this," he said, defiantly.

"Oh, he'll hear all about it, Konstantin. Probably tomorrow. He'll read all about it in the paper. About the big shootout in the Aleutians, and how three Russians were killed trying to find a shipment of heroin Jimmy Lasorda smuggled into Dutch. Tell me the name of the person in Anchorage who gets the heroin, the guy Lasorda passed it to. You tell me his name, I let you live."

The wounded man looked around wildly. "I don't know. I was never told." He paused. Then with a dawning realization, "*Three* Russians were killed?"

"Yeah, the three of you. The two stiffs upstairs and you. You killed Verna. And you tortured and killed Isabel Castro."

The man's eyes widened. "Please. For God's sake. Don't kill me."

"I'll bet that's what Isabel said. She probably begged you not to kill her."

The man started to shake. "I don't know who the person is in Anchorage. But if I tell you the name of my boss in Brooklyn, will you let me live?"

"Sure. Tell me the name, you live."

"Gasparov, Gennady Gasparov," the man rushed to say. "We call him GG."

"Gennady Gasparov," she repeated. "Why don't I believe you? Huh, Konstantin? Doesn't really matter anyhow." She stood, backed up a dozen paces, and raised her pistol. "It's time."

Shouting from the B and B made her pause and look toward the building. Charlie Dana sounded a million miles away. "Sasha, for Chris sakes. Don't. Stop. Don't do it. Don't do it."

She watched Charlie, heard his plea. She flashed back to the Anchorage pedophile pastor she had disposed of. That bit of vigilante-ism had caused her a short-lived bout of contrition, a fleeting onset of remorse. But she easily came to grips with both of those kindred feelings when she weighed the man's crime and the benefits to society of the churchman's elimination. She hadn't been proud of herself. But neither had she felt shamed by her action.

Now, the sound of Konstantin Zhuganov's bowels giving way brought her back to real time. The man was crying out for his mother. Sasha looked again at the FBI agent then turned and shot Arkady/Konstantin twice in the center of his chest.

"Fucker. You fucking killer," Charlie yelled.

Detective Sasha Kulaeva stood quietly for a moment then went to the dead man. She rolled him onto his stomach, clipped off the plastic tie with her switchblade, and put the pieces in her pocket. She picked up the man's pistol, cleaned off her own fingerprints, put the gun in the corpse's hand and, using his finger, fired a shot into the B and B's front wall.

She looked up at Charlie. "You can call the police now, Agent Dana." Her voice seemed dead to her.

~~~

Leonid Bulgarin, cousin to Boris Bunin, had been tuned into the police frequency since five that afternoon. He was praying that the pair of passengers he had flown to Dutch Harbor were staying out of trouble.

Leonid knew the two men, knew the kind of work they did for Boris. And he also knew the big blond man who came to collect them. That one, that brute, Kostya Zhuganov, had ordered the pilot to stay put and be ready to fly away with little notice. Leonid would follow orders. He knew better than to disobey Zhuganov.

The pilot was at his wit's end. He blinked spasmodically and jumped at every sound coming from the field next to his plane. His shoulders rose and dropped as though operated by an invisible puppeteer.

This is not what I signed up for, he thought, recalling the events of the autumn, 2004, lunch with his cousin in

Manhattan. Boris had offered to set him up in an air taxi business in Alaska. Although Leonid had been skeptical during the calamari, by the time the cannoli and coffee were put in front of him, he had been successfully seduced. The capper came when Boris hinted at the possibility of flights to the Russian Far East, to Vladivostok and Khabarovsk. Leonid imagined himself atop an airy kingdom, jetting around the globe. *A dream job,* he'd thought then. *Not so dreamy now.*

And when he brought the news home that night to his wife, she went ballistic. "Getting involved with Boris Bunin is a one way ticket to an early grave," Dorotea warned, not for the first time. "He's a gangster. A murderer. I'm begging you, Leo, begging you, do *not* take his money."

His wife's warnings fell on deaf ears and within a few years, Grizzly Air, his new Alaskan air taxi business, was doing just fine. The original two Beechcraft became a fleet of several medium-range aircraft that catered to oil company executives as they flew back and forth between Anchorage and the North Slope. Alaska's oil patch paid handsomely.

As did the great outdoors. Leonid flew Japanese and Swedish hunters and anglers to Alaska's wilderness where they fished in unnamed waters and hunted animals whose heads came to adorn woody dens in Stockholm and Tokyo.

And several times a year, he flew out to the Bering Sea, to St. Lawrence Island. There, he reconnoitered with an Eskimo man—a boat captain—and took receipt of an oil-skin-wrapped parcel, sometimes two.

Those were the flights that caused Leonid to lose sleep. He didn't fool himself about what he was collecting. He knew. And that certain knowledge caused his flights back to Anchorage to be excruciatingly nerve-wracking. And, of course, he never mentioned any of this to Dorotea.

Sitting now in his plane and glued to the radio's police band, the pilot recalled that during that fateful lunch, Boris had noted—a throw-away comment, really—that Leonid might occasionally be called upon to provide unspecified assistance in some unspecified future. When pressed, Boris had been vague.

Leonid had succeeded in shoving that part of their conversation to the back of his brain. He never imagined that unspecified assistance might require his participation in the 'wet work' that often—at least according to Dorotea—characterized the Bunin business empire.

But here he was, listening intently to the police frequency, praying *not* to hear anything that would indicate that his passengers and the local police were getting to know one another.

He didn't sleep, wouldn't dare shut his eyes, had to be alert and ready to get the Cessna Caravan off the ground at a moment's notice. He left his pilot's seat once an hour to pace around his craft, to pee, to stretch. Luckily there was no one around. No one within a mile. He'd landed at a long-abandoned airfield north of town, a relic of the last world war.

Around eleven, eight hours after they had landed, the airfield remained dead quiet, the only sound, an occasional spattering of rain that gently thrummed against his plane's fuselage.

Then, far in the distance—*Oh God, please no*—he thought he heard popping. Popping? Gunshots? *Please let it be fireworks. Or a car backfiring. Not gunshots. Please.*

He strained eyes and ears through the darkness in the direction of the sounds. There was nothing to be seen. Then, once again, three more pops, then a long silence, maybe five minutes, then two more pops, then one, then silence again. He climbed into the cockpit and listened with his entire body to the police band. Almost immediately, it crackled to life with the unthinkable—all available police vehicles were told to converge at an address, report of multiple shots, possible fatalities.

"Fuck me," Leonid screamed, his armpits dampening. *"I am royally fucked,"* he shouted heavenward.

He would've loved to crank up the engines and get the plane airborne. Clear out. Head home. He could be back in Anchorage by first light. He knew, however, that was not an option cousin Boris might allow him to consider. *Don't even go there.*

The pilot had to wait, to verify what was going on. He took his smart phone into sweaty palms and called Brooklyn. He reported what he had just learned over the police scanner and was told exactly what he knew he would be told—don't move until the men had returned. He closed his cell phone and stayed put.

Over the next several hours, as the sky in the east lightened, the pilot lived in his radio and heard a steady and often conflicting recounting of what was going on. Around six in the morning, the game was over. The score: three men dead, initially identified as Russian, one dead American woman. Leonid called Brooklyn and reported the bad news. His marching orders came at once: "Get out, right now."

Leonid was in the air in less than three minutes, heading back to his home in Anchorage. He fully expected a bitter round of "I told you so," from Dorotea. Maybe they could sell the business and go back to Russia. Maybe. Probably not. Permission from his cousin would not be forthcoming.

Gaining altitude over the Aleutian Chain, Leonid put the plane on autopilot, cupped his face with his palms, and began to sob. *Dorotea's going to kill me. I am so totally fucked.*

~~~

Within twenty minutes of Charlie Dana's call to the local police, most every one of Dutch Harbor's emergency first responders were swarming inside and outside the B and B: all thirteen members of the Police Department, including two off-duty patrolmen and a part-time dispatcher; a retired Alaska State Trooper from Fairbanks visiting his ex-wife; four firemen, two paid, two volunteer; five EMT/paramedics; three doctors—a cardiologist, an obstetrician, and an eyes, ears, nose and throat specialist; four nurses; and three city councilmen, one in pajama tops under his hastily thrown on hoodie. They were milling, staring. Some who had never seen the bloody aftermath of what bullets can do to human flesh had raced to the side of the building to give back their dinners.

Only the Chief of Police, Stanislaw Babiarsz, born in Lodz, Poland, and a former Chicago South Side policeman, seemed to know what to do. The big boned, five-foot-ten, two hundred pounder, with close set black eyes under a single dark brow had seen scores of gun shot victims. From the Windy City, after all.

The chief first instructed the medical technicians to verify that none of the four people on the ground or in the building with bullet holes in them was still alive. He roped off the body in the parking lot, ordered 'crime scene' tape to surround the house and grounds, had all non-essential personnel herded beyond the tape, and told them all to go home. None did. He left his forensic team to sort out the mess of bodies, while he met with the two survivors—an exceedingly calm Anchorage detective, and an FBI agent who seemed on the verge of collapse. He asked the federal agent to wait while he interviewed the policewoman.

Babiarsz led Detective Kulaeva around the remains of Verna Westinghouse and into the B and B's kitchen. He closed the sliding doors and sat down opposite the Anchorage policewoman. He wondered about her name. *Kulaeva. Russian? And the three dead men, apparently also Russian. What gives?* He opened his notebook, pen in hand. "So, Detective Kulaeva. Exactly what the fuck happened here?"

Sasha explained that the Russians were stick-up guys, come to rob anyone staying in the B and B. Were armed and threatening. Killed the hotel owner. She and the FBI agent tried to arrest them. They resisted. A gun battle ensued with the obvious bloody consequences. "That's pretty much it, Chief," Sasha concluded.

Babiarsz listened and took notes. *If that isn't the craziest fucking story I've ever heard* he thought. Especially after she explained that she and the federal agent had come to Dutch Harbor to interview the crew of a *Russian* boat from which an American fisheries observer had disappeared. *Lots of Russian shit,* the Polish-born cop thought. *Hate those mother fuckers!*

The Chicago Police Department veteran knew for a dead certainty that there was something seriously flawed about the woman's account, major details she was obviously leaving out. But the police chief understood he didn't have the juice to challenge her story. She was an APD detective sergeant, after all, and the man, an FBI agent. Stan Babiarsz, having been schooled in the murky and labyrinthine workings of Chicago's PD, knew enough to take their statements as given to him. He'd pass them up the ladder.

After hearing her oral account, he asked the police-woman to leave the kitchen and write out her statement. Then it was Charlie Dana's turn.

If the woman had been the picture of tranquility, the federal agent seemed a basket case—visibly quaking, wrapped in a blanket that should have warmed him, given the spring-like weather. The FBI agent appeared to be listening, but when Babiarsz asked for details, the light in Charlie's eyes dimmed.

Babiarsz knew from the bullet holes in the upstairs door that the fed had participated in the shooting. The chief was more interested in what had occurred in the parking lot. "Tell me, Agent Dana. What did you observe from the window?"

Charlie stared at a point on the floor, shook his head. "I didn't see what happened. After Detective Kulaeva ran downstairs, I went back into my room, sat on the bed, and called the police."

"Uh huh. And how long did that take? For you to call the police?"

Dana stared at Babiarsz. "Dunno. Few minutes, maybe. Maybe longer." Dana crossed one leg over the other, then reversed the process.

"So you didn't see anything, right? But you must have heard the shooting from the parking lot?"

"I'm not sure. I was pretty . . . not with it, I guess."

Babiarsz waited a minute for more information, but the FBI agent had apparently said everything he was going to say. *Okay,* the chief thought. *Looks like a conspiracy of silence.*

"Thanks, Agent Dana. Let me have your written statement, please."

Charlie nodded.

The chief completed his note taking, left the kitchen, and met with the medical crew examining the body of Verna Westinghouse.

Sasha rejoined Charlie in the kitchen. Neither spoke. He kept his eyes turned away. She made coffee, brought him a cup and placed it next to him. He seemed indifferent to both the brew and the gesture.

Sasha left him and found Babiarsz upstairs. His medical team had two body bags open, ready for filling.

"Chief. Any chance Dana and I can leave town tomorrow on the morning plane? That's what we planned to do. Unless you need us for anything else."

Babiarsz thought a moment. "Sure," he said. "Go rest up. I know where to find you if I need you. Take care of Dana. He's a wreck."

Sasha returned to the kitchen and told Charlie to get himself packed, they were leaving in a few hours. He rose and walked by her, still swaddled in his bed's heavy comforter.

Towards eight that morning, Police Chief Stan Babiarsz took a needed break, left the massacre site and walked to the edge of a field that bordered the B and B. He found a butt-comfy small boulder and sat himself down, hidden by the surrounding tall grass. The air was nippy, but revivifying. He took a cigarette pack from his pocket and removed a spliff, the half-tobacco, half-marijuana blend that he favored. He lit up and inhaled deeply, holding the smoke in for five seconds.

Two more puffs and the eye tic that had come on while he was listening to the woman cop's fairy tale disappeared. He exhaled. *Nothing like this shit. So glad it's now legal!*

Babiarsz was having trouble making sense of the previous night's blood-letting. And he wasn't looking forward to the clusterfuck of problems the follow-up investigation would present—an Anchorage cop, *without* jurisdiction in Dutch, shoots and kills three people. Which police department handles the Officer Involved Shooting investigation, his own or the APD? And what about the mandatory administrative leave, and the required turning-over of the cop's weapon?

He twisted his neck, took another long drag, held it in. He needed breakfast and a nap. *Exhale.* Then he'd begin to sort it out. *Inhale.*

~~~

Rose Nakamura slept poorly and awakened hardly refreshed. She looked at herself in her bathroom's mirror. *Death warmed over.* There was a foul taste in her mouth. She brushed, then flossed, then gargled with Listerine. *A little better.* She showered for fifteen minutes in water as hot as she could stand. After donning fresh clothes, she realized she was starving. She made herself scrambled eggs and toast, followed by peach yogurt with a banana and blueberries.

She turned on the TV. The newscaster was talking with great animation, appeared ready to jump through the screen. Rose watched, not believing what she was learning—the shooting deaths of three Russian men in Dutch Harbor, killed late yesterday evening while attempting to rob a bed and breakfast. *I know that place,* she thought. *That's where Jimmy and Iz stayed.*

She kneeled in front of the TV, cranked up the volume. The newscaster promised an update from Dutch Harbor within the next hour. When he concluded and went to another story, Rose switched the channel. She listened again as the details about the robbery were repeated. *Robbery? Bullshit. They were at the B and B looking for Jimmy's last load of heroin. And now they're dead.*

Rose suddenly recalled the out-of-place sounds that formed the background of the Russian man's phone conversation of the previous night—wind shield wipers and foghorns. *He was calling from Dutch Harbor. Now he's dead.* She began smiling for the first time in a week. *A chance. Jesus Christ, a real chance.* She went to her computer, looked up Alaska Airlines and booked the early afternoon flight to Los Angeles. Then she packed quickly, drove to Jerry's Fast Bonds and arranged bail for her former boyfriend, soon to be her decoy.

~~~

They sat in separate rows in the tiny, half-full airport lounge, waiting for the call to board the morning flight back to Anchorage. Because of strong cross-winds whipping off the Bering Sea, takeoff had already been delayed an hour.

Charlie sat in the front row, staring through a bank of windows. Outside, a red and white striped windsock was being buffeted.

Sasha sat two rows back, holding a cup of under-brewed coffee. Next to her on the floor was a large duffel bag stuffed with heroin.

Charlie remained turned away from her. She'd seen a lot of his back the past few hours. She thought he looked like hell and stupidly told him so earlier that morning.

As she watched, he sat up in his chair, cleared his throat, swiveled in his seat, faced her squarely, and announced, decisively and loudly enough for her to hear, "No more, Sasha. We're done."

Three other passengers—woman, man, young girl— tuned in. They were sitting at the end of the row between Sasha and Charlie. They were drinking coffee from Styrofoam cups and were eating day-old blueberry muffins. Their heads began tennis-courting back and forth, each wondering how the woman might react to the very definitive proclamation made by the man. They suspected he was either her boyfriend, lover, or even spouse. She didn't let them down.

"Fine by me," Sasha said, glaring at the man. "Why don't you go ahead and tell Emmitt what happened last night. Let him know what a horrible person I am. You know what he'll do, Dana? He'll give *me* a medal. And then he'll turn around and ship *you* out to some cornfield in Iowa. You can go investigate the break-in at the local silo."

The threesome exchanged glances. *This is so cool! What could have happened last night between Sasha and Dana? And who was Emmitt?*

When the man called Dana didn't respond, the woman continued. "What the fuck you think police work is *really* about, *Agent* Dana?" her voice way too loud and her language way too provocative for airport café, early morning small talk.

The three passengers pretended they hadn't heard and dove into their muffins. But each bent a little closer to the conversation. *Police? Agent Dana? Great!*

Charlie looked at Sasha with as much venom as he could summon up on an empty stomach. He noticed the three people in the next row pretending not to be listening. He thought to give them a 'mind your own fucking business,' but reined in his anger. He craned toward Sasha, and in a whisper, "You slap the shit out of Rose. You threaten to drown Rudy." He dropped his voice even more. "And you cap it off by shooting an unarmed and defenseless suspect."

Sasha got up and walked slowly and deliberately to the end of her row, moved up one, and came to sit in back of him. She leaned toward him and hissed, "Rose? She's lucky I'm not getting her fired for lying on her work application. And Rudy? That heroin shooting, heroin dealing prick. He's going to jail for at least a five spot. And the one in the parking lot? The one who tortured and then murdered Isabel Castro? The one who used his own special brand of cigarettes to burn her breasts? The one who stuck a needle in her ass, and gave her a heroin and cocaine cocktail? Enough to kill four people, the ME said."

Sasha paused and caught sight of the eavesdropping family. They drew back from her scowl. They were being cut out of the best part of the conversation and were indignant. Although their eyes couldn't meet hers, their ears were still on full audio alert.

"You with me, Agent Dana?" Sasha whispered. "You want to tell me that scum sucker last night wasn't worth killing? You need to get your head out of your ass and come into the real world. He deserved *exactly* what he got. And you know what, Dana? You know what? I couldn't be *happier* that it was me who was able to administer the *coup de fucking grâce.*" She sat back, glared at the three spectators, and in normal volume declared, "Do it again in a minute."

The trio of breakfasters looked at each other. *Do what again in a minute?*

Charlie stood, walked to the end of his row, and bought himself a Butterfinger from a vending machine. The intercom squawked to life with the news that the morning flight was ready and passengers should proceed to the boarding gate. He retrieved his briefcase and bag, without a glance at Sasha, and started for the gate.

She rose, collected the contraband, her small suitcase, and followed after him.

The family of three trailed close behind.

Charlie stuffed the candy wrapper into a trash bin and paused at the boarding gate. "Don't worry. I won't mention your methods to Emmitt. Or to anyone. Your secret is safe with me. But I won't work with you another day."

"It's a free fucking country," Sasha said loudly, handing her boarding pass to a scandalized ticket attendant.

9

Katherine Manfredi always put up a good front, front being part of her therapeutic practice. She listened attentively, smiled encouragingly, and gave sound advice when appropriate. And for the first ten years of her practice, she found her work gratifying. Each new client presented a unique set of challenges. But with time, those challenges began to blur. One person's perceived inadequacies were reflected in the next client's. The trauma experienced by one child devastated by an abusive parent was echoed in the recounting of ten other brutalized childhoods.

Recently, the psychologist found herself fully alive only when given the chance to work with someone whose singular problems elicited genuine excitement—problems that might continue to engage the therapist after the fifty-minute session was up.

The arrival of Detective Alexandra Kulaeva in Katherine Manfred's office seemed to the counselor a god-send. The existential events in Dutch Harbor piqued the therapist's imagination, aroused her curiosity. Manfredi believed that her client's revelations would transport her to places she was rarely allowed access, a world apart, a violent and compelling world. The therapist hoped that the policewoman would fill in the thrilling details, details only sketchily described in the media. She had never worked with anyone who had been in a situation where gunfire had taken lives. She was excited about having a window into the drama of a deadly struggle.

With it all, the counselor scolded herself for being overtaken by what she thought was an unprofessional sense of curiosity, a desire to live vicariously through her patient's near-death experience. *I'm just as bad as the kids addicted to their video war games.*

Manfredi considered phoning Sasha, ask about her well-being, but then decided against it. Better if the detective came on her own to unburden her heart and conscience from the weight of having just shot and killed three men.

~~~

The shootout kings, carrying a heavy parcel of white powder, were met at Ted Stevens Anchorage International Airport by their two bosses.

"My God, you two!" was Emmitt Esterhazy's initial greeting, smiling and embracing first Sasha then Charlie.

Without comment, Sasha handed the parcel to her boss, Jack Raymond. The Detective Captain took it, weighing it in his hands.

"Incredible. Hard to believe."

"We got lucky, Jack. In more ways than one," she said.

Esterhazy looked closely at Charlie and Sasha. "You two alright?"

Charlie said nothing.

"We're cool, Emmitt," Sasha said. "It was no fun."

Raymond took his detective by the arm. "OK. Let's you and I go deliver the package to the lab. Maybe the techs'll put it on speed dial and get us some preliminary results by this afternoon." He turned to the FBI agents. "We'll be in touch with you two soon. Go relax, Charlie. You look beat all to hell."

Charlie nodded and let himself be led off by his boss. Esterhazy skipped through the terminal.

Raymond walked Sasha to his car and put the package in the trunk.

They drove out of the airport, past the Alaska Aviation

Museum. Raymond kept his eyes on the road. "Rudy Castro's bail is set at two hundred Gs. He ain't got it. His lawyer's a PD, Jepson. Know him?"

"Yeah. Little goofy but he'll give his client good advice."

"Cooperate, or else." Raymond cleared his throat. "Anything you want to tell me about the shooting? Better with me now than coming out later."

Sasha answered quickly. "Nothing there, Jack. Not a thing. By the book. I gave them warning, announced I was police, told 'em to drop their weapons. They made to fire at me. I shot 'em."

"OK. What about the third one? I've gotten some news from Babiarsz, the chief out there. Might be problems with the wounds. Busted nose."

She shook her head. "Nothing. He was fleeing. I shot at him from the window and caught him one in the ass. Ran downstairs and went after him. Called to him again. He turned and fired off a shot. I shot back. Charlie was there, looking from the window. He'll corroborate everything." She held her breath.

Raymond looked over at his detective. "That's not his story."

Sasha kept it together. "No? Whattya mean? What'd he say?"

"Dana told Babiarsz he didn't see a thing, wasn't watching from the window. Says he went into his room, sat on the bed, waited a moment, then called it in."

She tried not to seem relieved. "Wow, that's a surprise. I didn't read his statement. I thought he was watching from the window."

"No. It's just you, Sasha."

"Well, it's like I told you, boss. It was legit."

Raymond avoided looking at his detective. *Cognitive dissonance. Not a bad thing sometimes.*

"Who's handling the Officer Involved Shooting investigation?" she asked.

"That's being worked out. Babiarsz is in touch with Juneau. Office of Special Prosecutions. He thinks his department'll probably wind up doing it.

"So, *his* cops, not ours, will handle the OIS?"

"Looks like it," he said.

"They won't find shit, Jack. Not to worry."

At the crime lab, Lupe Dellarosa, the tech on duty, couldn't mask her excitement.

"If this is the real thing, it'll be the single largest seizure of hard drugs in the state's history. I'll get you a prelim soon as I can. But it has to go south, to the lab in Seattle for confirmation."

"Sure. Thanks, Lupe," Raymond said. "You can reach me any time. Sooner the better." He turned to Sasha. "Turn your weapon in. Then go home. You get a mandatory four days off. With pay, of course. Get some sleep. Babiarsz'll contact you soon. And if the shit in this package turns out to be the real thing, get yourself ready for tomorrow's press conference that Emmitt's planning. It'll be a three ring circus."

~~~

Boris Bunin was in his kitchen, pacing back and forth, a throw-away phone in his hand. He was talking to Mehmet Ozil. Their conversation was punctuated more by long silences than by words. It was time for careful thought.

Ozil finally said, "The news this morning, Boris, is incomplete. Only scattered details about how the men died at the hands of the FBI agent and the Anchorage cop. If it comes out that they've really recovered the goods, things'll get more complicated. Fast."

"I hear you Mehmet. Listen, my friend. I'm trying to control this dumpster fire from here, but if you feel you need to become invisible until we learn what information the men might have given up before they were killed, feel free to do so. That'll be your call."

"Thank you, Boris. I've got a private plane ready and waiting. My family's out of town. All in Europe. Artun and I can fly away at a moment's notice. Let me just see which way the wind's blowing."

"As I said, Mehmet, that's your decision. What about the other two, the woman's brother and her girlfriend?"

"We're watching the woman, see what she does. If she's seen the news, she may believe Denis is dead. She may think she's off the hook, may try to clear out. But let's not panic. None of the three men who were killed knew of me. At least, I hope they didn't."

~~~

Sasha turned in her weapon at the station, then drove home. There, she opened her MacBook Pro and began a search for Gennady Gasparov, the name Konstantin Zhuganov had given her in the misguided hope that information would save his life.

She would have preferred to do this at the station where she'd have access to the specialized search engines available to law enforcement. But that was impossible. If it were discovered that the Russian had provided her a name, then her account of their meeting in the B and B's parking lot would be discredited.

She hadn't believed him then, and the longer she searched through the meager Internet resources available to her, the more she became convinced that '*Gennady Gasparov*' did not exist.

Zhuganov had offered Brooklyn as a place where the alleged crime boss supposedly lived. She Googled *'Russian Mafia Brooklyn'* and spent the next hour learning about the émigrés, many Jewish, who were that group's early organizers. She made a list—gleaned from online newspaper stories—of suspected Russian mob bosses in New York City: Balagula, Bunin, Ivankov, Nayfeld, Fainberg. Those names meant nothing to her. A dead end, so it seemed.

~~~

The doorbell of Charlie Dana's apartment had been rattled into silence by the Good Friday earthquake, and no one in the last fifty years had seen any reason to fix it. You wanted someone inside to come and open the door, you knocked. And right now, someone was doing exactly that. Charlie knew who it was and didn't welcome the interruption. He was spread out on his naugahyde couch wallowing in a deep depression, staring vacantly at his television. He was listening without interest to the young woman who was wailing at America's Got Talent's four judges. The audience whooped stupidly every time the singer tried for a high note. Three of the judges seemed engaged. Howard Stern looked bored.

The knocking at the door came again, more insistent this time. Charlie continued to ignore. He felt himself a prisoner to the events in Dutch Harbor. He had been a witness— more than a witness, an accomplice—to the murder of a suspect who should have been arrested and made available for questioning. He'd watched as Sasha interrogated the man, presumably found out what she wanted to know, then murdered him. And later, when he was questioned about it, he'd claimed *not* to have been a witness. *CYA Dana!*

When the Unalaska police arrived, and Babiarsz questioned him, he had a chance to do the right thing, but did not. He could have easily refuted Sasha's fabricated account of the shooting in the parking lot. But when asked, he had remained silent. *Deaf, dumb, and blind. Definitely dumb.*

And again, returning to Anchorage from Dutch Harbor, he could have set the record straight, to pull a George Washington/cherry tree. 'I cannot tell a lie . . .' *It turns out, however, I can lie, and I have lied to the cops and to the Bureau. And most of all, to myself. Deeper and deeper.*

There was another reason for his silence, for his complicity. He was bedeviled by her. Or, at least, had been at the time. He'd felt a definite something going on. Maybe more than sex. *That would have been new.* He believed she had felt it, too. In the B and B, another few minutes without interruption and who knows where things might have led? Now, however, that moment was gone, those feelings had evaporated and were replaced by a sense of revulsion, a deep resentment toward the woman who was capable of cold-blooded murder, and who had flipped his world upside down.

The pounding on the door continued and now a voice, "Charlie. Open up. It's Melanie. Open up. Please, Charlie."

"OK," he shouted. "Coming." It took him three tries to bounce up off his couch. Once on his feet, he grabbed the remote and shut the TV off just as the crowd was booing Stern for calling the woman's effort, "a poor example of yodeling."

"Coming," he said again, shuffling slowly toward his front door in stockinged feet. He hesitated. He knew he was lousy company tonight, and that Melanie, for all her good intentions, would probably not provide balm for his bruised ego. Truth is, he didn't want to be roused from his self-inflicted funk. He rested his head against the door.

"Melanie. I'm a mess right now."

A long silence from the other side, then, "You want me to go, Charlie? I can go," Melanie said in her sweet and slow southern drawl. The sound of her voice warmed him. He couldn't bring himself to dismiss her. He opened the door. "Hey, kiddo."

Without crossing over the threshold, she spoke in a voice full of compassion, "Hey, Charlie. It's all over the news. Dutch Harbor. It must have been awful. Want some company?"

She was dressed in her waitress' outfit. She had come straight from work, her unkempt red hair framing an expression of deep concern. He thought she looked as lovely at that moment as any woman he had ever known. "Thank you for coming, Mel." He stood back and reached out a hand to her. She took it and held it tightly. He pulled her closer and shut the door. Melanie took his hand and placed it on her breast. Charlie closed his eyes and let his forehead sink against hers. He imagined the million freckles dotting Melanie's alabaster breasts. A sense of deep shame brought a bitter taste to his mouth, at the same time as his erection pronounced him ready. *Louse.*

~~~

The adrenaline washed away around eight that night, and its absence left Sasha feeling squeezed, raggish, and with an overwhelming sense of fatigue.

The rush from the discovery of the heroin at *The Sea Turtle*, then the shooting, and the ensuing antagonism between herself and Charlie had all helped to push her to the edge.

She'd already spoken with her daughter, assuring Robin that she had returned from Dutch in one piece. Robin was *not* reassured by her mother's soft-pedaling. Sasha admitted to her that it had been frightening but had shied away from filling in many details, side-stepping the ones that would not pass legal challenge. Only after she promised to fly out as soon as possible were Robin's misgivings allayed.

Sasha then called Katherine Manfredi and made an appointment. She wanted to speak about the shooting, to unburden to someone who could be counted on to keep her secret and not judge her. She wasn't looking for absolution. She wasn't pleased with what she had done, but at least she was at peace with herself.

Too tired to eat, all she wanted was bed. And a beer. Maybe a couple. Maybe six. She craved the oblivion that came with the alcohol bender. She knew it was a fool's errand, but she was driven to go to her fridge anyway, knowing that there wasn't a chance in hell a beer would appear, all icy and delish.

She recalled, vaguely, having drunk the last one the evening before she and Charlie left for Dutch. *Charlie,* she thought. *Don't make me laugh, girl. You only wanted him for his body. And he felt the same about you. Still . . .*

Her fridge-quest yielded only a half-full quart bottle of pink lemonade, bought a month earlier when her daughter was in town for a weekend sleep-over. It'd have to do. She gave the bottle a swirl, unscrewed the cap for a cautionary sniff—not the worst thing she'd ever smelled—then took a long swallow, shivering at the tartness. She moved to her kitchen table and settled down onto a chair, gripping the bottle with both hands. She began sorting out the events of the past two days.

The shooting, of course, was prominent. She'd never *officially* killed anyone. Never shot anyone in the line of duty. Never even drawn her weapon.

She wasn't worried about the Officer Involved Shooting investigation. She didn't know who in Dutch Harbor would be conducting it, but she had faith that her snow job to Chief Babiarsz would hold water. Especially since Charlie claimed *not* to have seen anything.

Up until now, she'd avoided thinking about the shooting. Too frightening. But sitting within the familiar confines of her own home, she felt safe enough to bring up the memory. She recalled every one of her actions, emotions, and thoughts, down to the smallest detail.

Before the two Russians entered the B and B, she'd experienced a jolting panic, an increase in heart rate, a confused thought process that clarified only when she heard the downstairs screen door slam shut.

She heard them come up the stairs, pass by her room. Then, decisive action, unthinking, by rote. Five seconds, five shots. Her hearing had not yet recovered from the blasting noise.

Immediately after the two Russians were down, she was overcome with a flooding sense of relief and thankfulness. She had survived a brief but insanely intense fire-fight. Peering down at the men she had shot, she experienced a dizzying elation, a kind of whoop-de-do, look at me. I'm alive and these two pricks aren't. Hooray for our side!

And strangely, she also felt a sense of gratitude. The bad guys had paid the ultimate price and she was grateful to have been responsible for their removal from the rolls of the living. She needed to keep that thought to herself, however, buried deep. Not a subject for her future post-shooting compulsory counseling sessions with the department. *Do I even share those thoughts with Katherine?*

Then, the parking lot where she caught up with the third Russian, the one who had tortured and murdered Isabel Castro. Sasha was able to parse that memory into its component pieces. She could recall every word the two of them had spoken, every change in the Russian's facial expression and in the tone of his voice. Before shooting him, she remembered thinking, *"I am Shiva, destroyer of demons, the avenging angel."*

Sasha closed her eyes and brought to mind the man's final moments: Konstantin on the ground, wounded in the thigh, a young man realizing that his life was now being measured in moments. The look in his eyes as she raised her weapon—undiluted terror as the abyss opened in front of him. She heard his bowels give out. He had called for his mother. A brief interruption when Charlie shouted from the window. Then the execution. And again, Charlie screaming at her. He had witnessed the whole episode, start to finish. *He's seen the real me. Do I give a shit?*

She took four long swallows of the lemonade, puckering at the tartness. Tomorrow, a press conference and the hope that the Boy Scout would continue to keep his mouth shut.

She took a quick shower. She rubbed herself vigorously dry and pajamaless, crawled into bed.

Before falling asleep, her thoughts returned to Charlie in the bubble bath and what had grown so robustly beneath the bubbles. *He'll never let me get that close again. The hell with him!*

~~~

The OpEd page of the Anchorage Dispatch News said it all.

> With a population of just over three hundred thousand, Anchorage is large enough to be able to claim most of the problems of similarly-sized communities in the Lower '48: gangs dealing fentanyl and meth, road rage, drunken brawls, wife beatings, child abandonment, corrupt and/or inept politicians, huckster clerics. The usual ills associated with today's advanced societies.
>
> Through it all, however, we've remained a relatively small potato town.
>
> But this . . . the news coming out of Dutch Harbor . . . this is very big potatoes, indeed.
>
> Even the sourdoughs—the folks who remember when the forest began a scant mile

from downtown, the folks who can count on the fingers of one hand the number of Anchorage's pre-war paved roads—even they have never really seen anything quite like this on their precious 'Last Frontier.'

The events being reported from the Aleutians are simply too juicy to believe: over twenty-three pounds of a white powder thought to be Manhattan-grade heroin now in the hands of the local FBI; three dead Russians; a dead American resident of Dutch Harbor caught in the crossfire; and two heroic law enforcement officials who outgunned the bad guys. Can you believe it?

The morning after their return to Anchorage, FBI Special Agent Charles Dana, and Anchorage Police Department Detective Sergeant Aleksandra Kulaeva were wheeled onto center stage, along with their bosses.

The media was out in force: all of Alaska's major papers, the wire services, the network television affiliates—all crammed into a small conference room at FBI headquarters in downtown Anchorage.

Special Agent in Charge Emmitt Esterhazy, resplendent in a navy blue suit over a cream colored shirt, a light blue and mauve striped tie, and a pale rose handkerchief in his jacket pocket strode to the bank of microphones like Caesar entering Rome, a bounce in his step, confident and downright sassy.

In his eight years as the Anchorage Field Office's SAC, Esterhazy hadn't given his superiors in Washington any reason to be unhappy, and considering the problems in his last assignment, they were more than ready to find fault. But if there were no complaints from Quantico, neither was there much cheering. The next few minutes would change all that.

Standing at the podium, Esterhazy made sure he had his left hand resting at all times on the dozen tidily wrapped packets arranged on the table next to him. That hand told the tale: *He* had the heroin. The FBI had it. The pushers didn't. The mob didn't. And your local Drug Enforcement Agency absolutely didn't.

After he finished his opening remarks, he gave the floor over to the APD's Captain Jack Raymond. The policeman had little to add other than praise for his detective. He chose not to mention other, closely related aspects of the case: the murder of a Fish and Wildlife biologist whose beaten and burned body was found recently in a meadow north of town; the victim's relationship to an American fisherman lost off of a Russian trawler under suspicious circumstances. The snoops in the Fourth Estate would eventually ferret out those connections, but Raymond wasn't about to help them. He promised the media more details as they became available and turned the mic over to his ace detective.

Sasha was smiley, but tense. The several cups of overly sweetened and very potent coffee she had drunk since awakening had seriously focused her brain. The down-side was a case of caffeine jitters. She gripped the podium tightly, fingers squeezing, nails scratching the pine wood lectern.

She, too, was brief. She acknowledged the close cooperation offered to the Anchorage police by the FBI. She noted with deep appreciation the help extended to her by Special Agent Charles Dana, towards whom she now turned and nodded a thanks.

When the man pointedly ignored her peace offering and continued to stare at the floor in front of him, Sasha turned back to the press. She thanked them for their interest and retired to the back of the dais, to stand beside her boss.

Charlie was next up. He mumbled a few quick *'thank yous'* and promptly withdrew, never mentioning Sasha. That omission was not lost on either Raymond or Esterhazy. Nor on many of the press who sensed the palpable enmity Dana was emitting toward his partner-in-glory.

A final visit to the podium by Esterhazy who promised more information by the end of the day. As soon as he made to leave, questions were shouted up to him from the press.

"Have you identified the Russians? Were they Alaskans? Where did the heroin come from? Where was it going? Was it intended to stay local? Does Anchorage have a heroin problem? How did Dana and Kulaeva happen to be in Dutch Harbor? Can we have more details about the shootout?"

Esterhazy waved off the questions. "Nothing more for now," he said. "We'll be in touch with you soon." He and the other three crime fighters exited through a side door. Two FBI special agents remained in the room to pack up the contraband.

~~~

Across town, the director of the DEA's Anchorage office was watching the live feed of the FBI's triumph. It was torture.

Nolan Cardozo was dressed only in striped boxer shorts. His longish hair, usually beautifully styled, hung in uncombed hanks. He needed a shave. He smelled of booze and nervous sweat. He picked at the lint in his belly button. A mess.

He held a large tumbler, half-full of Glenlivit 25. His third of the morning. He took a long swallow, in fearful anticipation that a call from D.C. would be coming in any time now. *Jesus!*

He'd phoned in sick this morning, wanting to watch the FBI's hastily called press conference without having to face the sneers from the backbiting bastards who manned his office. They were probably joking to each other right now about his absence. But he could live with that. He already knew who the big mouths were, the jokesters, the Fifth Column. He knew their names. And by the end of the day tomorrow, he'd know exactly which of them had said what.

He'd know because the first thing he did three years earlier when he took over the Anchorage office was to find out who on the staff could be coerced into being his mole. What would it take? A promotion? A raise? Fully comped trips to wherever? Extra time off?

Nolan soon found his man, Lionel Pinkwater. *Ambitious little turd.* The man was easily enticed by his boss into becoming the resident snitch. In return for a yearly paid trip to Maui, Pinkwater provided the DEA director with regular updates about the loyalty—or more often, the disloyalty—of Cardozo's subordinates.

The TV showed a gloating Emmitt Esterhazy. Cardozo despised the man. *Preening prick.* And next to Esterhazy, stacked on a table, lay a huge cache of heroin, heroin that by all rights should now be in the DEA's evidence lock-up.

Esterhazy introduced Detective Kulaeva.

Cardozo knew the woman, now a media darling, dubbed *'the shootout queen.'* He suspected she was a lesbian and knew for a fact she was a serious boozer. He was certain her boss didn't know about her drinking. But Cardozo did, and at some point in the not too distant future, that bit of intel might prove useful. *Hey, it worked for J. Edgar. Worked for Stalin. Know everything about everybody. Then you had leverage. You don't get to the top by playing footsie.*

Cardozo's phone rang. He put the TV on mute and reluctantly picked up his cell—Estelle, his ex-wife, in Coral Gables. Hers was the last voice on planet earth he wanted to hear this morning. He let the call go to message, un-muted the TV and cranked up the volume so he wouldn't have to hear her usual complaints about their son, Billy, flunking out of NYU; or her brother-in-law, Morrie the Moron, slapping Estelle's sister around; or not having enough ready cash to cover her weekly massage. *Shit!*

On the TV, Esterhazy introduced Dana, his agent.

Cardozo watched the man shuffle toward the mic and mutter something barely intelligible. *Probably PTSD. Pussy!*

His cell phone chimed again. Cardozo looked at the screen. *Christ. Springfield. DEA Central.*

He took a long gulp of the scotch, then another, finishing off the drink. He tilted to the side and farted twice, then picked up his cell phone, ready to receive a deluxe, District of Columbia ream-out, probably by Assistant Director Donny 'Can I suck your dick?' Hitchcock. *Ass licking homo.*

~~~

The two women were lunching at Villa Nova, a hole-in-the-wall restaurant known for some of the best Mediterranean cuisine in Anchorage.

"I spoke to Esterhazy this morning, after our press

conference," Sasha said between mouthfuls of pasta alla putanesca. "He gave me a rundown of the three talks he'll be giving at the conference in Vladivostok. Two'll be for English speakers, so no problem there. But the third one is for Russians only, on cyber security. That's the one where a good chunk of the vocabulary is beyond me. I was hoping you might give me a hand with some of the tough stuff."

Elena Markova used a piece of bread to sop up the sauce from her veal scaloppini marsala. She wolfed it down then wiped her lips. "I can help out, sure. Be glad to. Why don't you text me the phrases and topics this afternoon and we can talk about some of the specialized language that might come up. We can actually start this evening, if you like."

"Thanks, but I'm flying out to Big Lake later this afternoon, to my family's spread," Sasha said. "Won't be back for a couple days. I'll text you the essentials."

Sasha had worked with Elena several times and knew she was the State Department's preferred simultaneous translator for all of that agency's needs on the West Coast. Which is why she'd been picked by the DEA's Nolan Cardozo to accompany him to Vladivostok for the second half of the crime conference.

Markova was tall and full-bosomed, with long and shapely legs, light blue eyes and very short blond hair. She filled her glass with wine and went to pour some for Sasha.

The detective placed a hand over the glass. "Trying to cut down."

"Guess I'll have to do all the heavy lifting myself. I'm pretty sure I can manage," she said, taking a long swallow. "You don't know what you're missing, Sasha."

"I know exactly what I'm missing, Elena. I have to

fly this afternoon." She lifted her glass of water and tipped it toward the other woman. "Here's to you," she said. "Now, tell me all about your work. How's it doing?"

Elena took another swallow. "Work? Sucks. Way slower now than when I started in '88, when glasnost and perestroika were taking root. In those days, every Alaskan and his brother thought he could make a fortune doing business in Russia. They stormed my doors, needing two-sided business cards, brochures, contracts, every kind of document, all translated into Russian. After about three years, it started dawning on folks that the Russkies didn't have a clue about the western business model. Their infrastructure stank, they couldn't write a contract to save their lives, had a crappy banking system, and generally couldn't find their new capitalist asses with both hands." Elena paused to finish off the last bite of her veal, followed by another gulp of wine. "And there were all kinds of other problems."

"Like?"

"Like the idea of fair dealing. Those days, the Russians had trouble living up to their promised obligations. Like honoring the contract they'd signed. And meeting deadlines. So, one after another, Alaska businessmen took it in the shorts trying to deal over there."

"Any different today?"

"Some. The main difference is that we've learned, we've adapted to the way the Russians operate."

"How's that?"

"Well, where American businessmen pretend they're legit, that they deal on the square, Russians don't even bother with the pretense. Corruption, kickbacks, bribes, outright theft, is all integral to the way they do business. That's how the oligarchs made off like bandits, splitting up the spoils after the fall of communism. With the connivance of the government, naturally. And it goes right to the top, too. Putin's supposed to have squirreled away over seventy billion and has a palace on the Black Sea. But the lumpen prols turn a blind eye. They like their leaders strong and the niceties of democracy just get in the way. So, we've had to learn the hard way."

"And when people come to you to prepare their business documents . . .?"

"I tell them to be extra, extra, super careful, to not take anything at face value. Everything gets written down and signed. Everything! And if you decide to invest, make sure you go in with eyes wide open. With that warning, I've done right by my clients." Elena made room on the table for the flan and espresso that were just arriving. "You're flying to Big Lake."

"In a couple hours."

"Probably the perfect place to recupe from all that shit out in Dutch."

"I'm hoping."

~~~

Police Chief Stan Babiarsz watched the press conference on his living room TV. He just finished savoring his way through the remains of his wife's breaded cutlets and cabbage rolls. A pair of Alaskan Amber beers helped him digest some of the weirdness he had just witnessed at the packed media happening.

Babiarsz was only mildly surprised at what he saw stacked next to the podium—a great pile of heroin being caressed by a grinning SAC. *The woman cop had somehow overlooked letting me know about that in her account of the shooting. Oh well.*

He'd been snowed before. Wasn't the first time. He'd witnessed large doses of obfuscation, double-dealing, and outright lying during his twenty-two years as one of Chicago's finest.

The policeman hadn't been fooled for a second by the bullshit story the woman detective had told him—that the Russians had come to the B and B to stick up the place. Really? Even a rookie patrolman would have seen right through that one. And Babiarsz was no rookie.

A few hours after sorting through the bloodbath at the hotel, he started calling around, trying to trace the movements of the three dead men and the two Anchorage cops. By the end of the day, he believed he'd put most of the pieces together.

It began when Sean Carmody, owner of *The Sea Turtle*, called to tell him that the package of heroin rescued by the two cops had been deposited in his restaurant's deep freeze. The depositor was Jimmy Lasorda, the American high seas fisheries monitor who had somehow disappeared off of a Russian fishing boat. The police chief thought it not at all coincidental that said vessel just happened to have been parked in Iliuliuk Harbor, and that its presence here was what brought the two cops to Dutch in the first place. *Curiouser and curiouser.*

He knew the Russian trawler had to have been ordered into Dutch by the Coast Guard. He contacted Butch Kozol, the Guard's public information specialist, and learned that he and the two cops had been aboard the fishing vessel investigating the disappearance of Lasorda. *Okay. Starting to piece it together. Slowly.*

Babiarsz was fairly certain that the three dead Russians were *not* stick up artists. He reckoned they were in Dutch—the police chief hadn't a clue how they got here—to try to find the bundle of heroin the two Anchorage cops had stumbled upon at the restaurant. The same heroin that had been fondled on TV by Emmitt Esterhazy. *Let's see,* Babiarsz thought. *Lasorda was probably bringing the shit into the country from Russia, on the ships he worked on as a fisheries observer. He stored it in his buddy's icebox. On his next tour at sea, Lasorda goes missing. How and why, no one knows. Is it connected to the heroin? If I had to guess, I'd say so. The Anchorage cops come to investigate his disappearance. They find the heroin. Three Russians come looking for it. There's a shooting. Dead Russians, a dead B and B owner. And the FBI now has the heroin. I think I got most of it. Except, we got a problem. A big one. I need to call my colleague in Anchorage and give him the bad news.*

Nine years earlier, Detective Captain Jack Raymond had gone the extra mile for Stan Babiarsz when the Chicago policeman phoned, introduced himself, and explained that he was considering a job offer in the Aleutians. Might Detective Raymond perhaps provide some insight?

For the next hour, the Anchorage cop told the prospective hiree what to expect if he took the job in Dutch Harbor. Raymond ended the call with a recommendation—if Babiarsz really wanted to learn what crime was like out there, and to laugh his ass off at the same time, he should Google 'Dutch Harbor Police Blotter.' "You won't believe it," Raymond said.

Babiarsz was grateful, and when he and his wife

showed up two weeks later on their way out to the Chain, they brought Raymond an unexpected gift—seven pounds of Chicago-made Polish sausage, right from Kurowski's on Milwaukee Ave.

Their friendship was cemented that evening when the wives, Marie and Louisa, cooked up a storm—Polish sausage for starters, Copper River red salmon for finishers.

Jack Raymond, almost tasting his retirement, sat in his office. His door was open. Low noises and conversations from the squad room filtered in. He held his unlit pipe between his teeth. He'd been listening for the last fifteen minutes as Stan Babiarsz told him what he, Raymond, had already suspected. It was a discouraging story, one that almost broke the detective captain's heart.

"Can you please run through it one more time, Stan? I just need to hear it again. You don't mind, I hope?" Raymond bit down on the pipe.

"Not at all, Jack. I'll go through it point by point. Stop me with any questions you might have, anything at all you believe we may have overlooked or somehow misconstrued."

"Fine," said Raymond.

Babiarsz began. "The story your detective told about what happened upstairs in the B and B checks out. Well, sort of, anyhow. She said the two men came down the hall and passed the room she was in. She said she came out of the door behind them and ordered them to drop their guns. When they didn't and turned and began to raise their weapons, she fired three times at the nearest man, hitting him all three times, twice in the chest and once in the upper arm. She said she then fired three times at the man farther down the corridor, catching him once in the neck, once in the body. Dana, the fed, shot through the door of the room he was in. There were eleven holes in the door. Two of Dana's bullets apparently hit the second man, one in the pelvis, one in the knee. Both of the Russians were killed without either getting off a single shot. Looks like they got sandwiched in a cleverly arranged cross fire."

"Alright. I can see it," Raymond said. "But you said, 'sort of.' That her story about what happened upstairs checked out, but only 'sort of.' Tell me again the problem."

Raymond heard Babiarsz sigh into the phone. "Well, the only problem with the story from upstairs is that one of the Russian men, the first one she shot at, the one with the two bullet holes in his chest . . . one of the holes, the one in his heart," Babiarsz waited a beat, "had powder residue on his chest. Close range, Jack. My forensic team thinks probably less than two feet. That'd be inconsistent with the rest of her story about how far she was from the men when the shooting started." The Dutch Harbor cop waited. When he didn't get a response from the other end of the line, he continued. "Now, I'm thinking, and this is just a supposition, Jack. That the man was down and she approached him and . . . looks like she may have just finished him off."

"That'd be my guess, Chief," Raymond said slowly, gnawing on the stem of his pipe.

"Might still have been a threat," Babiarsz said, in defense of Detective Kulaeva. "But the shot, the one leaving the powder burns, was a through and through. And we found a hole in the floor under him." Babiarsz hesitated. "So . . ."

"Might have been a threat," Raymond repeated, not believing it for a minute. The Russian had already been shot once in the shoulder and once in the middle of his chest from less than ten feet. *A threat? Not likely.* "OK, Stan. Now the rest."

"Well," Babiarsz began, "the rest of her story, Jack, is pretty fucked up. Actually, *very* fucked up. The thing upstairs—the powder burns on the guy's clothing—she might have a little wiggle room there. But out in the parking lot, with the third man, your detective's story simply doesn't hold up. And part of her problem, like I told you before, is that Dana said he didn't see anything. Said he was busy phoning it in and too shaken to look out the window. Sounds like a load of crap to me, but that's his story. So we only have your detective's account of what happened in the parking lot. And there's the problem."

"I'm listening, Stan."

"She reported to me that after the two Russians were shot upstairs, she heard the downstairs screen door slam close. She went to the window, saw she couldn't open it, kicked out the glass, shot at the fleeing man three times, striking him once. That, by the way—the breaking glass part and the number of shots—we can corroborate from the next-door neighbors. They live a distance away. The first gun shots, the ones upstairs in the B and B, woke them. They said they ran to their bedroom window, opened it, and looked toward the hotel. They can't see the place from where they live, but they claim to have heard things pretty clearly. Young couple. She's a doctor, he's a nurse. No hearing problems for either one. We both know that witness testimony can vary like crazy. But these two seem dependable. Anyhow, they say they heard glass breaking, then three shots. That corresponds to what your detective reported."

So far, so good. But here comes the shit, Raymond

- 285 -

thought. "OK. I'm with you."

"Right. Your detective says she pursued the third man. She actually told me, and I'm going to quote her account to you Jack, off of her written statement. She wrote, 'I ran after the wounded man, caught up with him in the parking lot, ordered him to drop his weapon. He was lying by his car trying to get the door open. He turned and fired once at me. I fired at him twice, striking him in the chest both times.' Those're her words, Jack. I just read 'em to you."

"Got it. Explain to me again the problem, Stan."

"The problem, problems really, are many. According to your detective, she was fired upon once and responded right away with two shots of her own. The neighbors, however, the doctor and her husband, heard things *very* differently. They said they heard the glass breaking and three shots from the window. Right?"

"Right," said Raymond.

"Then they said there was a lapse of time before they heard any more shots."

"How much time, Stan?"

"I questioned each of them alone. Standard procedure. They both say there was a lapse. The man thought maybe six minutes between the shots from the upstairs window and the next shots he heard. The woman said maybe as long as seven minutes." Babiarsz waited for Raymond to absorb the information. Again, nothing from the Anchorage end. Babiarsz continued. "That's a different story from your detective's account. According to her, after firing the three shots from the window, she ran downstairs, chased after the third Russian, ordered him to drop his weapon. He turns and fires. She returns fire, killing him. We're talking here a minute, maybe ninety seconds max from the time she shot him from the upstairs window to shooting him in the parking lot. Not six or seven minutes."

"Go on, chief," Raymond said, closing his eyes. *Christ!*

Babiarsz plowed on, compassion in his voice. "In your detective's account, the shots she exchanged with the man in the parking lot should have taken only a few seconds. He fires one. She returns fire right away, two shots. But the neighbors say there was *another* time lag and the grouping of shots was different. They say that after several minutes, they heard *two* shots, one right after the other. Bang, bang. Then a gap of about a minute, then a single shot." Babiarsz waited several beats. "You get the picture, Jack?"

"I do, Stan. I get it."

"And there's the business of the dead man's broken nose. No explanation offered by your detective and no physical evidence at the scene to explain it."

Raymond didn't know what to say.

"I'm an old school cop, Jack. I know how things work. So do you. Here's what's going to happen at my end. I've spoken to Special Prosecutions in Juneau, told 'em that we're taking charge of the OIS. I got a couple sergeants out here, good guys, who'll do it. I'll give 'em your detective's statement to work from. What I've just gone over with you is in my hand written incident report. It's not going to get transcribed onto my computer. At least, not right away. No one else has seen it yet and no one but you has heard it. I'll send you a copy in the mail. I'll keep the only other copy. I won't show it to my two guys, unless they ask for it. And since I've already had a long talk with 'em, they're not *gonna* ask for it.

Will this work for you?"

Raymond exhaled, thinking, *Babiarsz is no fool. A Chicago cop. An old pro. He knows exactly what happened. And so do I.* "Yeah, Stan. That'll be fine. I'll let you know how we proceed. Meanwhile . . . I owe you one. Big time."

A light laugh at the other end of the line. "I'll be in town day after tomorrow for that crime conference. I like the steaks at Club Paris."

"You're on, buddy. The chateaubriand and the oldest bottle of wine they got. I'm grateful."

"Take it easy, Jack. See ya in a couple days."

"See ya, Stan. And thank you again."

Raymond hung up and looked around his office. He spun around in his seat and surveyed his wall of commendations. *Do I talk to her? Do I confront her? Or do I forget about it and just push through to retirement? I'll be so glad to get outta here.*

10

Just past noon, Rudy Castro walked out of the Fourth Avenue Jail, a free man. He tossed his day pack in the back of Rose's hatchback and got into the passenger seat. He closed his eyes and relaxed onto the head rest. Five minutes later, when he opened them, they were driving south through town.

"This ain't the way to Palmer," he said. "What's goin' on, Rose? Why we goin' this way?"

She stared straight ahead. "What's goin' on, you dummy, is that we're on the way to the airport. When we get there, I fly away and you will officially be outta my life." She paused. "But I'm leavin' you the car."

Rudy was thunder struck. At the intersection of International Airport Road and Jewel Lake, he rediscovered his voice. He toned down the shouting, thinking he'd try sweetness. "After all we been through, Rose. This is how you treat me?" he asked softly.

Rose drove onto the airport's 'Departures' lane. "Rudy, you are such a royal dork. Check the glove compartment. There's an envelope with five hundred bucks and a reservation at a place out of town where you can lay low. The Frontiersman Motel, in Palmer, right off the highway. I got you a room there for a week. You can hide out. After that, you're on your own."

She pulled up in front of the Alaska Airlines' doors, left the car idling, got out, and walked to the rear of the hatchback. Rudy joined her.

"Rose. For God's sake. What am I supposta do?" he whined.

She didn't answer. She pulled out her purple roller bag and telescoped up the handle.

Rudy put out his hands, pleading, "Where are you goin'? When am I gonna see you again?"

"See me again? How 'bout never?" she said, then turned and rolled her bag into the terminal.

In a black pickup parked further down the line of cars, the driver and passenger watched the former boyfriend/girlfriend.

Mehmet Ozil spoke to his cousin, "I'll follow her inside, find out which flight she's on. I'll call Brooklyn. You take care of him."

"No sweat," Artun said. His cousin got out of the pickup and walked toward the terminal. When Artun looked back toward Rose's car, Rudy Castro was still standing there, screaming.

"Bitch. Bitch. You fuckin' bitch," the junkie shouted after his departing former girlfriend.

Three baggage porters stopped what they were doing and stared at the man. They shook their heads and laughed quietly to each other.

Rudy stormed back into the idling Honda and raced off. The pickup eased into the traffic behind him. The tracking device stuck under the Honda's rear bumper allowed Artun to stay far behind.

~~~

Rose was traveling light, had packed only enough to fill her carry-on roller bag. She'd arrive in LA around seven p.m., grab the airport shuttle to Union Station, Amtrak to Tucson, then bus into Mexico and make her way south. She thought about the large Japanese ex-pat community in Bolivia. *Why not?*

She'd decided to bail Rudy out and let him fend for himself. She hoped the search for him would occupy the Russians, even to the point where they might possibly lose interest in her. *Could work. If he only takes my advice and drops out of sight. The longer the better.*

~~~

Artun Ozil was enjoying himself immensely. The spring day was balmy, the view driving north on the Glenn Highway was calming. Broad vistas of mountain and flatland, winding rivers, wispy clouds. *Someone should paint this*, he thought. And half a mile ahead, a red Honda sped north, driven by someone with a bull's eye on his forehead.

They drove over the Knik River and a few minutes later, came to a major split in the highway. To the left, Wasilla, where Russia is apparently visible from certain front porches. To the right, Palmer, and beyond that, the Canadian border. Rudy took a right. Artun followed, wondering if the man intended driving out of Alaska. His cell phone rang. Mehmet.

"She's waiting for the non-stop to Los Angeles. Leaves in half an hour. Arrives at LAX at seven thirty. I'll watch her board and wait 'til the plane pulls away from the gate."

"OK," Artun answered. "The guy's turned off on the road to Palmer."

"Keep on him. I called Brooklyn. Gave them the woman's arrival time in LA, described the clothes she was wearing, sent them a photo."

"Right. I got this end. I'll make us kebabs tonight. I got us some baklava from that place on Northern Lights. What's it called?"

"Turkish Delight. See you later. Be careful, cousin."

Artun ended the call as hunter and prey passed the State Fairgrounds and a few miles later, the Honda turned off on East Arctic, into Palmer. After a few blocks, Rudy entered the parking lot of the Frontiersman Motel.

He drove past the lodging and pulled up in front of a set of golden arches. He watched through his rear view mirror as Rudy entered the motel's office. A short time later, he came out with a key card in his hand. He got back in his car and drove around the side of the motel, still in plain view of the pickup's driver. Rudy pulled up in front of a staircase, collected his day pack out of the hatchback, took the stairs to the motel's second floor, and let himself into the last room on the landing.

Artun reached under the passenger seat of the pickup and felt around for a small flight bag. Inside, he found a suppressor and a Walther pistol. The weapon was a favorite of his since he saw Sean Connery use one in *From Russia With Love*. That would have been in 1969. He was eight-years-old. He and Mehmet had snuck into the Emek Sinemasi in downtown Istanbul. What a theater! What a film!

Artun screwed on the silencer, checked the pistol's magazine, chambered a round, kept the safety on, returned the weapon to the bag, and stowed it carefully under the seat. He looked up at the arches and smiled guiltily, started up the car, and entered the drive-through.

When a pimple-faced boy wearing a paper hat stuck his head out the window, Artun ordered an extra large French fries and a jumbo Coke. He waited patiently for his order while watching Rudy's front door, no more than fifty feet away.

~~~

A short, bony young woman with straight, shoulder length blue and red hair, sat in Terminal 6, LAX. She was waiting for the Alaska Airlines direct flight from Anchorage.

As usual, the concourse around the C gates was packed. Kids scooted between rows of bored passengers—napping, noshing, reading—killing time before their flights.

The woman was dressed in fresh workout clothes and scuffed Nike running shoes. If anyone asked, she was waiting for the Alaska Airlines flight to San Francisco, takeoff at 9:15 p.m. And she had a ticket to prove it, though she had no luggage.

She'd been collected two hours earlier from her apartment in Venice, near Abbot Kinney Boulevard. She'd climbed into the back seat of a blue Chevy four-door and greeted the other passenger, an older man with a great, round head, a set of broken teeth, and very little left of his once blond hair. They knew each other, had worked together twice before.

The girl took out a vial, a pocket-sized mirror, and a MasterCard. She opened the tiny bottle and poured a small mound of white powder onto the mirror, then used the credit card to shape four lines. The man, meanwhile, took a dollar bill from his wallet and rolled it up. The woman offered him first snorts. When he finished, he passed the mirror back. She inhaled her two lines of cocaine, wet her finger, wiped it across the mirror, then massaged her gums with her dusty digit. "Waste not," she said.

"Kinda short notice," the moon-faced man said. "I was nearly out the door, ready to take my kids to a movie."

"I only got the call, myself, a couple hours ago. They sent a photo and a description." She passed him her iPhone. He studied the photo for a good minute. "Got it," he said, handing back the phone.

~~~

About five thirty, Artun broke down. He couldn't help it. His stomach was rumbling. He drove back around the arches, got in line again, waited behind a car full of high school kids, and when it came his turn, ordered the double cheeseburger with double onions, hold the mayo. And fries again. And another Coke. *Fuck it.*

Half an hour later, he checked his watch. Six o'clock here in Alaska. Seven in LA. The woman's plane would be landing soon. He took an empty pizza box, brought for the occasion, put on a baseball cap and a light windbreaker. He took the Walther out of the duffel bag and made sure the silencer was snugly screwed on. He flicked off the safety, placed the weapon in the box, got out of the pickup and locked it. Then Artun went to deliver Rudy Castro's last pepperoni and pineapple combo.

~~~

The red and blue haired woman watched as passengers from the just-arrived flight from Anchorage began flowing into the waiting area, heading for baggage and the exits.

She reached into her pocket, withdrew her phone and punched up the photo of an Asian woman, late twenties, dark ponytail, wearing a red sweater, jeans, and a brown leather vest.

She'd be carrying a red purse and towing a purple roller bag.

As soon as Rose Nakamura appeared, the waiting woman phoned her partner outside the terminal. "She's here. She's dressed exactly as advertised. Can't miss her. I'm following. If she goes to collect baggage, I'll let you know which carousel. But I'm pretty sure she only has the one carry-on, a purple bag. So be ready at the exit. If she stays in the terminal or moves to another one, I'll call."

"I'm close," the man replied.

Rose entered the very long and bare tiled hall that separates the arrival/departing gates from baggage at Terminal 6. She reviewed her itinerary: the FlyAway Shuttle Express from here to Union Station; then the AMTRAC to Tucson; the Tufesa bus across the border, to Ciudad Obregon, in Sonora; finally a cab to Alamos, where she had friends. There, she'd plot her next move.

She passed through the baggage area, crowded with passengers from Alaska, awaiting their luggage. She headed for the exit and in a few seconds, emerged onto a broad sidewalk crowded with hundreds of coming and going travelers. In the street, noise and congestion, lines of waiting cars and taxis, hotel and rent-a-car shuttles weaving in and out.

A traffic cop pointed her in the right direction. She began walking toward her shuttle, a hundred yards down the sidewalk. The woman in the workout clothes followed her easily, closing to within a few yards. An older man with a round head fell into step with her. He was carrying a daypack. He offered it to the woman, but she shook her head. "Not here," she said. "Too crowded. Let's wait a bit."

Rose walked briskly to the shuttle bus with 'Union

Station—Express' lit up above the front windshield. She boarded.

"I'll get on," said the man. "Meet me downtown."

Without a word, the woman peeled off and headed for the blue Chevy that had been slowly trailing them.

Rose was starting to relax. The threat the Russian man had delivered in the parking lot had just about done her in. *But now he's dead. And I'm alive. And I'm on my way.*

The ride to Union Station—via three of LA's always crammed freeways—took less than an hour. Rose exited the bus, tipped the driver, and entered the beautifully styled, 1930s-built, railroad station. She thought briefly about walking over to Olvera Street for a Mexican meal, but chose instead to eat at the Traxx Café, inside the terminal. She ordered two appetizers: a Waldorf salad and jumbo prawns. Over dessert—Mexican chocolate flan and an espresso—she reviewed her train's timetable. The Sunset Limited that would take her to Tucson was set to leave at 10:00 p.m.. She'd reserved a private compartment and hoped to sleep most of the overnight to Tucson. She left the good looking young waiter an extra large tip, then started for her train.

~~~

The next morning, the young woman with the rainbow colored hair opened her Los Angeles Times. On the third page, lower right, she read about the death of an Asian woman at LA's Union Station. The victim was crushed and mangled under the wheels of an arriving Amtrak train. Investigators identified the victim but weren't releasing her name. Police learned she was on her way to Tucson. An accompanying photo showed EMTs wheeling her body toward a waiting ambulance.

The young woman closed her Times and punched a number on her cell phone. When someone at the other end picked up, she asked, "Seen today's paper?"

"Not yet," a man answered. "What's up?"

"Take a look," she said. "We made the third page."

"Shit," he laughed. "Same as last time. When we gonna make the front page?"

~~~

Mother and daughter stood on the Big Lake homestead's landing field, locked in each other's arms. They hugged for a full minute. They had spoken just once since the events in Dutch Harbor.

Robin pushed Sasha to arm's length, looked her up and down, checked to see that all of her mom's parts were still in place. "You're okay?" Robin asked.

"Physically, fine."

"Physically fine? And the rest?"

Sasha took her daughter's face in her two hands, kissed her on the forehead. "I'm tired, jumpy, and shaky. The mental side, darling daughter, I'm coming to grips with."

"I saw the press conference," Robin said. "You looked so tense. I thought you were going to rip the podium in half."

"Nothing gets by you, does it? I thought I had masked that pretty well." Sasha put her arm through her daughter's as they slowly walked from the airfield. "Actually, it was a coffee overdose. I wanted to be up for the conference, even though I felt pretty much like a limp rag. I've hardly slept a wink in almost two days."

"The other guy, your partner out there . . . Dana?"

"Charlie Dana."

"Yeah. He acted so weird. I mean, he mumbled, didn't look at you, even though you thanked him for his help. What's up with that?"

Sasha took her time replying. "It was the first time he'd ever been in a shooting."

"It was *your* first time, too," Robin added quickly.

"True. But he's not a street cop. He's mainly an attorney, supposed to keep the other FBI agents current on the law. We just happened to get put together. The shooting was scary. Real scary."

"And you're still working together?"

"No. Not any more. He's got other things to do."

Robin began walking faster, pulling her mom. "Hurry up. Viktor's waiting to see you. He's made borscht."

"Beet or cabbage?"

"Beet. In your honor. How long you here for?"

"Just 'til tomorrow. We leave for Russia in a few days. That crime conference. Be there a week or so. But as soon as I'm back from Vladivostok, I'm taking time off. I'm putting in for leave. Maybe half a year."

Robin stopped in her tracks and almost shouted, "Will we fly every day?"

"Every mother-lovin' day. Promise."

"Most everyone's away," Viktor explained at dinner that evening. "Up at Beluga Lake, getting the lodge ready for the season. A big bunch of New Zealanders are due in mid-May.

Little early for hunting, but we're not going to talk 'em out of coming."

"Just as well there's no one around here right now," Sasha said. "I need to chill, sleep, eat, catch up with the two of you, and sleep some more. I'm fried." She looked at her daughter, "Tell me about your flight training. Still bumping heads with the instructor?"

Robin smiled. "Viktor and I got that sorted out. I'm actually working more with Uncle Terry. He's teaching me to tune the 172, the Skyhawk."

"Ask your uncle if he wouldn't mind giving my plane a once over. Running a little rough. No rush. I want to leave it here. I'll pick it up when I get back from Russia, in ten days or so. Meanwhile, maybe granddad'll give me a ride back to town tomorrow."

"Leave about nine?" he asked.

"Settled," said Sasha. She stared at her daughter. "So, I got a question that I've been meaning to ask. How come I call this gentleman granddad and you get to call him Viktor?"

Robin looked lovingly at her grandfather. "Feels right," she said, taking her bowl to the stove and ladling herself another portion of borscht. She laid the dish on the table then went in back of her mom and hugged her around the neck. "Is that a problem for you, *Sasha?*" she asked, growling in her mother's ear.

Sasha laughed out loud and relaxed back into her daughter's embrace. "God, I am so happy to be home."

She awoke at eight the next morning, the sleep at the homestead, as always, deep and restful. She dressed quickly and went back to Viktor's cabin where she found a carafe of coffee and a stack of toast. And two notes: one from her daughter, gone to school, wishing her a safe back-and-forth to Russia; and the second from Viktor reminding her they were leaving for Anchorage at nine and that they'd grab breakfast en route.

Two hours later, at Red Robin Gourmet Burgers in Wasilla, Sasha ordered Arctic cod and chips. Viktor went for the soup and sandwich combo. Both ordered cherry Cokes. They waited in silence until Sasha took a deep breath.

"Granddad. I'm seeing a psychologist. I've started getting some stuff off my chest. I can talk to her. Nice lady. She asked if I had anyone else to confide in. She recommended it, actually. I thought of you."

Viktor carefully sipped a spoonful of steaming clam chowder and smiled playfully at his granddaughter.

"Why always me?" he asked. "When you were eight you confessed about having taken Marnie's Lego set. Your cousin was very upset. And at fifteen, you took her boyfriend and felt the need to once again confess your pilfering to me. What have you taken of hers now?"

"Marnie's safe. This time, it's all about me. Me and my life." She dipped a piece of cod in tartar sauce. "Granddad," a long pause. "I'm a drunk. A drinker. A drunk, I guess."

Viktor didn't react immediately.

"Did you hear what I said?"

"I'm not deaf," he answered testily. "My knees are shot, my hips are done for, my right shoulder aches every time I chop wood, I can't climb into my own plane, damn it, but my ears, dearest granddaughter, still work. I heard you say you're a drunk. Or a drinker. Not the strangest thing in the world, considering your Russian heritage."

"You're Russian and you're not a drunk. None of our family is. Only me."

He considered a long moment. "It seems to me that there are drunks and then there are heavy drinkers.

"And the difference?" she asked.

Viktor sat back. "Full-time drunks drive their snow machines into open water. They beat their wives and children, shoot at the village police officer, then claim they can't remember anything because they blacked out. And then there are the part-timers, folks who drink to excess every now and then, maybe because their life is intolerable. They can go along pretty okay for days, maybe weeks, then something trips them up, and they fall off the wagon. I learned that idiom—fall off the wagon—from your grandmother. No one I ever knew spoke English as beautifully as my Virginia. And after forty years of marriage, she spoke pretty damn good Russian, too."

Sasha smiled at the mention of her grandmother, at whose skirt-side she'd been raised.

"So, darling Sasha. I ask you now for a self-assessment. Where are you on that drunk-drinker scale that I just described?"

"Well. I'm not the beat-my-wife, beat-the-kids kind. At least not yet. Although the other day, I was hung over on the job and screwed up badly. Gary saved my rear end. Again. And I'm smart enough not to take my snow machine out on the lake before the ice has been judged thick enough, mid-January. I'm more the kind who finds getting bombed an occasional and easy escape.""From?"

She thought a minute. "From a life that I hate some of the time. Maybe more than some of the time." She began bending her straw into odd shapes.

Viktor sipped his Coke. "Your husband was an exceptional man, Sasha. Exceptional. You were different around him. Softer, sweeter, much nicer to be around. And sober."

"You're right. I used to be nicer. I liked myself. In the two years we were married, Robin helped me learn to like myself in ways I never knew I could. He put up with such bullshit from me. In the beginning, before we were married, I'd butt up against him. But he never felt he needed to oppose me. He worked his judo on me, not resisting, just stepping out of the way of whatever silly wave I was stirring up. He always let me win. And then one day, I realized that winning wasn't all it's cracked up to be."

"From a cranky, bitchy little girl, to a gentle and accepting woman."

"Cranky? Bitchy?"

"I'm being kind, Sasha, my love. You were all that and worse before you met Robin."

"I admit it. And since he's gone?"

Viktor started on his sandwich, took his time, and finished a mouthful. "I'm not a counselor. I'm not sure what to say and what not to say. I'm not even sure that the full-time drunk, part-time drinker idea I just described is valid. But because you are my favorite grandchild—don't let the others know—I need to tell you something. You've developed a hard shell since Robin's death. Which I completely understand. I know you need to protect yourself. You've been deeply and maybe permanently scarred. I get that. I also felt that need for self-protection after your grandmother died. Still do, a little. But there's something else going on, isn't there?"

She finished the last piece of cod. "Yeah, there is.

Robin validated me as a person. And as a cop, too. Here I was, trying to make it in a man's world, trying to be a tough, capable policeman. It was way harder than I thought it'd be. But he made it okay for me, helped smooth the way. Gave me a ton of confidence. We'd talk about our work and it was clear that he admired my take on things. He wasn't just playing the role of supporting husband. He *really* appreciated and valued my views on his investigations. It was like he was saying, 'I'm a trooper and my wife's a cop. And she's every bit as competent, maybe even more so, than I am.'"

"And when he died?" Viktor asked. "What happened at work?"

"You can imagine. It wasn't the same anymore. That validation, that pat on the back, disappeared. It was like I had to start all over again, proving that I was worthy to be a cop. Which is why I'm reluctant to seek advancement. Jack suggested the other day that I should apply for a lieutenant's job. I know I'm ready, but the other detectives at the station don't. So, to save myself further aggravation, I try to avoid the limelight, even when I believe, in my heart, I deserve it. Does that make any sense?"

"It does, even to an old crank like me. You know, Sasha, your life is like a pendulum. Back and forth, from one extreme to another. Maybe you can find some center ground?"

"Not sure, granddad. Where do you think I am on the pendulum right now?"

"You're at one extreme and I think you drink to cope, not only with your loss but with your loneliness. I think you want someone close but you're afraid to open up, afraid of being vulnerable, and you feel you are too . . . too complicated maybe. Too ornery. Too fearful, perhaps. Too much baggage.

Have I got it right?"

"For the most part. But I think I'm worse off than that."

"Perhaps you're saving part of your confession for the psychologist you're seeing."

"I am. Some things I'm not too proud of." More twisting of the straw. "You mentioned the wagon, falling off and staying on. Lemme see what it's like to stay on. See if I can manage without booze."

"I'll drink to that," he said, sipping at his Coke. "And now it's my turn to confess."

"What have you done now?"

"What I've done is flown my last flight. I think seventy years in the cockpit is quite enough, don't you?"

She was speechless.

~~~

"I hope you've brought me good news, Taras Dmitrich."

"The Turk called. The woman's brother has been eliminated."

"Good. Very good," Boris said. He relaxed behind his den's desk. "How did it happen?"

"The Turk's cousin."

Boris smiled. "The always dependable Artun. And what about the brother's girlfriend?"

"Also."

"Artun again?"

"No, no. She ran. Flew to Los Angeles. Nasty accident at the train terminal."

Boris raised his brows. "That skinny little bit of thing? What's her name?"

"Irene."

"Irene. How much?"

"The usual. Fifteen thousand."

"A bargain. So, where are we now in this giant mess? Ozil should be feeling better. Shouldn't we be able to sound the all clear?"

"We can. Those four connections to the Turk have been eliminated."

"Wonderful. Maybe the worst is over. I'll call him right away, talk about new arrangements." Boris regarded his long-time friend and brother-in-law. The man was as down in the dumps as Boris had ever seen him. He knew that Taras and Kostya were close in ways only twins can be close. They grew up in Odessa, attended the Fontanka School for delinquent orphans. Taras, despite being younger by twenty minutes, had always assumed the status of big brother. He often had to rescue Kostya from his poor decision-making, most notably after the stupidity at the Dubrovka Theater. When Kostya was dismissed from his sinecure with Russia's Federal Security Services, Taras came to his boss and vouched for his twin.

Reluctantly, Boris had agreed to sponsor Kostya, to bring him to America, to put him to work.

In spite of his initial qualms, Boris had to admit that the man had performed well at the simple jobs assigned to him in Brooklyn and further out on Long Island. Kostya's methods were decidedly crude, but eminently effective. So when someone was needed to go to Alaska to recover the American fisherman's last shipment of heroin, Taras had put forward his brother's name.

The bodyguard shook his head. "I'm to blame, Boris Davidich. I should have foreseen this."

"My fault, too. Taras. It was my call to send him. I gave your brother a job for which he was not suited." *Kostya is better off dead,* Boris thought. *Because of his bumbling, the fool brought about not only his own death but the deaths of two of my most trusted men. Dammit! But what's done is done. I have to take care of Taras. He needs closure. And in our world, closure comes only with revenge.*

11

For anyone else, this would have been a tough audience. But Nolan Cardozo knew how to get this kind of a crowd lathered up. He understood better than their own spouses the problems and stresses of the working lives of the folks listening to him this morning. The several hundred international law enforcement personnel gathered in Anchorage for the *Sixth Annual Pacific Rim Conference on Organized Crime* shared a common understanding about their work: they were barely holding the line.

What they were hearing from Cardozo was hardly new information. This was a pep talk, a call to arms, not much more. Everyone in the hall understood that. But in spite of their long-held cynicism, the policemen gathered here could dare to feel a small twinge of optimism. They knew that Cardozo represented an American organization—the Drug Enforcement Agency—that had money, resources, and reach. They felt encouraged by his fiery rhetoric, on display now.

> *"Today's international crime cartels can compete on virtually any level with any country's law enforcement apparatus. They can compete in the area of sophisticated communications and in methods of transportation. Today's criminal cartels are very adept bankers and money managers. And in strength of arms, I don't have to tell you that they often out-muscle us."*

Cardozo was just warming up, working the dais like Jagger painting it black. He removed his jacket, loosened his tie and rolled up his sleeves.

> *"You heads of international police forces grapple daily with worsening news: how narco-terrorism poisons*

the political system; how white collar criminals skim billions each year with the witting help of financial institutions; how organized crime extends its reach, touching every household in your countries with illegitimacy and corruption; how smugglers control your borders; and how overburdened court systems are daily losing ground. The best we can say is . . . we're holding our own."

At the rear of the packed hall, Detective Sasha Kulaeva entered quietly, name tag in place. She had come fully awake only at ten this morning, feeling relaxed and encouraged by her tell-all the day before with her grandfather.

A waiter directed her to the far end of the crowded hall. She began snaking her way around the tables, acknowledging acquaintances, exchanging greetings with some, nodding to a few, avoiding others.

She stopped for a long several minutes at the Alaska State Troopers table where she recognized colleagues from her early days in Sitka. They had heard about the shooting in Dutch Harbor, were eager to inquire about her well-being, and applaud her work. She thanked them, promised she'd get back to Sitka soon for a visit. As she was saying her last goodbyes, she heard herself being hailed. Emmitt Esterhazy, several tables removed, was calling to her.

Wending her way toward the FBI table, she drew admiring looks from a pair of swarthy delegates, their nametags showing them representing the Santiago, Chile Police Department. She gave them her most alluring smile. "Hola, muchachos," she threw at them. The men—one more handsome than the other—could barely contain themselves.

Sasha waved demurely and continued on.

Esterhazy had seen her performance. "A trail of broken hearts," he said as she drew near.

"Those two? Dime a dozen," Sasha said, sliding into a chair and greeting the other three agents at the table, Charlie Dana conspicuous by his absence. *Do I care one way or the other? Not any more. Long as he keeps his mouth shut.*

Esterhazy gave her an avuncular once over. "You're looking exceptionally lovely today. I'm actually surprised to see you here. I thought you might take a pass on this meeting, given the rough time you and Dana had out on the Chain."

Sasha searched the table for food. "I didn't want to miss any of Nolan's speechifying. I heard a bit just now. For someone whose agency has just gotten scooped," she exchanged smiles with Esterhazy, "he's actually still sounding pretty in charge."

"You gotta give him that," Esterhazy said. "Galvanizing the troops in his own inimitable fashion is his strong suit. Saying nothing new, of course. But he's saying it with panache! That's the important thing, Sasha. It's not what Cardozo says, but how he says it."

Sasha knew better than to respond. *Maybe we can get out of the building without the two directors provoking each other.* She reached over and took a skewered prawn off of Esterhazy's plate and dipped it in a small dish of what she supposed was Hoisin sauce. "I'm wondering how he reacted to our press conference. Must be pretty unhappy at being one-upped."

Esterhazy allowed himself a sly smile. "Unhappy doesn't begin to describe the mood of our esteemed, local DEA director. Word from inside his office says he was spanked by DC and is taking it out on the underlings."

"Poor baby," Sasha said, finishing off the prawn and wiping her mouth with a starched cloth napkin. "Had lunch the other day with Elena Markova. We're prepping for our work in Vladivostok. She's helping me with the cyber stuff."

"Great. We'll have fun in Russia."

Sasha remembered her boss' warning about the FBI chief being available. She diverted the conversation. "Our case. How's it moving?"

"We're working on getting a handle on the heroin, trying to find out where it came from. My bet's Afghanistan, though you can't rule out South East Asia. And we've got the information the Coast Guard guy, Pozol, gave us."

"Kozol."

"Yeah, Kozol. He sent us Lasorda's work history. Also the names of every American fisherman who's worked on Russian fishing boats. We've contacted the National Marine Fisheries Service about the previous thirty-three times Lasorda shipped out from Russia. Plus, I've been in touch with Interpol in Moscow about the Vladivostok side. See if they can't help. Russia's had a heroin task force since '07, but between you me, I don't place a lot of faith in it."

"Neither do I," Sasha said. "What I hear about Vladivostok is that it's running a close third behind Moscow and St. Petersburg in crime stats. Sure, we can ask for help from the locals, but you're right. We shouldn't expect much. Especially with you-know-who as the mayor over there."

"Kollantai? A crook from the word 'go.' And a dangerous one, to boot." Esterhazy got to the last prawn just as Sasha was reaching for it. "Still, the main question remains—where does the heroin go once it's in Anchorage."

Sasha trolled the table for more leftovers. "And really, the only one who can help is Rudy Castro. What's his status? Gonna cooperate?"

"Maybe. Maybe not," Emmitt said, gnawing the prawn off the skewer. "He's over at Fourth Avenue. Jepson, his PD, is trying to make him see the light, urging him to cop a plea. The DA, though, wants him to do some time. Castro, naturally, is objecting. Thinks he's got something to trade. We'll see."

Sasha slid a plate of pirogi closer, speared one and began carving it up. "How 'bout the dead Russians? Do we know who they were?"

"The bodies were flown in this morning from Dutch. We got mobile prints at the airport and sent 'em back east right away. If these guys are in the system, we should hear back soon, maybe tomorrow if we're lucky."

"Great, although I don't think we'll be able to connect them to the vanished Jimmy Lasorda," she said. She moved Esterhazy's plate in front of her. She finished the pirogi and started on a ricotta-stuffed crepe. "Dana and I interviewed everyone on board. Not a single out-of-tune note from any of them. We agreed with the Coast Guard, with Kozol, that unless we find something new, it'll go down as an accidental drowning. Best we could do."

"That's what I figured," Esterhazy said. "By the way, I spoke with the chief out in Dutch, Babiarsz. No problem for you out there, is there?"

Sasha kept her face neutral. "None that I can foresee. It was a righteous shoot. Guy was running, spun 'round and fired. I returned fire. I'm cool."

"Happy to hear it. We're working on how the three Russians got there in the first place. We're in contact with the FAA about flight plans in and out of Dutch over the past several weeks. Very little they could tell us because the airport out there is uncontrolled, doesn't have a tower. Planes avoid each other by using a common radio frequency to talk to each other. Anyone can land at any time. So we're contacting pilots who might have flown out there during that period. See if they saw anything. Lots of flights. Lots of pilots. "

Sasha noticed her partner making his way to their table. He looked seriously upset. "Hey guy. What's up? I thought you weren't planning on coming today."

Hernandez pulled up a chair. "I wasn't." He rubbed his face. "Bad news. Rudy Castro made bail and disappeared."

Sasha sat back, forkful of crepe half-way to her mouth. "How'd that happen?"

"Girlfriend, Rose Nakamura, came up with cash for the bond. Twenty grand. Rudy walked yesterday, around noon. His PD called to let me know. He went to the jail but his client had bailed. Jepson was as surprised as I was."

"Any line on where he might be? Have you spoken to Rose?"

Gary shook his head. "She's also flown the coop. We've staked out her place in mid-town, Castro's Hillside house, and his sister's apartment in Earthquake Park. We've also got a BOLO out for her car."

Sasha sagged, tossed her fork onto the table.

"It's not all bad," Gary said. "Crime lab called. The prints off the hundred dollar bills you got at the B and B? They match the ones on the syringe taken from the woman's butt."

"Good news," she said, realizing that the guilty verdict she had rendered in the parking lot had now been corroborated and the execution of Konstantin Zhuganov, in her eyes, justified. *Shot the right guy! Case closed.* Next to her, Esterhazy raised his arm and waved to someone. She turned to see. Charlie.

The agent began making his way to the table, but stopped short when he saw Sasha. The SAC pulled out a chair for him. Charlie sat, avoiding looking at his former partner.

Esterhazy laid a hand on his arm. "I wanted to tell you earlier, but I didn't get the chance. I'm recommending you for the Bureau's Shield of Bravery. Quantico's already read the account I sent them of what you and Sasha did out on the Chain. They wanted me to recommend the award, which I'm happy to do. Congratulations."

Charlie fiddled with an empty cup and saucer. "Really?" was all he said.

"Yeah, really. And one more thing. I want you to come to Vladivostok with me. Help me out at the conference."

"I shouldn't take the time off. I'm behind in my work here at the office."

"The hell with the work. You're coming with me to Russia. Beef up your CV. It's settled."

On the stage, Cardozo was finishing with a rush.

"Ladies and gentlemen. This is war! Crime is proliferating at levels thought unthinkable just a few years ago. If we don't take it seriously and if we don't mobilize all the community resources at our disposal in waging this war, we are sure to lose it. The enemy is tenacious, cunning, and utterly ruthless. We, acting together, must be equally cunning, equally tenacious, and equally ruthless in our single-minded quest—to stamp out international organized crime on the Pacific Rim."

The audience burst into applause, many rose to their feet. Esterhazy stood out of politeness but didn't clap. Sasha continued to work on her crepe while the object of her indifference stood and made toward the exit. She watched as Charlie stopped three tables away and began talking with a very attractive woman from the Tokyo Metropolitan Police. Sasha shrugged. *What else is new?* She got up, and together with Gary and Emmitt, began a slow shuffle to the doors, stoppered to a standstill. She felt someone come up to her from behind. She stopped and turned.

"Hola senorita." A beautiful baritone belonging to one of the cops from Chile. The man inclined his head slightly and extended his hand. "Tomás Morales."

"Aleksandra Kulaeva. Mucho gusto." She reached for his hand and was floored when he took it and pressed it to his lips and kept it there for a good three seconds.

Sasha was dazzled. *I could get used to this.*

He released her hand. "I have a meeting right now that will occupy me throughout the afternoon and evening. But if you will be in Russia for the rest of the conference, perhaps we might meet there for dinner?"

Without thinking, Sasha answered. "I would like that very much." She wanted to say more but found herself tongue tied. She turned to see her partner and Esterhazy leaving the hall. "If you'll excuse me, now, Tomás. I, too, have work. See you in Vladivostok. I hope."

"I look forward to it. Hasta luego," he said. "Until then."

She smiled and reluctantly left the Chilean. When she got to the exit, she looked back. He was still standing there, gazing at her. He bowed his head once again. She did the same and, feeling happily light-headed, left the auditorium.

She came out into a huge, high-ceilinged atrium filled with leafy shrubbery of all sizes and a copse of thirty-foot high trees. There were glass sculptures in closed cases as well as the obligatory scattering of stuffed Alaskan fauna: brown and black bears, wolves and wolverines, eagles, geese, and puffins. There were a dozen large tables covered with conference literature, bottled water, urns and carafes of coffee next to piles of fresh fruit. Scattered easels showed workshop room numbers and the agenda for the rest of the day.

Charlie and the Japanese delegate had exited the auditorium in front of Sasha. The two walked arm in arm and appeared to be basking in each other's company. They stopped to chat next to a stuffed polar bear standing on hind legs. They stood close to each other.

Sasha couldn't damn Charlie for being a two-timer since they hadn't done the beast with two backs even once. Though they'd come close. She considered bringing it up later that afternoon at her meeting with Katherine Manfredi.

At the far end of the atrium, a burst of laughter broke from a small crowd of well-dressed men and women. At center stage stood a large man with a mop of wavy blond hair, dressed in a beautifully cut dark suit. Roman Kollantai, the Mayor of Vladivostok and host of the second half of the conference, was holding court. He had a parental arm around a young woman, short, dark complected, curly black hair, wearing sunglasses. He was introducing her to the other delegates.

Sasha knew of Kollantai by reputation. Like many Russians who managed to survive the bumpy road from Gorbachev to Putin, the mayor of Vladivostok was a deft juggler. He nimbly changed roles as the need arose: Communist Party apparatchik, populist leader, new capitalist-cum-oligarch, and through it all, an unforgiving and ruthless mobster. The urbane and cunning mayor of Vladivostok was reputed to have fingers in many enterprises, and a few, actually, legitimate.

One of his entourage noticed Sasha and pointed her out to the mayor. Kollantai looked her way, smiled and did his imitation of a gunslinger's fast draw. He mouthed a 'pow-pow,' then blew smoke from his imaginary six-shooter's barrel. The men around him laughed. "Annie Oakley," he called to her. More laughter. The young woman with Kollantai raised her sunglasses onto her forehead and didn't bother looking at Sasha.

Standing next to his partner, Gary also saw the woman.

"Wonder if she drives a blue Mercedes?"

Sasha nodded. "Wouldn't doubt it."

"Not much we can do about it here," he added. "But once you're in Russia, think you might have jurisdiction?" he laughed.

She laughed along with him. "I didn't have jurisdiction in Dutch and look at the shit I'm in."

"You'll be fine. Listen, Sash. I got some work back at the office. I'll touch base later."

"Talk to you," she said.

Gary left and she and Esterhazy strolled over to a table heavy with baskets of fresh fruit. Sasha grabbed a bunch of red grapes, Emmitt opted for a banana. Before they could pretend that they hadn't seen him, a smiling Nolan Cardozo came over, hands in his pockets.

"Hello Emmitt," Cardozo said, focusing on the FBI chief and ignoring Sasha.

Sensing a battle of the behemoths, she retreated a step, out of the direct line of fire.

"Hiya Nolan," Esterhazy answered lightly. Then, unable to resist, the FBI chief stormed in with an uppercut, "Heard you got an earful from D.C. the other day."

Sasha winced and moved further away.

Cardozo visibly rocked back on his heels. He withdrew his hands from his pockets and made his fingers into fists. His mouth froze into a rictus while the muscles along his jaw worked up and down.

Esterhazy, smiling wolfishly and gazing at the DEA director, worked on his banana. The stare-down continued for half a minute before Cardozo was able to answer. He stood up straighter, seemed to puff out. "So how come you didn't let me know?" he demanded.

Esterhazy put on a puzzled expression, looked at Sasha, as if seeking a clarification of Cardozo's baffling question. He spent time finishing the banana, then dropped the peel into a trash container. He wiped his hands carefully with a napkin.

"Oh, right," he said. "You must be referring to the twenty-three pounds of heroin in the *FBI's* evidence lockup." Esterhazy grinned a nasty grin, and then very slowly, enunciating each word, "Now why the fuck would I let you know?"

Sasha closed her eyes. *Maybe I can save myself if I just back out of the free-fire zone.*

Cardozo glared at his nemesis, his brows lowering. "Why? Here's why, Mr. FBI Special Agent in Charge," he snarled. "Because drug trafficking falls within the purview of the Drug Enforcement Agency. My agency. That's why."

Esterhazy weighed the DEA director's answer. "So you're telling me that if the situation were reversed, you'd let me know? 'Zat right?"

Cardozo's expression indicated he didn't get the question. Esterhazy had another go.

"Let's say, Nolan, the DEA, your agency, has a line on a domestic terror cell. You're all set to make a bust. But you'd hold off, right? You'd drop everything and get on the horn and let us folks at the Bureau know. Right? Because you understand that domestic terrorism is within the purview—that's the proper word, isn't it, Nolan? purview—of the FBI. And you'd want to do the right thing, wouldn't you?"

When Cardozo didn't respond, Esterhazy blew out a small breath, *phhhh*, at the DEA director. Sasha thought Cardozo might launch a physical attack on the FBI chief, older by at least twenty years. But Cardozo held himself in check.

Esterhazy looked around, saw Charlie sipping coffee with a female delegate. "Charlie," he yelled, "C'mon, gimme a ride back to the office."

Charlie looked over, put down his cup, began making apologies to the woman. She seemed annoyed that her new friend was being called away.

Sasha couldn't help smiling, imagining the woman's final words: *Maybe later. Come by my room. I'll make miso soup and udon noodles. We'll have fun.*

Esterhazy looked at Sasha, then at Charlie and the Japanese woman. He leaned toward the detective and whispered. "Green doesn't become you, Sasha. Leave it. I'll talk to you later." He walked over to his agent and the two men headed for the exit.

Green? Sasha thought. *With jealousy? Unh-uh. I've left it, Emmitt. Charlie's yesterday's news.* She snapped to and realized she was now alone with someone who resembled Vesuvius on a bad day.

"Tell me something, detective," Cardozo said quietly.

Oh shit. "What's that, Director?" Sasha tossed a couple grapes into her mouth.

The DEA chief sneered. "Does your boss know you're a closet drunk?" Cardozo's mouth formed an ugly scar, then he turned and walked away.

Now it was Sasha's turn to recoil, unable to swallow, the grapes jammed in her throat.

~~~

Hugo Mertens and Alan Casper were patrol sergeants for the Dutch Harbor Police Department. Although they had been cops for a combined twenty-eight years, their experience with homicide was limited—Mertens had investigated two, Casper, one. Neither had ever worked an Officer Involved Shooting probe.

Their boss, Police Chief Stan Babiarsz, had described to them the jurisdictional problems. He explained how they were stuck with the dirty job of investigating the shooting of three Russians by an Anchorage detective.

"Those pieces of shit are better off dead," Babiarsz had noted to his sergeants. "But we need to do our due diligence."

The two men began their OIS investigation by reading the statement the woman cop gave to their chief.

"Kinda stinky," Casper said. "We're supposed to *believe* her, that the Russians were there to rob the people at

- 319 -

the B and B? Man, does *that* not fly."

"I agree. Total bullshit. But I'm not sure it's our job to question that part of her story," Mertens said. "Whatever the hell they were there for, I think we're only supposta assess whether or not our department's policies were followed so far as the shooting's concerned."

"OK," Casper said. "She wrote that she gave them warning, the two upstairs. They brought up their weapons, she felt herself in imminent danger and shot 'em. Cut and dry. I'll buy it."

"Me, too," said Mertens. "I don't see any contradictory evidence. And the third one, the guy in the parking lot? Seems the same, according to her statement. Says she ran after him, told him to halt, he fired, she fired. They dug his bullet out of the side of the bed and breakfast."

"Yeah, but what about the dude's busted nose?" Casper asked.

"Musta got broke when he fell. After he got shot."

"Makes sense."

"I wish the FBI agent . . . what's his name?"

"Dana."

Mertens nodded. "Yeah, I wish Dana had seen it go down, could support Kulaeva's statement."

"No, it's just her."

"Alright," Mertens said. "And according to the Anchorage crime lab, the fingerprints from the dead Russian in the parking lot were on a needle stuck in some murdered woman's ass, the one they found in a meadow north of Anchorage."

"Looks to me like this Kulaeva saved the taxpayers a load of money, took care of a killer."

"That's what it looks like. You go, girl."

~~~

Katherine Manfredi was in her front yard, playing the good gardener, on hands and knees, digging into the pungent spring soil. She rose when she saw Sasha pull up across the street.

"You're early," she called to her client, wiping earthy hands on her gardening apron.

Sasha got out and remote-locked her car.

"I lost track of the time. Hope it's not a problem."

"I would have liked a heads up, but as long as you're here . . ." Manfredi walked to the arbor that served as a passageway into her yard.

Sasha paused at the gate. "Katherine, I'm alright. I know I shouldn't be but I think I am. At least I got through the mess in Dutch in one piece."

"Quite an ordeal," Manfredi said, taking hold of Sasha's right hand, and leading her into the yard. "Let me wash and change out of these work clothes, then I'll brew us some coffee."

A quarter hour later, patient and therapist sat in Manfredi's office, coffee mugs at hand. Beyond the room's broad bay window, the western sky—seen through the therapist's forest of cacti—was a cloudy rose-orange. Several minutes passed while each woman considered a way to begin the conversation.

Sasha finally spoke. "There's a lot to tell. An awful lot. I'm not sure where to start. Or what to include. I mean, things happened out there that have never happened to me before, and I'm still processing. Isn't that what I'm supposed to be doing, Katherine? Processing? And right now, I'm feeling a little . . . I don't know . . . tight, I guess. A little like *not* sharing. Which is crazy because I called you as soon as I got back, thinking I had *a lot* to get off my chest."

"I'm sure it's difficult sorting out your thoughts and feelings. Those were highly unusual events out in the Aleutians, even for you, a trained and veteran policewoman."

"Trained and veteran? Is that what I am? I guess. It's funny in a way. This was the first time I've ever had my gun out of its holster. Isn't that weird? Nearly seventeen years a cop and this is the first time I've ever drawn my pistol." Sasha rose and walked her half-empty cup to the kitchen, topped it off, then returned to the living room, pausing against the kitchen doorjamb. "Tell me something, Katherine."

"Sure."

"You may not be able to answer–privacy and all–but I'm wondering if any of your clients ever talk to you about crimes they've committed?" Sasha lightened her tone. "I'm not looking for names or specifics. I'm not playing the arresting cop here. But I'd really like to know whether you've heard about criminal activities."

Manfredi sat back and searched her ceiling. "I think I can answer in a general way. The short answer is 'yes,' I've heard about illegal activities. I've seen hundreds of clients with all kinds of histories, all kinds of baggage. And criminal activities, every now and then, are part of the conversation. But if you're wondering about therapist-patient privilege, I can assure you that I have never, ever breached a confidence. Nor would I."

The detective kept her expression neutral. "Tell me, if you can–you can keep it vague–the kinds of crimes folks have confessed to you, things, maybe in the range of Class A or B felonies."

"Well, other than murder and kidnapping, I'm not at all sure what crimes fit into those categories. I had a client once who threatened to kill her boss. Verbally and several times on email. Didn't do it, but spent some time in jail just the same."

"Did any of them show remorse? Did they feel the slightest twinge of guilt about what they'd done?"

"Some of them sincerely regretted their acts. For others, it seemed all they needed to rid themselves of any guilt was to verbalize to me their transgressions."

"Interesting," Sasha said. *So, we've danced around the problem. I've laid the groundwork. What do I do now?* She took a seat on the bay window and decided. *Not yet. Not ready for the confession.* "You know something odd? I hadn't thought of this before, but my pistol—it's a Glock nine—it felt lighter when I was holding it than it ever had before. I'm waiting for the two Russians to come up the stairs and I wasn't sure I'd loaded the magazine. I freaked, had to feel for it. It's silly because just a minute before, I'd checked the clip, shoved it in and cranked a round into the chamber." Sasha closed her eyes. "I fired six times at the two men. Two . . . three at the man closest to me and three at the second Russian. Missed only one time. I could see the bullets hitting where I aimed. It's a memory I guess I'll probably always have." She looked out the bay window, onto Cook Inlet's sun-streaked waters. "I've shot game before. Lots. Moose, caribou, deer. Shot a seal once down in Prince William Sound, near Tatitlek. But always from a distance, always far enough away so I didn't really see the bullet as it punctured the flesh. But I wasn't more than a few feet from these two guys. I can see the hole the slug made in the first man's shirt as it went into the side of his shoulder. The force of it was unbelievable. He was a big man but he got spun around. And the second guy, I fired into his chest and almost lifted him right off the ground. You could hear the bullets striking the men. But I think maybe I'm imagining that. Shouldn't have been able to hear anything over the gunfire."

Manfredi sat as quietly as she could, absorbing and cataloging every detail. *This is so cool.*

"As soon as the Russians were down, I ran to the end of the corridor, to the hall window. I had to jump over the two dead men. They were piled on top of each other. From the window, I saw the third man running toward his car. I fired three rounds at him and hit him once in the back of his thigh. A lucky shot at that distance. My partner'd been shooting through the door of his room. I think he hit the second man."

As the light in the west dimmed, casting the room in shadows, Sasha's tone of voice became more intense. "The guy in the parking lot screamed like crazy. But the two upstairs hadn't made a sound. I'm thinking they died instantly. It all went down pretty fast. Probably no more than four, five seconds, if that."

"This is the first time you've mentioned your partner, the FBI agent," the counselor said.

"Right. Charlie."

"Charlie?"

"Charlie Dana. The Boy Scout. I'm not sure he's a good cop, though he thinks he is."

"How's that?"

"He thinks we should play by the rules."

"Shouldn't we?"

Sasha squirmed in her seat. "Forget him. He's not important. But something happened today. Bad. I thought I'd hidden my drinking. Apparently I haven't done such a good job. Turns out the head of the local Drug Enforcement Agency knows I drink. He cornered me, told me so."

"Anything you can do?"

"I could stop drinking. I'm actually trying to sober up. I visited with my grandfather. We talked. For his sake, I'm trying to clean up."

"It's a good start."

It was now twilight in the room, the sun having sunk behind the mountains across the Inlet.

"I got a bunch more, Katherine. Can I save it for next time?"

Manfredi lit her desk lamp. "Of course you can. Any idea when that might be?"

"When I get back from Russia. We're leaving tomorrow. Might be readier to talk about some stuff than I am now. I'll call."

"I'm here."

When she was alone, Manfredi took up pen and yellow pad and for the next hour filled up eight pages of notes, writing without pause. She skipped lines, leaving space to add comments later on.

Although she was fascinated by the very specific details of the shooting, the therapist believed Sasha's questions about confessed crimes and contrition were the most important topics they discussed. Manfredi took three full pages to write down that part of the conversation.

The therapist also noted how calmly her client had recounted what should have been a terrifying and chilling event. Under such circumstances, the psychologist had expected to see someone demonstrably agitated, shocked by the events, shaky, teary. But here, just now, the opposite. Sasha had recounted the shooting with cool dispassion.

Manfredi re-read her notes and spent twenty minutes adding between-the-lines remarks, questions to herself, things to think about. Compared to the more mundane problems of her other clients, this was terrific stuff, exciting stuff! She couldn't wait for her next session with Detective Kulaeva.

~~~

Gary drove Sasha to the airport. Both cops were in a partial funk, their case only half solved. The fingerprints on the syringe stuck in Isabel Castro's rear end matched those taken from Konstantin Zhuganov, the third Dutch Harbor Russian. But the disappearance of the bailed Rudy Castro had left them foundering, making it nearly impossible to trace the heroin connection in Anchorage.

Gary parked in front of the Jet Blue doors. "Got everything you need? Doesn't look like a lot for a week," he said, pulling Sasha's small roller bag out of the trunk.

"Everything except my piece. Had to turn it in. But even if I had my weapon, no guns allowed in the new Russia."

"You were thinking you'd need one?"

"You never know. Vlad's a rough place."

Gary's cell phone rang. He checked the number and hit green. After a brief listen, "Say again, I didn't catch that." He turned away from the traffic and covered his off-ear.

Whatever was repeated caused him to shake his head in frustration. After a minute, "Thanks Mr. McKimmey. I appreciate the call. I'll get back to you."

Sasha heard him say 'McKimmey,' and saw the look of defeat on her partner's face. "It's Rose, isn't it?"

"Dead in LA. Crushed on the tracks at the train station. McKimmey said he heard from the LAPD. They found her Fish and Wildlife ID and got in touch with him this morning. She had just gotten off the non-stop flight from here."

Sasha felt leaden. "LAPD have a line on what happened? Accident? Foul play?"

"Not a one. Loads of people around but no witnesses."

"Sounds like good planning," she said, rubbing and twisting her neck. "Rose, you silly little bitch. And Rudy? We gotta find him, Gary, before the Russians do, or *he's* dead meat, and our case will be, too. He's got all the answers."

"Everyone's looking for him, Sash. Esterhazy's mobilized the feds into a national search."

"Alright. Listen, I gotta go. Keep the faith, pardner." She gave him a hug.

He returned a long squeeze. "Stay cool," he said.

"'Stay cool?' Sounds like code for 'stay sober.'"

"That, too."

"I'm trying, Gary. Really, I am. See you in a week."

~~~

Sasha sat next to Elena Markova during the first leg of the trip to Russia—the three-hour flight from Anchorage to Seattle.

"You comfortable with the cyber vocabulary?" Elena asked.

Sasha glanced over the list of technical terms Elena had prepared for her. "Pretty much. Thanks for the help."

"My pleasure." Elena stopped a passing flight attendant and ordered another split of a so-so California Bordeaux.

Sasha took note. *That'd be number three. But who the hell am I to count?*

The attendant looked at Sasha. "Something for you?"

"Sprite, please."

When she left, Elena said, "You've no manners, Sasha. You're letting me drink alone. Again."

"I like the stuff too much. Need to cut back. I actually promised my grandfather."

"That's a good girl," Elena said. "I should have listened to *my* grandfather. He told me to find a rich man who would make me laugh. Jesus, did *I* not listen."

The flight attendant returned with their drinks.

Elena sipped. "Tell me something. The FBI agent, Charlie . . . what's his name? Dana? What's he like?"

Sasha assessed the variety of answers she might give. After consideration, she came up with a measured response. "Generally, a good guy. Good looking in a screwy kind of way. Bright. Can be funny. Can be charming. Perceptive about some things, clueless about others. What else? He likes women."

"Alright. So far, so good. Were you two involved? Or are you now? I know you were working together. Went through all that shit in Dutch."

Sasha smiled at the memory of the B and B bathtub. "We weren't involved. Might have been, but Russians got in the way. No loss, really. Why? You interested?"

"I saw him at the conference in Anchorage." Another

pause. "And yeah, I'm interested. Can you introduce me?"

Sasha laughed out loud. "That would be the kiss of death, Elena. You'd be DOA if *I* introduced you."

"OK then. Maybe I'll try to shanghai him in Vladivostok."

"Go for it. I think he'd probably enjoy the experience. Actually, I think he'd *love* it."

~~~

Boris Bunin smiled up at his long-time friend. "Taras Dmitrich. I have some interesting news for you."

The bodyguard remained tight-lipped, brooding, standing in the Bunin den, peering through a large picture window facing the East River.

Boris looked up from his computer screen. "I've just been to the web site of this crime conference in Alaska. You're aware of the event, are you not?"

"I've read about it. We know some people attending. Friends as well as recent enemies."

"Did you know that the second half of the conference starts in a few days in Vladivostok, Kollantai's fiefdom. Perhaps you should attend."

When Taras shrugged his indifference, Boris went on. "I've just read over the list of delegates going to Russia for the second part of the conference. The list has been modified slightly since the last time I looked. Seems an Anchorage police detective and an FBI agent will be attending. Interested now?"

The expression on Taras' face grew dark. His body stiffened.

"I called Vlad this morning," Boris said. "Spoke to Kollantai. He's agreed that you can come and do what you must. I've made plane reservations for you. You're leaving this afternoon. You'll get there tomorrow night. Back three days later. That ought to be enough time, don't you think?"

"Plenty of time," Taras said quietly. "What help can I expect from Kollantai?"

"Not a great deal. He's not overjoyed about having to absorb all the problems that might follow the deaths of two international policemen at a conference he himself is hosting. You can understand his delicate position. He wants to remain as far removed as possible. He won't provide any muscle, but he'll get you weapons, a car, information, and a safe house if you need one." Boris scrutinized Taras. "You won't need a safe house, will you? Please, Taras. Not like your brother. No torture. Just quick and clean and come home." Boris leaned forward. "We've known each other a long time."

"A very long time, Boris Davidich."

"When you were working for my father, he used you for all kinds of tasks. But since you've been married to my sister, not so much."

"Actually, none at all. You've kept me off the street." Taras hesitated. "I know what you're thinking, and you're right. I *have* been away for a long while." Taras paused. "I know my brother was stupid, impetuous, violent when he didn't need to be, unsophisticated, crude. A jerk. But we were twins. I'll manage. It'll be quick and clean."

Boris nodded his blessing. "Good. So, on your way. And bring my sister something fun from Russia. A fur perhaps?"

"Wouldn't think of returning from abroad without something for Raisa."

~~~

They were five hours out of SeaTac, high above a night-darkened Pacific and halfway through the ten-hour flight to Tokyo's Narita Airport, courtesy of All Nippon Air. Both women were happily into their dinner. Elena had already finished her own flask of sake and was working her way through Sasha's. Between bites of sashimi, Elena asked, "You're a policeman . . . er . . . police*woman*. How'd the hell did *that* happen?"

Sasha put down her chopsticks, the flying fish roe temporarily abandoned. "On my sixteenth birthday, me and a bunch of friends were camping by the Talkeetna River. We were smoking pot and we all got busted by a park ranger. I had two fat joints stuck in my back pocket. My family went bonkers and decided I needed to take my medicine. They didn't lift a finger, no lawyer to help me beat the rap. They even let me spend four nights in the McLaughlin Youth Center in Anchorage, the holding tank for teens. An eye opener and my first real taste of the criminal justice system. When I got to court, the magistrate went easy on me–first offence and all–gave me forty hours of community service. It was a blessing in disguise because part of it included two ride-alongs in police patrol cars. I got hooked, then and there. When I told the folks at home I was going to do criminology and then become a cop, they couldn't believe it."

"And you were all of sixteen?"

"Knew what I wanted," Sasha said, returning to her tobiko.

~~~

Flying Air France eastward across the Atlantic, Taras was torn, nervous, jittery. The assurances he had given Boris had vanished, replaced by self-doubt. He was seriously considering getting off in Paris and returning home straight away. He'd phone Boris, tell him he'd reconsidered the need for revenge. *"After all,"* he'd explain, *"me and my dim-witted twin brother had never been that close. And the murder of two American policemen just for the sake of revenge? What if I get caught? What of Raisa? No, thanks. Too many unhappy consequences."*

Taras believed his change of heart wouldn't substantially alter his relationship with Boris. On the contrary, he felt his honesty would be appreciated. He sat back and reviewed his life with the Bunins, drawing upon memories he'd not recalled for years.

In 1985, when he was nineteen, he found work in the Russian merchant marine, despite never having been to sea. A full grown, six-foot four-inch, two hundred pound rough neck, he'd talked his way into the boiler room of a rusted hulk out of Novorossisk, on the Black Sea. The good ship Prospero was bound for Tampico carrying a cargo of deep sea drilling gear for Pemex, Mexico's state-run oil company.

He was diligent in his work and was duly rewarded with shore leave when they made port in Mexico, three weeks later.

His shipmates did what sailors have always done when they hit dry land—spent their wages in bars and bordellos. But he dreamt of a better, richer life and began hitchhiking north. After a month of dodging the Federales, he wound up in Tijuana, just across the border from California, USA.

Because he was now well-dressed, he hardly got a second look from the US Customs agent. She was a very short, round woman who had to crane her neck upward to take in the young man presenting his American passport for inspection. The document had been issued three years earlier to sixteen-year-old Henry Raymond Thompkins, of Wichita, Kansas. The agent looked at the photo of Henry at sixteen and determined that the man standing in front of her had grown even more handsome over the past three years.

"Welcome home, Henry," the customs agent said.

He nodded, smiled and, under his breath managed a "Thank you."

Had the border control officer asked him the simplest question in English, the jig would certainly have been up. But she surveyed the long line of people waiting behind him and decided that the young man's passport was in order. "Right through those doors," she directed, waving him into America.

Four days later, he arrived by train at Penn Station, in Manhattan. He heard Russian being spoken by a pair of well-dressed older women and inquired in which part of New York City most of their countrymen/émigrés lived. They told him Brighton Beach, Brooklyn. He took the subway and by two o'clock that afternoon, he stood among a dozen older Russian men playing chess under a shady stand of pitch pine trees, not far from the ocean.

He watched, waited, engaged a few of the kibitzers in small talk. He took a seat on a bench next to a man of about eighty years whose loose, wizened skin hung on his bones. He wore a Panama hat and a short-sleeved, flowered shirt. His yellowed teeth and fingers and his hacking cough were testament to a life devoted to tobacco. He introduced himself, extending skeletal fingers.

"Jacob Yakovlovich Ginzberg, formerly of Samara. Nice to meet you."

"I'm Taras . . . Archenko. From Odessa," he replied.

The old man looked at his watch, dangling around his thin wrist. "Time for a late lunch. I could eat a little something. You?"

They walked to the Gambrinus Café and ordered borscht and beef stroganoff. Ginzberg all but inhaled his food.

Later, heading back to the chess arena, he asked the geezer about the Russian mafia in the area.

Ginzberg was purposely vague. "Mafia? You hear about them, for sure, but . . . who knows?"

"Well, I'm interested," he answered. "How might someone get introduced to people in that line of work?"

"Are you nuts?" Ginzberg asked. "If I knew that, which I don't, do you think I would share what I know with you? Hah!"

"No, of course not. Forgive my stupidity. But certainly there must be a place, a night club, a bar

close by where such men meet."

The old man blew out a sigh of disbelief and rolled his eyes. "This way, meshugge," he said.

Fifteen minutes later, they were on Brightwater. When they came abreast of Third Street, the old man stopped, nodded directionally, "A hundred meters straight ahead, on the left. The Krasny Dom. And mazel tov," he said. "One more thing. Pretend we never met." Ginzberg shuffled away.

That night, around nine, he showed up at the Krasny Dom, a cavernous, dimly lit and raucous bar. Over the PA system, Vladimir Visotsky was singing The Ballad of Truth and Lies. A quartet of drinkers around a small table were singing along. He strolled over to them, joined in, and when the song ended, posed a few questions.

Ten minutes later he was fighting for his life in the alley behind the building. Two men, not quite as large as he was, but obviously well versed in bare knuckle fighting, were administering a well-deserved ass-kicking to the nosey punk kid.

He gave a good accounting of himself, and escaped with only three broken ribs and the left side of his face swollen and bloody.

He returned the next night. This time, he was escorted, at gunpoint, to the local mob lieutenant who was intrigued by his brash behavior. The brigadier, Zhenya Karatayev, sat on a table, his legs swinging back and forth. He leaned over and stuck a thin bladed knife half an inch into the upstart's right nostril. He was in a chair, wrapped, mummy-like, neck to toe in duct tape.

"I saw Polanski do this in Chinatown. He cut Nicholson a new nose. You'd like maybe the same?"

"No thank you very much, sir, Mr. Karatayev. I definitely would not like that."

The local mobster appreciated that the boy was polite, liked that he knew when to back off, liked there was no braggadocio. He also liked the young man's size and the fact that his two boyeviki on the previous night had not had an easy time subduing the youth.

"How is it, Taras Zhuganov, we find an American passport and a tidy sum of cash in your pocket?" Karatayev asked.

"I borrowed it from someone in Acapulco."

The brigadier grinned. "And weren't you nervous that the owner, this Henry Thompkins, would alert the police or the American Embassy?"

"That wasn't going to happen," he said.

"And why is that?"

"When I left him, he was in no condition to report anything to anyone." He raised his eyebrows. "Ever," he concluded.

Karatayev, an excellent judge of goon/muscle, began slicing at the duct tape that bound the young man. "I think we have a place for you, Taras."

Stretched in a first class seat, the bodyguard now remembered the bravado that had characterized his younger days. Twenty-five years earlier, as a member of David Bunin's muscle crew in Brooklyn, Taras had willingly done anything demanded of him: breaking arms and legs, smashing faces into unrecognizable masses, and drowning four members of a rival gang in the Head of Bay, out by JFK.

So who's the jerk now, he asked himself? *Who but a jerk would place himself in jeopardy in order to avenge the death of someone he didn't love or didn't respect?*

And if he decided to continue on to Vladivostok? What then? He'd meet Kollantai, get squared away, find the two who killed his brother, dispatch them, and return home. Would it be that simple? Never was.

He tipped forward in his seat, cupped his face in his hands, and held his head.

The woman next to him in the window seat shifted her body toward Taras, as if to strike up a conversation. Her roughly handsome row-mate appeared distraught, eyes shut, lips moving slightly, muttering to himself. She spoke, "Probably nothing I can do, but I'll make the offer anyway."

Taras didn't react.

The woman hesitated and tried again. "If there is anything I can do to help?"

Taras raised his head. "Sorry. What . . .?"

He had noticed her as soon as they boarded but had not yet spoken to her. Now, here she was, late forties, dark eyes and burnished ebony skin, dressed in casual but expensive clothing. Her tastefully elegant jewelry was an arrangement of gold and pearls. And a French accent.

"I thought I'd offer a friendly ear, if that's what you're needing. If not, I'll shut up and mind my business."

Taras liked what he saw and appreciated the offer. He smiled at her. "Thank you. I got caught up, making a list of things to take care of. I'm okay, thanks."

"Good to hear," she said. "I'm Christine D'Arcy." She

didn't extend a hand, but kept both of them folded, regally, on her lap. Her demeanor was relaxed, confident.

"Taras Archenko, from Los Angeles," he answered. "On my way to Paris to visit my brother."

"Taras? Isn't that a Ukrainian name?"

"It is. Not many people know that."

"When I was at the lycée, I read *Taras Bulba,* by Gogol."

"A good read. And you? From your accent, I'd say you're a French speaker, but not from France. I'm going to guess Montreal."

"Actually, Martinique. You know it?"

"In the Caribbean? That Martinique?"

"That's the one," she said, smiling at him. "What's your work, Mr. Archenko?"

"Security."

"Exciting. People? Business? Computer networks?"

"All that," he said, not offering more.

"Do you have a card? I might be in need of your services."

"Never carry them. Don't need them. These days, we have more business than we can handle. Word of mouth works for us."

"Even so, how long will you be in Paris?"

"Not long."

"I live in the Seventh Arrondissement, on Rue Mazarine, near St. Germain. If you're free, perhaps you can stop by, see what kind of home security system you might recommend."

Taras inclined his head and smiled at the woman. "Perhaps."

~~~

"I'm going to burn these clothes as soon as we touch down," Elena announced as they settled into their seats for the last, four-hour leg of their trip, Tokyo to Vladivostok.

"I'm also feeling overripe," Sasha agreed, getting a whiff of her body and making a face.

Their conversations over the past day and a half had flowed easily back and forth in Russian and English.

Sasha thought Elena's Russian was flawless, far and away superior to her own homegrown, non-academic, and much more vulgar version.

Elena explained that she'd earned a full-ride scholarship to study her native tongue at the Middlebury Institute of International Studies, followed by a post-graduate stint at Moscow State University.

"The two years in Moscow were a gas," Elena said. "I'd been there several times before but never for very long. When I was a kid, visiting relatives, the place always seemed so oppressive and uptight. Too much cement and way too many lousy cars. But when I had the chance to study there, the place really blossomed for me." She drifted into a dreamy reverie.

Sasha watched her. "A pleasant thought?"

Elena's smile became wistful. "Maksim. Yum. What a sweetie. But no ambition. He wanted nothing more than to be a lawyer for the Ministry of Interior. Ho hum." Another moment and she snapped to. "Enough. How about you? Where'd you study and who'd you fall in love with on campus?"

"Went down to Washington, to Pullman for criminal justice. No boyfriends to speak of. In those days, I was pretty standoffish. Always been too tall for a lot of guys, made me feel like a geek. Anyhow, finished up in four years, came back and applied to the police training academy in Sitka. They were hard up for women recruits that round, so I lucked out. Finished close to the top of the class and got hired right away by the police department down there."

"Is that where you met your husband? I thought I heard he's a Trooper."

Sasha took her time, asked herself when, if ever, she'd be able to handle questions about her dead husband without diving into a tub of 'poor little me.' She nodded an affirmative. "Yeah. Met him in Sitka, at the Academy. He was a trooper." Pause. *Just say it!* "He died."

"God, I didn't know that. I'm so sorry," Elena said, flustered, embarrassed.

Sasha reached over and touched her arm. "Please, don't feel . . . I mean, it's alright. *I'm* alright. We had a daughter. She's nearly a teenager."

"Nice. And I have a son. He's nineteen. Just finishing his freshman year at Lewis and Clark. Something about sustainability. Strange thing, he can't speak a word of Russian."

"And your husband?"

Elena's caustic grin said it all. "He doesn't speak Russian either."

"No. I meant . . . what about . . .?"

"I know what you meant," Elena said. "Hubby's long gone. He was around just long enough to plant his seed, then picked up and skedaddled. And a good thing, too. Wasn't rich, wasn't funny."

"Shoulda listened to your grandpa."

Elena laughed and looked out her window. Nothing but the Sea of Japan.

~~~

The Aeroflot Airbus A330 was over Siberia. Lake Baikal, Russia's holy lake, thirty-five thousand feet below, sparkled like a precious gem.

Taras closed his eyes and recalled the last hours of the Air France flight, JFK to Paris. They were flying at night over the Atlantic. The cabin lighting was subdued. He and the French woman had shared a blanket, under which they did as much to each other's private parts as hands can do. And when they arrived in Paris, he accompanied the woman to her home, a block from the Seine and a stone's throw from Notre Dame. He was there for twelve hours before he took his leave, promising to keep in touch.

That brief stop in Paris had served to boost his self-confidence the way a casual, sexual encounter often did for him. The doubts that had plagued him vanished. He felt refreshed, vital, and more than up to the task awaiting him. In a way, he was now looking forward to Vladivostok, to the challenge.

12

In 1935, two hundred Midwest families were recruited by FDR to travel to the Territory of Alaska to farm the Matanuska-Susitna Valley, just north of Anchorage. Fertile land, suitable for potatoes, beets and cabbages. Maybe even dairy.

They were known as the Palmer Colony and their efforts met with only limited success—the expense, the difficulty of farming, and the severity of the climate all being determinative factors.

One of the first structures built to accommodate the Colony's new arrivals was the building now called *The Frontiersman Motel*. It had begun as a temporary living space for some of the newly arrived pilgrim/farmers from Minnesota and Michigan. But as folks began to establish their own homesteads on land given to them by the federal government, *The Frontiersman* was used less and less.

Over the next several decades the building changed ownership every few years. Because of its configuration–thirty-five rooms, many with small kitchens–it was always some kind of a live-in-lodging, either for tourists, for Boy Scouts attending the yearly jamboree, or for people coming from faraway to attend the end-of-summer Palmer State Fair.

Each new owner brought a new name: *The Way Inn, Bob's Place, Your Highway Home*. In 2011, a Korean family bought the structure and rechristened it *The Frontiersman*.

Now, almost eighty years old, the building was still sound, *mostly*: a sturdy, cement foundation, walls solidly fashioned out of well-cut, fifty foot spruce logs, and a steeply pitched roof that defied snow accumulation.

But the floors . . .

For some reason, the original builders had skimped on

the floors. The original two-by-six joists that supported the second story had long ago begun to sag, leaving most of those upper rooms with floors that drooped and bowed. Not even close to level.

The severely tilted floor in Room 16 soon led to a shocking discovery directly below, in Room 8—a dull, red liquid began staining one of the walls of the lower room.

The occupants of Room 8, Mavis and Truman Schneiderhorn, from Green Bay, Wisconsin, had come to Alaska to visit their dentist son and his new wife. The visitors failed to notice the discoloration when they left their room just before nine in the morning. They drove up to nearby Hatcher Pass to the long-abandoned Independence Gold Mine. They took the tour, lunched at the lodge, and spent a pleasant late afternoon watching the last of the season's cross-country skiers meander across the alpine bowl.

The Schneiderhorns got back to their room about six in the evening. The first thing they noticed when they opened the door was the smell. The second, the wall in back of the TV was streaked in red, right down to the floor.

Mavis speculated that they were painting in the room directly above them. Truman walked over to the wall and inhaled. "Smells like someone just offed a pig." He looked up at the ceiling, where the red liquid was collecting on the molding. A single drop fell, splattering Truman's left shoe.

The manager of the motel, Kang-Dae Bak, was called to bear witness. The first generation Korean American, a recent graduate of the University of Alaska Fairbank's nationally rated computer science department, was confounded. He dashed out of the room, up the outer stairs, along the walkway, and after banging on the door to no avail, let himself into Room 16. At first glance, the curtained cubicle seemed to be in order. But when Bak flipped the lights on, a pair of sneakered feet could be seen jutting out from behind an ancient, vinyl Barcalounger.

The former honor student didn't really want to see more, but coaxed himself toward the chair, in back of which, and pushed against the wall, was the crumpled body of a man. Bak could clearly see the three holes in the victim's chest, and one in his forehead. The motel manager pulled out his cell phone and called 911.

~~~

A large samovar, perched in the middle of the Hyundai Hotel's dining room, was audibly bubbling. A dozen sleepy-eyed delegates carefully carried their cups of scalding tea back to their breakfast tables. Piped-in Russian folk music floated in the background.

Emmitt Esterhazy sat alone at a table set for six. He was preparing to dig into a bowl of yogurt and fresh fruit when he spotted his translator and favorite Anchorage cop.

"Sasha, darling. I didn't expect to see you up and at 'em this early."

She pulled up a chair, parked her tray of food, sat and poured herself coffee from a carafe. "Why not? I'm usually an early riser."

Esterhazy crooked his head sideways, looked at her skeptically. "Well, I just figured that . . . you know, you and Charlie . . ." he added, smiling wickedly.

Sasha sat back, puzzled. "What're you talking about Emmitt? Me and Charlie? Me and Charlie what?"

The FBI agent ate a large spoonful of yogurt and

blackberries, followed by a second one. He liked drawing it out, enjoyed keeping Sasha on edge.

"What's on your mind, you old fart? Spit it out," she said.

Esterhazy wiped his mouth. "Well, Charlie didn't come back to our room last night. So, I just assumed that you two had patched things up, put behind you whatever it was that happened in Dutch Harbor, and . . . you know," he gestured vaguely with his spoon.

Now Sasha relaxed, smiled and let out a huge, "Aha!"

"What's that supposed to mean?"

"Elena didn't come back to *our* room last night either. On the flight over she said she was interested in him. Said she might shanghai him."

"Aha," Emmitt echoed. "That explains it. So, does this mean that you and he have gone your separate ways?"

She dolloped a load of jam onto a piece of black bread, spread it around with a spoon.

"C'mon Emmitt. We were never on the same page. Besides, I told him that I'm saving myself for you."

Esterhazy sighed over-loudly. "If I only thought there was the slightest bit of truth in that."

"Of course there isn't the slightest bit of truth in that Emmitt. I'm way too tall for you."

"Yeah, but. . ."

"Yeah but nothing. Eat your yogurt."

"So, Charlie's moved on. And you?"

"Playing it loose, like always. Shopping around."

"That cop from Chile, for instance? The one who corralled you at the end of the conference in Anchorage."

She sat back, surprised again. "How'd you know about that?"

He finished the last spoonful of yogurt and leered at her teasingly, "All FBI. All the time."

"I bow to your greater intelligence gathering," she said.

"Thanks for the acknowledgement. So, we off to the port soon?"

The taxi rolled off the dockside highway onto a side street lined with drab buildings.

"This is it," the cabbie announced, stopping in front of the Slaviansky Bazaar. Sasha told the driver to wait, they'd be back in fifteen minutes. He grumbled something unintelligible.

The name of the hotel was carved in flowery Cyrillic into a chipped, marble slab over the entrance. Six concrete steps led up to large, unadorned landing in front of a set of heavy wooden doors that creaked open just as Sasha and Esterhazy arrived atop the landing. Two brawny men exited, dressed in navy pea coats, dungarees, and woolen caps. They didn't have a full set of teeth between them. They looked at Sasha hungrily, stepped aside, smiling. Sasha returned their smiles. One of them, a grizzled tar of fifty-some years, held the door open for her, removed his cap and bowed. "If you please," he said.

"A gentleman," she congratulated the sailor.

"Do my best," he answered in a tobacco-raspy voice.

The room they entered was no more than fifteen feet wide by twenty feet long and stank of tobacco, cabbage, and cheap vodka. Three forlornly ancient armchairs were pressed against a wall, begging to be set on fire. A staircase off to one side was covered with threadbare carpeting. A pair of naked light bulbs, stuck in ornate sconces, did little to illuminate the chamber.

At the far end of the room, the front desk was enclosed by a tightly meshed wire cage. Inside, sat a large, bald man of indeterminate age. He wore Trotsky glasses and had a wispy, salt and pepper beard. He wore a yellow shirt, buttoned to the throat, long sleeves rolled up. In one hand, cupping his leaning head, was the lit stub of a cigarette, the smoke drifting up into a paint-peeled ceiling. In the other hand, a worn paperback. He put down his book and watched them approach.

Sasha went first, Esterhazy lagging behind. The clerk gave her a surly look.

She noted the title of his book and beamed at him. "Eugene Onegin," she said, then gave the man the first lines of Pushkin's classic, known to every Russian reader on the planet: *"My uncle, what a worthy man, falling ill like that and dying."* She paused, allowing him the chance to jump in. He jumped.

"It summons up respect. One can admire it, as if he had been trying," the man replied, beaming back at her. "Can I help you?" Much nicer now.

"I hope so," Sasha said, taking a photo of Jimmy Lasorda from her coat pocket and unfolding it for the desk clerk's inspection. "Do you remember this man? He's stayed here in the past."

The clerk's smile faded even faster than it had appeared. "Ah, the American fisherman. Poor man. I heard he had an accident."

"Right. He went missing while working on the *Pyotr Veliky.*"

"Too bad for him. Worse for Captain Vronsky. He got beached yesterday, soon as he hit port. Hadn't even come ashore when he got his notice."

Sasha frowned at the disquieting news. She was planning on seeing Vronsky the next day. She made a mental note to find a suitable gift for the forcibly retired seaman. She tapped her finger on the photo. "Did this man stay here often?"

"Occasionally," the clerk answered.

"Alone?"

"As far as I know."

"Anyone ever come to visit him?"

The man smiled through his beard, took a last drag off the stub of his smoke, and crushed it out in an overly full glass ashtray. Taking his time, smoke curling out of his nose, "Not that I ever noticed."

"No friends at all, maybe a girl, young, dark?"

"Not that I ever noticed."

"Did he stay in one particular room?"

"Moved around."

"It's a ways from here to Pier 26, where the *Pyotr Veliky* berths. Any idea how he got back and forth?"

"No idea."

"Maybe someone came and picked him up."

"Not that I ever noticed." The clerk yawned and reached for his book.

Sasha looked back at Emmitt. "Nothing," she said in English.

The man in the cage repeated, in English, "Yes, nothing. So, I go once again to my Pushkin. Farewell to you." He picked up his book, resumed his head-leaning posture, and continued reading.

As soon as the two inquisitive foreigners were gone, the clerk made a call.

Outside, the day had turned overcast. A strengthening ocean breeze brought with it the decaying harbor odor of long dead fish, long ago spilled diesel fuel, and a million broken barrels of who-knows-what.

"Nothing," Emmitt said, trying to imitate the clerk's English accent. "Now what?"

"Now, I've got an errand."

They returned to their waiting taxi, the driver slumped across the front seat, dozing. He came awake when his passengers got in. "Let's drive along the dock," Sasha said, handing him a hundred-ruble note.

He took them to Nizhneportovaya, the street that paralleled the dock. Huge cranes were lifting forty-foot long, multi-colored shipping containers onto immense barges, stacking the steel boxes five high. Ferries and fishing boats came and went, and a flotilla of moored war ships was a reminder of one of the port's main roles: home to the former Soviet, and current Russian, Pacific fleet.

Paralleling the dock stood a line of stores selling goods in support of the port's maritime needs. Sasha told the driver to pull over next to one of the largest.

"Back in a flash," she said.

After ten minutes, she returned.

"What's in the box?" Emmitt asked.

"A real find. Something rare. He'll love it. But for now, you can buy me lunch. And after that, I'm napping."

~~~

Taras was beat. Very little sleep in Paris, then three and a half hours from Paris to Moscow, a four hour layover at

Sheremetyevo, and another nine hours to cross Russia to Vladivostok. Aeroflot Airlines, not famous for pampering its passengers, didn't make the last leg easy, not even for first class fliers.

They landed about seven in the evening at Knevichi, Vladivostok's international airport. Taras was met there by two men whose beautifully tailored suits did in no way disguise the fact that they were thugs. They told the American that they had been sent by Roman Kollantai, the mayor of the city, who would like to meet with him right away. Would the gentleman please accompany them to their waiting car?

Taras would have much preferred a shower and a decent meal–the Aeroflot rubber chicken leg resisting digestion–but knew he could not refuse the invitation.

Forty minutes later, he was delivered to the mansion/ fortress that was the home of the mayor/crime boss of Vladivostok.

Roman Kollantai was swimming in his twenty-five meter, indoor heated pool.

Taras took a seat in the humid room, steamed-over windows allowing only a gauzy view of the mansion's extensive gardens. He fought to stay awake, loosened his tie and after five minutes of watching Kollantai glide smoothly through the water, removed his jacket. Another ten minutes passed before the swimmer finished on the opposite side of the pool and climbed out.

The visitor took stock of his host. Roman Kollantai was thick set, heavily muscled and moved like someone who could take care of himself. Taras knew the details of Kollantai's rise to the top. The mayor began as a mid-level party functionary under Gorbachev, then graduated into enforcement for Sergei

Larionov, Vladivostok's crime boss in the 1990s. And when his patron was arrested and killed while in jail in 1998, Kollantai's campaign to replace him was quick, violent and effective. *A dangerous and unforgiving man,* Taras reckoned.

Kollantai toweled off and donned a full-length, blue, terry cloth robe. He threw a towel around his neck and looked back to see his visitor. "Taras Dmitrivich, is that you?" the mayor yelled.

"It's me, Roman Vassillich."

"Welcome to Vladivostok and to my home," Kollantai said, walking toward a wet bar built into a poolside wall. "Something to drink?"

"Cold water, Mr. Mayor, if possible. Thank you."

Kollantai took a handful of ice cubes, dropped them into a tumbler and filled it from a large bottle of Evian. And for himself, he poured some kind of red juice into a second ice-filled glass. Kollantai drank most of it, refilled, then advanced toward his guest. "Good to meet you at last, Taras Dmitrivich," Kollantai said, handing his guest the water. "Boris Davidich speaks about you glowingly, says you are reliable. Is that so?"

Taras kept it friendly, kept his gaze fixed on his host. "It's true, Mister Mayor."

"Let's hope so. Come sit and let's talk about why you are in my city." Kollantai indicated a pair of cushioned chaise lounges. The two men sat across from each other, a glass table separating them.

Taras drank most of his water, then began, "As Boris Davidich has told you, I'm here on family business."

"Right. A personal vendetta. Some people killed your brother and you want to kill them."

"I hope to keep it as uncomplicated as possible, Mister Mayor."

"Aye, there's the rub," Kollantai smiled. "You understand that 'uncomplicated' is a relative term. For you, no problem. You kill these two people and return to your Brooklyn safe haven. For me, however, I'll have to swim through any shit that might surface should you screw up. The problems that could arise out of a poor effort on your part might seriously jeopardize my business. After all, you're asking permission to use my city as your personal shooting gallery. Normally, that is not a request to which I might object. But today and for the next few days, more than four hundred policemen from all up and down the Pacific Rim are here, thinking they have come to a safe place. Imagine their surprise and annoyance if they discover that the opposite is true. They'll leave my city with a bad taste in their mouths. And when someone might ask them, 'Tell me about Vladivostok,' what do you think they might say?"

Taras didn't venture a reply.

"'Vladivostok?' they'll say. 'Wouldn't get caught dead there.' You follow, Taras? Those are some of the complications *I* might expect."

Kollantai finished his glass of juice and placed it on the glass table. "But Boris Davidich and I have worked well together in the past. We're doing great things right now in the present, and hopefully, will continue to prosper into the far and distant future. He asked me–as a personal favor–to allow you to carry out your project. I explained the downside. He understood. Boris is a smart man, not much escapes him. His father's son. You worked for his father, David, isn't that so?"

"Yes, I did."

"A good place for an apprentice." Kollantai smiled, then rose, took up his glass and walked back to the wet bar. He refilled the tumbler with ice and juice. "Before this arrangement, Boris and I were on fairly equal terms. But now, because I have agreed to his request, your boss is in my debt. He understands and accepts that. You follow, Taras?"

"I do, Roman Vassillich. I am appreciative of your generosity and understanding, because of which, I, too, am in your debt."

"Good, Taras. I'm glad we understand where we stand." Kollantai finished his drink and put down his empty glass. "Now, because of the sensitivity of the situation, there is only so much I will do for you. I'll provide you with weapons–your choice, of course–and a safe place to run to, if you need to run. And these." Kollantai took two items from his robe: a conference name badge, and a small square of plastic with *'Hyundai Hotel'* written across it.

"This is a master room key for the hotel where you'll be staying. Everyone from the conference is there. Beyond these few things, there is nothing I will do. I'll provide no men. God forbid you should get caught, Taras, because there will be no rescue. You'll be totally on your own. Understood?"

"Understood, Roman Vassillich."

"For now, I've reserved a room for you at the Hyundai, under the name on this badge, the name Boris sent me, Archenko. An interesting name."

"My soccer coach in Odessa, at the Fontanka."

"Ah yes, the Fontanka. The school for trouble-making young men. Are you a troublemaker, Taras? I hope not."

Taras was silent.

Kollantai took a long time assessing his guest, then

continued. "The conference opens tomorrow. I am to give a welcoming talk in the morning. My daughter, Alla, has taken a room at the hotel. She'll find you at breakfast and help you identify the two people you're looking for."

"Thank you, Roman Vassillich. For everything."

The mayor smiled a warning. "You will be discreet, Taras. You will do what you need to do as quietly as possible. And I emphasize 'quietly.' Don't get caught. Do what you must and then go back to Brooklyn."

"Trust me, Roman Vassillich."

"We'll see," said the mayor.

~~~

Sasha was stretched out on her hotel room bed, wrapped in a robe. She had just emerged from an hour-long bath. Next to her, Elena's bed remained unslept in, unsat upon. *Let her have some fun.*

She thought to rejoin Emmitt where she'd left him, an hour earlier, at the hotel's bar. She resisted the temptation. She was trying to be good, the promise to her grandfather winning out. By a whisker.

She reached for the house phone, hesitated. She let her hand rest on the receiver and after a minute of yes/no, finally picked up and punched in a room number.

"Good evening," said a voice on the other end in beautifully accented English.

"Good evening. Tomás?"

"No, this is Alejandro. Wait a moment and I'll get Tomás."

Sasha could sense the man smiling. She imagined his

message to Tomás: *"It's that big, blond detective woman. The one from Anchorage. I think she's hot for you. Maybe you'll get lucky tonight."*

"Hola. This is Tomás. Who is this please?"

In for a penny... "Hi Tomás, this is Detective Aleksandra Kulaeva. From Anchorage? *Jesus Christ! Why the full title, why not just Sasha?* Tomás, I'm wondering . . . you think we might dine together tonight?"

They were picking at the food. The spring rolls had already been shunted aside after a single bite. And it was only due to heavy applications of soy sauce that the plates of noodles, rice, cabbage, and mystery meat were at all edible.

"I should have known from this place's home page," Sasha said. "They hardly had a single word spelled correctly, in Russian or English. That should have been the tip-off."

"In Santiago, my home town, the Chinese food is far superior," Tomás explained. "My partner, Alejandro—he answered the phone this evening—he and I go *la chinesca*, what you call China Town, at least twice a week to eat. The cafe we go to is owned by the Kwan family." Tomás paused, laughed quietly.

"What's funny?" Sasha asked.

"Well, I thought we wouldn't talk shop, but . . . Anyhow, we're in there one afternoon, a few months ago, having lunch. Mrs. Kwan comes and sits at our table. She's over eighty and doesn't weigh eighty pounds. She tells us that a rowdy bunch of teenagers comes in on the weekend, demands food, and then doesn't pay. She asks if we can help."

"What'd you do?"

"We helped."

Sasha could imagine several remedies. "And what, exactly, did you do?" she asked, pushing away her entrée.

"We had a talk with the young men."

"A talk?" She recalled how she and Gary 'talked' to Rudy Castro at the Alyeska Prince. *Rudy, where the hell have you gone to?*

"I asked them if they had ever been to the football stadium at Viña del Mar. They understood the reference."

"I'm afraid I don't."

"In 1973, your CIA forced Allende out of office and cleared the way for the right wing dictator, Pinochet. He ordered all opponents of his new regime rounded up and brought to the football stadium. They were put in cages on the field. From there, many of them disappeared."

"Looks like the kids got the message."

"They seemed to."

"I'm sure you can be very persuasive, Tomás. I don't think I'd like to be interrogated by you."

"I would love the chance to interrogate you, Sasha. But I don't believe you'd crack. You'd be difficult to break," he said, sweetly but seriously.

Sasha hid her discomfort. *That's something Charlie would say. Tomás sees it in me, too.* "Not so hard, Tomás. Trying to soften up a bit."

Over cups of spiced tea, Sasha learned that the Chilean was a man of surprising contradictions: a policeman when he should have been a banker; a bachelor when he should have already been married to any of the numerous nubile, wealthy, and well-placed young women of his hometown; and a radical socialist when by money and lineage he should have been an arch-conservative.

When it was her turn, she told him about her family life, her daughter, the death of her husband. She was surprised and gratified it had all come out so easily.

The diners took their time walking the five blocks back to the hotel, delaying their return as long as possible. When it began raining, however, they sped up and arrived at the Hyundai more wet than not.

The confidence that Sasha had felt about her near hook-up with Charlie in Dutch Harbor was not spilling over into the current situation with the Chilean policeman. Her unease must have been apparent.

"I enjoyed myself immensely, Sasha," he said. "I hope, if you have the time and the desire to spend more time with me, we might see each other again before the conference is over."

"I also had a lovely time, and yes, I would very much enjoy spending more time with you." *So coy, so virginal!*

"If I might, I'll escort you to your door."

Sasha was taken aback. *I don't think I'm ready for this.* She was saved when Emmitt Esterhazy came out of the bar, and walked toward her, teetering slightly.

"I appreciate the offer, but I see someone I need to talk to."

Tomás looked toward the FBI director. "You'll be in safe hands with Director Esterhazy," he said.

"I hope to see you tomorrow, Tomás. Sleep well." She touched his arm and watched him make for the elevators.

Esterhazy came up to her, a huge grin on his face. He nodded a questioning glance at the departing Tomás and was about to speak.

"Not a fucking word, Emmitt," she cautioned him.

He pursed his lips and ran a closing, zippering finger

across them, unable to hide his smile. "C'mon, I'll buy you a drink."

After a quick, backward glance at her dinner partner, Sasha allowed herself to be drawn to the bar where a small clutch of conferees had gathered. They greeted Sasha loudly and made a space for her in their midst.

Esterhazy signaled to the bartender. "Gin 'n tonic for me." And to Sasha, "Whatcha drinkin' m'dear," his words running into one another.

"Sprite," she ordered. "Trying to cut down."

"Always a good move," he agreed. Then his expression soured. "Listen, I got some bad news this evening."

"Do I have to hear it?"

"Afraid so. Rudy Castro was discovered in a motel in Palmer. Shot all to hell."

"Shit! There goes our case." She signaled to the barman. "Bring me a beer, a Baltika if you got one."

~~~

Armani-suited and handsomely coiffed, Roman Kollantai declared himself *"honored to be the host of this historic event."* He wished the delegates a successful four days. At nine-fifteen, he thanked everyone and invited the conferees to a buffet breakfast in the hotel's adjoining dining room.

Sasha began making her way to the food. She was alone, ravenous, and sober—only the one beer the night before. She had awakened early, felt refreshed, yet conflicted. The death of Rudy Castro put a giant STOP sign in front of the APD's heroin trafficking case. Hard to know how to proceed.

At a personal level, however, she hadn't stopped

thinking about the evening before and the easy and entertaining time spent with Tomás.

She took up her tray—porridge and nuts, kefir and berries, black bread and jam, and coffee—and scanned the room. She found who she was looking for at an out-of-the-way table—the two Chilean amigos. She made a casual beeline.

They stood as she approached, clearly captivated at her having had the good sense to single them out.

"Might I join you?"

The South Americans fell over each other in assuring her that that was perhaps the only reason they were in Vladivostok in the first place.

"Great," she said, smiling at the both of them, a second or two longer at Tomás. *Elena had the right word for it, 'yum.'*

The other man introduced himself as Alejandro. "I believe we spoke last night," he said, pulling out a chair for her.

"We did," she said, sitting and unfurling a napkin onto her lap. "How clever of you to find Tomás for me."

For the next thirty minutes, the three new friends chitchatted their way through breakfast, trading questions about their homes.

"No," Sasha hadn't been to South America.

"Yes," both men thought to return someday to Alaska.

At the end of the meal, the Chileans promised to be her personal guides if and when she ever were to come to their country. For her part, the two of them would be her guests at the fly-in fishing camp her family maintained in the deep Alaskan outback.

Towards ten o'clock, both men made leaving motions.

"We have a seminar we need to be at," Alejandro said. "White collar bank fraud." He put his hand over his mouth to stifle a fake yawn. "Thank you for the wonderful company," he said, and excused himself.

Tomás lingered. "I had a memorable time with you last night, Sasha. I'm ready to do it again."

"Me, too, Tomás. I'm visiting a friend this afternoon, and I need to be back at the hotel for work, at five. I'll call you after I'm done." *The second I'm done!*

"I'll wait by the phone," he said, smiled and took his leave.

Alone now, Sasha was in dream-mode, Tomás being the main feature. She was finishing her third cup of coffee when a movement at the far side of the dining room attracted her attention. She looked up and spotted someone familiar, someone she was sure she knew—a very large man standing in the doorway, looking into the room. Although she could see him clearly—nice suit, no tie, handsome in a beefy kind of way—she couldn't place him. He was looking away from her, off to his right, at the group of tables on the far side of the room. At that moment, Roman Kollantai entered, accompanied by the same young woman from the Anchorage conference. *She of the blue Mercedes?* Sasha wondered.

The mayor paused next to the large man, spoke a quick and quiet word to him, then continued into the dining room. The young woman, however, remained by the man's side. She inclined her head toward the last two tables next to the window, said something to the man, then rejoined Kollantai. The man now moved several paces into the room and seemed to focus on the very last table. Sasha followed his gaze. Seated at that table were six breakfasters: four members of the Australian delegation, and with their backs to the man, Elena Markova and Charlie Dana, elbow to elbow.

Sasha felt a creeping disquiet about the man's intense scrutiny, but dismissed the feeling. *Comes naturally with being in Russia.*

She thought instead about Charlie and Elena hooking up. Did she give a damn? Not really. She actually felt glad for both of them.

Another glance at the man in the doorway. Sasha was certain she knew him from somewhere, had seen him recently, but couldn't find him in her memory's contact list. She put him out of her mind after he turned and left the dining room.

~~~

Wearing a nametag that identified him as Artyom Archenko, delegate from the Khabarovsk Region Border and Coastal Patrol, Taras Zhuganov sat in back of a half-filled lecture hall, just off the main lobby of the Hyundai Hotel. He was nervous, his knee bouncing, a hint of perspiration on his forehead and upper lip. The psychic boost he had gotten from his encounter with the French woman in Paris had evaporated. The meeting with Kollantai had brought him back to the reality of the situation. Once again, he felt as if his years of being on the sidelines was working against him. Without looking, he reached down to the floor and found his Guess shopping bag. In it, under a light sweater, he felt for the silenced pistol. His clammy fingers grasped the cool steel. He shivered.

The lecture—on plans for a more advanced finger-printing database—was being wrapped up by someone called Cardozo, the director of the Drug Enforcement Agency in

Alaska. Taras, however, had not focused on the presentation, but rather on the two people who had killed his brother: Cardozo's translator and the FBI agent sitting several rows in front of him. The two had been identified by Alla Kollantai that morning at breakfast.

When the lecture ended a few minutes later, Cardozo and his translator got clear of the crowd and went out into the hotel's lobby. They headed toward a bank of elevators but were caught half way by the FBI agent.

"Where're you two headed?" Charlie called to Elena and Cardozo.

"The roof top restaurant," Elena said. "Come along. Mid-morning coffee and cake."

Cardozo turned sideways, shrugged his eyebrows.

Charlie caught the man's gesture. "I wouldn't want to intrude if the director wants to make it a working snack."

"No problem," Cardozo said breezily. "I'm not too hungry anyway." Then to Elena, "I'll catch up with you later. We're at it again at one-thirty. Same lecture hall."

"Fine. See you then," she said.

Cardozo left them and made his way to a group of delegates getting an early start at the bar.

Elena and Charlie walked to the elevator. She pushed the 'up' button, glanced at him, and let the back of her hand slide carelessly over his. "I'm not much hungry either," she said. "My room's empty. Sasha's gone visiting. Won't be back anytime soon."

"You mean we'll actually have a bed this time?" he said, laughing.

She punched him lightly on the arm. "Brute. I thought we did nicely."

"We did, didn't we?" he conceded. "We could even order room service."

"I'd have to work up an appetite first."

They entered the elevator and were joined by a large man carrying a Guess bag. He nodded to them. Charlie thought he looked stressed, seemed to be hyperventilating.

The elevator doors shushed closed.

~~~

From his right side perch in the old Toyota Corolla's front seat, the cabbie looked back through the rear view mirror. He saw a woman dressed in European clothes, almost certainly a foreign delegate to the conference. But when she began speaking to him in flawless Russian, he did a double take. "You speak like a native."

"My first language," Sasha said. "My grandfather was a Soviet pilot in the war. Went to Alaska in '45 and stayed."

"A very wise man," the driver said. "So, where're we headed?"

"North end of town. Tsimlanskaya Street." Sasha pulled out the copy of the Google Map she had printed the week before in Anchorage. She leaned over and passed it to the driver. "Look here. It's by the old aerodrome."

He took the map and looked it over. Then he closed one eye, tilted his head back, and finally nodded. "Got it. Pretty far though. Ummm, let's say . . . fifteen hundred rubles."

Since the cab had no meter, Sasha knew the price was negotiable. She did a quick calculation. Even given the declining value of the ruble, she thought a twenty-five dollar fare was a tad high. "How about twelve hundred? It's really not that far."

The cabbie swiveled to face her. He wore a battered green beret, pushed back on a head of frizzy gray hair. He had bulbous dark eyes, a prizefighter's nose and ears, and a three-day growth of beard. "Ma'am. I've got a family. Wife, three kids, all wanting some kind of vacation come summer. Tell you what. I'll throw in a short tour of the city and I'll go thirteen fifty."

"Let's roll," Sasha said, sitting back. "I'm Alexandra Petrovna Kulaeva."

"Marat Karlovich Stepansky. Pleased to meet you."

"Tell me something, Marat Karlovich. Last time I was in Russia, there were huge billboards and neon signs on the sides of all the buildings. You know the ones I mean: *'Leninism: the road to prosperity,' 'Socialism is our destination.'* And my favorite, *Stalin is our savior.'* But I'm not seeing any of them."

"They've all been taken down. I'm not sure there's a single one left in town. About the only reminder of that time is the statue of Lenin in front of the railroad terminal."

"Lenin still standing, huh? Have you been to his mausoleum in Red Square?"

The driver looked at her in the mirror. "Haven't yet had the honor," he said.

Sasha wasn't sure if he winked. "Tell me, where were your parents during the war? Here in Vlad?"

"My parents were born after the war, in the '50s. But my grandmother was here. My grandfather was in the army. He drove a lorry. He was killed trying to relieve the siege of Leningrad, on the ice road on Lake Ladoga." The driver shook his head back and forth. "Fucking Germans," he said with vehemence, turning and spitting out the window.

Sasha had seen the gesture before, knew that among Russians, at least the older ones, it was a common reaction when Germans were mentioned.

On Peter the Great Street, they stopped at the city's war memorial, in front of the Chapel of St. Andrew. Steps led up to a raised star out of which flames could be seen.

The driver turned to his passenger. "The city couldn't pay the gas bill for the eternal flame. But in 2011, Medvedev himself came to reignite it. He told the gas company to stick it, even though they were owed over two hundred thousand rubles by the Pacific Fleet, the owners of the memorial."

Though the morning was cool and misty, there were several old men, some obviously in their nineties, clustered around the monument. Many wore navy and army medals on their overcoats, reminders of the war. She believed Victor would feel right at home sitting with these men. He'd always called it The Great Patriotic War, never World War II. He said that because twenty-five million Russians died defending their country, they'd earned the right to take credit for the victory.

"You ready to go Tsimlanskaya Street?" the cabbie asked.

"Let's do it," Sasha said.

~~~

All three passengers exited the elevator on the fifth floor. Neither Charlie nor Elena had paid much attention to the tall man.

Taras paused in front of the lift and watched his two intended victims as they walked to the end of the corridor and entered a room. He followed down the hall and noted the room number: 506. He thought to wait a few minutes before paying them a visit. He continued the few steps to the end of the corridor, entered the stairwell, and took the fire exit stairs down one floor. A moment later he was in Room 404, the one rented to Alla Kollantai.

"And?" she asked, breathlessly, going to him as soon as he entered.

"They're in 506, shacking up." He took out a handkerchief and wiped his mouth and palms.

"Sounds perfect."

Taras began pacing. "I'm not sure . . . I don't think it's so smart to take them here in the hotel. I'm thinking maybe, it'd be better . . . I'll wait for a better opportunity. Too many things could go wrong. I mean, if their room is shaped like this one, I'll walk right in on them. They'll see me right away."

"I asked about the rooms when I checked in. In 506, you walk into a short corridor that leads to the main room, the bedroom is beyond that. You'll be ok. They won't see you when you come in."

"But what if they've latched the door?"

"If they did, you wait for another chance. If they didn't, you're in."

Taras licked his lips. "And the noise the electronic lock'll make. They'll hear it buzz."

"I doubt it. They'll be too busy with each other in the bedroom." She sat on the bed and beckoned to him. "Come, sit by me."

Taras walked over to the young woman, pausing in front of her. She patted the bed next to her. He sat.

She reached across his wide body and took his right

hand and moved it onto her thigh. "This may be the best chance you'll get. They're together. Go do the two of them right now," she said. "Then come back . . . and do me."

Taras moved his hand down to Alla's crotch and began to gently rub. She settled back and gave him free rein. After a minute, "Go, now," she said. "Do it quickly, then come back to me."

He stood and looked around the room. "You have anything to drink?"

~~~

Sasha's cab pulled into a narrow street not far from the waters of Amur Bay. Both sides of the road were chockablock with small, obviously well-tended private homes, each with its own particular fence or wall: some quarry rock, some picket, a few hedge rows dividing the lots, all looking nicely cared for. Berry bushes were leafing out all up and down the street.

"Sweet little things," the cabbie said. "Built by the navy, maybe fifty, sixty years ago to house the captains and commanders of our Pacific submarine fleet."

"Lovely. Who lives here now?"

"Still seamen. But more shipping and fishing than military."

"Pull over at Number 26," Sasha said. From her wallet, she fished out three, five hundred ruble notes and passed them to the driver. "Keep the difference, Marat Karlovich. Thanks for the terrific tour and have a great summer vacation with your family."

The driver nodded his head in thanks. "I appreciate it, Sasha Petrovna. I really do. Enjoy your time in Vlad."

"Thanks, that's the idea," she said, getting out of the taxi.

As the cab motored away, the front door to Number 26 opened and Captain Yury Vronsky came out onto his small porch. He was wearing faded dungarees, a bright red shirt, and high, felt slippers. He smiled broadly and waved a greeting to her.

They were sunk into deep over-stuffed armchairs, ancient antimacassars on the backs of the chairs and hand-crocheted doilies, fugitives from Czarist times, on the arm rests.

Vronsky's house was solidly built, with thick walls, wooden plank floorboards, and heavy timbered ceiling beams and lintels. There were three large portholes that gave out onto the front garden, now glistening brightly after the morning's drizzle. Scraps of wood were burning in the stone fireplace. The room was toasty and smelled of freshly picked sweet peas. A polished ship's chronometer sat above the fireplace and softly ticked off the seconds.

Vronsky rested his feet on an ottoman, Sasha's gift in his lap. He lovingly caressed the wood and brass sextant.

"The store owner guaranteed it was from the *Sedov.* Supposed to be a famous ship."

"Indeed, one of the *most* famous. It's the largest sailing ship in the world. A four master. It's still used as a training vessel for naval students."

"I'm pleased you like your gift, Yuri Gregorich."

"Very much." He placed the sextant on an end table, then rose, walked to the mantel, and took down a large, framed photo that he brought to his guest.

She saw a thirty-foot motorized boat, moored to a pier,

with Vronsky and several other people on deck, all waving, smiling at the camera.

"I bought it eight years ago and have been fixing it up, little by little. I keep it in Bolshoi Kamen, across Ussuri Bay. Takes a while to drive there, so if I go, it's for three or four days. I prefer going when the weather's rough. I take the boat into the bay, drop anchor and sleep on board, pretending I'm on a stormy Sea of Okhotsk. I sleep like a baby. Silly me. And when the weather is fine, my family and I go fishing. A joy." He returned the photo to its place of prominence.

Sasha sipped from a mug of hot tea between bites of apple cake served on an elegantly fluted china plate.

Vronsky-the-chef smiled. "You're enjoying my cake. I made it this morning."

Sasha raised her fork in salute. "Excellent, really excellent."

"I learned to cook as a young man, in the galley of a Soviet mine sweeper, based right here in Vlad. The more people I had to cook for, the better the food got. I was famous. Smirnov, the fleet commander himself, asked me for this recipe."

"And naturally, you gave it to him."

"I had a choice?" he smiled.

Just then, the front door opened and a stocky young woman burst in, wearing jeans and a blue and white wool sweater under her rain slicker. Mounds of curly red hair framed her round face. The woman appeared surprised at seeing Sasha, then walked over, offered her hand and introduced herself, "Viktoria Yurevna Romanova. I'm the captain's daughter."

And when Sasha spoke her own name, the woman broke into a huge smile. "It's you," she answered, her voice filled with excitement. "The American policewoman. Papa hasn't stopped speaking of you since he got back. It's 'Aleksandra Petrovna this', 'Aleksandra Petrovna that.' He won't stop." She looked at her father.

Vronsky squirmed slightly but was able to reply, "Vika, dear, I might have mentioned her two or three times."

"Two or three times? Very well, papa. Perhaps I exaggerated." Viktoria showed Sasha a set of raised, red eyebrows. She removed her coat and scarf, piled them on a chair, and helped herself to tea and cake. She found a place on the raised hearth, then turned a sunny face to their guest. "So, Aleksandra Petrovna, papa said you're here for a conference. Is it the one downtown, at the Hyundai? I drove by there early this morning. All those official looking people looking . . . so very official."

"Right. Your Mayor, Kollantai is presiding. And it's Sasha, please."

"Happily. I'm Vika," she answered. "But *Mayor* Kollantai?" Vika looked at her father.

Vronsky waved his hands as if to dispel a bad odor. "Our *notorious* mayor. The crook! Worse than Nikolayev, another mayor, a gangster and a murderer. He tried to run and got caught in Panama."

"I saw Kollantai in Anchorage," Sasha said. "He was with his daughter, I think. A young woman, native-looking with short dark hair?"

Vika nodded in mid-sip. "That would be Alla. She's not quite twenty. The original wild child. Doesn't work, doesn't study. Just spends her father's money. I've heard she wants to be part of his business. And I *don't* mean politics. Thinks of herself as heiress to his empire. Lots of boy friends. Plays hard. *Very* hard." Vika gave Sasha a look to indicate what kind of 'play' she meant. "She even drives hard."

Sasha smiled. "Let me guess. A four door, blue Mercedes."

"Amazing. You've been here a day and you've already seen her driving around?"

"No, no. Not driving. I saw her this morning at the conference with her father. And a week ago in Anchorage. I've heard about her choice of cars."

"Of course," Vronsky said, snapping his fingers. "She's the one my first mate described, the one . . . ."

Before he could continue, Sasha held up a hand to him.

"Oops. Sorry," the captain apologized.

Vika caught the interplay. "Oh ho. Sounds like police business."

"Something like that," Sasha admitted, then changed the subject. "Your father says you're a teacher."

"I am. I train other teachers how to teach Russian language to indigenous peoples—Evenk, Chukchi, Koryak, Nanai, even Eskimo. Actually, I'm just finishing up a workshop here in town. We brought in folks from up and down the coast. They're all going home this evening."

"They're all flying?"

"Right. Mostly to Khabarovsk, some further north. Why?"

"Just curious."

~~~

Carrying his Guess shopping bag, Taras used the emergency fire stairs to walk up a floor. He paused on the landing outside the fifth floor corridor, and went over in his mind, step by step, what he was about to do. He hoped they'd latched the door. Then he'd be off the hook, at least until he could come up with a different plan. But something else was nagging at him. He was certain he had overlooked an important detail. What was it? *Can't think. Shit!*

He opened the fire door, came into the empty corridor, and eased over the carpeted floor to stand in front of Room 506. He could just make out subdued sounds from within. He withdrew the pistol from his pocket, steeled himself and inserted the master key card. No green light! He tried again. Again nothing. One more time. The light flashed 'open,' accompanied by a buzz that seemed to echo thunderously up and down the corridor. He paused a moment, listening for some reaction from the room. When he was certain the buzz had not alerted the targets, he carefully pushed down on the door handle, entered a short hallway, and helped the door swing closed behind him. The layout was as Alla had described—the hallway, the living space, then the bedroom. The sounds coming from the bedroom were now amplified. He heard the two of them panting, working into each other. Taras passed through the living room and inched toward the bedroom door, his weapon leading the way. He peered cautiously into the room. They were naked, having sex on the bed. Kulaeva was on top of Dana, her back to Taras. She was sitting up, grinding into the man's groin, her short blond curls bouncing in time to her movements. Dana's eyes were closed, head tilted back, fingers squeezing her hips. The two were grunting, moaning, each lost in their own pleasures.

Taras' heart was racing, his mouth dry, his palms clammy. His pistol had a red laser pointer that he attempted to center on the woman's back. But his shaking hand would not keep steady. He took a double grip on the gun, aimed, and fired off two quick shots. The first bullet hit the woman between her spine and her left shoulder blade, the second in her right side. Blood from the lower wound spattered the man beneath her. She threw up her hands toward the ceiling and without a sound, fell onto the man who now opened his eyes in wonder and disbelief.

Taras hurried toward the bed, weapon pointing at the FBI agent. The woman's body was draped over Dana's torso, blood flowing freely onto the bed. Dana saw the man advancing and tried to twist away. Now from point blank range, Taras fired once into the agent's left side, halfway up his rib cage. The force of the bullet caused the FBI agent to grunt loudly, to convulse, casting the woman off to the side, leaving his body exposed. Now, from directly above the man, Taras fired three more times into his upper stomach and chest, each shot producing a new torrent of blood.

It was done. The killer stared down at the butchery, trying to catch his breath, trying to swallow. Dana was clearly dead, but the woman might still be alive. He knew he needed to finish the work with a shot to her head. He stumbled over to her, and placed the silenced barrel against her temple. The sight of her wounds and the smell of blood caused a sudden wave of nausea to overtake him. He lowered his weapon and let it hang by a single, trembling finger. With labored breath, he backed up to the wall opposite the bed and collapsed against it. He gagged, turned and staggered into the bathroom. He knelt down and threw up into the tub. He turned on the faucet, hoping to flush away his vomit. He succeeded only in coating the inside of the tub with puke. He came out of the bathroom and took one more look at the bloody mess on the bed, felt his gorge rise again, and forced it back down. He needed to get out of the room. He rushed to the hallway and yanked open the front door. A man! The one who had delivered the lecture, standing there with his arm raised, ready to knock. Each was shocked to see the other. Taras seized him roughly by the collar, hauled him into the room, kicking the door closed. He threw him down onto the carpet, fell on top of his chest, and closed his hands around the American's throat.

Cardozo beat futilely at his assailant's arms, clawing at his wrists. He tried to free the man's fingers from around his neck, but the brute was directly over him, pushing down and squeezing with incredible force. Now, short of breath, the DEA director tried to gouge at his attacker's eyes, but his reach fell short. A moment later, Cardozo blacked out.

But Taras was not done. He knew that if he released his grip too soon, blood would return to the brain and consciousness would follow. He maintained his strangle hold until his arms began to tremble from the strain. Finally, the killer relaxed, letting his arms fall limp. Sweat dripped off his nose, his heart thumped like a jackhammer. When he was finally able to catch his breath, Taras rose, stepped over the body of the dead American, took his Guess bag, and went to the door's peephole. The hall in front of the room was empty. He opened it cautiously and put his head out, looked both ways down the corridor. No one. He lurched out of the room and stumbled to the staircase, descending two and three steps at a time. He came out on the floor below and hurried toward Room 404.

Alla had left the door ajar, allowing him to enter easily. Taras rushed into the room, laughing hysterically. He fought for breath, dropped his Guess bag, and put both hands to his face.

"Did you do it?" Alla asked.

He nodded, still laughing, and wiped his brow with his sleeve. "Done."

She went over to him, looking up into his wild-eyed face. She put her hands on his chest.

Taras was a foot taller. He peered down at her, grabbed her at the waist, and lifted her up to lip level.

13

At approximately a quarter past one, a housemaid made a surprising discovery in Room 506.

"The door was open," forty-eight-year old Hermione Bondarchuk later told the police. "I push a little bit and call into the room. 'Hello,' I shout. 'Anybody home?' "When nobody answer I try to open the door some more but something is in the way. I push hard and stick my head in to look. A man is on the floor. He has a blue face. His eyes stick out. And his tongue. And I know it's gotta be me who's gonna clean up all that vomit and blood."

By 1:27, Doctor Bogdan Voroshilov, the house physician, had determined that all three people in Room 506 were dead, two by gunshot and one, apparently, by strangulation.

By 1:32, elements of the police *and* militia *and* state security were on the way.

By 1:35, Yelizaveta Kuryagana, a reporter for the English language Vladivostok Times, was on the fifth floor, smart phone chronicling for her readers and for posterity the furor around Room 506.

And by 2:20, the crowd of conference delegates at the front desk was ten deep, the international cops trying to pay their bills and get the hell out of town.

~~~

As Sasha was about to dig into a second piece of Captain Vronsky's apple cake, her phone jangled. She excused herself and pressed the cell to her ear. She listened, rose and rushed to the far end of the living room, her back to her hosts. She asked rapid-fire questions in English and three minutes later, turned, ashen-faced, to her hosts. She tried to form words, but could not.

Vronsky recognized his guest's distress. He went to the cupboard and half-filled a small glass with brandy, then took it to her. "Drink," he ordered, helping her hand move to her mouth. Sasha drank a sip, then a swallow.

"What's happened, Sasha?" Vika asked. "Tell us."

Sasha's voice came out choked. "There was a shooting at the hotel. Three people . . . from Alaska. They're dead. Elena, my roommate. Charlie Dana. You met him on the boat, Yury Gregorich. He's dead. And the head of the Drug Enforcement Agency in Anchorage . . . dead."

"Vika gasped and retreated a step. "Impossible."

Vronsky took Sasha's now empty glass. "Another?"

"No, no. I can't. I have to think. Give me some time. Please."

Vika and her father retreated to their own places as Sasha flopped into her armchair, a hand covering her eyes. A minute passed before she spoke, "It was him. The man in the hotel. It was him. I know who he is now. I know who the killer is."

"What man? Who is he?" Vika demanded.

"Someone I thought I recognized this morning at breakfast. Someone . . . Perhaps it's on the news. Can you turn on the television, Yury Gregorich?"

Two local channels were broadcasting live from the street in front of the Hyundai Hotel. Reporters were describing the scene. One was an attractive woman, heavily made up, dressed ultra-modishly in a full-length red slicker and red beret. She spotted someone who had just arrived and walked toward him. The camera followed her.

"Here's Chief of Police Yagoda," she announced to her

listeners as she stuck the mic in front of him. "Dragan Yefimich, can you tell us what happened? What have you learned?"

Yagoda, short, bald, and bespectacled, looked shell-shocked. He couldn't stop blinking and biting his lip. "From what I've learned, there was a shooting. Earlier this morning. Here at the Hyundai. Three people, all delegates, I think, to the conference, were killed. Two were shot, and the third . . ." The police chief went pale. "We believe the third victim . . . was strangled to death."

The reporter's entire body flinched. "Do you have the names of the victims?"

"Yes. No. Well. We know who they are, but at this time, no, their names are not . . . we need to contact their kin."

"You said they were delegates. From what countries? Any Russians among them?"

"No comment on that."

"Where did the murders take place?"

"In one of the hotel rooms."

"Have you been able to identify the assassin?"

Yagoda's eyes went wide. "No comment."

"Were there any witnesses?"

"We are questioning . . . asking anyone who might have seen something, anything."

"And the motive."

"No comment. That's all for now." The chief stumbled off, heading into the hotel.

~~~

"That's enough," Sasha said.

Vronsky turned off the TV. The room was silent except

for the tick-tock of the chronometer and the rain beating lightly against the porthole windows.

"The man I saw this morning—the one I'm certain killed the three people—I saw him with Kollantai and his daughter. They spoke together. She, Alla, pointed to Charlie Dana's table. Elena, the woman who was killed, was sitting next to Charlie. The man was watching the table the entire time." Sasha sat up straight, then stood. She automatically patted her side where her holstered weapon ought to have been. When she found nothing, she looked dumbly down at her waist. *Christ! Still in the station, locked up.* She looked around, then focused on Vronsky. "I need your help, Yury Gregorich. Yours, too, Vika."

"Certainly," Vika said. "Anything."

Vronsky echoed his daughter, "In any way, at any time."

"It could be dangerous. For both of you."

Vronsky smiled. "My dear Sasha. I was able to survive fifty years on the Bering Sea and much of the North Pacific, some of the most dangerous waters on our lovely planet. And I've lived to tell the tale. If you need my help, you may ask. Please."

Sasha went to the window and carefully peered out, then turned back to her hosts. "I believe my friend Elena was killed by accident. I'm sure the killer thought she was me."

~~~

"You cocksucker," Kollantai screamed into the phone. "You decided to take your revenge *in the fucking hotel room!* You were supposed to find somewhere relatively quiet, a place where the bodies wouldn't be discovered so soon. And in your rush to save your ass, you left the fucking door open. The dead Americans were discovered immediately."

Kollantai looked to the other four men in his office. He held up his cell phone. "This American jackass thinks he's a drone pilot. Thinks he's a Predator missile. Collateral damage? Just a simple and forgettable byproduct of war. No big deal for Mr. Shoot-em-up. Three people dead," the mayor shouted, spittle spraying from his mouth onto his phone and across his desk. "And two of them not even *supposed* to be dead. Say something, Zhuganov, you piece of shit."

Taras was sitting on Alla's bed, the mayor's daughter next to him. They were both naked. He held his phone so Alla could hear. He called up his most apologetic tone of voice, "Roman Vassillich. I fucked up. No two ways about it. I am deeply regretful."

"Well since you've apologized, I suppose it's okay. No big deal. Right? I'm supposed to let it slide?" Kollantai stomped around his large office. His four men backed up, pressing themselves into the walls. The mayor stopped next to a small bar, laid the cell phone down, put it on speaker, took up a bottle of Absolut and poured himself a jolt of the Swedish vodka. He downed the drink in a single swallow, then wiped his mouth with his sleeve. He leaned over the cell phone and shouted, "You killed the *wrong* woman! The devil knows where the *right* one's hiding. Why don't we just shut down the entire fucking city and do a house-to-house search so you can get revenge for her shooting your good-for-nothing brother? Would you like that? And let's not forget the other man you killed. The one you strangled. Only a Drug Enforcement Agency honcho. Brilliant."

The Mayor of Vladivostok began to vigorously rub his

face, his head, his neck. He looked up and signaled to one of his goons. The man came over, stood in back of Kollantai, and began massaging his boss' shoulders. The mayor let his head sink down while the masseur did his thing. After a minute, Kollantai looked up, moved the phone closer. "Alright. You. You prick. Stay at the hotel until you're ready to leave town. Then get the fuck out of my city and never come back."

~~~

"I can't go to the police for help, for obvious reasons," Sasha said.

"No explanation necessary on that account," Vronsky said. "They're bought and paid for. Totally corrupt." He went to the fireplace, reached his hands in and rubbed the heat into them. "If you need a place to hide, you're welcome here."

"Thank you. That may be necessary." Sasha hesitated. "Do you remember, Yury Gregorich, when we were on the *Pyotr Veliky,* talking about our families? You told me about your father. You said that after the battle at Kursk, he and the other soldiers went to the battlefield and collected all kinds of souvenirs. You recall?"

Vronsky looked long at her, seemed to be weighing what Sasha was asking of him. "Just a moment," he said, and without another word, went into the kitchen.

"I know what papa's gone to get," Vika said. "I don't like it, Sasha. I'm afraid for you."

"I'm also afraid, Vika. Believe me. But I can't let it go. I simply can't."

From the kitchen—the sound of the scraping of furniture being moved was followed by the squeaking of wood being pried. A moment later, Vronsky returned, carrying a small, beautifully carved wooden box. Using a kerchief, he wiped the box clear of dust. "I carved this myself, more than thirty years ago. Teak that I traded for with a seaman I knew from Java."

"Wonderful craftsmanship," Sasha said.

"Thank you, but it's the contents that will interest you."

He placed the box on the ottoman, opened it and swiveled it toward her. Two bulky shapes were wrapped in soft pieces of red velvet.

"Don't be shy," he said, pushing the box in her direction. "You know what these are."

Sasha took up one of the objects, held it on one palm and with her other hand, carefully folded away the velvet. A gleaming German Luger pistol lay exposed.

Vronsky removed the second hand gun and the box's inner tray to show what lay beneath—three magazines and a small leather pouch.

"I've kept the magazines empty. I didn't want to stress the springs." He opened the pouch and poured bullets into his palm. "There are only nine. Both pistols are in perfect working order. I fired them each, one time, three years ago. I take them apart and clean them twice a year, in July, on the anniversary of Kursk, and on my father's name day, in November." His tone became cautionary. "You cannot get caught with these in your possession. It would mean certain jail. If you need to, you can discard them."

"I'll take one of the pistols and one clip. And I'll do everything in my power to return them to you, Yury Gregorich."

"Fine, if you can. I would appreciate it. But do what you have to do, Sasha."

Vika had watched the whole conversation with growing concern. "What are you planning?"

Sasha took Vika's hands in her own. "I need a ride into town."

"I have my van. You can use it as long as you like. I'm leaving this evening with my teaching cadre. I'll be gone for ten days."

Sasha came alert. "To Khabarovsk?"

"Yes. Most of my teachers get off there. But why the sudden interest in my flight plans?"

"One last question. Questions, really. First, can you get me to Provideniya? And then, can I get a boat from there to St. Lawrence Island?"

Vika smiled. "Yes to both. From Khabarovsk, you can fly to Magadan. Once there, it's a short flight to Anadyr. And from there, you can catch a charter to Provideniya. You might have to wait, but eventually, you'll get there. I know someone in Provideniya, a former trainee of mine. She can put you up. As to boats. I know they sail back and forth. The Eskimos have been able to do that freely for a few years. But I don't know when boats leave, nor how often."

"Then that's how I'll get home. I can't fly on a scheduled airline. The man or men who killed my friends could be waiting there for me. But if I can get to Provideniya . . ."

"You can get there in two or three days if you make decent connections."

Vronsky had been listening to the arrangements. "Why don't you stay here with us until Vika's flight? Why must you go back to town?"

Sasha sat and began feeding bullets into the Luger's magazine. "The man killed friends of mine. That cannot go unpunished."

Vika and her father looked at each other in alarm. Vika knelt by her new friend. "Sasha. What can you be thinking?"

"I have half an idea. We'll see if I can invent the other half." She pushed the magazine into the Luger, chambered a round, then picked up her phone and punched in a number.

~~~

Tomás Morales sat on a wooden bench in the middle of Sukhanov Park, three blocks from the Hyundai Hotel. He huddled under a small umbrella, scant protection from the light but persistent rain that had begun an hour earlier. Although his head and shoulders were relatively dry, his shoes were now soaked through, the damp penetrating to his socks. He kept eyeing the gravel path that cut the park diagonally in two. He was waiting for the American policewoman. The night before, she had awakened something in him, something that, at the age of forty-four, he supposed had gone into permanent eclipse. He was charmed, and he felt intoxicated by the notion. The Chilean was so caught up in thinking about Sasha, he hardly noticed the older Russian woman, a *babushka*, slowly making her way toward him along the path, the sound of gravel scraping under her boots. He followed the woman's progress as she drew near. She was wearing a well-used overcoat. The frayed, bright scarf that covered her hair also masked her face. She stopped at the bench and sat. "Thank you for coming," she said in English.

This gets better all the time, he thought. "You're

welcome," he answered, grinning. "Wonderful disguise, Sasha, but why?"

She unwound the scarf. "Someone wants to kill me."

From the pained expression on her face, he didn't doubt it. His amusement vanished. "Who and why?"

"The same person who killed the three people this morning at the Hyundai is looking for me. The woman who died, Elena Markova? That was supposed to be me. I'm certain of it."

He took a moment to digest the news. "I can help you leave town, get you to the airport."

"No, no. I'm not leaving yet. I have something to do at the hotel. That's where I'll need you."

"Tell me how I can help."

"Listen, Tomás, a confession." She paused. "I'm not your usual policeman."

"From our two meetings—at dinner last night and at breakfast this morning—I never for a moment imagined you were."

A rumbling peal of thunder barreled across the city. They both looked up as the drizzle became more insistent. They huddled close, arms touching, thighs touching, looking out through the rain.

"I'm going to find the man who killed Elena," Sasha said decisively.

"And when you find him . . .?"

She hesitated, then went for broke. "I'll deal with him myself. I dealt with his brother, last week, in Alaska. A murderer, a torturer, and a dealer of heroin. Which is why the man today is hunting for me. Revenge."

Tomás assessed her words. "Perhaps we are not as

different, Sasha, as you might imagine. Now it's my turn to confess. Six years ago in Valparaiso, I *also* dealt with three men. Kidnappers and child pornographers. I believe we are the same kind of policeman."

She felt comforted. "It'll be pretty obvious soon, if it's not clear already, that the dead woman is *not* me. When that happens, the man will renew his hunt for me. Meaning, I have to find him first."

"It's unlikely he's acting alone, without some kind of help from someone here in Vladivostok," Tomás suggested.

"Exactly. At breakfast, after you and Alejandro left, I saw him in the dining room. He knows Roman Kollantai. They spoke. And he also knows the mayor's daughter, Alla. While they were together, she seemed to be directing him to the table where my friends were sitting. She could very well have been helping the man identify his targets."

"It's all speculative," Tomás said. "Couldn't hold up in court. But then, what you're planning might never get that far. How will you find him?"

"I think Alla Kollantai might help us."

~~~

She was the perfect cover. No one would think twice about questioning someone in the company of the daughter of the Mayor of Vladivostok.

Taras and Alla left the hotel's lounge and strolled, holding hands, past the small handful of police and medical personnel still in the building. The killer and his accomplice passed unnoticed, heading toward the elevators.

Seated in a corner of the lobby and hidden by a small

forest of indoor shrubbery, Tomás and Sasha spotted Alla and her companion. As soon as the elevator's doors closed, the two policemen emerged and walked toward an exit that led to the hotel's garage. It took only a minute to find Alla's blue Mercedes. Ensuring they were alone, Sasha took the butt of her pistol and smashed out one of the taillights. Then she used the Luger's prominent front sight to scrape a large X in the driver's side door.

They returned to the lobby, Sasha to her foliage-protected hideout, Tomás to the front desk to report the vandalism.

The desk clerk knew whose car it was and called up to the owner. He looked at Tomás with a pinched face. A shiver of his shoulders indicated that the shit was about to hit the fan.

A furious Alla Kollantai stormed out of the elevator and up to the front desk. There, she met the very handsome man, one of the delegates she recognized–from Bolivia, she thought–who had reported the ugly case of defacement. The man volunteered to accompany her into the garage to survey the damage.

Walking slowly around the Mercedes, Alla was livid, swearing a blue streak. She allowed herself to be escorted back into the lobby and gave the Bolivian a warm smile,

"Thank you so much. You've been very kind," she said, then turned, and walked toward the elevators.

Five minutes later, Tomás was back at the front desk, carrying a small bottle of brandy he had just purchased in the hotel's gift shop.

"The young woman, Miss Kollantai, is naturally upset about the damage to her car," he told the desk clerk. "I've bought her a bottle of brandy. Perhaps you'll see that she gets it?"

"Of course, sir," the clerk said.

Tomás then slid a fifty Euro note over the counter, toward the man. "Or perhaps I might deliver it myself," the suave Chilean suggested.

The potential bribee glanced briefly at the bank note, placed a palm over the paper currency and made it disappear. "Room 404, turn right off the elevators, toward the end of the corridor, sir," the clerk whispered.

Taras was asleep when Alla returned to the room. She was worn out and chaffed, the brutish physicality of her new bed-mate was taking its toll. He'd pushed, thrusted and jabbed like a novice teenager, unaware that there was someone else involved. And once he had spent himself, he rolled off her and fell into a deep sleep.

Alla took a quick shower, donned a bathrobe, and took up her smart phone, eager to see who had called, who had posted her on Facebook, who might have Tweeted. Her electronics were interrupted by a soft knock at the front door.

She put her phone on the bedside table, went to the door and looked through the peephole. That good-looking, very sweet Bolivian again, waving a bottle of brandy. *Nice man.* She opened the door, intending to tell him thanks, maybe some other time.

But before she could utter a word, a woman in old clothes siezed her by the throat, pushed her roughly back into the small hallway and shoved a pistol deep into her stomach.

"Not a peep," Sasha growled to the petrified young woman, propelling her into the main room. The large man Sasha had seen that morning was spread-eagled across the bed, snoring nasally.

Tomás quickly and quietly searched the room. He found the Guess shopping bag, checked the contents, and took it to Sasha.

"What we've been looking for," she whispered. Tomás went through the man's clothing and came up with a billfold and cell phone. He checked through the wallet but found no identification, only a variety of paper money. He collected Alla's mobile phone from the lamp table, then whispered something to Sasha.

She nodded her approval. "Great idea, Tomás. Go for it."

He stepped in front of the young woman and began to undo her robe's sash. Alla resisted and earned a wicked backhand from the Chilean.

Sasha grabbed a hank of Alla's hair and yanked back, pressing the Luger deep into her side.

"Do what you're told, bitch. Daddy's not here."

Now, a more pliant Alla allowed the man to undo her sash. Sasha forcefully pulled the robe down from in back and pushed the naked young woman toward the bed.

"Get in and wake him up," Sasha directed, pulling off all the blankets to reveal the man's nude and muscular body. Alla lay down and pushed on the man's shoulder. He mumbled something but didn't awaken. "Taras," she said loudly into his ear, "Wake up." She continued pushing until the man came around. He looked at Alla, saw the panic on her face, then glanced around the room. Two strangers, one, a woman pointing a gun at him, and the other, a man holding the Guess shopping bag. And now, too late, much too late, Taras Zhuganov, former muscle for David Bunin, remembered what he had overlooked, the thing that had nagged at him as he approached Room 506: he had forgotten to wear gloves, and because of that amateurish oversight, he had stupidly left his fingerprints smeared all over the weapon in the shopping bag, and on Room 506's door handle and bathroom. It was a mistake that doomed him. The realization made him squeeze shut his eyes and fall back on the pillow.

"Alla, move over," Sasha commanded. "Put your arm around his neck."

The young woman reluctantly complied.

Sasha took out her smart phone and snapped photos of the couple, directing Alla to adjust her position. Neither of the two seemed overly enamored with the other. Taras obviously was not ready for anything sexual. Sasha reviewed the photos, then sent them, with a short explanation, to Tomás, to Emmitt Esterhazy, to her partner Gary Hernandez, and to her boss, Jack Raymond.

After pictures of the low-caliber and staged porn were shipped off, Sasha took Taras' phone. "Let's see, who you've been talking to." She hit All Calls. "Two local and two international calls to the US, with 212 prefixes. New York City. If I call these numbers, who'll answer? Your boss? Your kids? Mom? Maybe your wife? Or should I just send them these photos of you and cutie pie?"

Taras' huge body visibly shrank. "Please." .

"OK. No photos for now. I'll keep them for future reference. But let's call anyhow, see who might answer."

Sasha dialed the first New York number. Someone picked up but didn't speak. She'd wait out whoever was on the line. After a minute, a man's voice, "Yes?"

"Taras would like to speak to you, but he's indisposed," Sasha reported, then closed the line. She looked at Taras.

"It was a man. Know who it might be? Maybe Gennady Gasparov?"

From Taras' puzzled expression, Sasha confirmed what she suspected when the man in the B and B parking lot—trying to bargain for his life—had given her a name. An invented name, it appeared.

"Let's try the second number," Sasha suggested.

Someone picked up after the first ring. "Taras," a woman's voice, anxious. "Taras, dearest? Are you there?"

Sasha winced and closed the phone without speaking. "A woman. I'm guessing that was the missus. She sounded distraught."

"And the local numbers, Sasha?" Tomás asked.

"There's just one, called twice. Dollars to donuts it's Alla's father. That right, Alla? Taras and your dad been sharing secrets?"

"You bitch," she hissed at Sasha. "My papa . . ."

"Your papa?" Sasha interrupted. "Your papa's gonna see photos of you naked in bed with Taras here, the fuck-up who's going down for the murder of three American cops. Those photos should get you in real solid with daddy. Whattya think Vladimir Vladimirovich, sitting in the Kremlin, is gonna think when he discovers your father and Taras have been chatting?"

The fight went out of Alla. She covered her face with her hands.

Tomás took Alla's and Taras' cell phones and copied the numbers into his own phone. "Anything happens to you, Sasha, Taras' friends in New York, and the local mayor, and every media outlet between here and D.C. gets these photos."

"At last, Tomás. I'm feeling a little better," Sasha said.

"I think we have what we need, Sasha. Time to bring in the police."

"There's a problem, though. Cops in this town can't be trusted. We call them without witnesses to the arrest, Taras'll skate. And Alla, too." After a moment's thought, she took up her phone, dialed, and connected with someone. At the end of the short conversation, she smiled at Tomás. "We're cool. The FBI'll be here shortly, along with three other folks he was having a drink with. When they get here, we'll leave and they can make the collar."

A few minutes later, Emmitt Esterhazy and his current drinking buddies—three members of the Sapporo Police Department's Special Assault Team—arrived in Room 404.

When Sasha gave the Japanese a questioning look, one of them answered in perfect English, "We are all team captains in Sapporo's version of your SWAT. Trust us to maintain order." The man bowed slightly. Sasha smiled, returned the gesture, and then explained the situation. She opened the Guess bag, showed Esterhazy the weapon.

"A *real* smoking gun, he grinned. What else?"

She looked at Tomás. "Anything else?"

"One more thing. I think you should take both Taras and Alla's cell phones. Proof that Kollantai and Taras were talking to each other. It'll be further insurance for you."

"I like it," she said.

"What's your plan?" Esterhazy asked her.

"Get outta Dodge. Get back home. See my daughter."

"Can I help?"

"I don't think so. But thanks for everything." She bent over and hugged the smaller FBI agent. Esterhazy emitted a low *grrrrr*.

"Calm down," she said. "You're still too short for me."

Esterhazy gently disengaged. "God, you are *so* mean."

Sasha and Tomás exited the elevator and fell into step, heading toward the hotel's entrance. She was still wearing Vika's mother's vintage clothes, scarf around hair and neck. Since she couldn't return to her crime-scene-room, the clothes on her back constituted her entire wardrobe. She knew she looked shabby. Didn't give a damn. She felt as if she were floating.

Once outside, they made a hard right and walked along a broad, shrub-lined path, toward the side of the building.

"A friend of mine is coming to collect me. She'll be here any minute," Sasha said.

"And? That's it? No more help needed?" he asked lightly, but with serious regret showing in his voice and in his expression.

"No more help needed, Tomás. At least for now."

"Perhaps in the future?"

"That would be nice. Thanks for everything, Tomás. Couldn't have managed without you. I mean it."

"It's the least I could do in repayment for the thrilling afternoon. And for last night."

"But nothing happened last night," she joked.

"On the contrary. Much happened."

Sasha was at loss about how to respond when the rattle of an overtaxed engine caught her attention. A green van rounded the corner and pulled up opposite the two. Vika, in the driver's seat, seemed greatly relieved to see her new friend.

Sasha signaled her to wait, then turned back to Tomás.

"The future? I have trouble enough with the present." She stepped closer, wrapped both arms tightly around him and held him for half a minute. She kissed him lightly on each cheek, disengaged, and began moving toward the van. Hand on the door handle, she turned back to him. He looked forlorn. "Hasta la vista, Tomás."

"Hasta la vista, Sasha. Espero que si. I hope so."

She got in the van, looked back at him one more time, blew him a kiss.

Vika started off, made a U-turn, and got onto the highway leading to the airport. She looked at Sasha. "Some kind of gorgeous," she said.

"Yeah, I noticed. And sweet. And smart, and . . . everything. I'm missing him already."

~~~

Emmitt Esterhazy and his three Japanese drinking partners delivered Taras Dmitrivich Zhuganov to the police, along with the weapon. An hour later, the apprehending quartet stood in the lobby of the Hyundai Hotel in front of a crowd of reporters.

Asked for details about how he and his colleagues had tracked down the murderer, all four men were vague, to say the least. But it was enough for now that the alleged perpetrator had been apprehended along with the murder weapon.

If the capture of the murderer galvanized the members of the media, the presence of Alla Kollantai in the room with the suspect electrified them.

Under normal circumstances, the Vladivostok police would have found the means to spirit away the trouble-seeking young woman. They'd done it before on several occasions. But the circumstances here were far from normal. The presence of scores of international law enforcement personnel—those who had not already fled—forced the local police to act like police. Accordingly, the mayor's daughter was taken into custody. Whether she was an accessory to murder or simply an innocent and unwitting bystander remained to be determined.

Alla's father, at home, was being fed a telephonic account of the proceedings by people on his payroll—three policemen, a reporter for Vesti News, and a member of the police's forensic team.

The usually clear-thinking and decisively-acting mob boss of Russia's third largest crime cartel had suddenly developed a severe and uncontrollable twitch in his neck.

14

Boris grabbed his phone and pressed it to his ear. No sound. Nothing. He waited. "Yes?" he finally ventured.

A woman's voice: "Taras would like to speak to you but he's indisposed." The line went dead before Boris could respond.

He suspected who the caller might be and the realization made him shudder. If it was the policewoman from Anchorage, then things were now monstrously fucked up, possibly irretrievably so, and his brother-in-law and best friend might be beyond help.

Hoping that his worst fears might *not* be realized, for the next two hours Boris attempted to reach Vladivostok. Finally, a desperately unhappy mayor came on the line.

"Taras has been taken. Arrested in the hotel. He'll be charged with the murder of three Americans. The weapon was recovered in his room. Actually, it was my daughter's room. She was also arrested. It couldn't possibly be worse."

Boris squeezed his cell phone with one hand and began gnawing at the knuckle of his other hand's forefinger.

Kollantai let the news hang for several beats, then continued, "This is nearly beyond my ability to control, Borya. I've heard from Moscow already, from Konovalov, the Minister of Justice himself. He's sending someone out to collect Taras."

Boris knew at once that there was no saving his friend.

Kollantai read his counterpart's thoughts. "I'm certain Taras is loyal to a fault, Borya. But he is now in custody. No telling what he might say, given the right incentives to talk or the proper administration of persuasive means. Do you follow?"

"Yes, I'm following, Roman."

The mayor's voice was stressed. "We don't have much

time. The man from Justice will be here tomorrow, by late morning. If he takes Taras to Moscow, I'll be helpless. We'll be helpless."

The two crime cartel leaders let a long silence stretch out their phone conversation.

"If there is something you'd like to say, Borya, please say it," Kollantai prompted, a note of sympathy in his voice.

Boris Davidovich Bunin felt a lump form in his chest. He remembered the first time he met Taras, when he served as enforcer for his father, David. And Boris recalled how radiantly his sister, Raisa, used to smile up at her fiancé.

"Are you there, Borya?" Kollantai asked.

"I'm here." A long pause, then, choking back his tears, "Do what you must, Roman. Call me when it's done."

"One more thing, Borya. The woman, the policewoman. She's gone."

Boris considered for barely a second. "Track her down, Roman. She needs to die slowly." He put the phone down, his fingers shaking. He cursed himself. *My own damn fault. Stupid, stupid, stupid!*

He sat, paralyzed by the bad news. His oldest friend was as good as dead. With his own permission and collusion, Taras' would be killed in the jail where he was being held, before he might be arraigned, before he might be flown to Moscow, and before he might be tempted to make a plea deal with the Russian Minister of Justice.

Boris felt drained. What could he tell his sister about her husband's death? What lies would he have to invent to ease the hurt for which he himself was responsible?

In a daze, he went searching for his wife and found her in the living room, reading. He sat down next to her.

"Borya, the look on your face tells me you're bringing me bad news."

"Taras."

"I'm listening."

He told her everything, leaving out no detail. Larissa was annihilated, sobbing. Through tears, she reminded Boris that it was Taras who was responsible for their meeting, sixteen years earlier. For half an hour they held each other and wept.

~~~

Vika steered her van onto a large field covered with weeds poking through the dirt—the airport's version of long–term parking.

"What about the pistol, Vika. I forgot about it. How do I get it on the plane? Or should I leave it with you?"

"Don't worry," she said. "You're not flying Aeroflot. We'll be leaving from the domestic end of the terminal. The security there is nonexistent. Trust me, Sasha. Very few people own guns in Russia—at least compared to your country—so getting onto a plane with a weapon won't be a problem. Besides, you should hold onto it as long as you're still in Russia."

"You're certain?"

"Totally. C'mon."

Walking through the parking lot, Sasha made sure she remained well-disguised, hidden deep within Vika's mother's clothes. They entered the terminal and proceeded to the domestic, very crowded, far end.

Vika was greeted by a group of women, all dressed

warmly, ready for the flight that would take them home to Khabarovsk, four hundred miles to the north. Vika introduced Sasha as a friend of a friend, a writer of mysteries, gathering information about the Russian Far East, especially along the Pacific Coast.

Several of the women showed real interest and let Sasha know they'd be happy to help. She thanked them and promised to be in touch.

Their flight was due to leave within the hour. Sasha found herself a seat in the midst of the women, her back to the large hall, her hand never far from Vronsky's treasured pistol. *If I have to use it, God help me. I'll never get out of this country. And if they decide to upgrade baggage security . . .*

~~~

Sergo Bolkonsky, Kollantai's number two, stood in front of his boss.

"It's all arranged, Roman Vassillich. I've spoken with the chief of police. Yagoda assured me there would be no problem. He guaranteed that Zhuganov will be eliminated within the next few hours."

"And the woman?" the mayor asked.

"She's disappeared. Didn't even check out of the hotel. Gone."

"Go after her, Sergo. Find her. Finish her," Kollantai said. "And bring me word as soon as the work at the prison is done. Now send in my daughter."

Alla Kollantai slunk in and buried herself in a deep sofa across the room from her father.

"I've spoken to the public prosecutor," he said. "In

order for him to release you into my custody, I had to assure him that you would cooperate fully. He's prepared to let you out of this mess as a favor to me. That puts me in his debt. Given that the man is a pile of stinking pig shit, being in his debt does not please me. You follow?"

"Yes, papa. Thank you."

The mayor was glum. "I blame myself, entirely," Kollantai confessed. "You are stupid, spoiled, entitled, and without education. But it is I, ultimately, who am responsible for your behavior. If your mother–bless her name–were alive, you would be a different person. Of that I am certain. But she is not, and here you are, a half step in front of the law. Caught fucking a murderer."

Alla summoned up a face of ultimate contrition and innocence. "Papa, I didn't fuck him. I swear to you. He came to my room after the shooting. He was raving, delirious." She hugged a bolster to her chest, hoping to deflect her father's withering accusations. She wanted to suck her thumb, wanted to climb into bed with her favorite teddy bear, draw the covers over her head, and sleep for two days.

Her father picked up a framed photograph of his wife, dead from cancer eight years earlier. The picture showed him and Anfisa on their honeymoon in Madrid, outside the Prado. The mayor placed the photo back on his desk, fiddled with his wedding ring, spinning it around his finger. He looked over at Alla and spoke to her in a voice he knew would get her attention, "So, my good-for-nothing daughter. It's now the end of April. Summer classes at State University or the Far Eastern begin in June. You will take two classes. Choose your own major. Then in the fall, full-time. You will be driven to school and picked up at the end of each day. There will be other restrictions as I see fit. If these arrangements are unsuitable for you . . ." Kollantai pointed to the door.

Alla nodded her agreement, felt relieved. But in spite of her overriding desire to protect herself at all costs, she felt obligated to warn her father. "Papa. The woman took my phone and Taras' also. She was able to see that you and he spoke. Twice."

Kollantai slowly straightened in his chair. The fearful consequences of that information becoming public made his butt cheeks squeeze shut. "Get out. Don't leave the house," he ordered.

When Alla was gone, Kollantai summoned back his number two.

"Sergo, when you find the American policewoman, destroy all cell phones in her possession. Search for her everywhere. All exits from the city. Follow her, if need be, to the ends of the earth. Get those phones."

~~~

A hard rapping at his front door awoke Yury Vronsky. He had been dozing fitfully in one of his deep armchairs, feet up on the ottoman, toes pointing to the scattered embers glowing in the fireplace. He looked up at the mantle where his chronometer read a quarter past nine in the evening, a bare few hours after the events at the Hyundai Hotel.

He threw off the afghan, rose, and walked stiffly to one of his porthole windows. What he saw made his stomach churn—illuminated by the porch light were two men, unknown to him, dressed in dark suits. They stood in the rain, each holding an umbrella. He had no doubt why they had come. He closed his eyes, counted to ten, and went to the door, opening it part way.

"Yury Gregorovich Vronsky?"

"Yes."

"Police," the man stated, flipping his wallet open and showing his credentials. He made a move to enter but the captain remained solidly in the doorway. Rebuffed, the man glared down at the shorter Vronsky. "There was a woman, an American police officer, whom you apparently know."

"Correct."

"Is she here."

"Was here this afternoon, for a visit. Came to give me a retirement gift. Then left." Now with more courage than he felt, "And why should this be of any concern?"

The two men looked at each other, the rain spattering loudly on their umbrellas. The second policeman stepped forward. "Listen to me, Captain Vronsky. This woman, this American, this friend of yours who brings you gifts, she's wanted as a witness to the murders that took place earlier today at the Hyundai. You know about that?"

"I follow the news."

"And you say you don't know where she is, is that what you're telling us?"

"That's exactly what I'm telling you. No idea where she is."

"If we were to come in right now and found the American woman, that would have very serious consequences for you, Captain Vronsky. Harboring someone wanted for questioning can bring severe penalties."

"Come in," Vronsky suggested, stepping aside. "Look as long as you want. As I've already told you, the American woman is not here."

"Perhaps she's with your daughter, the teacher?" the first man suggested.

Up until then, Vronsky had told the truth. Now, however, he was backed into a corner. He felt his mouth go dry. He wanted to call up some saliva and swallow but knew it would alert the men. "Why would this woman be with my daughter? They don't know each other. Never met." Vronsky hoped the noise of the rain on their umbrellas masked the series of small farts his nervous bowels were producing.

"If you see this American woman or know where she is, you'd best let the police know."

Vronsky couldn't speak, only nodded.

The first man said, "You're supposed to start working at the surimi plant next week. You don't want to jeopardize the job."

Sasha's warning that he could get into serious trouble by helping her came back to him with a rush. *Fuck it.* "I told you what I know," he said. "If I see her, I'll be in touch."

The two men gave the captain a long look before turning and leaving. Vronsky watched them get into their car and drive off. He was able to swallow. *Worse than a Force 10 gale. But I'm still standing.*

~~~

Three of the men ordered by Sergo Bolkonsky to find and kill the American policewoman and recover her cell phones arrived at Knevichi Airport just after 2:10 a.m., the morning after the shooting at the Hyundai Hotel.

The terminal building was under subdued lighting and was all but deserted—a handful of sleeping passengers and only a janitor, an older woman water-mopping the floor. She was wearing over-sized tennis shoes, army surplus fatigues, a bandana around her hair, and a sweater obviously knitted for the boys called to defend Stalingrad. She had an unlit, half-smoked cigarette stuck in her mouth. When she saw the men, she paused in her work, and called to them, her throaty voice echoing in the near-empty hall. "No one's here. No planes 'til tomorrow. Come back in the morning." She resumed her mopping but continued to eye the men.

One of them, Vadim Bezukhov, walked over to the woman. "Good evening, grandma." When she didn't reply, he spoke again. "We're police. We're looking for a woman, an American. We think she might have flown out of here this past evening."

The janitress stopped her work and looked the large man up and down. "Who the hell are you kidding? You don't look like police. You don't act or sound like police. Move away, I have to mop where you're standing."

Bezukhov, clearly confused, turned to his two partners. One stepped forward and forcefully wrested the mop from the woman's hands.

"Listen to me, you old bat. We're gonna ask you some questions. We like the answers, we'll leave. We don't like 'em, I'm gonna shove this mop handle up your ass."

She straightened and sneered, "I bet you'd really enjoy that, too, you fuckin' perv." She took out a book of matches and lit her cigarette. "Ask," she said.

"The woman we're looking for is tall, with close cropped, blond hair," Bezukhov said. "She might have flown out of here in the company of a group of other women, maybe teachers."

The janitress took back her mop. "I need to buy more smokes. Lots more."

Bezukhov took out his wallet, produced a hundred-ruble note, and held it just out of her reach.

The old lady eyed the bill. "Bunch of women flew out of here about six last evening, for Khabarovsk. Coastal Aviation. Should have landed there maybe three, four hours ago."

"When's the next plane there?"

"Aeroflot has one just before eight in the morning, but it's usually crammed full."

"And after that?"

The woman seemed put out. "What am I, a fuckin' travel agency?"

"And after that?" Bezukhov repeated, taking a menacing step toward the woman.

"Bunch of flights at eleven thirty." She reached over, took the bank note, stuffed it into her back pocket, dipped her mop into the bucket of water, and looked to the men to move from the spot she was intending to clean.

Once outside the terminal, Bezukhov called in and reported.

~~~

The morning after Emmitt Esterhazy and his three drinking partners had collared Taras Zhuganov, the FBI bureau chief was sitting by himself, picking at breakfast in the hotel's sparsely filled restaurant. He was more than slightly hung over, a tom-tom throb behind his eyes, his appetite all but gone. The death of his agent was weighing on him. The FBI director's rotten mood was only somewhat eased by the arrest of the killer. Esterhazy wondered how justice would be dispensed in this country. He wasn't hopeful.

His blue funk was interrupted by Roman Kollantai. The man, looking seriously rumpled, dragged himself through the dining room and fell into a seat across the table. The Mayor of Vladivostok had a hangdog expression on his face.

"Mr. Director," Kollantai began. "I am so deeply sorry about the loss of Agent Dana. It's tragic."

Suspicion being at the core of FBI work, the Anchorage SAC couldn't help feeling that this visit was not being made solely to commiserate, to console. There was something else going on. He drummed his fingers on the table, and waited for Kollantai to continue.

"I fear I have distressing news," the mayor said.

Esterhazy sat back. He had an idea what the 'distressing news' might be. "Mr. Mayor . . ." he said, inviting the man to continue.

Kollantai wagged his head. "Mr. Director. It's my unhappy duty to tell you that it seems that Zhuganov, the man you captured yesterday, is dead. He was killed late last night while in custody at the prison on Partizanskaya Street. He was stabbed to death by another prisoner while in the shower. We don't yet know who. I have my best men investigating. It's awful. I am so deeply disturbed."

Esterhazy was not surprised. "That *is* disturbing news, Mayor Kollantai." But the federal agent couldn't let it go unremarked upon. "This is not the first time something like this has occurred to a high profile prisoner in your custody."

No reaction on the face of Roman Kollantai, rendered immobile by the memory of past problems with prisoners held at the Partizanskaya.

Esterhazy went on. "I'm referring to Sergei Larionov, a major racketeer in your city. You remember him? Also stabbed to death while in your jail, in 1998."

Kollantai cracked a small smile. "Larionov? Yes. I recall the name. He was well before my time, however."

"Really? I thought I read somewhere that you worked for him. Perhaps I'm mistaken. But tell me, Mr. Mayor. You still have the weapon with the man's fingerprints. You can still prove he was the killer."

Kollantai shook his head in wonder and disbelief. "Mr. Esterhazy, sir. You won't believe what has happened. Some fool in our forensic laboratory has, by an act of sheer idiocy, destroyed the weapon. He included it in a shipment of old boxes of evidence that were earmarked for disposal. I can't imagine what he was thinking. Naturally, he's been fired. So I'm afraid the pistol is gone."

Esterhazy riveted the man with an unblinking gaze. *You mother fucker. If I had you in Anchorage, I'd rub that sanctimonious smirk right off your face.* "Mr. Mayor. An agent of mine was murdered yesterday in your city, in this very hotel."

Kollantai didn't respond. He sat there, his large body swaying in his chair.

"You and your daughter were seen talking to the murderer at breakfast yesterday, an hour before my agent and two other Alaskans were killed. A strange coincidence, wouldn't you agree?"

Continued silence from the Mayor of Vladivostok.

Esterhazy's appetite had returned. He spread gooseberry jam over a piece of dark bread, took a bite, then went on.

"Did you know, Mr. Mayor, that in my country there

are about three hundred million guns in private hands. All kinds. Handguns, shotguns, assault rifles. We like our guns in America."

Kollantai nodded, was able to speak. "I know you do, Mr. Director."

"We do, indeed." Another bite of bread and jam. "Do you know how many people are killed by guns every year in my country?"

"I would guess many thousands."

"Good guess. Actually, over thirty thousand. Sadly, many of them are innocent bystanders. You know that expression, Mr. Mayor, innocent bystander?"

"I know it," Kollantai answered, not sure where the conversation was heading.

"They were shot accidentally because they were in the wrong place at the wrong time."

"How very unfortunate for them."

"Quite unfortunate." Esterhazy put aside his slice of bread, paused and bent across the table. "Mr. Mayor, if and when you ever again step foot in my country, you must be very careful not to become an innocent bystander."

Kollantai gave the FBI agent the thinnest of smiles. "Mr. Esterhazy," he whispered, "that sounds like a threat."

Esterhazy got to his feet. "Ya think?" he asked, tossing his napkin onto the plate in front of the Mayor of Vladivostok before walking off.

~~~

Sergo Bolkonsky stood by the wet bar at the side of the mayor's pool, ready to report to his boss about the search for

- 409 -

the American policewoman. It was a few minutes after noon, a full day after the events at the Hyundai.

Roman Kollantai had returned from meeting with Emmitt Esterhazy, still smarting from the insolence of the American FBI director. The Mayor was working off his anger and frustration in his pool, swimming at a faster pace than usual. He was thinking about the state prosecutor sent by the Kremlin to collect Taras Zhuganov and take him back to the capital. Well, that wasn't going to happen, unless the man wanted to collect and interrogate a corpse. Kollantai was able to smile at the notion. *Stranger things have happened in our legal system. The old days in the Lubianka . . . .*

When Kollantai emerged, panting, from the water, Bolkonsky approached. "We have a lead on the woman. Vadim was at Knevichi last night. She apparently flew north to Khabarovsk, possibly in the company of a group of teachers. Vadim and two others flew there an hour ago."

Kollantai vigorously toweled off, then dropped into a chaise lounge and drank the iced juice drink that Sergo had poured for him. "Khabarovsk? What's she thinking?"

"Perhaps she'll try to catch a plane from there to South Korea, to Seoul. It's only a two hour flight."

"Alright. Keep an eye on the airport in Khabarovsk. But my gut tells me that's not what she's planning. The woman's from Alaska. I think she'll try and get to some port, way up north, on Chukotka, and then somehow, get home from there." Kollantai finished his juice drink. "Here's what, Sergo. If she's heading north, then the next places she has to fly to are Magadan and then Anadyr."

"The Kerensky brothers are in Magadan," Bolkonsky said. "They've helped us before. But I wouldn't necessarily count on them. Yefim's half a drunk, and Danilo, a whole one."

"But can they handle this? She's a tough bitch."

"I'll call, find out."

~~~

Danilo and Yefim Kerensky—life-long sots of the kind who fall down, throw up, and wallow in their own vomit—were born and raised in Magadan.

Their father, Rodion, during his short life, had been a bootlegger, dealer in stolen property, loan shark, numbers enforcer, purse-snatcher, and sex offender. In 1953, while living in Moscow, he was arrested for child molestation and shipped to the opposite end of Russia, to the Magadan gulag on the Pacific Coast, in those days the center of an immense forced labor, gold mining enterprise.

After Rodion had served his eight-year sentence, he remained in Magadan, working his life to a frazzle and himself into an early grave. The only bright spot in his exceedingly drab existence occurred at the end of each month—pay day at the lumber mill—when he'd stumble into one of the local brothels and groan his way through a drunken hour with one or both of his favorite whores. The prostitutes, Yana and Liubov Bazarov, sisters from Irkutsk, each bore him a son.

Rodion denied his paternity, but the women, as it happened, were also favorites of the local police chief. The cop persuaded Rodion to accept his fatherhood.

The apples not falling far from the tree, Rodion's two boys grew up on the border between licit and illicit. But unlike their inept, often incarcerated father, the two were able to thwart the best efforts of the local constabulary and never saw the inside of a jail.

By 1990, with Rodion now mercifully dead, the brothers Kerensky had established themselves as the go-to hoods in Magadan's crime community. Danilo was the muscle, and Yefim, as far as nature would allow, the brains.

Their sphere was generally limited to Magadan, but once in a while, they were chosen by Roman Kollantai for simple stuff, jobs that wouldn't tax the brothers' limited talents.

Yefim Kerensky, suffering the after effects of the day-long bender and brothel-creep he and his brother had enjoyed the day before, sat in the office of his auto repair shop, near Magadan's shore. He held the landline phone in a shaky hand. "I understand, Sergo. Don't worry. We'll find her. She's as good as dead." He hung up, and after a short search, found Danilo passed out in the back seat of a Lada sedan into which the Kerenskys were supposed to be putting new brake linings. They were a month behind. Yefim shook his brother awake.

"C'mon, Danushka. Sergo has a job for us. Sober up. We gotta find a woman."

Danilo Kerensky grumbled, opened blood shot eyes, burped, turned over, and resumed snoring.

15

Sasha and her escorts arrived in Khabarovsk without incident about eight in the evening. Vika's colleagues were collected by their families, leaving her and Sasha to find makeshift sleeping arrangements in the terminal. The two women slept poorly, never getting comfortable on the waiting area's wooden benches. Next morning, they boarded the early flight to Magadan and arrived on the coast of the Sea of Okhotsk before noon,

Vika went directly to the Aurora Air counter and bought a pair of one-way tickets for the short hop to Anadyr. The women were wrinkled and cranky and had three hours to kill before their flight. They shambled into the terminal's café where they fortified themselves with rounds of stale coffee and staler sweet rolls.

Two toughs working for the Kerensky brothers spotted them immediately. The goons—Anton Oblomov and Lavrenty Shutov—were sitting at the airport bar, just across from the café. They saw the women arrive and watched as one of them went to the Aurora counter, made a purchase, and returned to her table.

"Back soon," Shutov mumbled.

"What's up?" his partner asked.

"Gonna find out where they bought tickets to."

Shutov walked to the Aurora counter and began to question the ticket agent. The woman shook her head, frowning. Shutov leaned across the counter and whispered something. The woman's eyes widened in fright. She answered the man. Shutov rejoined his partner.

"On their way to Anadyr, one way. Plane leaves in a couple hours. It's the daily non-stop. They got the last two tickets. Damn!"

Oblomov kept his eye on the women. Strangely, the big blond—*must be the American*, he thought—was staring directly at them. She took out her cell phone, punched in a number, waited, then wrote a quick text. Oblomov feigned indifference, then warned his partner, "Don't look, but the blond woman, I think she made us."

It was all Shutov could do *not* to look.

"Lemme call it in to the garage, see what the guys want us to do," he said.

By the time the Kerensky brothers had sobered sufficiently to drive to the airport, it was noon. The target had flown away an hour earlier.

Yefim went to check with the Aurora Air agent. He spent a minute and returned to his cronies, all smiles. "No problem," he reported. "We know she's gone to Anadyr. And from there, she bought a ticket to Provideniya for tomorrow night. Soonest we can get to Anadyr is tomorrow morning. Which is fine. Me and Danushka'll fly there tomorrow and wait for her to show up for the Provideniya flight."

Satisfied grins all around. The Kerensky mob drove back to town, to their favorite bar to while away the rest of the day.

~~~

Roman Kollantai was overcome with foreboding. His mobile phone was ringing, showing Alla's number. And since he knew his daughter's cell phone had been confiscated by the American policewoman, he didn't want to answer. But he simply could not ignore the call. He hit the green. The screen showed a text message with enclosures. The message from the American woman could not have been clearer: "Spotted some of your friends just now. Fuck with me again and these pictures go viral."

Kollantai opened the first photo: his daughter and Zhuganov, naked in bed. The mayor closed his eyes and began a high-pitched keening through gritted teeth. He scanned the remaining five pictures—more of the same. The Mayor of Vladivostok slumped into his chair and reached for his cell phone. He dialed Boris Bunin, spoke a few words, and forwarded to his Brooklyn colleague the warning text and set of photos. The mayor ended the call abruptly, then flung his phone across the room. It ricocheted off a lampshade, hit the wall, and bounced to the carpeted floor. Kollantai shouted for his number two.

Bolkonsky came quickly into the room, saw the cell phone on the carpet, and tiptoed to stand in front of his boss.

"Listen, Sergo. We need to call off the search for the American woman. Where has she been tracked to?"

"Only as far as Magadan. Vadim and two others should be landing there soon. When they arrive, they'll coordinate with the Kerenskys."

"None of that matters any more. Call Vadim and the Kerenskys. The search stops right now."

"But I thought . . ."

"*Right now, Sergo!* Let the woman go."

"Got it. Getting in touch with Vadim's no problem. The Kerenskys, another story. They don't have cells. Only their office number."

"Just do it."

"Will do. Anything else?"

"Yes. Find my slut of a daughter and bring her here. Drag her by the hair if you have to. Even if you don't have to."

~~~

The Bunin household was deep in mourning. Boris' sister was inconsolable. At the news of her husband's death, Raisa had collapsed. Boris wondered whether it was a blessing or a curse that she and Taras never had children.

He'd shut himself away in his den. He knew he bore full responsibility for his brother-in-law's death. The call from Kollantai and his announcement that he'd called off the search for the American woman had shaken Bunin to the core. Everything was falling apart. He scanned, once again, the photos the mayor had sent him: Taras and a young woman, naked in bed, in a variety of poses. Boris had never met Kollantai's daughter but he made the connection. He thought immediately of his sister. *Raisa must never see these pictures. Nor Lara, either.* He imagined the American policewoman who had sent them would have distributed them to a few trusted people. That's what he would have done. If anything happened to the woman . . . *Nothing must happen to her.*

He was sunk into an all-consuming bout of self-flagellation when Larissa entered the room. Boris glanced up, startled. He stared at the phone in his hand and deleted the email as casually as he could manage. Then he cursed himself for his obviously furtive actions, certain to draw his wife's attention and interest. He looked up blankly at Larissa. She walked to the desk and stopped, hands at her side. She searched her husband's face, trying to read his expression. He seemed distant, lost to her. Boris couldn't hold her gaze and looked away. His wife waited a moment, giving him time. When he continued to stare beyond her, she turned and left him.

~~~

The Kerensky brothers arrived in Anadyr the next morning and confirmed that the charter north to Provideniya was leaving late that night. They had the day to themselves.

They scored two liters of a tolerable *samogon* from a cab driver, bought sandwiches and pickles and wound up sitting in a park through the afternoon, enjoying a warming springtime sun. Yefim, in charge of the dirty work, cleaned his pistol, a Makarov PM, an old reliable from Soviet days.

Towards sundown, they arrived at Anadyr's small airport, well before the departure of the charter flight to Provideniya. The waiting room was unoccupied. They still had half a liter of the home brew. They sipped judiciously and nibbled at the last pickles.

~~~

When Sasha and Vika arrived at the Anadyr airport, eight other people were in the waiting room: three older Chukchi women, a pair of middle-aged Russian men, and a couple with an infant.

"Plane on time?" Vika asked, as they sat themselves.

Sasha checked her watch. "It was supposed to leave at midnight, but it's been delayed 'til one. We have a couple hours yet. I get to Provideniya around dawn tomorrow."

"You'll be in good hands. My friend, Marya, will meet you. When I phoned her, she said the American visitors from St. Lawrence Island are sailing back in a day or two. You're lucky to make such a quick connection."

"Very lucky," Sasha agreed.

"My father'll be glad to get his pistol back," Vika said, patting her carryall. "I'm not surprised he gave it to you. He really likes you."

"It's mutual, Vika. You two saved my ass! I can't thank you enough." Sasha checked her watch again. "Listen, you don't have to stay and wait with me. Go on back to the hotel room. I'll be fine."

"You're sure?"

"Positive. Let's say our goodbyes."

Vika used her cell phone to call a cab. "Be here in five minutes."

They rose and stood opposite each other, holding hands.

"I'd be dead, Viktoria Yurevna, if not for you. For my sake and especially for my daughter's sake, I'll always be grateful."

"When I meet Robin, at Christmas, we'll celebrate."

"I've got you arriving in Anchorage in mid-December, staying with us for at least three weeks. Not a day less."

"That's the plan. I'm not sure I can convince papa to come. He's never loved flying very much."

"Do your best. He and my grandfather need to meet."

The two embraced once more and said their goodbyes. When Vika left, Sasha resumed her seat and let her head collapse onto her chest. She was exhausted. She sensed movement in front and in back of her. Before she could summon the strength to open her eyes and look up, something slammed across her shoulders, knocking her forward. She saw stars in a crazy quilt of rainbow colors and was overcome with nausea. Before she fell out of her seat, the person in front caught her and lifted her onto her feet. A blast of boozy breath washed across her face and served to bring her back to semi-consciousness. Her vision was blurred but there was no mistaking the pistol in the man's hand. Sasha began shaking uncontrollably.

"Let's go," the man hissed into her ear.

She looked to the other passengers for help. Surely they'd seen her being attacked. But the Chukchi women and the couple with the baby were all looking the other way, ignoring her.

The person in back of Sasha took a steely grip on her left arm with one hand and with the other, took hold of the back of her pants and lifted her, so that her feet were just scraping the floor. He began shoving her toward the door.

"We're gonna walk outside and get in the car," said the man in front of her, the one with the pistol.

Sasha didn't have to ask where they were going or what the future held. She was conscious enough to be furious at herself for not being more alert. All she could think of was her daughter and the hole that would be left in Robin's life.

On the sidewalk outside the small airport, Vika was waiting for her cab. The banging of hastily flung open doors brought her attention back to the building. She saw Sasha being hustled toward a car by a man holding what looked like a pistol. He pushed her into the rear seat and followed her in. At the same time, the second man got in the front, behind the wheel. As they were pulling away, her taxi arrived, its headlights reflecting off the rear of Sasha's car. Vika yanked open the cab's back door, and vaulted in. Using the same lines she'd heard in a dozen films, she commanded the driver: "Follow that car." She reached into her purse and pulled out a five hundred ruble note. "Don't lose him," she ordered, handing the bill over the seat.

"I'm on it, lady," the driver said.

~~~

Georgy Kutuzov, pensioner, widower, veteran of forty-five years of mining all up and down the east coast of Russia, was taking Blackie for his evening constitutional. The thirteen-year old Labrador's rear end had long ago given out and the evening walks the two had been taking since the dog was a pup had become markedly shorter. Which was fine with the pensioner. The man's feet were killing him. He needed new shoes, but his paltry pension . . . .

Kutuzov had to pause every five minutes to let Blackie recover his strength. They stopped for a rest next to a large empty field on Ozernaya Street, at the edge of town. He could hear the pounding of the ocean on the shore, half a kilometer to the east.

This section of Anadyr had always been Blackie's preferred toilet. When he was younger, the Lab liked to romp in the nearby woods. These days, however, the romping was a dim memory and the woods an impossibly distant fifty meters away. The dog contented himself by doing his business in the tall grass near the street.

As Kutuzov waited for Blackie to sniff out appropriate dumping grounds, a car drove up and parked half a block ahead of them. The graveled road had only a single light pole at each end of the long block. The pensioner was barely able to make out three figures as they emerged from the car. All were wearing dark winter clothes. One struggled slightly. They headed for the woods. Before they had gone twenty meters, a cab pulled up in back of the first car, someone jumped out and began running toward the group of three, yelling at them. The taxi drove away.

Danilo Kerensky was pleased at how smoothly all this was going. The woman didn't seem to give a shit about her fate. *We'll get to the woods*, he thought, *Yefim will put a bullet into her brain and we'll drive back home. We'll call Kollantai, receive from him a 'job well done,' and in the next few days, a tidy sum'll come by courier. Easy. But wait a second! A cab and some crazy bitch running towards us, yelling at us to stop, shouting that we'd dropped something at the airport. What the hell's this about?*

Blackie had found his spot and was just starting his business, undisturbed by what his master was observing so intently—the group of three people were close to entering the birch woods. The person running after them, shouting, was now upon them. Then all hell broke loose. Gun shots. Many of them. Kutuzov ducked as low as his arthritic knees would let him. Blackie, his hearing not what it used to be, continued his business. A minute later, Kutuzov raised up and saw two figures making their way through the grass. One was supporting the other. They arrived back at the car, got in, and drove off.

The pensioner was petrified. Four people went into the forest, then shots, two came out. And the other two? He looked around in panic, but didn't see a soul running to the scene. No lights coming on in the darkened apartments, three blocks away. No sirens. No witnesses.

Blackie had finished and now looked up at his master

and gave a little yip, as if to say, "I've done my duty. Can we please get the hell on home now?" Kutuzov stooped over and rubbed the Lab lovingly behind his right ear. He spoke quietly to his best friend, "We're not going home quite yet, old pal. We have some shopping to do first."

~~~

Being Roman Kollantai's number two was usually a plum job: tons of perks, loads of money, women by the carload.

Occasionally, however, like now, Bolkonsky hated his work, wished he were somewhere else, anywhere besides where he was—standing in front of the mayor and having to deliver extraordinarily bad news. Bolkonsky thought to start on a positive note: "I was able to contact Vadim in Magadan. But, after that . . ."

A pause long enough for Kollontai to look up from his desk. "And . . .?" he asked, suspicion edging his tone.

"And . . . things got hairy."

Kollantai scowled. "I don't like that word, Sergo. I don't like it when things get hairy. Explain."

"I tried to contact the Kerensky brothers at their garage. But no one answered. And neither of those jackasses has a cell phone, so I couldn't call them to stop searching."

"So?"

"So . . . they apparently found the American woman in Anadyr. Or she found them. Or something . . . ."

"Or something?" Kollantai screamed.

Get it over with, Bolkonsky ordered himself. He licked his lips. "The brothers are both dead. At least I think they're dead."

Kollantai shook his head, trying to make sense of what he was hearing. "You're not sure they're dead?"

"Well, it's like this, Roman Vassillich. Two men were found dead this morning in the woods on the outskirts of Anadyr, near the sea. They were each shot to shit. They apparently had been robbed, pockets turned inside out, no wallets, no ID. No watches. No weapons. And no shoes."

"No shoes?"

"Right."

"So how do we know it's them?"

"They had shirts with 'Kerensky Brothers Garage' patches sewn on the pockets. So, I guess we can assume it's them."

"She shot them? But how?"

"She's good, Roman Vassillich. She shot Bunin's three men in Alaska, grabbed Zhuganov here at the Hyundai, and now she's finished off those two knuckleheads."

"And she took their shoes?"

"So it seems."

Kollantai realized the terrible implications of what he'd just been told. If the American policewoman believed he was responsible for this attack on her—no matter the outcome–her threat to release those damning photographs had to be taken seriously. If she goes to the press, his daughter will get caught up in that ugliness at the Hyundai and there won't be much he'd be able to do to counter the visual evidence against her. And then, once Alla was in custody . . . a Pandora's box he didn't have the stomach to consider. The little bitch might even flip on him to save her own skin.

He needed to contact the American woman immediately, to explain. He dialed the number of his daughter's cell. No answer. He texted. Nothing. He tried repeatedly for the next half hour with the same results, rehearsing what he would say to her—that it was a terrible mistake, that he had called off the search but those drunken Kerensky blockheads didn't get the message. Please . . .

"It's possible her battery's dead. Or she doesn't have cell service," Sergo offered.

"Yes, possible," Kollantai said, dejection filling his voice. He had to get in touch with the woman, quickly, before she might make those photos public. The single only solution that occurred to him was distasteful in the extreme. He'd have to contact someone close to her, then beg, grovel, eat a yard of shit. God in heaven! No choice, though. He found the Hyundai Hotel's number and after a brief hesitation, swallowed his pride, his honor, his reputation, and made the phone call.

Someone answered. "Hyundai Hotel. How may I help you?"

"Connect me to Emmitt Esterhazy's room," the mayor demanded.

"I believe Mr. Esterhazy is at the bar. I can connect you."

"Yes, please. Hurry."

After three rings, an answer, the bartender.

"Yeah?"

"This is Roman Kollantai. Let me talk to Emmitt Esterhazy."

"At once, Mr. Mayor," the bartender said.

A few seconds passed. Kollantai heard a loud 'bang' as if the phone had been dropped. Another long wait until someone came on the line.

"Thish iz Emmi Esherhazy shpeakin'. Whoozis?"

~~~

Because of the events in Anadyr, Vika decided to accompany her friend the rest of the way. As their plane broke through the clouds and began its descent toward Provideniya, the women got a glimpse of St. Lawrence Island, fifty miles to the east, a stone's throw. They were able to see the shoreline where three welded aluminum boats lay at anchor.

"American, by their look," Vika said.

"Christ, I hope so," Sasha replied.

Marya Kinegak, Vika's student, was waiting in the small Quonset hut that served as Provideniya's terminal.

After quick introductions, Sasha asked, "Those boats on the shore, Marya, they're American?"

"They are. They arrived last week. About a dozen St. Lawrence Islanders came for a spring potlatch. They'll be returning home tomorrow morning."

"Can I meet with the captains of the boats before I do anything else?"

"Of course. I know them all."

Marya led them down to the shore and brought her guests to one of the boat captains. The man, of indeterminate age, was short and stout, round bodied, round faced, roundly smiling. He guaranteed there would be room back to St. Lawrence Island. He refused payment, happy to help out a fellow American. Sasha was incredibly relieved and now allowed herself to be steered back to Marya's home where her host had prepared lunch. They dined on a hodge-podge of native subsistence foods and standard Russian fare: walrus stew, dried salmon strips, and smoked reindeer.

All accompanied by hard tack, strong tea, and the Russian equivalent of a Twinkie.

The shootout in Anadyr had frayed Sasha's already tightly stretched nerves. She begged off after lunch, changed into the sweat pants loaned to her by Marya, and curled up under a sealskin blanket. *Warmer than eiderdown,* was her last thought before she fell into a long, deep, and dreamless sleep.

She slept through the day, rising only for a light dinner. Then, back to bed and awaking just before dawn. She dressed, threw some cold water on her face, and joined Vika for breakfast: buns coated in margarine, hard boiled duck eggs, more salmon strips, and tea. After breakfast and a sincere thanks to her hostess, Sasha and Vika made their way down to the beach.

The morning was soft and sunny, the waters of Provideniya Bay were dead calm. *Thank God for small favors,* Sasha thought.

The shoreline was crowded with St. Lawrence Islanders and their Russian relatives. The Americans were busy loading the subsistence foods and gifts they were bringing home.

Sasha found the captain with whom she had made arrangements.

"We'll be off soon," he told her. "You can park yourself up front." He pointed to a small enclosure built into the prow of the vessel. It was covered by a blue tarp stretched tightly across a framework of PVC pipe. "There are wool blankets inside. It gets chilly on the open ocean," he said.

"Wonderful," she said, then turned to Vika. "I don't know how to thank you."

"Don't worry about it. I'll have lots to tell my father."

"What about the pistol?"

"It's right here, in my purse. Only a single bullet left."

"He'll wonder about the missing eight rounds."

Vika looked out to the sea. A small colony of sea gulls reeled and darted overhead. "I'm not sure I'll give him all the details. We'll see."

Sasha took hold of Vika's hands. "I'll expect to see you soon, very soon, in Alaska. Right?"

"Very soon," Vika said, stepping forward and giving her American friend a final hug.

Sasha broke away, climbed aboard the boat and gave her savior a final wave. Then she crawled forward into the jerry-rigged front cabin. There were several burlap bags stuffed with eider duck feathers, cardboard boxes filled with food and gifts, two large oil-skinned-wrapped parcels, and seven frozen reindeer quarters. She was able to muscle the reindeer, the boxes, and the parcels aside, then sank into the feather-filled burlap bags. She covered herself with the blankets and relaxed. She heard the final farewells, the revving of the outboard engines on the transoms of each of the three boats. A moment later, she felt the keel of her boat scraping the bottom of the gravel shore, then the vessel tilted as the mate hauled himself on board. The boat slowly backed away from shore then swung about. Sasha felt the craft's forward motion, the up and down as the boat slid easily over the water. She was cradled to sleep and only came awake, hours later, when she felt the engines idle back. They were slowing down. Soon, a hard bump. One of the other passengers, an older woman, peered into Sasha's sleeping chamber.

"We're here," the woman announced.

Sasha climbed out of the shelter. They were on a beach.

An American beach. The St. Lawrence Island village of Gambell was visible from the coastline, a steep set of hills backing the village.

The afternoon was warm and golden. Sasha looked back to the west, over the just-traversed ocean. The high cliffs of Russia, above Provideniya, fifty miles away, were a dull, slate gray in the afternoon light. She checked her watch—six and a half hours since they'd left. She eased herself stiffly off the boat and dropped onto a pebbled shoreline. She helped several of her fellow passengers disembark, then looked around, taking in the scene. Skeletal remains of walruses and bowhead whales were strewn along the shore. A string of ATVs, each pulling a large, wheeled wagon, drove up. Several young men wearing waders got off and walked down to the boat. One clambered aboard and began handing down the reindeer haunches, tilting the raw meat over the side onto the backs of the other young men.

Several of the passengers helped with the unloading, carrying the burlap bags and cartons to the waiting ATVs. The two oil-skin wrapped bundles were the last things unloaded. They were left next to the captain. Sasha came over to stand by him.

"Beautiful day for an ocean voyage," he said. "I don't think I've ever crossed when the sea's been so calm."

Sasha couldn't reply, couldn't find words. She was overcome. The joy of being on her home soil, away from Russia, was indescribably delicious.

Another ATV drove up, pulling a smaller wagon. A young woman hopped off the vehicle, ran down to the beach, and threw her arms around the captain.

After a moment, they broke apart, gazing at each other

with great affection. The captain turned to Sasha. "This is my granddaughter, Julia Kopanuk. She's in her last year at university." He regarded her proudly. "She's studying to be a nurse."

Julia smiled at Sasha. "Come," she said. "If you're going on to Anchorage, Grizzly Air is due to land in a few minutes. Leo, the pilot, likes to get in and out in a hurry, so we'll need to get you and these two bundles loaded quickly."

"Let me give you a hand," Sasha offered.

#